Battle for Andromeda

A large and fearful dragon-like creature flew towards them from another direction and silently settled on the path in front of them, blocking their way and halting their progress.

'If you wish to survive their chambers of pain, quickly get on my back.'

Utterly confused by all the strange occurrences about them, they mounted its back. After passing many large mountain ranges, it approached a cave that was sited close to the apex of the largest peak. That cave could not be seen while the dragon was in the air above the mountain.

Within that cave was many of the dragon-like creatures, but there were a few aliens and humans. Lumak soon realized that he could not communicate with Gemmi, so he quickly released his hood and attempted to breathe the air. After sampling and testing, he gestured to Gemmi and she released her hood.

The dragons spoke without moving their lips.

'I am Algo. You have been transposed to a place between universes. This is a link between ours and yours and a type of prison created by our superiors. Only the vilest of creatures are placed here, within the shadows of Hades.'

The Chronicles of Osmaron series

First Edition

Chronicles of Galaxy Osmaron

Battle for Andromeda

The wars against the evil Nano-bot Javols
have begun with a vengeance.

By

Adrian Graye

Nutralian Publishing
http://nutralianpublishing.com

nutralian
An imprint of Nutralian Publishing
5 Brayford Square, London E1 0SG
http://nutralianpublishing.com

This paperback edition 2013
B00005555

First published in Great Britain by
Amazon Kdp 2024

ISBN 978-1-0687902-8-7

Printed and bound in Great Britain by Amazon KDP Publishing.

A CIP catalogue record for this title
is available from the British Library.

To all those who believe in Universal Existence and respect the lowliest of life; for like babes, - they are the beginning.

Table of Contents

Part 3
A Changing World

Part 4
The New Titans

Part 5
Battles Rage

Part 6
New Titans on the war path

From the ANACHROMAGNON - The book of final light.

'My love of all things will outlast even the memories of those I truly love.'

God lives in the hearts of all forever,
Evolution itself is beyond nature.
The stream of life does flow.
Invisibly it flows, its spirits to and fro.

By Siend Seno of Mond.

Prologue

Less than fifty years after his departure from Andromeda, Dracma had arrived in the galaxy of Triangulum. That painful journey was initiated by his brother several decades before. After an intensive search of his home galaxy, he had located one of the main ancient Hexolyte bases. It was the last one used by his creator, Father Dracos, over 2 billion years before.

Soon after, three main bases including the one at the nucleus of that galaxy was repaired and their ancient portals made fully operational and linked. After transferring his entity to one of the containment tanks for rejuvenation, he was aided by the Feloween and their many robots to engineer a new encasement cloak for himself and his brother, Lupher, still in Andromeda.

He was pleased with his newer and improved form and abused the Javols body that he had possessed all those years for containing his being. Finally he had no further use for it nor the need to suppress all of its endless desires and cravings.

He had accidentally acquired its form during the Javols' invasion of that cave in Andromeda and had always detested its rapacious nature. Nevertheless that serendipitous encounter had released him and his brother from perpetual confinement, albeit without even the Javol's knowledge.

After a period of joy for his eternal release and cursing for the memories of his hated experiences of the recent past, he sacrificed all reminders, including the Javol's body into the hottest plasma pit he could create. Then he began to revive all the dormant entities in many of their hidden underground caverns. Those had been placed in perpetual sleep before their masters departure from that galaxy in ancient times to Andromeda, but with the promise that their leaders would one day return to release them.

At that time they were chased relentlessly by their powerful and resourceful enemies, the Patriarchs, and had decided to close their operations until they found a way to destroy their persistent enemies and put a permanent stop to their constant meddling.

However by so doing they had aided their capture and had spent several aeons within containment tanks that had been previously laid by the hated Patriarch Aron and his son Jull on Endor's moon. It was meant to be their eternal prison until their accidental release by the ravenous copying Javols. Javols always craved to take new technologies apart for knowledge. Sadly, those two interfering Javols' bodies were immediately possessed and modified for their immediate survival. After that possession the original identities were liberated, never to trouble them again.

Since the turn of the 22nd century on Earth, over 300 million Earth humans had left with their belongings for the Andromedan Galaxy. The fall of planet Caefon and certain inducements had made Infilates consider it their best move. They knew of the Javols and their threat to civilization and Earth. They also considered the risks while living on fortified Caefon, in a galaxy infested with Javols. Yet, they had nowhere else to go.

Earth's population would be limited to only 500 million humans in the future and they would suffer the same faith as their predecessors; having little choice but grow old and die. However that age limit would gradually increase with the introduction of more advanced technologies in their new settlements.

The Son of Destiny had given all Infertilates or Infilates a second chance, with the option of renewed youth. It allowed them the ability to become fertile again and procure their own families. He was their trusted saviour and they would do virtually anything to fulfil his wishes in the process.

Since their arrival on Caefon, the Osmaronites had transformed the desolate world into a fortress with many distant probes to observe the movements of their enemies. However temporary peace remained in their sector of Andromeda. The Javols had turned their attention elsewhere thinking their galaxy to be completely safe and secure. They were also planning the invasion and conquest of the galaxy Triangulum, to where their former masters had departed.

Observation probes had placed the first wave of Javols just three decades away from Earth, but it was also considered that other more advanced types had overtaken the primary force and were now infiltrating The Milky Way Galaxy (Osmaron) to prepare the way for their numerous invaders. With the ability to change into virtually any shape or form, those new types could infiltrate the many facets of Osmaron's civilizations and possess those in high position.

Slowly, the underground assault within Andromeda had continued from Caefon and other worlds at the outer galactic rim towards its centre where most of the Javols remained. During that phase all Javols' bases would be taken over and replaced by Federation Drones. It was hoped the Javols would not be aware of that operation until it was too late.

Having devoured all of the opposing advanced civilizations within their galaxy, Andromeda, the Javols now relied heavily on slave farming and synthesized foods. Because of improved farming methods and technologies, they had become less aggressive. That was because they also consider their galaxy completely free of any threat. After all, they had not received positive communication of a single sighting of their enemies for many decades.

The Federation had turned their plans to securing Osmaron. During that phase many advanced weapons had been devised, installed and mothballed.

Earth's population had been reduced as planned from its original 11 billion to under 500 million. Finally the time had arrived for a leap in genetic engineering. A few humans would be given advanced minds and bodies to surpass any known primal forms. Those so chosen would be programmed from conception to take control of the universe. Those in control realized Earthly mankind had too small an IQ to make correct decisions in line with The Greater Purpose. Neither did they want Earth to return to the old days of barbarism, global warming and over population.

The Grand Council under consultation from its Supreme Macron (MAC) and many respected scientists on Planet Eden weighed the situation, comparing several human genes and finally decided to use the Earth type as a basis. It was also a requirement that those so chosen be related to senior married Councillors. Several donated their genetic information and just three unrelated members were initially chosen.

Science and technology had increased to such an extent on planet Eden that virtually anything was possible. The Lodorians, with the help of the Son of Destiny, now a Grand Lord himself, had devised massive machines for the creation or rehabilitation of dying stars. Such machines could be modified and used as weapons to destroy a complete stellar system if need be. Presently they had the knowledge to destroy a complete galaxy.

Despite their incredible abilities, they preferred a basic human existence in a clean and near perfect environment, with its many social activities and games. However they would sometimes transform into another alien to experience a new state of being. Such transformations could be done in virtual space or in real space when taking a holiday on an alien world. Despite the dangers, they were truly immortal and any damaged body parts could be quickly replaced or a completely new body created. To the chosen few, ageing was a thing of the past and it was seldom possible to find a human on Planet Eden that appeared older than twenty five.

The Macrons are very advanced and conscious computers that run civilization throughout the Federation of Worlds.

Presently, three ancient Patriarchs, now in the form of three superior human intellects exists on Earth. They are called Headrons and control the Macrons for the benefit of Earth's inhabitants.

Although quite young, they are guided by their personal Macrons and family members for advise. Earth would be their first toy for play. From its more primitive and hostile environment it is hoped they will learn to appreciate the problems associated with primal existence and the importance of human kind and other so-called lesser life-forms.

Knowledge of the Javols were not initially given to them. That aspect they would find out for themselves through evidence, logic and deduction.

After his return to Earth, Michael, the genetically engineered son of George Peterson, found the evidence. As an historian, among numerous other qualifications, he had probed the recent past and found many discrepancies which led him to the Ancients and then their enemy, the Javols.

Earth is finally ready to take her place in the Federation and is given the name, Solaria. From henceforth she would be the hub of all activity within Osmaron, our Milky Way Galaxy. Eden would henceforth be concealed and used as the paradise planet of residence for all the Lords of Osmaron. Here, they would build their golden palaces and visit planet Solaria (Earth) through the numerous long-range portals as and when necessary.

The City of Terminus on Mars would now be used as another scientific and military base for the Federation. It is presently the capital of our Solar System.

Michael the young Headron has deduced the beginning of a more advanced type of Javols and their planned invasion of Osmaron. He must locate them and gather evidence before all systems can be placed on alert.

PART 1

Return of more Ancient Patriarchs

CHAPTER 1

Sylon on Tuil, a different meteor

Earth time... unknown, a near repeat of circumstances.

Place... the city of Sylon, on planet Tuil somewhere within the galaxy of Triangulum.

The new city of Sylon on planet Tuil had expanded in leaps and bounds since its inauguration over fifty years before. Unlike Pron, which was over a thousand years old, with its constant congestion, unhealthy smog and quaint means of vehicular transport, Sylon had been specifically built around the latest portal technology that was based on many new concepts found on Planet Eden. Eden was presently the seat of power within the galaxy of Osmaron, known to many of Earth's inhabitants as the Milky Way Galaxy.

The Tuillians had designed their ancient cities in the ways of their ancestral architects; two thirds underground and the remainder plus additions and extensions towards and above the surface. The most critical areas were deepest underground. That way they avoided the previous high death rate from the occasional meteoric bombardment every third year of their worlds progress about its parent star.

During the past century they had installed many orbiting satellites for early warning and matter diversion. There were also several orbiting platforms with mounted plasma projectors. Those would intercept the meteors and in the process create large super heated craters and jets of matter, to alter their orbits. Most of those new technologies they had gained from the advanced Octans in Osmaron. Presently they were the real technologists of the Shadites who were committed to assist worlds like Tuil from impending disaster. Lord Faemon, the Ploran, was presently in charge of that side of business within the Greater Purpose. However they were also aided by the Lodorians and Polokans.

As a result, all those recent introduced technological measures protected Tuil from those past dangers, making it possible for its civilizations to live on their planet's surface, even during the third year of the expected bombardments.

'Sire, we have received warning of a large meteor in sector seven approaching at great speed from deep space,' Toran announced. He was the son of Nogad who had died during a previous strike.

'Set several scanners and keep an eye on its current position. I want a complete analysis in composition, spin, and approaching velocity. Also check for small objects following. Our new high gain sensors will be able to detect an object the size of a small pebble. Set primary drones to intercept at one hour before critical distance. Keep me informed!' Controller Wyman, Cleman's elder son ordered. Like Nogad, Cleman was killed during a previous strike.

'All data has been entered into our targeting computer. Now we wait!' Toran fiddled with a few knobs and buttons while Wyman checked the flat screen monitor at his location.

'Dam it! Six croes (about 7 miles) across, It's even bigger than the one that killed our parents. And 100,000 croesons (110000 miles per hour). If she strikes that monster will put pay to all life on our world.' Wyman continued scratching his forehead while waiting for new inspiration.

'Sire, we have no choice. It's too massive for our usual weapons. They will not put a significant dent on that moonlet.' Toran was worried in case the fast moving object passed beyond safe distance.

'This is definitely not a normal one. We've never registered one with such a high velocity before. Not in the last 1000 creons (1600 years). I wander where it came from?' he murmured still scratching his forehead.

'Sire, it's approaching critical distance. Shall I give the order?' Toran was impatient and churning in his high seat.

'I suppose you'll have to, it's our only choice,' Wyman replied, realizing it was their only backup system.. Once fired that weapon required half a day to recharge.

Toran pressed a red button on his panel and the secondary screen came to life showing the large lump of rock approaching his station. It was rotating about a common axis and determined to do the most damage to anything in its path including his world below. It followed its course with many other companions, some as large as buildings.

The large space station on which they stood began to rotate and move to a more suitable position in space. It had to be lined up with the trajectory of the target to be most effective and at near light speed it soon arrived at that optimum position.

'We are on target, Sire. Weapons primed and ready to fire. Graviton beams are ready to repel all smaller objects and debris,' the screen displayed.

'I Think it's time I said a prayer in case things go wrong and there is no need for those beneath us to know about the evil one that approaches,' Wyman murmured to himself. Then he knelt for prayer, but in silence. Suddenly the orbiting station rocked slightly as the gravitron fired and intense beam. All the smaller objects had been vaporized. Because of the sudden jolt Toran was thrown across the room but soon regained his stance and nerves.

'Quick, Toran! Go and do it manually. You are closer to the control panel. Go!.....Go!.... save all our lives!' Wyman said and waited. Toran slid down the almost virtual stairwell and entered the master control room. That weapon was supposed to be automatic, but remote was badly damaged from a previous encounter. He soon found the transparent housing with another red button that was meant for use during an emergency. He broke the glass and pressed the button just in time. There was a massive roar which shook the station and in an instant the large moonlet was as hot as the centre of a star. It and its companions soon vaporised into one enormous explosion. Then once more everything went still, including those on that faithful lookout station.

'Thank God for that!' Toran whispered as he realized the death of his father on a previous encounter because of smaller objects. However the Gravitron given to them by Lumak had made a substantial difference and saved their lives.

Since then they had utilized micro robotics in many of their cities' functions and utilities, making the new environments more comfortable and pleasant for its many citizens. However only their better citizens were allowed within its heavily secured enclosures, and those most trusted senior members of their society were issued with special portal passes for that purpose.

Sylon had been constructed within a transparent and sealed dome, acquiring virtually nil pollution from the filthy atmosphere of the industrial planet outside.

It was the first dome city to be built in that manner and if found satisfactory, the process would be replicated throughout the planet. Such dome habitats would be built everywhere, until all its occupants, including wild life, was isolated from the poisonous atmosphere. Then the complete biosphere would be slowly cleansed and detoxified over a period of several generations. It was also an ideal way to control population growth by adding certain chemicals to their water supply and imported foods.

The gigantic machines for the cleansing process were already being constructed on designated sites throughout the planet. After their completion, almost all industrial processes would be sited elsewhere on barren worlds. Such were the processes of planetary re-modelling when large indigenous populations could not be evacuated elsewhere.

The new portal technologies learnt from the Osmaron Federation had allowed them a way out of their problems of industrial pollution and Global Warming, providing their population was kept within specified limits. Technological advancement was usually a great incentive for population reduction and the Federation was good at solutions while dangling a carrot.

With Lumak's ingenuity and assistance, they were finally able to transpose their operations on moons and dead worlds over many regions of space well within their lifetimes.

Unlike Earth's conversion, which had mainly failed because of its severe overpopulation, their planetary ruler, Toccor IV, passed laws prohibiting any form of unprotected coupling for the purposes of procreation. By so doing, only those with a procreation license could produce offspring.

The penalty for breaking that law was banishment to the hostile penal mining world of Tribor IV within their system. That method of birth control was preferable to seeding their planet's environment with bio-engineered bacteria as with the Terminal Disease on Earth, or the use of sterility drugs. Everyone of age would be issued protective kits and informants given extra privileges.

His people would be judiciously informed of all the facts and lawbreakers would swiftly suffer the consequences of their impetuous actions. It was during that time that they were informed of the dreaded Javols by Lumak. That gory transmission was meant to shock them into a correct decision.

Once the majority had accepted their present course, the process of population reduction would continue until there was a planetary safe balance. During that period some fertile couples would be randomly selected for procreation, giving every obedient family the same chance.   The knowledge of the approaching Javols had made all Tuillians very compliant and many began to consider their long term survival in light of those dangers.

GEMMI DOFF

Shadite Gemmi Doff had lived in her new apartment in Sylon for several years.

'Thank's, whoever you are for recommending me for such a beautiful apartment,' she murmured, before crawling towards the kitchen for a drink. She never realized it was her old friend Lumak. He had assisted her people many times in the past and was one of his request from the emperor.

Once again she strolled unto the circular cushion and felt more comfortable than she had been for ages. She had only recently arrived to her home world from yet another mission for her Grand Lord.

She was now a grade 2 Shadite and had been assigned to many

important missions for the Greater Purpose, including the present one on her home world. Of all, the most memorable was with Lumak and Plato. That was during the evacuation of the Feloween from their nova catastrophe on Misoran II to Romera IV. She could also faintly remember another mission with Lumak, but whenever she tried her mind became a blank. It was almost as if those memories were blocked. Although she had met Lumak several times since, he had always been on urgent missions.

She pondered those thoughts and soon fell into deep slumber. Then she found herself in a falling nightmare. Just before she crashed unto the ground below, there was a burring noise in her head which took her out of sleep. She realized it was her brain implants informing her of an incoming call. She allowed the communication, while struggling from her bench to select her favourite beverage for that time of day.

'I must have been under for six hours. I didn't realize I was so tired,' she thought.

'Gemmi! It's me, Lumak. I decided to pay you a short visit. Nothing urgent, but I might need your assistance for something important.'

'Lumak! What a pleasant surprise. I was just thinking of you, Plato and old times.' She hadn't seen him in years.

'Nowadays I'm based in Osmaron!'

'I hear it's a fantastic place to be these days.'

'Yes, presently we are very busy. Are you hitched yet?'

'No! But had a few affairs. These days I don't have much time for long-term relationships. Anyway, I love the Shadite's life too much for that.'

'That's my girl, always sensible about everything. I think I shall take you to Osmaron to meet my wife. Then you can have a long holiday with us.'

'That will be fab.'

'Do you like your apartment?'

'I love it! How did you know?'

'Ha! Ha!' Lumak laughed.

'It was you who recommended me for this beautiful place.'

'Yep! They owed me a few favours and I called one in. Hope

you like it. Anyway, I'm on my way up.'

'Please make it soon.' she replied. She down-loaded the address information and broke the link.

Once again Lumak's incredible ship materialized in a myriad of multi-coloured lights just outside the main building and many of its brave local inhabitants, including their little children, went to view the strange inexplicable occurrence. Soon there was a large crowd of Speell on the scene to observe and comment on the strange aberration.

They were a very inquisitive race and relished a journey into the unknown. However the shock of the alien human figure walking through the walls of a ship without a doorway was to them truly gross and beyond reality. Many took to their multiple heels from that unexpected shock.

Since changing into the human form many decades before, Lumak had adopted that one on a more permanent basis. He didn't relish the process of changing into an alien form every time he visited a different world. There was also the relearning of all those sensual perceptions and the evolved modes of travel and manipulation. He would only forego those transformations if the environment was not a natural one and he required those changes to survive like its inhabitants over a lengthy period.

He knew their language well, so he released the hood behind his neck to reveal his human features and called them to him.

'My beloved friends of Sylon, there is no need for fear. I am Shadite, and I am here to visit an old friend. She is Siend Gemmi Doff, and I am told she lives within this local building.' He spoke in their language. Lumak was wearing black but not his famous Shadite's Cloak.

'My God! He is Shadite!' one of the local ones shouted and many began to murmur amount themselves.

'Where is he from?' shouted another.

'I am from the galaxy you call Fondle, and we call Osmaron,' Lumak replied.

'All the way from Fondle. Is that really possible?' the first one exclaimed.

They halted their progress in the direction away from the ship and began to get close to observe the strange alien form.

They had heard of the Shadites and knew they were messengers of a higher order within the universe. Anyway, that is what they were thought in school, but other than their own Gemmi Doff, they had never seen such a strange one before. Many came forward to feel his blacker than black garment. Then it suddenly changed into a brilliant white before their eyes.

'Who will look after my ship for me?' he shouted and everyone in that crowd, included the kids, lifted their forward right arms.

After spending time with the large crowd and answering their many questions, he took a local portal and were transferred to Gemmi Doff's apartment.

'Woo... What a surprise! A human surprise!' Gemmi Doff greeted. Despite her initial foreboding, she had grown used to the human form over the years. She herself had tried it during her visit to Eden in Osmaron for her implants, and had found it quite acceptable.

Seeing him completely vertical, while being horizontal in her large caterpillar-like form, made her think how dissimilar both species were. Yet, the human one was a lot simpler. Being vertical it occupied less horizontal surface and was a lot less cumbersome in getting about. Also, they took up a lot less space in crowds. Yet their voices and some facial features were similar.

'We have an important trip ahead of us. For that one you must become human again. I shall take you to Eden, where you will be transformed and briefed. From what little I have been told, your galaxy and its peoples are in immediate danger.' She closely observed his human features and realized he was not in his usually happy disposition.

'That bad, eh!' she replied.

'Do you remember that time we visited the barren world of Riporan III? It was the planet with the strange Hexolyte underground installations.'

'Yes! I do! How could I ever forget! It was the one with the good demons, and I wanted to complete that mission to see where it led,' she replied.

'I said we would take up that quest again, at some future time when we were not on urgent missions. I have now been given the go-ahead by the Grand Lord himself and after all this time, would like you to be my historian and archaeologist once again. Plato is also part of this campaign and will join us later, after he has completed his current mission.'

'Wow! After all this time? I was worried then and I am still worried now. Well, if I'm needed, my humble person is at your command, Sire. But I must first inform my cousin Prann. He is running a local black ship. He can take over in my absence. Anyway, my job here is almost completed. I had to map out our world for siting more dome environments,' she replied, in her usual humorous manner.

'Prann! I haven't seen him since that mission. Let me contact him for you.'

Lumak soon contacted Shadite Prann and explained the situation to him and he agreed to fill in.

'Hi, Pal. Long time no see. We must get together soon for some timely celebrations.'

'Getting together again will be great. I look forward to it,' Prann replied.

'By the way, I need Gemmi for an urgent mission and would like you to supervise her present project.'

'That's no problem. I have the right person for that job on board ship.'

'In that case, thanks, and see you soon!'

No one ever refused Lumak who was Grade 1.

Gemmi had grown to love Eden on her previous visit and knew she would be very well cared for at Sarah's palace as before. But she took along a few carvings and perfumes as gifts. Anything else would not have been relevant in her new human form.

Several hours later they arrived in the palace grounds on Eden and were received by Sarah.

After a brief rest, she was taken to the Macron, Mac, where she was transformed into a most beautiful human female with more advanced brain implants.

CHAPTER 2

The ancient Hexolyte base revisited

It was not long before Lumak and Gemmi were summoned to Little Osmaron to be in the presence of the Grand Lord of the seventh part of the known universe. They transposed through the magnificent crystal enclosure and found themselves in a brilliantly lit room. Presently that satellite moonlet orbited planet Eden and remained perched above Eden City in a geostationary orbit.

'I brought you here to inform you of certain changes within the master plan. The Hexolyte, Dracma, has recently arrived in Triangulum with the intention of reviving his demon kind to plague the universe once again.

'He will use whatever means available for that purpose. You are to locate all their main bases within the local galaxies and install hidden H-wave communicators so that their progress may be monitored.

They filled their special super fast reconnaissance and surveillance ship with all the provisions it could hold and were soon on their way back to Triangulum. This time they headed directly to its nucleus to investigate a white dwarf star. That one had been pinpointed on the alien's map several decades before during a previous excavation.

'How do you feel with your new body and its superior implants,' Lumak asked, knowing it would have taken several days for her to recover from the system shock of being human and in getting used to her new senses.

'Just a little strange and groggy. I'm afraid, this time it's a little less intense. Perhaps it's because I did it once before. I'll need a little more sleep than anticipated, so I hope you don't mind if I remain inactive for a little while. Otherwise I might not be of much use to you for a couple days or so.'

'That's quite ok. Using just LPDs, it will take us three days to get to where we are going and this ship is on automatic, so you can sleep as long as you wish. When we get to our destination I will give you a nudge. I have placed you in virtual, so enjoy some restful music and images with a little tranquillity while you rest,' he said and she nodded and fell fast asleep, to be subconsciously awakened into a virtual world of an Alice-in-Wonderland adventure.

She had taken special booster drugs to speed the process of humanization, but those also had the side effect of making its subjects sleep during the re-configuration and learning process. However the virtual program was also designed to enhance the drugs by placing her new human mind in simulated adventures, many of which were survival orientated. Original herbivores and non-predatory life-forms always had problems when changing to predatory types like humans. It was partly to do with the balance of hormones in their systems. However once the change was made they grew to like the social experiences in that body format.

Lumak had on board an analytical computer that he had programmed for the specific purpose of plotting that area of the universe in space and in time. By so doing, he could find the precise location of any known stellar body up to tens of billions of years in the past.

That computer was linked to the ship's own navigation computer and Lumak's brain implants.

After another three days, they arrived at their destination near the nucleus of Triangulum.

'You can have it! You Hexolyte bastards!' Gemmi shouted, furiously. But she slowly opened her eyes to view the strange cabin with Lumak at its controls.

'Sorry captain. I just had a fight with a few Javols and a couple Hexes. You took the Javols out and I terminated their superiors.'

'Ah! You are finally back with us. Those were the final images in your conversion program. They were meant to kick start you back into the real human world,' he replied, smiling. She awoke from her deep sleep with much better coordination and an appetite to match. Her implants were also more finely tuned and could now be linked with the ship's computer. Feeling somewhat guilty for her absence, she decided to assist, but she soon found there was nothing to do with Lumak's brand of advanced technology.

'How long have I been under?' she enquired, still in a slight daze.

'Only two days. We have about another to go.' She viewed the enormous galactic bulge through her linked implants.

'Commander, do you think there is intelligent life in this part of the galaxy?'

'It wont be natural. The radiation levels out here are far too intense for natural evolution. Too many heavy nuclei and cosmic rays shooting about. Any life out here will be robotic, microid or perhaps an elemental form.

'Javols or Hexolytes would relish this part of the galaxy. However, they also require a constant supply of primal life for their sustenance. So they would prefer an area just outside the nucleus.

'You know, evolution has very little to do with random radiation, which if anything, impedes the process. Evolution has purpose and is more to do with the will of a self-aware entity, desperately wanting a specific change to enhance its survival causation. It might take numerous generations to attain a specific goal and pass it, but it is never random. Well, not random in the long term. If a condition is not suitable for us we will not remain under those conditions but move to another more acceptable environment. That applies to all life-forms, even microbes. They will continually move away to more acceptable environments and will themselves to adapt. Therefore, it's a strong will that matters.

'It's like a wanting to climb a mountain or fly from branch to branch. Only those specific muscles and bones would be developed and shaped for that purpose. Radiation could not assist such a process because the parts of their genes relevant to those muscles and bones would not be specifically targeted by random radiation. That wanting, to get away from a predator or even to get a prey, would over many millennia change the life-form into a more suitable type for that type of wanting in its survival causation.

'A planet does not evolve life. Only life evolves life. A dead planet, even with an active atmosphere, will always remain a dead planet. However, the moment life is introduced unto that world evolution will begin. Life is usually introduce when certain building blocks like proteins and nucleic acids fall unto a planet from outer space during initial stages of planetary evolution. The stellar processes involved are quite complex. Nevertheless, this incredible process tells us that every living thing holds a special living entity within its person which makes it self-aware.

'In the case of prey and predator. The prey will sense its natural enemy and attempt to device a better method of survival, by better protection and defence and finding a better means of escape. The predator will devise better weapons and skills to locate and consume its prey. By so doing, a balance is met and both prey and predator survives together and in balance,' Lumak said, while Gemmi listened attentively.

'If that is the case, where did the original life come from to seed the planet and begin the process?' she asked.

'Like the heavier elements, the building blocks of cosmic life begins with a supernova or a giant star blowing off parts of its atmosphere. You know, giant stars exist as life givers. Anyway, during that time many of the heavier nuclei come together to form complex proteins and nucleic acids. Those in their many variety are distributed throughout space and are scattered everywhere within the galaxies by cosmic winds, meteors and comets to seed all worlds. However, only suitably parent worlds with a correct environment can nurture primal life,' he replied.

'Where does the special entity come from,' she asked, out of curiosity.

'Some think that a living entity is an indestructible bubble of space-time, which existed since the beginning of the Cosmos. They were the first building blocks of the Cosmos, which encompasses and permeates all things, being inter-dimensional. It was during that time that order came to exist out of chaos. That was even before matter and time existed. So you see, our innermost beings or identities are the oldest living entities in the Cosmos. Nevertheless, there are numerous identities and many that are non-corporeal that exist within what we call the Nexos.

However, many also exist within the City of Gohenna or Goh. Every thing that exist and can be given a name has an Identity associated with it.

'To further understand, you must think of an entity as a prime number. A number is unique in that it cannot be removed or destroyed. Can you destroy the number 4. If you could, no one would be able to add 2 and 2 to make 4. As a matter of fact, the whole system of numbers would collapse.

'In a similar manner, an Identity is unique and cannot be destroyed, but its inter-dimensional matrix can be enhanced through experience and corporeal change. That is because, there are numerous amounts of such individual entities in a body, thus forming the complete life force. Once they form a suitable cognitive matrix, the spirit in that form can continue its explorations to eternity. Like the numerical system of numbers, every Identity in the universe is needed to make it complete.

'You should further realize, that the whole Cosmos is composed of Identities and groups of Identities. Whether they be groups of atoms to form a particular substance or a group of sub-atomic particles to form an atom, and all those will have their own Identities. Since every Identity is unique, only one type of the same can ever exist within the Cosmos. That is why everyone of us are so unique. Even if an identical clone was made of you at this moment, your Identity would not be in it and it will have its own identity, simply because every atom in its body will be different to yours.

'Space is filled with visible matter and a similar amount of invisible entities which cling to ordered strains of matter. The more ordered, the more they cling. So I suppose certain types must prefer the symmetry of a DNA chain. Apparently, because of their self-awareness, there is an inbuilt desire to explore and modify. So evolution must begin with the smallest protein chains.

'Further, such an Entity or Identity has the strange ability to modify its environment by a strong desire or wanting. You know, all life is capable of altering the chaotic nodes of matter by thought. This is also the process used in evolution, a form of altering ones own matter to enhance its survival causation. Hence the reason why planetary life tends to form a symbiotic relationship with their planet,' She was surprised by his detailed knowledge of such unknowns.

Their small ship suddenly appeared above the planet but did not release its shields to become visible. Lumak was particular about their methods in case he aroused too many sleeping dogs.

'We must not leave evidence of our presence on any of the worlds we visit. That means we cannot disturb anything, not even the dust within their installations.

'Our cloaks must be fully vectored and surveillance units placed withing solid rock or within the walls of their enclosures.

'These small units are held within specially phased containers which will materialize minutes after they are activated. Three will be placed within each installation, although only one is required. Then we place micro probes in orbit about this world to relay the information.

'Because Hexolytes do not use electromagnetics, all links from their installations to our orbiting probes will be of that type. However, the probes are both electromagnetic and H-wave.

'Once the probes are initiated, they will transmit all received data to one of several randomly selected repeaters. That way, they will not be able to locate any of our collection bases within this galaxy. The ancient Patriarch's bases must also be probed in a similar manner.'

'Ok, Boss. Lets do the work!' she replied and they both vectored their cloaks and floated out of the ship's wall towards the planet below. Being almost massless and unaffected by the remaining atmosphere of the planet meant the special LPDs could automatically propel them at incredible speed toward their destination.

They selected a warmer area of the frozen planet. That area was the most turbulent and with a large gradient in temperature. Those conditions were good evidence of an ancient underground fusion reactor that utilized hot plasma from the planet's core. That method was common with Hexolyte bases, since such installations tended to utilized hot matter for the fabrication of the other elements used in manufacture and repairs of their maintenance robots.

'Another world of ice with a white dwarf! Could be as dead as a dodo! It's like I've been here before?' She had seen similar places before but had not realized she had been with Lumak on a similar mission before for the Grand Lord, but this one was more massive and appeared to be the enemies' main base.

'You could be right! It's like deja vu. Anyway, we must be careful! Parts of their bases could be booby-trapped, so seal yourself into your suit! Now we should save our batteries and normalize our suits.' Lumak communicated through her implants. He anticipated the worst, but she had already selected that mode.

Lumak soon located the main door to the outer cave. That entrance was on a steep rock face overhanging the sunken plateau. The flat rectangular area of grey sand he called the sunken sea, but there was no water in that area, just a dense mist that covered a thick layer of sand.

On analysis, the sand was found to contain particles of debris from an ancient city. Over the aeons it had been reduced by the turbulent weather into a wavy surface of thin sand.

'To avoid any of their more subtle traps, I think we should follow their natural routes and entrances until we find the door to their main control room,' Lumak warned.

She followed him until they came upon the massive door with a perfectly flat surface, but with no orifices, handles or projections. It reminded her of the similar one they had encountered on Riporan III and she cringed with horror when she remembered the sight of the rows of human skeletons on the other side of the door. Not to mention her experience with the demon Neramon probing her mind.

'To save our batteries we should normalize for now and use vectorization only when needed,' Lumak repeated.

From previous knowledge, Lumak knew the code they used for such locks and had fabricated a suitable electro-magnetic key.

He pointed the small device, pressed a button, the catch released and the door slid opened vertically. That was the only way they could enter normalized without tripping the many sensors. After all, it would have been the natural route taken by any one of its previous occupants. However Lumak and Gemmi could have normalize their bodies before entering and vectorize once inside.

While normalized, they would be vulnerable, so only one could enter and vectorize before signalling the other at the rear. As always, Lumak took the lead normalized while a very nervous Gemmi followed at the rear.

Without disturbing any of the local debris just inside the door, he un-vectorized and Gemmi followed in his steps precisely. She was a trained Shadite and knew the processes involved.

That entrance led into a small area with three corridors that diverged into the distance. From what they could observe the underground facility was endless, with an assortment of many containment tanks and numerous connecting pipes of all shapes and sizes. It was another Hexolyte factory, but this one was constructed on a larger scale.

Lumak viewed its immensity with awe and realized it was probably the main part of their universal factory for mass-producing Hexolyte soldiers. At least that was their intentions before their plans were disrupted by the Patriarch Masters aeons ago.

Nevertheless despite its dormancy, that base had been kept in better condition than the others that had been visited. Judging from the cleanliness of the place, it had an active contingence of robots that came alive frequently to service the equipment and their environment. Such robots were advanced enough to create and replace other robots or even to alter their designs to more efficient models. A type of robotic evolution.

'We must locate their main portal. Judging from the way the rows are organized, it could be directly below us, but we should enter via their trap-door. There is usually at least one on every level,' he advised.

After an extensive search at that level they found the hidden door. It was on the same level as the floor and relied on two near human weights on either side in order to be released. They had to normalize and face the dangers of whatever traps had been set in that area.

When they entered there was a whir as the trap-door lifted and the area began to move beneath their feet. That whole area moved downwards to the next level and stopped. Despite the scare, they did not re-vectorize their cloaks in case the process relied on their joint weights. They did when the platform completed its descent and stopped. So far they had encountered no booby traps in that part of the building. Perhaps it was because those areas were more frequently used by personnel and robots.

They took the local stairs to yet another level and found themselves close to one of the ancient hexagram portals. It was a large area with the floor surface engraved with the hexagram and circles. Above their heads were the many rods and amplifiers used by such ancient portals. There were several attachments that linked with the portal to receive material or make connection to other similar portals on distant worlds. All being part of a massive production plant, perhaps intergalactic in scope.

'This place is more extensive and larger than any of our previous visits. I hope there are no more of their elemental demons down here waiting to surprise us?' Gemmi was apprehensive while waiting for the worst to happen, but the place was as silent as the grave. Lumak kept his silence while probing the area for any motion, but there was none.

They approached the first of many hexagram circles along the straight and narrow middle path. That one led as far as the eye could see. The circle they beheld were enclosed by five small tanks along its outer periphery. Several lines radiated from the centre of that area to the tanks and cris-crossed into the sign of a star. On either side of the large circle were massive pillars which could be circumvented by small zig-zag routes around them. Those two routes bypassed the circle but were not the easiest. The shortest and quickest path was directly through the centre of the circle.

CHAPTER 3

Within the limits of Hades, a repeating time-zone

Their cloaks were fully phased, making them immune from any physical dangers, so they decided to take the easiest of the three routes which led directly through the pentagram. The moment they entered that area it became active and they found their forms being pulled by an irresistible force into the unknown. For a brief moment they were in complete darkness.

'Oh, My God! What's happening?' Gemmi yelled.

'I don't know where this is going to take us, but we must always remain close together!' Lumak shouted through his implants. He then retrieved a thin cord from his utility belt and quickly linked it with hers. The vertex was long and dark and during their transit to a place or places unknown they were virtually helpless.

On arrival they came to a sudden stop on a firmer surface within several large pillars. The blackness became a reddish sky with many flames and fires burning in the distant horizon. Yet, the place was not alive. No life energy could be detected anyway, not even their own.

'This must be Hell!' she complained. When she revectorized her cloak to full she stumbled over a small rock and began to roll down hill. Lumak soon began to chase after her while she triple somersaulted down hill amidst a small rock-fall. Yet she remained silent despite being somewhat ruffled.

'This is the first time I needed protection from my cloak. Thank goodness, I'm still in one piece!' Lumak checked her over but there were no broken bones or bruises.

'Yes, you are still in one piece! This place is almost as dense as an ocean'

'Where do you think we are? I have a strange feeling I've been here before,' Gemmi inquired.

'One thing I know, it's a place I've been before. This place does not appear to abide by our natural laws. It could be another completely different universe and one where life hasn't yet evolved,' Lumak replied.

'As bad as that. If that is the case, how will we get back?'

'If there is a way in, they should also be an exit. Also, if we've been here before there will be a way out. We just have to find it. I've mapped this area and our present location in my implant, so we can always return to our point of entry. That is assuming there is another timed doorway in this local area.' Then he downloaded the information to her implant.

While they walked in their chosen direction, the fires diminished and they found themselves in an ancient place or city. But the strangest of all cities contained boxlike buildings, many of which were twisted and contorted, and was devoid of all life. The many stacked box-like enclosures were of all shapes and sizes. Within the distance they could observe several dragons blowing what appeared to be blue flames of light at others. Using their inbuilt LPDs, Lumak and Gemmi took to the air and were on the way to where the dragons were. They took cover behind a large square pillar until that area became uncomfortable. Then they decided to move again. This time they were exposed to all and sundry.

'At least our LPDs work? But our suit batteries need recharging,' She was more settled although still apprehensive and tense.

'Keep close to me. We must try to make it to the hills over there!' he shouted amidst the noise and roar of the flames.

A large and fearful dragon-like creature flew towards them from another direction and silently settled on the path in front of them, blocking their path and halting their progress.

'You are precisely on time. If you wish to survive their chambers of pain, quickly get on my back!' it urged. Utterly confused by all the strange occurrences about them, they mounted its back. After passing many large mountain ranges, it approached a cave that was sited close to the apex of the largest peak. That cave could not be observed while the dragon was in the air above the mountain.

Within that cave was many of the dragon-like creatures, but there were a few aliens and humans. Lumak soon realized that he could not communicate with Gemmi, so he quickly released his hood and attempted to breathe the dense air. After sampling and testing, he gestured to Gemmi and she released hers. The dragons spoke without moving their lips.

'I am Algo. You have been transposed to a place between universes. This is a link between ours and yours and a type of prison created by our superiors. Only the vilest of creatures are placed here, within the shadows of Hades. This place was created at the beginning of time by our forefathers, better known to you as the Mesotrenes. We are what you would consider the better part of our species and are now considered dangerous rebels by our so-called masters,' the creature, Algo, said.

'So you guys are Mesotrenes? I once read about your people.' Lumak said, while giving the Shadites greeting with hands on heart and Gemmi did likewise. Then another dragon came forward.

'I am Melfa. You are lucky we sensed and caught you in time or you would have surely been devoured by Kator. He is in charge of this place and will shortly be searching for you and your companion. He can sense all new entities within this plenum and no one ever survives his gaze. However, you will be quite safe with us here for now.'

'Thank you guys for your help. I am Lumak, and this is Gemmi my close companion. We are also of the good part of our universe. That part we call the Greater Purpose and we stand for life, freedom, and order within the Cosmos, if those attributes also hold in this place. We were investigating one of the Hexolyte bases within one of our galaxies and found ourselves falling within this trap. Could you tell us of a way out?' There was a deep silence, then Algo spoke.

'To our knowledge, there is no way out of this cursed place or we would have taken it aeons ago. This scenario is constantly changing. Whatever plans were made seconds ago will not hold in the future. The fabric of this place will soon change to another, so it is not easy to create a fixed and stable form from its substance. Further, within this realm, time constantly repeats itself in one continuous loop. However, the temporal loops, although continuous, will exhibit slight variation to cope with new unexpected changes within this continuum.'

'How strange can a place be?' Gemmi was concerned.

'Our cave here appears to remain constant in time only because of a spacial generator. This device also prevents our enemies from locating us, because it shrinks our space and places us ahead of our enemies in time, but we are not completely outside of the temporal loop. Everyone of us wears the special headband which links our bodies with the device and to our own engineered continuum.' Algo informed.

Lumak was surprised and worried by his present ordeal. He had no idea that the Mesotrenes were dragons who existed in another, but not parallel universe. Neither did he know that the majority were not nice creatures. Their universe appeared to be the exact opposite of all things natural. With its own type of order. Even the substance of that plane was different, with the ability to shrink and enlarge.

When their universe clashed with ours many aeons ago, they had obviously created a hyper-spatial link between both universes, but it had since been removed from their end as part of an ancient agreement with our seventh universe.

During that period of upheaval, they imposed a negative effect on our seventh universe. It was at that time they were given the necessary technologies to enhance their survival and were made to return. They were very ancient and may have existed in a very strange universe which made them little suited to ours.

Since the Grand Lord ruled the seventh part of all seven universes, Lumak thought that Grand Lord Gerra would be somewhere involved in the bigger picture. However that place called Hades was within the sixth part of the sixth universe and was not under his lord's jurisdiction. Nevertheless, despite their occasional deja vu, they could not remember that they had visited that very same place before to collect the ancient Patriarchs Aron and others. The Grand Lord had previously erased their memories. Now unknowingly, they were back to collect the other members of Aron's family.

'It appears that a link still remain between our universe and yours, but not the other way around. I wonder why that is the case?' an astute Gemmi inquired.

'It was a condition met for services rendered many aeons ago. However, there was no requirement to remove the link at your end. Nevertheless, others may have found a way to use it for their own purpose of domination,' Algo replied and licked his leathery lips with his forked tongue, as if to lubricate them.

'You mean to say, the Hexolytes in our universe have made contacts with these demons over here as allies in their plans?' Gemmi inquired.

'Being Demons themselves, Hexolytes will be accepted and the demons over here always prefer change, particularly a new universe to experience and change for themselves,' Melfa said.

'Perhaps it might be possible to re-establish a link at our end for your safety. Since it appears to me that we fight a common foe. At least, it will release you from eternal bondage. Is there others like us on this in-between world?' Lumak asked.

'Since the beginning, many have been sent here, but few like you. Some have found ways to survive and others were absorbed into the whole. However, ones like you still remain within Hades. They are too powerful for Kator and have built their own defences against him and his hordes,' Algo said.

'Where do you think they came from?' Gemmi asked.

'I don't know. Many could have used this place as a type of eternal prison from which no one could ever return,' Melfa replied.

'Well if Hexolytes can have allies, so also can we! Can you take us there. I mean, to the ones like us?' Gemmi asked.

'They will not accept outsiders. They trust no one. Not even us. That is the reason why they have survived this long,' Melfa replied.

'Is it possible to communicate with them?' Lumak asked.

'Only if we share the same time and space. That will mean releasing our spacial generators, and leaving us open to the mercies of Kator and his demonic hordes. Only then can you communicate telepathically with them through one of us,' Algo replied.

'In that case, let us assist you towards our common goal and perhaps in a little time we shall find an answer to our present dilemma,' Lumak replied and they agreed.

Both were taken to a lower level within the apparently large cavern within the mountain. Then they were issued their own neck-bands which linked them to the causal generators. That way they would exist just outside of Hades time and space, but with the occasionally phased cyclic temporal connection at the start of each time cycle.

CHAPTER 4

Jot, the inter-dimensional entity appears once again

Jot had existed within Lumak's mind since their meeting decades before. That strange occurrence took place while on his way to rescue the Feloween. After his wanderings from his own dimension, Jot was cast out from amongst his own entities because of irreversible changes to his being. That was due to his acquiring certain dimensional viral attributes that he had unknowingly collected during his wanderings outside of his domain. Like any contagious virus, those irreversible changes could have become dangerous to his own kind if he remained among them.

After rescuing Lumak from their strange dimension, the only way he could survive in the material universe was to possess part of Lumak's mind. However, although Lumak had given the entity permission, Jot had hypnotized Lumak into thinking he did not exist. So Lumak awoke thinking it was just a dream. However since that time he had assisted Lumak in many of his scientific projects without his knowledge.

Jot had learnt much over the decades and because of his capabilities, knew infinitely more than Lumak about inter-dimensional structures or the lack of them. Because of the strange qualities of their new dimension, Jot could now survive outside of Lumak's person.

To make himself visible, he became a small point of light which increased in intensity to a small radiant blue ball. He bobbed up and down on the flat surface of rock they used for a table. He floated through Lumak's head and in an instant Lumak knew who he was.

'Jot, what are you doing here?' Lumak asked and Gemmi looked at the strange light on Lumak's head with utter surprise.

'Do you both know each other?' she asked, perplexed.

'I met him before I arrived on Trom. That was during the evacuation of the Feloween. It's a long story and I will tell you all about it one day,' Lumak replied, but he had his mind on more important thoughts.

Foremost in Lumak's mind was how to find a way out of the strange in-between world. If only he could communicate with others like him from his own universe? If those other humans in Hades could resist Kator and his hordes, also meant they were superior beings and could aid in his release from the Hexolytes' super-trap. But if they were that good, wouldn't they have taken the quickest route out of their eternal prison long ago. Or had they chosen the Hades path for themselves, because it was safer than some other choice? Lumak pondered those ideas until a thought began to grow in his mind.

'I've got it! I've got it! I think I have found a way out of here,' the thought said and by its mode and inclination he knew it was his old friend, Jot.

'What have you found, my friend?' Lumak asked.

'This place is between universes, which are themselves different planes of existence. It shares the laws and substance of both, albeit in a more chaotic manner. Being intermixed, their effects are reflected in the strange environment observed within this sub-plane called Hades. By unravelling and isolating those attributes, it will be possible to escape.

'It is possible to isolate residual substances from here that are part of our real universe. Then with that substance we can create an environment similar to our own universe which is very different to this one. By so doing, we should be rejected by this one. In a not too dissimilar manner to the way I was rejected from mine,' Jot said and Lumak smiled at the ingenuity of his little pal.

'That's an intriguing hypothesis, but risky. What if the ship blows up during the process of rejection?' Lumak replied calmly but with a smile.

'That is not possible! If it blows up, even more unwanted material will be present and the numerous fragments would be infinitely more difficult to remove from the system. Such substances cannot be created nor destroyed, only transferred to other places and certain substances will follow the more natural course to blend with others of their own kind,' Jot said.

'Pal, you seem to have it all in place, so why don't we try and see.' Lumak was finally convinced that Jot was on the correct track in finding a way of escape.

'Could you get Algo and his friends to design such a device?' Lumak asked.

'I am sure I can, with what little I've learnt from their type of technologies,' Jot replied.

'Well if you can do this, Pal, you will have me as your best friend to eternity. However, in the mean time I must locate the others from our universe before we can leave this place,' Lumak advised.

Because their human form hadn't changed significantly since their arrival, Lumak and Gemmi thought the only way they could make contact with the other humans was to merge with the original Hades and take their chances with Kator and his hordes. However once that step was taken they could only find Algo and his other companions again by merging with their space-time coordinates. That meant he had to take along an arm-band for the convertor that would linked them at the appropriate time. He also realised that all those in the proximity of the arm-band would be similarly transposed to the new temporal parameters. Nevertheless only when they approached the position of the cave could they be converted to the new microscopic dimensions.

They informed their companions of their intentions and stealthily crept away towards the southern regions. They assumed that was the place where the humans they sort would be found amidst many dangers. Apparently, their fortress occupied the southern part or south polar region of that strange in-between world. Their few Mesotrene enemies occupied the northern or northern hemisphere and Kator, its northern polar regions.

The world itself was barely ten kilometres in diameter. Worlds within the Mesotrene universe were somewhat smaller and there were no stars or galaxies, just planetoids of immense mass floating about in an ocean of a less dense and transparent medium. At lease that was what Lumak and Gemmi observed. Life in that realm received their energies from the strange medium that permeated its spaces.

Beyond the spacial curtain of the in-between dimension of Hades were those cratered worlds that extended to infinity. Mesotrenes existed in a myriad of different sizes within that universe. That was the only species that could evolve within its strange domains, and they took sustenance directly from the medium while travelling through its vastness. Yet, they were ancient and each species attained the knowledge of all others at the time of birth. It was as if the universe itself was a living entity and the perpetual ocean was a multiple of substances, including an interface for their universal mind.

There was a strong telepathic link between them and the universal medium, which permeated everything for its own survival causation.

'Siend, I never thought such a place could ever exist out of the weirdest nightmares and here we are,' Gemmi complained.

'I must agree, it's one of those experiences better done without, but we Shadites are constantly tested,' Lumak replied.

'Yea, we could be here on purpose. I have a strong sense that we have been here before,' she advised.

'Since time constantly repeats itself, it's hard to tell,' Lumak replied.

Lumak wondered about the strangeness of that world and could not fathom its depths. Neither did he attempt that course of action in earnest, because the process sickened and irritated him. After all, the environment was so utterly boring to any creature that needed the experience of beauty and variation in all their many shades. However the Mesotrene's real universe existed within their minds. They were highly creative and had conceived their own universe within a world of abstraction. That was because, in their real universe they had little else to do or appreciate. He also realized that was the reason they wanted other universes to explore.

Jot gave instructions to the friendly dragons for the types of enclosures he wanted and they were built in sections. The special field convertors were designed to change one of the structures to the precise material of the seventh universe. A second one of equivalent mass was to be configured in a different manner. That one would be left behind as its doppelganger. Only in that way could their bodies be transferred safely to their home dimension.

With spiritual entities like Jot, the process did not matter, because he was almost compatible with both universes and for long enough periods. Nevertheless he could not survive within the seventh universe on his own for very long without Lumak's assistance.

'Do you think the device will be ready by our return,' Lumak inquired through their mutual telepathic link.

'It will be ready by anytime when you return. This is because you will be outside of our time and we can adjust our temporal loop to contain those events,' Algo said telepathically.

'Stranger and stranger!' Gemmi replied, but patiently listened through her implants.

CHAPTER 5

Passage through Hades a second time

Lumak felt completely helpless in the in-between dimension of Hades. It was apparent from the time of their arrival, that his Shadite's Cloak, including all his weapons had stopped functioning. And that was not all, their forms were slowly changing to the stronger elements of that strange dimension. Even their LPDs had stopped functioning. Only their implants continued and they wondered when those functions would stop.

The more natural dragons of that plane were favoured with a bluish flame, which they utilized to reduce their enemies. By blowing the flame on their victims something was taken from them and they reduced in size. Whatever it was, gave the larger creatures greater powers over their minions and they increased in size. But they never carried the process to termination. Their victims were better alive than dead. After all, they could grow again and be further harvested, while they in turn would harvest those beneath them, ad infinitum. That was the only way they took real power from that dimension. But they could also draw energy from the strange spacial substance that propagated everywhere. Occasionally a dragon would acquire greater powers by chance and begin to dominate the others. That process of prey and predator within that singular type of species must have continued to eternity.

They had each been handed a special net by Algo for protection during their travels.

'This will protect you for a while as you travel southward. It will prevent them from extracting your elemental energies. Try not to get too close to the large ones. Their powerful breath can tear the net and constant attacks will diminish its protection. When you approach the southern fortress, switch the communicator fully on. It will amplify your thoughts and link you with theirs.'

For that important journey Lumak and Gemmi had transformed their bodies into the natural Hades types and had taken the eight kilometre route to the southern fortress. According to Algo, that area was filled with the smaller of his species and they would not pose a great threat in themselves. However whatever they observed would be instantly relayed to their superiors, who would soon be on their way to investigate. Even so, those dragons would not have entered a three mile limit imposed by the southern citadel. Nevertheless the two Shadites would be exposed to unwanted encounters during the first four kilometres of their journey.

Once they were released to the natural environment of that place, they walked with difficulty along the surface of the strange and rugged world. The dense atmosphere was similar to that encountered at the bottom of an ocean, with its many obstructions and changing currents. When they tried to increase their speed, their bodies slowed and when they slowed below a certain level their bodies speeded up. Nothing remain still in Hades. Not even the world they were on, for it constantly rotated. Like a gigantic ocean, the energy medium was meant for swimming, so Lumak sent a telepathic thought to Gemmi and like fish they both took to the dense water-like medium. To them the medium appeared perfectly transparent and colourless.

'I didn't realize we could float this way in this substance. Travelling like this is a lot faster but not as quick with wings,' Lumak said.

'This is almost like having fun, providing we are not eaten by a dragon-shark,' Gemmi commented.

'That's why the dragons are so nimble. Their bodies have been specifically designed for this environment,' Lumak replied.

They could watch thousands of dragons floating about and moving hither and thither. Ever so often a larger one would pounce on a smaller one and absorb its energies until it became a minute spec. However by that action it would have stirred a much larger one into action. Then that one would pounce to absorb its newly claimed energy, leaving it with an equivalent size of its previous victim. That way some form of order was maintained.

Lumak pondered the thought, that if they got larger and larger to infinity, why were there no giant dragons within that world and how did the little ones come into existence in the first place, since they all appeared to be of a single sex or perhaps even sexless.

The little dragons constantly moved their small wings for speed, with their webbed three fingered hands and tail for guiding them through the medium.

'I don't think they can harm us. We are not like them and are not composed of their strange chemistry. I think we should ignore them and carry on as if they didn't exist,' Lumak said, but Gemmi was not convinced. Soon after they were observed by a large dragon several times their size and like a desperate shark he moved towards them at great speed.

They dodged and darted hither and thither, trying to shake off the creature, but it persisted and kept on their trail. It might have considered them to be something special. A new type of living energy in its dimension to be sampled. After all, how often in its whole existence had such a lucky chance morsel occurred.

As they approached the southern region they could observe a ring of blue flames encircling that area and the once desperate dragon made a sudden last-attempt and dived towards them. He missed and in an instant changed direction and vanished. Not a single dragon could be observed within that region of Hades and the medium was perfectly clear.

'Oh! That was a near miss!' Gemmi exclaimed.

'I hope those here are more friendly,' Lumak replied, but continued onward.

Lumak switched his communicator on and sent a thought.

'I am Lumak the Shadite and have come from the Seventh primal universe of humans and others. I was brought into this strange in-between world of Hades by a Hexolyte trap. We are the new guardians of the seventh universe and need your assistance. There is much we can learn from you and we have information that will interest you. Can we discuss these matters?'

They felt a rumble within the spacial medium and a narrow passage formed within the local flames, but there was no reply.

They propelled their way towards the narrow opening, trying their hardest not to miss their landing at the neck of the dangerous flames. They assumed the strange flame had something to do with the energy elements of the Mesotrenes' universe and did not wish to experience its clutches at first hand.

Lumak was the first to land. Once he had gained a foothold, he guided Gemmi to his position. The flames soared on either side and had the powers to absorb their energies and reduce them in size.

'That was another close encounter. I just missed it by a foot. Did you know, this flame has no warmth or heat. It just penetrates and absorbs,' she said.

'How do you know?' he inquired.

'I felt it in my innermost senses,' she replied. Then he realized it was probably an extra sense.

They followed through the centre of the narrow passage with menacing flames on either side and above, which were assisted by more wandering currents that tried to move them either way. Despite their protective nets, the flames seemed to penetrate the core of their very beings. Yet, their protective nets held. Those flames seemed to engulf the complete area of the south polar region.

They soon realized that only human forms with the ability to walk could enter that area. One had to be firmly anchored to that type of terra firma to manoeuvre themselves through the narrow passages, and those dragons without any hind legs, had little knowledge of the concept of walking and could only float in the deadly inferno with its much slower currents.

CHAPTER 6

Patriarch's City beyond reality

As they approached the end of the path, the area about them began to fold and they found themselves falling into a bright light, not too unlike the sensation felt in an intergalactic portal. Suddenly they found themselves in an enclosed place with a large door. On the door was inscribed many ancient symbols that had been engraved unto it. The entrance opened to reveal a large transparent sphere amongst an infinity of Mesotrene worlds. The sphere itself contained a large city with many diverse life-forms. Even Mesotrenes could be observed within its large transparent bubble. There were numerous such bubbles containing their own cities, which were unlike the boxlike structures encountered on their arrival in Hades.

Like an immense bubble, the local city floated within the medium as if completely isolated from its influences and that area outside the city contained many dragons, but they were all of similar size and did not prey upon each other. One approached the couple to guide them into the city.

'I am Malfor. I have been ordered to guide you into the city of Gol. Our masters would like to meet you,' the creature said telepathically and they followed.

Soon a powerful voice thundered into their minds.

'You have been transposed to the seventh part of this universe of the Mesotrenes. This part is within what you call the Greater Purpose, and we have been informed of your arrival.' Then the voice snapped off.

Suddenly, Lumak felt more at ease within himself and sensed the dangers felt since his arrival in Hades were dissipating. However he would have felt a lot better within his own universe, even with lurking Javols and Hexolytes about. To him, Hades was the eternal hell, where his type could never fulfil a truly creative dream. Here, there was no beauty, no colour, no trees or other forms of life. He also wondered how any life-forms could live an eternity in such a vacuous environment.

The dragon took them to the only entrance of that transparent world with many waiting.

'You must wait here for your guides. They will take you to our Master's citadel within Gol.'

That dragon soon departed. Thereafter four creatures of light came forward. They were like large fairies, but appeared to be composed of light energy. They held Lumak and Gemmi by their shoulders and lifted them toward a distant palace.

'We approach the citadel of our masters. Clear your minds and prepare yourselves, because they can see through your every thought,' one of the beings said.

'The master awaits your presence,' another one said and dropped them on a white floor in the centre of the building. Then their guides left via one of the many entrances. There was a blinding light and from the brilliance walked an ancient Patriarch.

'Thank you for returning to collect us. I am Tellor and here is my wife, Carrol. You have been specially chosen to take us home.'

'You mean you are one of the ancient Patriarchs? The great Tellor of old?' Gemmi exclaimed. She had heard so much from Lumak about their great exploits against Hexolytes in ancient times, she just couldn't remain silent.

'Yes, we are the same! You came here before to collect my father Aron and brothers. All your memories were erased on your return for security reasons. The Hexolytes' base was rigged to bring you to us at an appropriate time. I am afraid, it was the only way.' Then Lumak realized the cleverness of such a device. It was the perfect path to their world, since only the right ones with good intentions would have found their way through. All others being taken to the worst places of that universal dimension.

'I thought you had died many aeons ago, but you live?' a surprised Lumak inquired.

'We all live. This is a place of eternity. Within its boundaries no one ever dies. We had to take this path without making our enemies too suspicious. We knew we would have to return in later times to secure our universe, and could not have taken any chances in case our enemies caught on. Neither would they have been suspicious of the use of their own base for our purpose. But we have also learnt of changes in our original universe.'

'What changes, My Lord,' a humbled Gemmi inquired.

'We can no longer exist within your universe in our original forms. However we have designed special containers that will hold our beings until the appropriate time of release, when we are given new bodies. Our Grand Lord has made the necessary arrangements for us.'

'So we are to escort you out of this place once again?' Lumak inquired, realizing their present mission had been planned from the start.

'Yes, you will be our escort. At this time, the rest of us will return with you. We are just eight,' Tellor said.

There was another flash and all his remaining family members appeared as if from nowhere. They were indeed very powerful beings and were twice the size of an average human. Their thick eyebrows lifted upwards and their foreheads were slightly bulged and more circular. Yet, their eyes were intense and piercing.

'I am very happy to have been given this great privilege and will always remain your humble servant until our safe arrival back within our home universe,' Lumak said and bowed.

Soon they encircled him and Gemmi, observed their strange attire for a while. Then they offered their powerful hands in friendship.

Lumak told them of his universe, and the way it was today and they were happy that the majority of predator species had disappeared, with the exception of the Javols, whom they had not met. He also told them of the rebels Algo and others, who had assisted him in his quest.

'Algo is also one of us. His task is to remain hidden and watch for all new arrivals. Shortly, he will lend his skills to our departure.'

'It's nice to know who to trust. We found them quite helpful,' Gemmi interjected.

'Your companion Jot has done well in designing a suitable containment vessel for our journey. A more detailed knowledge of which has been dispatched to Algo.'

'Yes, Jot is good at that sort of thing,' Lumak replied.

'Since you have initiated the doorway, no longer are we to remain prisoners within these realms beyond Hades. Nevertheless, we must not get carried away and allow the Mesotrene masters to possess this knowledge, or they could try to re-establish a link with the Hexolytes or another predator species as in ancient times.'

'Yes. That possibility also worries me.' Lumak replied.

'Their minds cannot penetrate beyond the bubble. It is like a separate universe within the Mesotrene's one. So there is no need to worry. It is their way, you know, and the way of their universe. They are not at fault, for everyone must be allowed free will to evolve in its own ways, as with prey and predator. Even the aging star must be allowed its freedom to explode into a nova and destroy many of its innocent children. That is the way of the natural order and we cannot change it. However, our duty is to uphold law and order and to prevent the strong from taking advantage of the week. Assuming the process does not threaten the long term survival of either by so doing,' Aron said. And Lumak realized the wisdom of his words.

'Yes, I understand your reasoning.'

'Lumak, our time here has not been wasted. Knowing our stay would be long, we decided to create our own temporal and spacial configurations. Once we had achieved our goal and were secure from the predators of this universe, we turned our minds towards unravelling the secrets of the Cosmos. During that process, we have achieved much and are better beings because of it. Believe me when I say, we are a lot more than what you see. This is only a representation of our former selves. Our persons have evolved well beyond form, but in a universe with little in common with our original. That is the reason why we have to attain the new material substance of your present universe before we can exist within its domain. In fact, we must be born again,' Tellor said, and Lumak understood his words, for they were within his own concepts.

'I just realized. I haven't eaten a thing in weeks,' Gemmi said and he realized he was not hungry.

'While here we are always eating. The energy you require for sustenance is always present everywhere and permeates all things. This whole universe is a living organism,' Tellor said and Lumak realized that most, if not all universes were alive, with their own internal organs like galaxies, stars and such like.

In the case of his own primal universe he thought it was more like a tree with branches of galaxies like leaves on some incredible multi-dimensional tree.

Lumak transferred most of his knowledge to their minds and very soon that area of the citadel changed into a place similar to Sarah's palace on Eden. They had created it for Lumak and Gemmi's comfort during their brief stay within that city bubble they called their world.

He soon learn they had become powerful beings and could at a moments notice translate their universe into any comfortable type. However they had to obey the laws of all natural universes and could not change their attributes or substance. But it didn't prevent them from altering their own bubble, since it had been created by them and obeyed their rules.

CHAPTER 7

The way out of Hades with more Patriarchs

They had to choose a precise time to leave that universe. First of all, they had to pass the roaming dragons that fed on all others, then avoid Kator and his evil hordes, and once in the protective cave, choose the precise time of temporal alignment between both universes.

This time they took a new route to the hills of Hades. It was completely different to their first and avoided the larger dragons. Nine large dragons follow to protect Lumak and Gemmi from the largest predator types within Hades. Those dragons held weapons that could repel any advances from would-be predators. Lumak and Gemmi held the eight small vials containing the entities of the eight chosen Patriarchs within their sealed cloaks.

Because of their incredible knowledge and powers, the Patriarchs were themselves considered Grand Lords of the Cosmos. However during the journey within universes they were vulnerable. They had to follow the same dangerous process out of hades as had been taken by Lumak and Gemmi on their way in. That journey would begin where Algo collected Lumak and Gemmi on their arrival and at that time no one could protect them from the wicked Masters of Hades. This whole process was precisely timed to the second.

Algo had moved his caves to another mountain closer to the exit plains. He could view that area directly and tell when the time was right for their departure. He also wanted a new position in case their original one had been compromised and reported by Kator's sympathisers.

Soon after their move he realized that it was indeed the case, when the dreaded Kator came thundering in with fifty of his best and most feared. They trampled and flamed that mountain until it was unrecognizable. Then thinking they had destroyed the minutest of their enemies' bases, moved on to reap more havoc elsewhere. That way Kator was always noticed and feared by his underlings.

The whole performance would be repeated on a daily basis, until some other sequence of events occurred during that exact time period and replaced it. However all other causal sequences within future time periods would remain as before. Even their conscious memories would repeat. Time in Hades always repeated with the rotation of their strange worlds.

Only the most advanced Mesotrenes could overcome that time repeating problem by creating their own worlds within their minds, and Kator was young and not yet that matured in his nature. It required much endeavour and training for anyone to gain powers over the natural environment of that world.

Lumak and Gemmi's arrival had altered the normal course of events on that world. It was as if they had taken a causal something with them from their universe which permanently changed everything. And while they remained, those changes would continue to affect the natural order and in the process change them to fit the newer one, so they had to leave as soon as possible before those changes became permanent.

That problem did not occur within Algo's cave nor Aron's fortress. Those places were technologically controlled and followed their own temporal loops. It only occurred when they were synchronized with the more natural and raw energies of Hades. But as it changed so also did they change to confirm to the new parameters.

They had been given the new location of Algo's cave and had arrived without any problems on route. The time chosen coincided with Kator's meditation period. During that time Mesotrenes were dead to their physical universe.

'Your special cloaks are being rejected by Hades. From what I have sensed, total rejection will ensue within two rotations of this world. We must therefore leave this place before then,' Jot advised.

'Is everything ready for our departure,' Lumak asked.

'We have been unable to test the process with this new one.

Only by our successful journey can this method be fully tested. However, if everything goes to plan, we should arrive at the original point of departure, within the Hexolytes' base and at the exact time that you left. To prevent a repeat operation of the trap, I have arranged for an immediate displacement away from the circle when we materialize.'

'Can we recharge our batteries before we leave,' Gemmi asked.

'Good thinking!' Lumak replied.

'They have already been charged. We are ready to go!' Algo replied.

'As on a previous occasion, from this moment on, you and Gemmi will not remember your experiences within this world. Neither will the transportation vessel remain. Only I and the sealed entities will retain that knowledge. However, with your permission...when I return within your mind again, you will be reminded of your mission and given a strong desire to return to Eden. At that time the entities and their containers will be removed from your cloaks without your knowledge,' Jot said.

'Wow! You are something, Pal. Do what you think is right to get us home and well away from this place,' Lumak replied and Gemmi nodded in agreement.

The transportation vessel was securely fitted to Algo's large back. Lumak and Gemmi was harnessed to Melfa's back. That way, if things got rough they could remain on board during their short trip.

The moment they left the hidden cave and their spacial generator bands released, they were joined with Hades. It was then that Kator sensed their presence. He and his horde of flaming dragons were soon on their way.

'Let us get these imposters!' he shouted. Once again they began burning everything in their path over the original mountain. Then they decided to follow their trail to the new location.

'Let's get them before they escape! Block all routes!' Kator shouted and many large dragons took strategic positions.

'They have found us out!' Gemmi cried, supremely worried as flames got closer.

Still they had to wait. Everything was timed so that the moment of their arrival at their point of departure coincided with the correct time within the temporal loop, so they had little time to spare after their arrival.

Now with flames all around them. While Algo settled, Melfa carefully lifted the transporting vessel off his back and placed it within the area of the four pillars. While in that position they were partially shielded from the flames. Then Lumak and Gemmi released their harnesses and landed within the area. They quickly entered the vessel and sealed the entrance. Once that was done, they switched their control hand-bands, which in turn did something to the vessel's controls. In an instant they had materialized within the ancient Hexolyte base on the world close to the centre of the galaxy.

'That was very close. I thought we were cooked for sure!' Gemmi exclaimed. Yet Lumak remained silent as if in a dream.

He stopped for a moment and realized he had completed his mission at that base. For reasons he could not understand he was unable to remember his recent past or of the previous steps he had taken. Yet, they were on their way back to the ship, so he assumed his mission within the base was completed and the detectors laid.

'You know I have the strangest feeling I've been somewhere and accomplished something significant, but for the life of me, I cannot remember,' he said while Gemmi patiently listened.

'I have the same feeling and think it was meant to happen that way,' she replied.

While they climbed the stairs they could observe many tanks opening to free the robotic guardians holding powerful defensive weapons and realized they had to make a swift getaway. Their suits were still vectored and they remained invisible. However they must have done something to trigger their awakening. It was as if they were being chased out of the place for some greater purpose.

'Something must have tripped their sensors. We must get out of here immediately!' Lumak yelled through their implants.

'Those strange rings in the portal could have sensed our presence,' Gemmi replied.

Either way, they were not going to remain and find out. Hexolytes were clever and would not have laid such obvious traps. After all, at that time in their ancient past they were waging a war with superior beings.

They couldn't be sure what other traps awaited their escape, so they vectorized and took the shortest route out of the area, which was vertical.

After laying the micro-probe in orbit about the planet and testing the system, they left in a hurry.

'We are to return to Eden before continuing with our present mission,' he said.

'Is there a reason?' Gemmi asked, realizing the unpredicted change in his transmitted thoughts.

'I don't know. I just have that feeling. There must be an important and overriding reason,' he replied and she understood. Jot had reclaimed his territory within Lumak's mind and had done his job by reminding Lumak of immediate changes to his plans.

As always, Gemmi made the perfect Shadite companion and both understood each other like brother and sister. That was despite the fact they were from completely different worlds and the most alien in origin to each other.

When they arrived on Eden, the Grand Lord sent his messengers to collect the eight small containers from their cloaks while they were asleep. During that time both had further loss of memory. After that, Lumak and Gemmi were none the wiser of their unscheduled visit to Hades or of the small containers that were safely hidden within the weaves of their cloaks.

CHAPTER 8

Back to Romera IV with apologies

Once again Lumak and Gemmi were summoned to Little Osmaron and in the presence of the Grand Lord of the seventh parts of all seven universes.

'I have received an urgent report from Prann of Tuil. He informs me that the Feloween on Romera IV are in trouble and have asked for you, Lumak, by name. In the name of The Greater Purpose, you are to discontinue your present mission and visit their world to assess their needs.'

'Yes, Metrasiend,' he replied, while bowing his head.

'Your cloaks have been recharged, but use your current mode of travel. Gemmi's assistance will also be required and both your presence will be felt and appreciated by many, so give it your best effort.' The Grand Lord gradually faded from view.

Lumak did not know what his new mission was about. Yet he realized the Grand Lord always held such details for a reason.

They took the same ship and were soon on their way to the target system within the galaxy of Triangulum.

'Back in home country, eh?' he said and Gemmi nodded.

'It's been a while since we trekked this part of the galaxy. It brings back some vivid memories.'

'I know. It was at that time you decided to become a Shadite. I hope you haven't any misgivings?' he said.

'No, No misgivings. Once I gained a taste for the job, I could never imagine myself being a normal citizen again.'

'Anyway, I've since adopted you as my sister, so anytime you need my assistance for any purpose, you just call and I'll be there,' he said and she hugged him.

'It's a good thing I didn't take you as a mate. This togetherness is a lot better,' she said and he agreed. Yet, unlike closer couples, they held no secrets from each other.

They soon landed in the main square of the small city. Amidst cheers and greetings they had arrived in the city of Trom on Romera IV. It had been called by that name in memory of their satellite Trom that still orbited around their dying home-world in another distant system. It had survived the nova and was useful during their evacuation to their present world now over 100 light years away.

In spite of everything that had occurred, they were still not settled on that world. It was completely different to their parent world, Misoran II, which was seventy five percent water. Contrastingly, Romera IV, was only twenty percent water and mostly desert.

They had attempted many types of farming, from fish to plants, but a combination of soil and pestilence had always resulted in failure. Being a crustacean life-form with a desire for large oceans and seas, that world had become a claustrophobic nightmare. They had heard of Lumak's successes on Tuil and wondered whether he could turn their present world around in a manner more livable by their kind. Anyway, Lumak was the Shadite responsible for saving their people when their star blew up and they had much respect for his brilliance in solving unsurmountable problems. As far as they were concerned, if anything could be done, Lumak would be the one to do it.

President Brai Saln was busy with foreign visitors from Tuil and asked his second in command, Pillor, to receive Lumak and Gemmi. He was also required to take them around the city and show them the disgusting conditions of the place.

The moment they left their ship they were greeted by the most innocuous smell and Gemmi immediately fitted a nasal filter. She never thought a place could smell that bad. It was like rotting meat and to further compound the problem, swarms of small black insects were everywhere.

'This is not what I expected.' Lumak complained while fitting a nasal filter.

'There is much water on this world, but most of it is tied up in its polar caps and humid atmosphere. If only we could release some of it,' Gemmi said and Lumak had an idea.

'We could build them a large city dome as with Sylon. Its environment could be controlled to rain and the inner city could be surrounded by a small filtered lake. Such a system could be self-sustaining, with any replenishment being attained through local condensation. By maintaining a higher internal pressure with sealed chambers and locks, bacteria and pest would be kept out indefinitely. As their population increases, more similar enclosures could be constructed to the same blueprint.'

'That's a fantastic idea. And the air within the dome can be seeded with microbes to enhance purification and deter those pests,' Gemmi said.

Pillor came forward to greet his important guests and crowds of the little creatures came forward waving their pincers while the visitors waved back. Even so, Lumak felt their unhappiness tinged with a sense of desperation. After all, they had been saved once before and didn't wish to became a dependent nuisance to anyone. They were a proud people and could not find a way out of their current problems without some outside assistance. Lumak felt proud in the knowledge that of all their past associations with others, he was the only one they had called for by name.

'Greetings friends! You see, we are back!' Lumak said and took Pillor's claw firmly in greeting.

'Forgive our present forms. This is called the human type and is the main one in the galaxy you call Plactorii.'

'Personally, I consider it to be a most outstanding one and am so pleased to have you with us. My president is busy, but sent me to receive you in his place. I hope your stay with us is a most pleasant one,' Toccor said and curtsied.

They were taken through the city and were astounded by the filth and debris throughout its many streets and passages. Their present levels of technology were very basic and had significantly deteriorated from when they were on satellite Trom.

It was as if they had given up all notions of advancement and adventure. It was like a monstrous disease of the mind that fed its victims with overwhelming apathy. Lumak was shocked by their situation and also realised why the good diplomat, Toccor, had decided to show them the city in detail. It was as if making a point of his dissatisfaction for the way things had turned out for himself and his people.

When the tour was over, he took them to the civic hall to meet the president.

Lumak had met president Brai Saln once before, when he was trapped in the underground bunker after the aftermath of the nova and the destruction of their original world. At that time Lumak's body was Tuillian and he knew he wouldn't be recognized. But Brai had heard much about one Lumak the Shadite and his friend Gemmi Doff and was looking forward to their visit.

They entered the large room dressed in their black Shadites' cloaks, with many senior members of government and they were cheered. Brai came forward to greet them and immediately took Lumak to the rostrum.

'So you are the famous one from Plactorii. I have since learnt you are all shape-shifters and can become any life-form at will,' Brai said, overwhelmed with emotion.

'We are capable of changing to almost any form, but that aspect is technological and not biological. We made this trip hurriedly and was unable to change to your form at such short notice. I trust you will accept us among you in our present state?'

Many came forward to greet the famous Lumak and he could sense their spirits lift, knowing he hadn't forgotten them and had taken a lengthy course to assist them in their hour of need. Then Lumak went to the rostrum to advise them.

'Having observed your situation here, I have found a suitable solution. With your permission, we have decided to build a new city within a sealed environmental dome. Within that city will be a large lake of pure water.

Its internal atmosphere and environment will be very similar to Misoran. You will also be given knowledge of some of our more advanced technologies. As and when your population increases, similar domes may be built to the same plan. In the mean while, we shall continue our search for a more suitable world.'

'It may take years to build such a structure and many of us are dying from the diseases of this cursed world,' one of the politicians shouted.

'Leave that problem with me and I can guarantee you a domed city within thirty of your days. In the mean while, Gemmi and myself will attempt to assess your other needs,' he replied and they wondered how it was possible to build such a structure in that time.

Soon thereafter, Lumak sent a thought to Sarah through the Mind and Venusa's ship appeared above their city. Its massive size overshadowed a large part of their city and they were in awe of its form. It landed in a local area and many robots and androids were released to build the enclosed city.

The ship delivered many crates of food and medicine and the surprised Feloween were soon organized in a supply and distribution program.

Lumak called a meeting of all senior members and informed them of progress and they were grateful for the incredible plan shared.

'How can we assist you in return?' the president asked.

'For myself I require nothing. For our organization I shall require a permanent base on this world. It will be a place of excellence where we can train our followers, so that they in turn can rescue others in trouble. Such a facility must be free of your jurisdiction, but I am sure many of you will join us in the common fight against prejudice, injustice and suffering.' Then Lumak removed the little black box from his cloak and the images of the Javols' destruction of Caefon was clearly displayed on the near wall.

To the Feloween those images were shocking and they responded to the gore images in silence.

'Many within other local galaxies have come together against our mutual fore. Since the destruction of Caefon, over three thousand years ago, they have been on their way to this and other local galaxies, and are soon to arrive. In order to secure this galaxy, we must quickly build our defences. Those technologies will be thought to your people in due course.'

'From now you should always be on your guard. They may visit at anytime!' Gemmi warned.

'Those of you who would like to know more about our organization are free to join. You will be well assisted in your efforts. For that purpose, I have decided to form an extension to that organization here on Romera IV. It will be one of our main bases in this galaxy for training our followers,' Lumak said

'As you see, we are few in number and poor remnants of a once great people. Could we be accepted within your noble empire, for the common good?' Brai Saln asked.

'We can only accept those that genuinely aspire to our ways and beliefs, and those will be trained to abide by our methods and rules. However, because of the interest shown among your people, we have decided to build a second domed environment called Edonia within the area of the plains. That one will be ruled by our organization, but can be linked to yours by an underground passage. Our ways will give freedom to all, including those that are not yet interested in our organization. By so doing, we can mutually assist, learn and gain from each other,' Lumak replied.

The two new domed cities of Misoran and Edonia were built and linked together by an underground system. Soon, both cities were enjoyed by their occupants. The Feloween had recovered from their many problems and were once again a race to be reckoned with.

Brai Saln remained president of the Feloween, but Pillor soon became one of Lumak's admirers and was made president of Edonia. He would take over that city in the name of the Greater Purpose.

During the months that followed Lumak realized the Feloween problems had been removed, and decided to submit his completion report to the Grand Lord in order to resume his original mission to locate the ancient Hexolyte bases in that galaxy.

Many of the converts had been trained and boldly wore the federation crest. A small army had been formed to defend both cities against the unknown, but in reality they were being trained to fight the Javols.

CHAPTER 9

Dracma's landing

In the years after Lumak and Gemmi's assistance, the Feloween had become very advanced and had turned their efforts to micro robotics, a technology they had since acquired from Osmaron. Many of their products were presently being exported to Tuil and other local worlds within their newly formed commercial federation. That same federation was discretely linked to Solaria and there was a constant transfer of trained personnel between both galaxies for supposed education and tourism. The Solarians in Osmaron realized the Triangulum galaxy was most likely the first to be invaded by Javols, since it was the main base of the Hexolytes in ancient times. Therefore they extended their immediate program to include Triangulum.

Despite the deadly diseases, pests and other serious problems, including one of severe pollution within the deserted city of Trom, a few of its resident families remained. They had accepted employment within the domed city of Misoran and commuted on a daily basis.

Those few Feloween had grown used to that way of city life and would have felt claustrophobic under the stricter regimes within any of the domed cities. However, special drugs were available to prevent infection by the more common diseases carried by pest, so that aspect didn't worry them.

One such family was the Wondii. They were one of the original rag-and-bone families and were well used to wandering the city and its surroundings collecting discarded objects of sellable value. Their parents and most of their elder family members now had steady and gainful employment within the domes. Those that were employed, financially supported the younger members and children. Therefore, the young were free to wander as their parents did previously, but instead did it mostly for fun. Those juveniles were very much like human teenagers and behaved in a similar vane.

The twin Tille and Bran knew every nick and cranny of that small part of their world. They enjoyed the excitement and trill while speeding over rough terrain with their fast mountain bikes. They would switch over to the chemically driven motors when necessary to make a quick getaway. However, they could quickly get to most places with peddles and enjoyed their freedom with all its dangers.

Amongst other things, they enjoyed chasing Morts. They were like a large jumping rat that could inflict a dangerous bite when cornered. Nevertheless, they never harmed or captured such creatures during the course of their chases. Baring accidents, those two were much too fast, nimble and agile to be stopped by any natural creature on that world. That was until they caught sight of a strange silvery object gliding across the distant horizon. From its spherical shape they knew it wasn't a Federation craft, so they changed gears and were soon on their way to investigate.

'It's got to be an alien craft!' an excited Bran cried while he leaped over a local drain.

'What if it's dangerous?' replied Tille with excitement.

'Then we shall have to be very careful!' Bran responded with excitement.

The strange craft landed on its three telescopic legs but there was no sign of an exit or door. The twins encircled the ship but it was seamless.

'We shall have to climb and check on top,' Tille advised.

'Oh, no! That means one or both of us will have to go home to collect some items,' Bran replied.

'It's only a hook and ropes we need. Two should do. Don't worry I'll go,' Tille said.

'No likely! I'm not going to remain here alone. We both go!' Bran insisted. He went close to the ship and placed his sensors on its metallic body, but no sound could be heard.

Before long, two hooks were fired and ropes strung across the ship. Then they used a special motorized device to climb the rope. They drew lots and Bran was chosen to investigate the upper part of the almost spherical ship.

As he climbed towards the top that upper part of the sphere

lifted. With utter fright he clambered down the rope as quickly as he could, jumping to the approaching ground to speed his descent.

'Bran what did you see? What was so scary?' Tilly inquired, nervously.

'I don't know. I just didn't like the smell and the inside of that thing looked like death itself,' Bran replied and Tille sensed his overwhelming fears.

They were soon on their bikes and darted in the general direction of Trom city.

'Brother... that was a close shave! They could be those Javol things for all we know. We have to inform dad. He will know what to do!' an excited Bran advised while they speeded alone semi rough terrain. The moment they arrived home the gasping couple got on the communicator to call their father.

'Dad, a very incredible thing has happened. A strange ship or flying object landed in the Pairen Valley near Blue Mountain. From its markings, it's not a federation type,' Bran said.

'Are you sure it's not an experimental balloon or a sampling drone?' their father, Koram, inquired.

'No Dad. It's made of solid metal,' Bran replied.

'Leave it until I get home. Don't tell anyone. Not even our own people and we can visit it later today. Such a thing can be worth a lot of money, you know, and we have many mouths to feed.'

An excited Bran soon became worried. He knew his father well and realized once he had an idea in his head for making money he was not easily deterred. That was one of the reasons he had become one of the most successful rag-n-bones in Trom. Yet, he feared for the safety of his father and other involved family members. What if that craft was in anyway linked with the feared Javols? With the assistance of his twin brother, Tille, he immediately decided to locate a couple of his father's old weapons in case there was serious trouble ahead.

The evil Hexolyte, Dracma, one of the heads of the Javols and the most feared of all Hexolytes had finally arrived in

Triangulum. That was after an unpleasant trip taking more than half a century. Having searched extensively through their system, he had located Romera IV, previously known to him as Pol IV. That world was once the original home world of his creator, Father Dracos. Presently the world was several billion years older since their creation and with the exception of its present inhabitants, most of its other life had become extinct during that period.

He viewed the ancient world and realized it had survived the aeons almost in tact and so did its star after all those aeons. Once young and blue but now, yellow and old. Nevertheless, despite the star's age, it was not too turbulent in its output. He also realized the star had another hundred million years or so before it showered the world for the last time with its death throws; for that was the duration of its remaining life before it went nova and became a white dwarf.

He himself was ancient in origin and knew much about the Cosmos and the evolution of such systems. He surveyed the world with his mind and could hardly believe the changes. The once fertile world with its many seas, oceans and intelligent life had deteriorated into a virtual desert with only one alien crustacean type and only a few smaller insect pests remaining.

Nevertheless, from the two large cities observed, their citizens were very advanced and could be made useful in his cause. After having observed them for a while, he decided to put his little diabolical plan into operation. For that plan to be enacted he had to land his ship in a secluded area and hope it would be observed and investigated. He could always fly away if things didn't work out in the manner intended. Nevertheless he realized such young life-forms were not too clever and always inquisitive enough to investigate. There he remained, like a most venomous spider waiting for his prey to spring his trap before he pounced.

After his discovery by the unlucky intruder, whose body he would soon acquire for his immediate needs, his first task was to locate the cave of Father Dracos and revitalize his being. Then he would dispose of his Javols' body remains, including all reminders of that wasted period of his life in Andromeda. Then with the aid of his new friends, he would create a special protective cloak. One that would give his being flexibility and the ability to transform into any primal type. Once that was done, his elemental form could survive an eternity even within the present universe. Once that initial survival phase had been completed, he could always recharge his being from the many elemental occupants within the underground tanks that had been left behind since his imprisonment many aeons before.

Finally, when everything was secure and portals repaired, he would send for his brother, Lupher. Then the universe would be theirs for the taking, or so Dracma thought.

As for now, he would store most of his elements away in the small storage tank that had been prepared for that purpose and use the personal side of his being to possess his next victim. Although somewhat degrading, it was necessary if he was to use the creatures of this world to assist him in his endeavours.

Dracma did not have very long to wait. Bran's father, Koram, had arrived in a large antique vehicle with his two sons to investigate their new find and had come prepared, with ladders and tools.

On first viewing, the ship was a lot more than he had bargained for and couldn't believe his luck.

'Boys... this time you've done your old man proud. What a beautiful craft. She looks more like a surveillance probe and could have landed here on automatic, to collect samples and other information. She could also have been sent by an advanced civilization to check for other advanced ones like us. But this has not been designed or made by any member of our federation, nor of any of our visiting friends from Osmaron, so it could be from elsewhere,' Koram said.

'But dad, what if it's dangerous?' a worried Tille interrupted.

'Leave it to me, Son. Our family is not in the junk collection business for nothing. All I have to do is locate a buyer, who will give us a good price. And sons, I have decided to let you both have a bigger share of this find, after the price is settled. Until then, you will both have to do as I say.'

'We must be very careful, Dad,' a frightened Bran advised, but his father was too excited to take any notice.

'Both you... stay here. I will check it out and when I'm ready, give you the all-clear.' Koram ignored them and began to scale the ladder.

Using a rope ladder, he entered the top and fell through a narrow passage which led into a highly reflective area at its centre. At one point he had to place a wad of rags across his face to block out the stanch within, but he persevered.

'This place stinks to high heavens!' he shouted but there was no reply from his nervous sons.

From what he could observe, the ship was about eight metres in diameter with a central living sphere of about three metres in diameter. Between the inner and outer spheres were many chambers that were shielded from view. Close to each chamber were buttons which when pressed, made their contents accessible to the central area.

Koram wondered why it was necessary for such an elaborate security system on such a probe. It was as if someone or something was holding prisoners in the chambers and that someone was the only one that could release them for its own purpose. There must have been about fifty such chambers. But they were separated by a more central area at the bottom of the sphere.

He pressed a button and released one of the chambers and was utterly shocked by what he saw.

'Sick! Sick! Sick!' Koram gasped with disgust, placing his right main claw to his face in an attempt to reduce the smell of the decaying carcass, with a strange human head almost devoid of any flesh.

Despite what he had seen, he assumed the creature had died from starvation on the long space journey and decided to clear all bodies out of the craft. After all, who in their right minds would give a good price for such a unique craft with dead bodies on board. He soon gave the all-clear to his sons and they were shown the inside of the craft and the dead bodies.

'We have to check every chamber and make sure everyone in here are berried out there. I think they are all dead.

'That's a good thing.... Means we don't have to bargain with anyone for the craft. Now its strictly salvage. And we being the first on the scene means its ours.'

'But Dad, have you searched the whole ship?' Bran asked but he was ignored.

'You Bran, get us three face masks from the car and some refuge bags from the truck, and dab them with alcohol. That should stop the stink from getting through.

'Tille, get us some overalls and plastic gloves. They are in the back of the car. It's going to be a messy job,' Koram said.

To their further surprise, they found all the other chambers contained the same bodies in different degrees of decay. If they had all died of starvation why were all the others not skeletons, and why leave only one behind to run the ship for such a long time. Yet, to Koram's way of thinking, it would be quite possible for some alien races to sacrifice themselves in that manner if food rations were very limited.

Sensing greater dangers from the large unit which he left for last, he sent the boys outside.

'Start burying the bodies. I shall lend a hand after I have opened the last chamber.'

CHAPTER 10

A new Dracma

As Koram pressed the button on the largest chamber, an immense black object or shadow came out from within it and rapped itself around him. Both struggled for a while as the Javols' microid body of Dracma oozed into everyone of Koram's orifices. Then Dracma made the relevant connections until he felt at one with his new mind. Soon the original would be no more.

Although he hadn't made a similar possessive transfer on any primal life-form since aeons past, to him it was as natural as walking and could not be forgotten. Of all the chambers, Dracma's was the only one that could be opened from the inside and that he did like a vicious predator when the opportunity arose.

'What the hell are you! What do you want?'

'I only want your body!' Dracma replied.

'Oh, My God....!' Koram cried, but it was already too late.

'Hoo... That feels a lot better,' Dracma laughed, while taking control of his new body.

'Sorry, but there is only enough room in here for one... so.. Good riddance you little insignificant fart.'

Then Dracma absorbed all his experiences and memories until only Koram's Identity was left. Then he pushed it out into the unknown.

'Freedom at last!' Dracma cried. All residues of Koram's life force was quickly absorbed within his own being. He cried out in a most ghostly manner that could have awakened the dead and Bran and his brother Tille stopped their digging for a brief moment and ascended the ladder to check what was wrong with their father.

Next to their father was a pile of Javol remains that smelled even worse than the rotting bodies. They assumed it was a pile of alien excreta that their father had removed from the larger chamber. The smell was too much and they immediately retreated to find their face masks.

'I have changed my mind about us selling this ship. I think it will be a lot better if we used it to explore the galaxy instead. Adventure is better than wealth and I think you lads might prefer that choice,' the new Koram (Dracma) said with seemingly scary eyes as if in a drunken state.

'Yes, Dad. That's brill, and we can visit Tuil and other major places of the federation,' Tille replied, while observing his father's strange disposition, but they were overwhelmed by excitement about the idea of having their own interstellar craft for sailing the stars.

'However, we must hide her properly. We don't want anyone nosing about our special find, do we? We are going to get some heavier digging equipment and cover her up for now until we can build a proper hanger,' Dracma said. He had adopted Koram's body very well and after a short while the boys were unable to tell the difference.

During the following years Dracma in the form of Koram used his super intelligence and powers to infiltrate Feloween society. It was not long before he became one of their leading scientists in micro robotics.

Dracma realized he had to behave himself and sacrifice his evil cravings for a time until he built his organization, so he became a most respected citizen. That was require while he gathered information on the more advanced systems within the local galaxies.

Bran and Tille was none the wiser of their father's transformation into the evil Dracma. Their father had done everything by the book and had made no one suspicious of his actions to draw them to himself.

With constant prompting from their supposed father, the two lads suddenly became interested in space exploration and had decided to join the federation space navy, where they were trained as captains. While in a living body he had virtually no problems with elemental seepage. That was because he had merged his elements with the living cells of that body. That way they could always be replenished. That would be enough until he visited one of the ancient Hexolyte caves for replenishment and a more permanent change..

Dracma was finally ready for phase two of his diabolical plan. At that time he would concentrate on rebuilding and refurbishing the ancient Hexolyte bases and portals on that world. For the commencement of that operation he needed many scientists and engineers in the name of his most dedicated followers, so it was time he began his religion with its satanic rituals and sacrifices. That type of religion always attracted the darkest few in any society. The way he had planned, that diabolical religion would eventually grow to encompass every civilization within the galaxy.

Initially, the rituals could be conducted in his master's cave, well away from civilization. His space ship could be made part of the ceremony and used to ferry his followers to their cavern which was located in the area of the black sunken sea.

The few chosen leaders of his sect were also his best scientists. They were initially bribed and corrupted by the usual temptations. Caught in greedy traps of their own making and promised the freedom of the universe for their unswerving and undivided dedication to his cause. Because of his superior ways and powers many began to respect him as their eternal saviour.

Dracma had planted many of his spies within the city domes and had used his influence to acquire information of the federation and their friends in Osmaron, but because of the stricter regime within the Edonia dome, whatever information he received from there was always somewhat vague and sketchy.

However, he sensed he was dealing with a much greater power behind those within the Edonia dome. He soon realized that their micro robotics and other advanced technologies had come from the distant Osmaron galaxy and were somewhat dismayed by that knowledge. He also realized that although the inhabitants of that dome was not currently available to him, they would not be too great a problem once he had gained power over the Misoran dome. Even so, he had more pressing matters to deal with and only those necessary for his immediate plans would be utilized.

Since his Primal body was always vulnerable and short lived, his most immediate plan was to engineer a special containment cloak to hold his entity. It would have to be tightly sealed against the environment and utilize the insulating materials his brother Lupher had developed to significantly reduce leakage of his elements. Yet, it must be flexible and allow him the ability to transform into any primal type of an equivalent size. That way he could further deceive his disciples and gain more popularity amongst the Feloween. He felt that although a primal body was useful in keeping him alive and informed, it was not always useful in imparting his superior powers to others. All those limited senses and emotions restricted his powers.

Three of his best microid scientists were put on the project, and before long they had created the necessary blueprints for the project. However they had to create the necessary processing equipment from scratch. That was because their technology was not yet at that advanced level.

One of the lower levels of their hidden cavern was soon converted, and a small production unit was up and running.

After much trial and error, the complex process had delivered the materials for the fabrication of the special garment. It was constructed from numerous types of microids which formed a material of many layers.

The cloak was self-repairing and included a special layer at the inside of the garment that would isolate Dracma's entity from the outside universe. It included a small nuclear power pack to maintain its many functions. That aspect also made it transparent for his many transformations.

Nevertheless even with such a cloak it was not possible to mimic every action and word of a primal life-form. Since the cloak acted as a sealed enclosure, normal eating and breathing was not possible, but those could be mimicked to a certain degree without consuming the food. Nevertheless, a small orifice was woven at a point corresponding to his mouth for absorbing his elemental nutrients from tubes, if and when necessary.

Not being of a material form, that part would have been released when charging his elementals from one of the storage tanks located deep within Dracos underground base. However while he remained within Koram's body, he would not have use for any such refills. A primal body always generated more than enough primary elements for a basic entity.

Even so, he was concerned with the frailty of Koram's primal body, with its tendency for infectious diseases and the occasional fatal accident. If the body died during his period of possession he would also be susceptible to death if no one was available for a possession.

Despite those risks, he realized that once he entered the microid cloak there would be no turning back. Its unique insulating qualities prevented seepage of his being and would equally inhibit his natural ability to possess other primal life-forms. For that reason, he decided to remain within Koram's body for as long as possible.

After the first prototype cloak was completed he sacrificed five of his most sincere followers during its testing. The process was carried out ceremoniously under the pretence of an unholy sacrifice to their gods. Those few had suffocated within minutes within its sealed clutches. When he was satisfied with its many functions, he ordered for three to be made. Those were engineered to a more improved specification. One he would use for himself at the appropriate time, one for his brother, Luther, and the other as a spare in case of damage or failure.

His next task was in repairing the ancient Hexolyte bases within Triangulum with their long range portals. He would then establish links from there to Andromeda and Osmaron. Then he would be able to release some bad demons unto the universe.

'Thank utter badness, our hated and disgusting Javol dogs cannot use such means of travel. Thank every evil badness in this sick primal universe that I have been able to dispose of that disgusting muck of a Javols' body. I can't believe I existed in it for so many millennia,' Dracma complained with utter hatred in his manner. Yet he realized that even without the use of advanced portal technology, the Javols would soon be arriving in droves within his galaxy. Those pathetic Javols would have to be dealt with before they began multiplying to eat away every last vestige of advanced civilization. They would eat every shred of life before he had a chance to use their technologies for his own long term plans of universal conquest.

As he figured out the problems ahead, he soon realized he didn't have much time to waste and had to come up with a plan for those invading Javols.

CHAPTER 11

A diabolical plan

When everything was ready, Dracma built the necessary transmitter and beamed a communication to his brother Lupher via the original MasterMind at the nucleus of Andromeda.

'My brother, everything has been secured at this end. Many of the original portals have been revived and linked. This is the location of an ancient one in your galaxy.

'You must repair it and add these new items to our latest specifications. The Praille will understand the new technology. But you must have everyone involved in this operation. Sacrificed them after completion. No one must be aware of our immediate intentions or long term goals. In due course, I shall despatch a containment suit and all necessary instructions for your regeneration in our original form,' the message said.

'Brother! Brother! Thank awful badness you have made it. Pity I cannot communicate with you from here at this time, there are too many listeners. But I shall follow your instructions to the letter, and trust we shall be together soon,' a happy Lupher thought. He was still at the MasterMind location in Galaxy Andromeda. Lupher immediately summoned his captain and a Timit woman was brought forward for pleasure and amusement. Afterwards, she was painfully sacrificed for his own amusement. After that he drank her blood as if it were vintage wine.

'That definitely hit the spot!' He threw the ceramic container to the sacrificial statue of himself and it shattered in many pieces.

Then as if drunk from the blood of his victim he outstretched his powerful arms and screamed to the top of his voice.

'Freedom at last! Freedom! Freedom! Freedom!'

Lupher soon located an ancient world just outside of the nucleus of Andromeda and instructed many Javols and Praille to repair and complete the installations there. The Javols were told it was to do with the development of a powerful weapon for the defence of their stronghold against future invasions and they were honoured to oblige in its construction for little reward. Nevertheless they were told to ensure the project was maintained under strictest security, with death to all those in the area who were not involved.

When that project was completed, it was given to the Javols as one of their main military bases for protection against any would-be invader, but they were non-the-wiser of the type of weapon or of its zero potentials in destroying an enemy. However they never questioned their MasterMind in such matters. Such rebellious attitude, if known, could quickly assign the offender to a hot plasma pit in one of the local entertainment and amusement arenas.

Very soon thereafter that area was closed from all Javols, under the pretence of certain types of energy emanations dangerous to their form, and robots took over the operations of all its underground installations. Thousands of Javols remained outside to guard their invaluable property. Since most of that world was habitable, farming was encouraged and very soon it was considered one of the best spots for Javols within their so called inner empire.

Lupher had made the equipment and tanks to his brother's specification. After testing the portal and retrieving the special encasement suit from Triangulum, he decided to set their final plan in motion. One that would keep the Javols together for a while and cause the eventual destruction of their Patriarch enemies from Osmaron and elsewhere along with their followers.

During that time, it was hoped, many Javols would be obliterated by their Patriarch enemies, never to plague the universe and destroy all primal life as before, but at the same time taking most of the enemy to hell with them. Lupher enjoyed the idea of setting the cat among the pigeons. The cats being the Patriarchs of Osmaron and the Pigeons the Javols. That way they could mutually destroy each other while he and his brother Dracma created a firmer foundation and grew their roots throughout the system.

After all, he and his demonic Hexolytes had always received more painful pleasures from the entrapment of advanced primal civilizations, with the ability to suffer pain through both mind and body. They would receive little pleasure from a universe devoid of primal life and filled with boring and uncreative Javols, after having eaten their way out of house and home.

Javol's were immune to pain as felt by most primals and could easily survive almost any disgusting environment indefinitely. However for that plan to work it was necessary to give the Javols more superior technology, to make the fight more equal. Perhaps his brother, Dracma, now in control of their bases in Triangulum would assist with that plan, or so he thought.

Since his detection of the fifth order entity in the Osmaron galaxy many cyclons before, and the strange occurrences within his own galaxy, he had placed his MasterMind on red alert. Since then he had tuned its every sensor for the collection of the minutest changes and disturbances in the fifth. The subsequent and unexpected disappearance of all humans on planet Caefon symbolised something was amiss. He realized all those anomalies posed a great threat to himself and his organization in that galaxy.

Soon after those strange occurrences, were the invasion of his galaxy by large black ships that were also from the galaxy of Osmaron. There were too many coincidences that didn't add up and everyone pointed to the local galaxy. That Osmaron invasion was too easily defeated, almost as if they had planned it that way. However that easy defeat was mainly due to his insight in placing the whole of Andromeda on alert and preparing his armies with more advanced technologies that had been created by his Praille and Thoraxi slaves.

Further, those large ships were unmanned and none of the enemy had been captured. Apparently, they had left Osmaron several thousand years before and with old technology that was almost equivalent to their current technologies. If they were so advanced thousands of cyclons ago, they would be much more advanced today.

Having considered all those factors, Lupher realized there were several unanswered questions. Foremost in his mind was the recent disappearance of the complete human population of Caefon, which he now assumed had been taken to Osmaron for some unknown purpose.

Suddenly he realized how inadequate and feeble his current situation was, with all his previous efforts being focussed to keep the useless Javols in check and under control through MasterMind. He considered the Javols to be the most incompetent morons that had to be kept in line to prevent them from eating and destroying everything. Thus, he realized he had to prepare a master plan in which they would all be sacrificed and hopefully most of his Osmaron enemies would go the same way at the appointed time.

And what a convenience it would be if his Osmaron enemies removed the Javols' plague for him from his dominions with their superior weaponry. He could always find ways to enslave the few remaining ones on route to Triangulum, perhaps by his own brand of advanced technologies. Thus preventing them from procreating and eating what's left of his parent galaxy. He must complete immediate plans and prepare to leave this dead galaxy of Andromeda well before the enactment of those plans.

In order to mislead MasterMind, two Praille computers were programmed to take the place of Lupher and Dracma. Its AI interface was designed in such a manner as not to arouse suspicions, and his many Javols' armies and their seniors that were stationed on that world were promoted and reassigned to their fleet. It was something they had always had a yearning for and an easy way to clear the main world of all Javols on a more permanent basis.

Luckily, Lupher could train the Timit men to take over their functions with translation helmets. Those few thousand Timits would be sacrificed by a suitable airborne poison after he was satisfied everything was functioning correctly on automatics when driven by their two computer drones. Unknowingly, MasterMind would transmit any queried observations on a tight H-wave beam to his new base in his home galaxy of Triangulum.

With MasterMind fully programmed and tested, and the

programmed termination of all major life on that world, the now free Lupher possessed a male Timit body then entered a thought into the portal controls and in an instant was within a similar one close to the nucleus of Triangulum.

Moments later Lupher was ported to another part of the galaxy. He was greeted by his brother Dracma in one of the underground bases on Romera IV somewhere below the sunken sea.

'You are not what I expected, Brother. Why change from a ruler to a slave,' Dracma laughed, while starring at the greenish human with reddish lips and sharp claws on webbed fingers.

'Brother, It was the only thing I could find to get me through the portal. Anyway, I have not destroyed its mind. I thought we would sacrifice this morsel together to mark a turning point in our plans and our present successes. I know how you like them and we can have a toast with their blood afterwards.'

'Brother! Brother! You think of everything!' a pleased Dracma yelled.

After celebration with some chosen natives and sacrificing a few more female Timits they had dispatched from Andromeda, Lupher decided to discuss certain matters with his brother. They never kept any secrets from each other, neither was there any pretence in their attitudes.

'Brother! Brother! Brother! I am so proud of you and your accomplishments with these natives in such a short time. Personally, although I did my best with the special ship, I had my doubts it would get you this far,' Lupher said.

'What do you mean exactly?'

'Well, there are always certain risks involved when travelling through space and it was not tested for such a long trip. Now I know the method works, so we can make bigger and better ones based on the same design,' Lupher replied, sympathetically.

'Luckily, Brother, I insisted on taking along a few Timits to keep me entertained on route. I had to savour each in turn for years. Thank utter badness they eat little and heal quickly. After their death, their blood made good drinking and their flesh made good eating. I never thought they could be so delicious. I have subsequently added them to a few of our special recipes,' Dracma said and Lupher looked amused.

'Brother! Brother! You are something else. Anyway, I think I have another brilliant and budding plan. One that will gain us power over all within these local galaxies. One that will curtail the aspirations and desires of our pretentious enemies in Osmaron and elsewhere, and allow us to fulfill all of ours.

'What plan is that?' Dracma inquired with great curiosity.

'From what I have observed here, it is not practical to build us a suitable army from these week Feloween, who are forever contented with their simple ways. On the other hand, Javols are a million fold tougher and more numerous. If altered in specification, they could become formidable warriors... in a manner that would make them a lot tougher and more intelligent than their predecessors,' Lupher said, and Dracma listened carefully to his plans.

'I have formulated a new microid virus that can infect a Javol and transform it into a different life-form, by altering its microbial and metabolic processes. By so doing, they can be trained to become our soldiers of the future, with the ability to transform their bodies into almost any form of an equivalent mass, even with changing colours, but without the limiting restrictions imposed by their natural urge to feed, specialize and procreate. Our new Muts will obey orders, feed on certain non-biological material and be non-replicating. That way, as in the past, we remain their masters and saviours.'

'You mean, they will be neutered by the virus, but retain their original memories?' Dracma replied with curiosity.

'Not exactly! During the infection, they will lose all their memories. From then on we shall retrain them to whatever type we need.'

'That's brilliant, Brother! Truly brilliant!'

'Soon, Brother, all our armies will pay and pay dearly! Ha... Ha... Ha...,' Lupher grimaced, filled with sarcastic humour.

'If that is the case, Brother, all our future problems are solved. But how to stop their parents insatiable appetites and multiplication?' a still uncertain Dracma quarried.

'They will all be converted to a single male type, without the ability to procreate. It's a simple change in their genetic coding during their transformation. All those selected will be reborn, reformed and indoctrinated in special sealed chambers. Further, each mutant Javol so formed will be given a life span of several thousand years. Time enough to conquer the local galaxies.'

'That means we can capture them on arrival.'

'Yes, Brother. After a long time hibernating in space, many tired and energy depleted Javols will soon be arriving from Andromeda. When they approach this part of our galaxy they will be directed by our supreme new MasterMind and led into our traps for conversion.'

'Ah! Ah! Ah! That's very neat. What a delightfully cunning and awfully bad guy you are!'

'In the mean while, Brother, we amass an army to infiltrate and disrupt our enemies here and in Osmaron. We begin to weaken their resolve until the time is right for us to rule,' Lupher said.

'How can you be so sure that such a complex and elaborate plan will work. After all, from what I have learnt, the Osmaronites are no simple minded Timits or wasteful and sadistic Javols. I am almost certain they are being manipulated by surviving Patriarch Masters, who have remained alive and active in their cause since the beginning, even during the period of our incarceration. During all this time they would have gained incredible knowledge by themselves and from their numerous advanced civilizations, whom they have nurtured. Brother, unlike us, they have not been unwittingly devoured in their blossoming prime by over zealous Javols.'

'That was a very unfortunate time in our lives that I seldom wish to remember. During that period we were also incarcerated and had to take that course of action for our mutual survival. We tried to contain the little Javol monsters as best we could, but our plans have paid off and finally, Brother, here we are, completely free!'

'After several eons of wasted time. These confounded Patriarchs will pay dearly for destroying our empire. Osmaron will not be far enough for them.'

'I know how you feel, but most of my plans have already been completed. The microid viral dust has been fully tested and optimized. The induction chambers are shortly to be constructed and after the building of new MasterMind on a chosen world, we shall be ready to propagate our spies to infiltrate our enemies' territories. Then there is the awakening,' Lupher said.

'What awakening?' Dracma queried.

'There are many of the great ones held in tanks and others suspended in eternal twilight. These we must release unto the universe for the common badness in the name of our most evil god Zetan. Our conquest will be much swifter if assisted by Hexil, Warlord Zaltan and others of his kind. They can also divert the efforts of our enemies while we find their weakness.'

'But those Demons were savages, with no table manners whatsoever. Don't worry, I see the funny side of that plan,' Dracma said with a broad grin and glaring eyes that could kill any mortal.

'Although more ancient and savage than ourselves, they will always remain loyal and grateful for their release to freedom. They are ideal for bringing chaos unto those remote areas of this universe that we are unable to reach during our campaign. Their location can be found, but many portals must first be repaired and relevant inter-dimensional links made before their release can be enacted.'

'I have a team of loyal engineers already on repairs and refurbishing,' Dracma replied.

'Brother, truly, you are always ahead of me with forward planning. You see, Brother, although we were apart our plans are one and merge together as if we are a single individual. It's true what they say about twins. Anyway, many plans have already been made and will be speedily enacted after the release of our first batch of mutant Javols. Further, with our new suits of encasement, everyone, including the worst elemental demons, can have one for a price.'

'We don't want these bums getting too powerful. Do we?' Dracma queried.

'Only the chosen few will have them. As you may have doubtlessly realized, the Feloween make good scientists but are small, weak and unsuitable for any type of aggressive behaviour. I place them in the same category as the Praille and Thoraxi. We must let them be for now, because I do not consider them a threat and any changes in their modus vivendi might arouse the attention of their Osmaronite friends. Further, their connections will be very useful for our spies and infiltrators in the future. During that time we can always import more Timits from Andromeda,' Lupher said and Dracma was amazed by the clarity of his brother's mind.

'I agree to everyone of your plans. As always, you are the genius planner, Brother. What can I say but compliment you on such an ingenious plan. Just tell me of my purpose in your great plan and I will comply! As I said before, You are something else, Brother,' Dracma said and busted into uncontrolled laughter.

'In that case, Brother, its your job to create the Supreme Mind. It will be like MasterMind, but a thousand fold more clever. I shall assist you towards that goal when I'm free. We already possess the plans for MasterMind, so that task should not be difficult. However, because we do not deal with numerous Javols, make it partially controllable by our mutants and train it for war against our enemies. It must work independently, to convert, train and control our new mutant soldiers while we turn our minds to more important matters,' Lupher said.

'Consider it done, Brother!' Dracma replied.

From that moment on both brothers turned their minds to the task ahead and very soon thereafter the blueprints for a supreme computer mind was completed. Such a computer could be expanded ad infinitum and act as the mother of all mutants. She would also control the collection of wandering Javols, their transformation by the viral microid and their induction and training.

CHAPTER 12

The first evil Muts are created

After several years of intense mental effort and the aid of the Feloween and others, many of whom he had corrupted with wealth for his assistance, Dracma had engineered a new containment cloak from a special kind of microids.

It was a type of technology they had learnt form another distant civilization in Osmaron. However, with that new technology he was able to make a flexible cloak that could completely seal his being and actively utilize ambient energy to maintain its shielding. Further, there was also a small nuclear power-pack for much greater demands in energy.

With that protective cloak, they could visit anywhere within the galaxy through their new portals. Like spiritual vampires, they were able to charge their beings from the many hidden containment tanks holding the elemental forces of their own kind, also kept in confinement since aeons before.

'Since the beginning, aeons ago, the mighty Zaltan, Borak, Kitz, Lotz, Hexil and others were imprisoned within Aron's tanks for eternity. We must find a way to detect and release them from their eternal confinements, by using our improved technologies and portals. It will be a necessary sacrifice for greater evil and utter badness in the name of our eternal god, Zetan.' Dracma said.

'The Patriarch Masters could not have imprisoned them for eternity without some means of free will. That is the universal law. By so doing they were given access to our portals. All we have to do is repair their links and release them, but not before giving them one of our special suits for a price,' Lupher said, while his brother Dracma listened and took note.'

'Are you sure? Those guys are badder than bad!' Dracma inquired.

'They will be free from bondage and will need our assistance to survive in this universe,' Lupher replied.

'Don't worry, Brother. All their cloaks will be booby trapped. Many have been sacrificed while testing their more intricate functions. And brother, we can add some more extras to their suits in case they get the wrong idea who is boss,' Dracma said and Lupher was amused by that idea.

'I never thought I would ever have seen my day of freedom. Now look at us with these incredible containment suits that can take the form of anything and with no fear of travelling hither or thither through the length and breath of this universe, even through walls, extreme cold and heat. What a vile garment,' Dracma replied, with an expression of happiness and contentment in his unique designs.

'The recent batch of Timit women seemed to have done you a lot of good. Ugly bad thing I took along a few for your awful painful indulgence and cruel pleasures since my last order, Brother. But my male Timit possession was the best sacrifice of them all,' Lupher remarked.

'After you screwed his neck off his shoulders, and fill our glasses, I thought I was drinking your blood and eating your flesh, Brother,' Dracma replied and began to laugh hilariously at that funny remark.

'I liked the way he grinned with his eyes almost popping out when I poked his head unto that pole. Ha! Ha! Ha! I can still see him now! I suppose your Koram would have been similar, but not as pleasurable. Feloween don't appear to have a great threshold of pain or much blood flowing through their veins. I think Timits are the best in the universe for such sacrifices. Ha! Ha! Ha!' Lupher laughed.

'Yet, I feel the deep loss for an old friend, or may I say, an old body. The Feloween Koram's body has been very useful to me. It allowed me fleshly pleasures with his kind, including his wives and concubines. These are pleasures I shall miss,' Dracma said, with disappointment.

Since his transference to the special microid cloak the body of Koram had been discarded. The mindless and lifeless body had been placed in a cryogenic chamber, in case it would be required some time in the future. However Lupher had no such ideas and compulsions and decided if a problem arose he could always possess any local primal with the right intelligence and form, and many such primals were always about.

They had spent many years together and had survived the ages by mutual help and assistance and in that way were tied together almost as one to eternity. Nevertheless they were extremely competitive and clever demons that could adapt quickly to changing circumstances.

Both were scientific and technological geniuses in whatever fields they chose, but seldom used their own hands to complete such ingenious tasks. After all, the universe was filled with their many primal slaves who they could utilize at will, even to the point of modifying them for their own purpose.

They soon realized that the Feloween were not a great threat once infiltrated with their doctrines, but their primal kind were not as capable as the almost indestructible Javols.

Then Dracma had an idea that would utilize the same microids, who could be programmed to invade a Javols body to transform its form into a much tougher and more flexible type without altering its original mental structure. That new and almost indestructible Javols' form they would use to conquer the present universe. They would contain some elements in their making that would make them fully dependant on their masters, but without the ability to reproduce outside of their laboratories without the interceding of their new Supreme Mind.

Soon thereafter, a large computer brain called SupremeMind was created. Its main purpose was to call all Javols to a specific location within Triangulum. Its intentions were to mislead those unfortunate Javols and make them undergo the conversion to the new mutant form.

Many of the original Hexolyte soldiers held in underground storage over aeons were relegated as nourishment and their elemental tanks added to those of their masters for their own sustenance. Because of the numerous quantities of such tanks, their two masters would be in food for many millennia until their located another source.

Nevertheless Hexolyte soldiers were not required in the present universe with its reduced elemental energies over the aeons. There were enough stray Javols for that purpose. Anyway, all such energies were rear and, precious and would not have sustained such armies for long. Further, the mutant Javols were much hardier and a lot more suited to their current plans.

PART 2

A Changing Earth now named Solaria

CHAPTER 13

Terminus City on Mars

Earth Time... AD2140

Since George, the Son of Destiny, and his gang moved from Earth to Mars about half a decade before, Terminus City had expanded to three times its original size and the Federation Base had been extended to over fifteen times. That part of Mars was sealed by a massive structure of domes and had become one of the most important cities in the solar system. The base alone occupied just over one hundred square kilometres of surface area, and included many shielded underground facilities, multistory hexagon buildings for administration, training and accommodation with defensive weapon stations. All of the miners and their families had been transferred from Caefon Dome to the new city and the Dome converted for vegetable farming and waste cycling.

The population of Terminus City proper had expanded to 1.8 million since her construction. Only eighty thousand were from the Martian mining families in Caefon Dome. All others were distinguished Fertilate families from Earth and they assisted in its administration and mining industries. At the present time portals were not used for the general public and travel was by underground LPD shuttle.

Presently many of its citizens included Andy's Specials who were assisted by androids to guard its many facilities, routes and corridors with plasma weapons. The androids could function in virtually any environment, so those moved freely throughout the colony and its external enclosures without the need for environmental suits. There were also a large contingency of roving Federation Warriors who overspilled the local base. Presently the whole of Osmaron was on high alert and awaiting the arrival of the first Javol swarms.

During this period the planet Mars was being reformed. Therefore there were numerous robot ships collecting ice and other elements and materials from the outer worlds and moon to enhance the Martian atmosphere. The numerous Magnatron satellites gave Mars a powerful magnetic field, that would repel the solar wind even more than on Earth. As the planets' atmosphere increased so it became more livable by its inhabitants. Most of the atmosphere of Venus was being extracted by more robot ships in the correct proportions and would form part of the Martian atmosphere. The idea was to reform both planets Mars and Venus at the same time. Although the process of reforming would take many centuries no one was in a hurry with Javols on the way.

The new Miners Guild was created as the main source of law and order and followed strict disciplines for living on a world almost devoid of atmosphere. Anyway, those survival rules had been well proven by miners over the decades and was adopted by the Son of Destiny for those reasons and also out of respect for his fellow compatriots.

Their chief justice was a Macron that dished out the law as written. It could only be overruled by their Mayor with many of his advocates serving its many precincts. Nevertheless Fertilates and miners were very responsible and fun-loving people and as a result, crime was almost nonexistent.

The main mining families were quite wealthy, thanks to certain agreements initiated by their lord, George Peterson, in their favour for minerals, and only responsible Fertilates with a specific purpose were allowed permanent accommodation on Mars.

George Peterson also the Son of Destiny, was now considered by all to be their supreme lord and saviour and everyone followed his laws and regulations without question.

The Supreme War Council of Osmaron was presently based in Terminus City. The Federation of Worlds had selected that course because it was inconspicuously sighted and on a world still incapable of sustaining complex life on its surface. Further, its hex structures were well insulated from the environment and emitted very little radiation, making that world the least attracted to enemy probes. That city was linked to all main worlds within the federation via concealed portals and those were used as the main terminal for security reasons, hence the name Terminus.

The Supreme War Council of Osmaron were not involved in politics and made decisions of inter-galactic scope. The predominant members were Grand Lord Gerra, Grand Lord Jull (George Peterson, Son of Destiny) Sarah, Cathy, Clair, Jon, Meron, Martia, Venusa, Lumak, Malik of Polok, Bailor and Volt of Lodor, Bawaki of Tarran and others.

Many represented their home worlds, most of which were sited within The Federation of Worlds and local globular clusters like Kalboron within Osmaron. For military and reasons of security, Caefon in Andromeda was considered part of Mars. It was however not represented by any of the Andromedans on the council, who considered planet Eden in Osmaron their new home. Thus allowing their original world of planet Caefon and their parent galaxy of Andromeda free access from Osmaron for the purpose of settlement by Infilates and other adventurers and explorers.

The sole purpose of the Supreme War Council was to defeat the Javols and all other predator species within the universe.

Andy Colman was now Commander in Chief of War, which made him responsible for all Specials, Federation Soldiers and military campaigns. Many of which were still active in Galaxy Andromeda.

Soon, many of the Earth's cities were in reck and ruin. The main coastal cities were covered by the rising waters due to Global Warming and other parts were taken over by aging Infilates with no desire for change. They had a motto that when they died their bodies were to be burnt with all their belongings, including their homes and properties, and roving gangs followed their final wishes. That was after their captured Fertilate sons and daughters had ransacked their homes for their most precious belongings. That way, several areas of any city could be seen smoldering at any time from the air. Also, many were set alight by their Infilate occupants who had decided to take the course of suicide instead of the alternative; which was leaving their possessions to their enemies, the real Fertilates, and their detested children.

More recently the incidents appeared to be well planned and coordinated, as large fires were initiated simultaneously withing different cities and in different continents in a manner that hindered the sparsely remaining rescue services. However, as if wishing to make a crucial point, only the central city areas were targeted.

During this period of unrest there was mass evacuation by Fertilates from the suburbs to the many dome enclosures for added protection and safety. Many of the dome enclosures were now full to overflowing and even the very wealthy Fertilates had taken to Satellite Gimbal, Eta and Terminus City on Mars.

However that was only the beginning of the Infilate's campaign. They had amassed many nuclear missiles and LPD ships for their day of finality. The one they called Day Zero.

'Commander, we have been summoned to council. I think the expected troubles on Earth has begun. They seem to be winding up to something serious. Our lord has sent for Clair. She is the only one that can clarify the future,' said the sweating Lieutenant Carlos Lopez. He collected his small computer folder and they were on their way to a local secret portal.

'Ah Andy, sorry for this unscheduled meeting. I think the trouble we expected on Earth has begun. Let me take this last short and set the game to hold,' George said and the golf club visibly disappeared from his hand and the vast course with its large club-house vanished, leaving in its place a beautiful scenery with cascading waterfall.

'You will have to deploy some more of your Specials to neutralize their worst elements. Take whatever measures necessary to rescue any of our captured Fertilates and prevent the sacrificing of any more families in their Hell Fires.

'While you are there, secure the Hearst Manor with automatics and assign Ulysses and Hercules to hunter-killer status. But I don't want them to use their nuclear devices to destroy any cities yet. You know how vicious those two Herculean Colossi can become when they are on the war path for their lord. Anyway, I think it's time they had some action. It will be a very dangerous mission, so note the relevant portals and issue life-savers to all your Specials, just in case,' George commanded. Then he took them into a room that looked more like a small chapel. It was used by Clair and her followers for meditation and was also driven by a special meditation Macron computer.

In their highly advanced mode of existence, it was very difficult to tell the difference between the real world and one created by virtual images. All the seniors of their society had brain implants which linked directly to powerful macron computers for communication, entertainment, education and other means. The implants increased their brain power twenty fold and also included several doctors in chosen subjects, which could be added to at will. Along with that they could tap into the combined knowledge of all such systems within the galaxy.

Clair, now a young woman, knelt in a white robe before the alter which comprised a large sword with two horned serpents on either side forming a figure of eight. Four of her disciples stood on either side of her person with their hands held together in prayer. There on the alter was the Anachromagnon or Final Book of Light in all its golden glory.

'Earth has reached the final stages of its conversion. From this moment, the Infilate remnants will cause much destruction and ruin before dispersing from their cities towards the four corners of the globe. Their remaining cities will be deserted and only our people that are protected in domes will survive the final assault. However, not all our domes will survive.'

'Can we evacuate those from the domes on our danger list?' George inquired.

'Yes we may. Here is a list!' She downloaded the long list to their implants.'

'So we are here at last, Sister?' he asked, realizing that inevitable stage of change was upon them.

'It is the case! From this moment, fences, barriers and all ownership of property is transferred to the federation through our lord. The cleansing of Earth will continue for just over one decade, until the world is divided into protectorate regions and ruled by our Headrons. For these reasons, Earth must be thoroughly cleansed, sector by sector, of all its remaining Infilates. Not a single one of them will survive the coming turmoil. This period marks the end of Earth as we knew it. After that its name will change to Solaria.'

George transmitted a thought to all the most powerful Macrons on Earth and the process was initiated. The Specials were now on full guard. They would be assisted by robots and androids to secure the dome habitats and release captured Fertilates.

'This period also symbolizes a change in emphasis and direction in our fight against the Javols. From henceforth, most of it will be directed from Galaxy Triangulum, because she has now become the weakest link in the chain for our survival. I have spoken in the name of the Greater Purpose. Let it be so,' Clair continued and they all placed their hands together and repeated her last sentence.

'Let it be so!'

Clair had an uncanny gift of knowledge and prophesy and used that gift to keep the great minds of Osmaron a step ahead in the fight against the Javols.

CHAPTER 14

Dangerous Earth

When the Son of Destiny was on Earth, many Infilates and politicians had turned to his organization, which upheld the principles of the Galactic Federation of worlds. In view of the Javol's intended invasion of our Galaxy, all intelligent civilizations had to be brought together in order to repel that most deadly of all enemies.

The Nano-bot Javols were not primals like humans, they couldn't be bargained with, couldn't be pleaded with and saw all such life-forms as food for the taking. Despite the threat that presently faced Earth, many old politicians and Infilates had too much to lose by way of power and wealth, and had opted for their own political independence in the face of overwhelming opposition.

Those stubborn few saw their stance as a way of defending their God-given-rights and would sooner die than give an inch to anyone, least of all the Solarians in the form of their Galactic Federation and its cronies. They even spread negative propaganda, that Javols did not exist and was a monster generated by the Solarians to misguide Earth, so that they could take their properties away from them.

All those wayward factions were called the Remnants. Yet, of all those Remnants, the rebel Infilates hated the politicians and scientists the most. Those hated few were mainly the professional Fertilates, who had not found a cure for the Terminal Disease in years gone by. All Fertilates, including the stray politicians hated the Infilates and considered them the scum of the Earth. The remaining Infilates on Earth numbered just under one million and the majority were over one hundred years old, chronologically.

These few remaining Infilates occupied the major cities of Earth and had full control over the remaining parts of New York, London, Paris, Tokyo and other major cities. As a matter of fact, any stray Fertilates found within any of those occupied cities was immediately executed in the most gruesome manner by Infilates. Nevertheless Infilates also had help from some young feral Fertilates who they had made part of their families in previous years.

Jerry and his wife Miranda were presently in control during the planet's transition and had remained on Earth to take an active part in maintaining control among Fertilates during a period of gross unrest. Almost all Fertilates and their families were quarantined in large environmental domes for their own safety, but there were many still living in remote areas that needed rescue.

With so many dead Infilates about, there were many deadly diseases like the bubonic plague, cholera and others running rampant among city populations with nonexistent medical care or drugs.

Many placed the blame of the re-contamination of Earth by such deadly bacteria and virus at the doors of Fertilates. After all, they were the ones in power and with the knowhow to engineer such contagious diseases.

The global Infilate population had reduced from about eleven billion at its peak to about one million. Many of the current survivors aged between one hundred and one hundred and twenty. Although an elderly population, many utilized organ transplants with rejuvenation drugs and had routinely exercised special rules of living that were issued in better times by their governments.

Since the break down of law and order on Earth, numerous Infilate gangs had been formed and taken control. Some of those gangs were controlled by politically driven renegade young Fertilates for power and wealth. Those Infilate gangs had very little to lose and were very hostile and savage towards all outsiders. Many had negotiated to form larger groups of gangs for their mutual survival. However without the ability to procreate and rear children, they knew their days were numbered and continued to loot, pillage and plunder.

During this time the large environmental domes were guarded by Primorphs, androids and guardian robots. Primorphs were a form of super microid robot, who could transform into the most ferocious animals. They aided the Specials in their campaigns against their Infilate enemies.

Because of their fear of Primorphs, Infilates would only attack the domes by air, and had adopted several LPD crafts and drones for that purpose. However Primorphs, with an array of beam weapons, could transform into almost any life-form, including giant bats with metallic claws. By so doing they could take to the air and quickly destroy the enemy by literally taking their craft apart in flight.

Further, all domes were surrounded by powerful plasma weapons, each with enough impulse energy to vaporize a large building on the moon from any visible point on Earth.

Andy had selected several thousands of his finest warriors, instructed their seniors and the federation space ship, Churchill. With many fighters they were now on their way to the ravaged home planet, Earth. Churchill was left in orbit, while they took the smaller fighting crafts to the surface.

As they glided over land to survey the damage, they couldn't believe the images they beheld of her once great cities like Paris, London, Tokyo and New York. Many were covered by the rising waters and those areas that remained were in ruins, with large areas smoldering in the aftermath of massive explosions.

As Chief Commander of War within Osmaron, Andy always led his Specials into battle from the front and to him, the problems on Earth was no different than fighting Javols. Having viewed many of the surface scans relayed from Satellite Eta and despite the numerous sporadic points of violence and destruction, he had little idea of the Infilate's true intentions or planned targets during the present uprising.

Since his period on Terminus, he had not involved himself in such planning for Earth, since it was deemed unnecessary in view of their falling population levels. Nevertheless he now realized that they had an arsenal of weapons, including aircraft and bombs that they could rain down on many of the local domed city environments. It would be their dying wish to take as many

Fertilates with them on their last and final journey to hell. All those thoughts worried him. Further, all his chosen Specials thought Earth to be the worst hell hole of the galaxy, with its roadside rotting corpses, endemic crime, rampant diseases and endless funeral pyres, and that was when they were not attacked by more roving gangs.

Andy knew that within a period of 10 years Earth would be free of its Infilate burden, but until then, his Specials would have to dig in and find ways to protect it's innocent Fertilates and their many domed cities.

On this particular occasion he would use the Warland Base as his point of command. From there they could reach almost every disturbance globally through intercontinental portals and their super fast Vipers. Vipers were the latest federation ships that were designed to move at high speed in any medium.

Portals had been fitted in the basement of every dome environment throughout the planet and every major city was associated with a fortified dome of the same name. Although there were storage caverns underneath the domes, many were presently stocked with defensive fighting crafts, domestic supplies and weapons, so only a few of their occupants could be evacuated to those areas.

Since the beginning of the recent unrest, most of the domes perimeters were secured with special sensors and underground defences, but they were still prone to attacks from the air, in particular, high altitude bombers. Those could explode nuclear bombs several miles above with disastrous results to all structures several miles below. All those ideas went through Andy's mind. Yet, the evacuation of close to five-hundred million Fertilates were completely out of the question, so he had to do the best with what he had and hoped that the enemy was not too determined or had not acquired too much dangerous technology.

'Please! Please! Can anyone out there help us?' Yet that voice stood out, so Stella kept listening.

'So many calling for assistance, Sir.' Stella nervously approached her commander.

'Yea, it's a big planet and most of them have communicators,' he replied unconcerned.

'My wife and family are to be roasted on their bonfires. If anyone can help, we are in central DC. They intend to make an example of us at noon. Please help us...Please!'

Suddenly the message stopped. Andy listened through his implants and continued undisturbed towards Warland.

'I suppose we are now within their local cellular communication range. Don't worry guys, we shall receive a lot more distress calls like this one before this day is through. Travelling this way, we can feel the current situation and get a better overall view of our poor world than via portals,' he calmly said.

'Sire, we must try to help them as soon as we can!' Stella yelled with distress written all over her face. She was a new captain and hadn't seen any real action before.

'Only as soon as we can, Captain, and we are not ready yet. Always take on a task you are sure of completing. Those Infilates will lay a trap and you will be the second to be sacrificed on their hell fires,' he said and she was silent for a while.

'I'm sorry, Sire, for that oversight,' she apologised.

'That's all right captain, just follow procedure,' Andy warned.

Their craft soon landed within the main complex in Warland Base near Washington DC and they were greeted by Chad, Ebony and her Amazonian gang of fighting women, Mallory, Roseanne, Carl and others. Several rows of uniformed Specials were standing at attention on the nearby lawn.

'So, the greatest and mightiest fighters in the galaxy are back together again?' Andy inquired in jest, with his usual broad grin, while glancing in the direction of his father, Mallory Colman.

'I don't know much about that, but we are ready to kick Infilate ass,' Ebony replied.

There they stood, all dressed in their fighting leathers with the Federation winged insignia on their left lapels glistening in the near noonday sunlight. In the distance they could view hundreds of super-fast fighting craft called Vipers. They were loaded with the worst plasma projectors and weapons known to the federation. On the other side of the parade was a glistening row of metallic looking Herculean Colossi. Those were the special Primorphs, over twice the size of any human and made of metallic microids.

'Wow! Are we really going to use these... against a few elderly Infilates?' Andy exclaimed, realizing how inadequate the last dying wishes and intents of a few unsatisfied Infilates were against the true might of the federation.

'Only if you give us the order, Commander, and we have to save every one of our domes, Sir,' Ebony replied.

'In that case, let's go to the operations' room and plan our strategies for our next mission. We have a family to save before noon today. I suppose, Sol-Newton is now monitoring all calls globally?' he said.

'Yes, Commander. They installed the Coms Macron for that purpose yesterday,' Mallory replied.

'In that case, I shall have all such messages relayed through our implants from now,' Andy said, and they were immediately connected through their War Macron to the one in Sol-Newtown.

'This one is going to be a very delicate operation, so I want Ebony and her gang to ready six Vipers. Since the upper levels of the White House is still secure and afloat, we shall use it as our drop-in zone if necessary. Each viper can take three extra fighters, so that leaves 24 soldiers plus equipment. We need 18 for the job, so we split into three groups of six.

Ebony and her gang will remain invisible over the White House and on standby in case we find ourselves in trouble or have to respond with force to clear the area before we can land the rescue mission. However, the rescue part of the operation will be done invisibly, with our cloaking suits. This is in case those poor hostages are rigged with micro-bombs, then we shall have to get close to them to de-vectorize our suits and become visible before we can ask them. We won't know until we ask them and if any of their captors are within visible range, they can initiate the bombs. So you see how tricky this operation can be,' Andy said and Roseanne placed her hands to ask a question.

'Why can't we use our intense EMP weapons to destroy their micro-circuitry. Such intense fields can render such bombs inoperable. We could also neutralize all electronic communication within the target area.'

'Yes Commander. I am sure we could, if we knew for sure that their captives were not wearing implants and pace-makers. But we do not have a complete picture of the situation on the ground and until we are fully updated with such knowledge it will be too risky. All we know is that there are five people tethered to wooden poles. Further, many of the captured Fertilates, not to mention, Infilates could have medical implants and pace-makers. They can kill each other and themselves if they wish, but I shall not have any of them on my conscience. So in future, all of our missions will be to save life and that also includes our poor misguided Infilates. Any more questions?' Andy said.

'You know, micro-bombs can also be constructed with level-switches and vibrating systems that are immune from radiation, like EMP. All the poor hostages have to do is move from their present location and they can have their heads blown off. So we can have a serious problem if we do not consider all possibilities. The way I see it, some might die during the rescue, but all will die in a few hours anyway if we do nothing, so those are our clear choices,' Mallory said.

'Any more ideas, anyone? Well, DC used to be my home town. That was before my place got flooded by the Atlantic, so I would like us to thread carefully. Further, while we are there we are going to be in the middle of Infilate gang territory, with many of their spies everywhere. So this can be considered a dangerous mission.

'Yea, we realize it's no picnic!' Ebony said.

'I suppose, all your Life-savers are up-to-date?. If not, you can stay behind and hold the forth until we visit Sol-Newtown tomorrow. I am sorry we didn't have much time to acclimatise and plan ahead for this one. Even our War Macron is not yet fully updated on the new parameters, so this one is our own little baby. These situations do occur and we are supposed to be Federation Commanders, with the ability to take whatever is thrown at us.

'Anyway, I wish us success on this our very first operation together on our blighted planet Earth,' Andy said.

'Is the unsubmerged parts of the city still in tact. I mean the areas near the White House,' Roseanne asked, with a hint of nostalgia for when she lived there several decades before.

'Other than the missing monuments, the high wall, the diverted river and the flooding, everything else appear to be in tact. Anyway, we shall see for ourselves when we fly over. But from the few satellite pictures I have observed, there is not much on offer. Since the last US president was assassinated, the Infilate gangs had taken over and many of the great buildings had been set alight. Good thing all of our great monuments and statues had been moved to the new cities in the Appalachian mountains. The White House only remains because it was turned into a refuge for the locals. The upper floors are now hospital, refuge and kitchen. Anyway, that building is also guarded by several Primorphs in disguise as spies. We can use them to observe the local population and relay any suspicious behaviour to us through our War Macron.

'Our plan is crude but simple. Taking all known factors into consideration, two groups, B and C, will take this route along the river wall. Ebony and her gang in group A will remain at what's left of the White House, aided by the Primorphs to gather as much information as possible on the plans, weaponry and methods of our enemies.

Group B, led by my father, Mallory, will take care of our backs. We make more precise plans when we have more precise info on the hostages. Now lets get ready because we move out at 10 precisely,' Andy said.

They all went to freshen up and secure their outfits and weapons.

CHAPTER 15

Along the dreaded river, Potomac

Vipers were truly amazing inter-galactic ships. Each contained its own Battle Macron which was the most advanced form of AI computer. It could quickly analyse a scene and plan several strategies depending on the requirements of the mission. Those ships had no visible controls and could only be linked to its crew through their brain implants. That process placed its pilots in Virtual Space where all thoughts and actions were at least 100 times faster than in normal space-time, for such were the technologies of the Federation.

While within Virtual Space, every external action or movement occurred at a snails crawl, and as a result could never be a threat. These ships could travel anywhere within our galaxy within ten minutes. They simply blinked in and out of normal space.

Their stellar drives were not based on the old LPD or Linear Progressive Drive inertial technologies, but were instead of the IDD of Inter-Dimensional Drive technology, so they could appear anywhere on Earth in the blink of an eye. On their forward nose were mounted two lasers for cutting, two gravitron beams for lifting and shearing and three plasma cannons, two medium and one large.

Despite all the technologies at their disposal, their Infilate enemies had little to lose and were known to be very tricky customers. Further, they could not use such weapons in case they took innocent life and only when a clear opportunity arose. Therefore, soldiers were required on such a delicate mission.

'Since the Infilates plan was to start bonfires at noon, and show the scenes on national TV to make their point, I don't think they will blow them up now. However, to be on the safe side, I want Ebony and her group to go to 2000 feet, scan the local area and neutralize all cellular transceivers and phones. Group B, under Commander Mallory, will also go to 2000 feet and neutralize all devices about the scene. Group C shall remain poised just above the target area. Once that operation is completed, my ship will quickly de-vectorize near the father. I can gain a foothold on the pole if I reduce my mass. Once I am stable, I can ask him about bombs and such like,' Andy said.

In a blink of an eye all local communication was neutralized and saturated with white noise and an almost massless Mallory descended towards the pole where the first hostage was tied.

'Oh, my god! Where are you from!' she yelled, but Mallory silenced her..

'We don't have much time, so listen to my words carefully and answer my questions precisely. Are you wired to micro bombs?' Mallory whispered while ripping the tape from her bound hands and feet.

'No micro bombs. But my eldest daughter..over there... is wired to a large bomb that is rigged to detonate if she is removed from that area. It's hidden in a large box and buried under wood and debris,' he said, nodding his head in her direction.

Once again Mallory became invisible and gave a command to Ebony to prepare to take measures against a large bomb, which was sited somewhere below the pile of debris and wood. In the mean time Mallory readied his ship's powerful gravitron beams to carefully lift wood and other inflammables from the area of the bonfire. Then he used the Laser to cut the chains that held them to the poles engineered for the purpose. Once that happened, their Gravitron beams would capture each inturn just before they fell from the poles. It was a very precise and delicate operation and could not yet be performed on the eldest daughter.

From their present positions they couldn't observe the wires and connections to the bomb. So Andy would have to visit her and check the connections below the pole.

The problem happened with Andy's sudden appearance on her pole. The moment he pealed the tape from her mouth she became hysterical and began to scream. He was not sure whether she screamed because of his sudden appearance on the pole next to her or just from the basic accumulated fright gained from her capture and present hopeless situation. Anyway, that scream did the damage. They soon had a group of young rebel Fertilates moving in their direction to investigate. To further compound the situation, the timer on the bomb had been triggered to go off in one minute and the count down had begun. Without further orders or questions, the restraints of the other four hostages were cut. Their bodies lifted from their poles and floated upwards towards four visible ships, now like gleaming silvery jewels above that location. Seeing the strange aberration in the area above the bonfire, the young rebel Fertilates did not fire their weapons but turned heels and ran away from that direction.

'It's a good thing there were no guards on the scene,' Ebony said through her implants.

'Just a stroke of luck. If there were, you would have had to silence them with your lasers. I'm afraid, although I will do my best to save lives, I'm not going to jeopardise good Fertilates for bad,' he replied.

Andy had re-vectorized and quickly become invisible again while searching for the bomb. He carefully followed the wires and soon found the device. It was a 2000 pounder and with just five seconds to go.

'Cut her chains and take us up now!' he shouted.

'Got her!' said a female voice in his implants and she short vertically from the pole like a bolt. There was a blinding flash of white light followed by an enormous explosion. Andy was not out of the area before the bomb went off. There was also a blinding white light. The light glowed as the powerful defences of his suit became active to shield his body from the blast. The nuclear forces involved were many times greater than the chemical explosives of the bomb and could easily have ended all life in the area of the bonfire. However, the girl was just beyond range and was only slightly singed by the resulting heat.

'Light that pile of remaining wood and junk with your plasmas or they might decide to use it again for some other poor hostage,' he said as he became visible from a cloud of dust.

'Commander! Is that you? Is everything all right?' a worried Ebony inquired and stunned to see he was still alive. Suddenly they were relieved.

'Yes! Despite everything, I'm still in one piece. Those suits are truly incredible. I didn't realize their nuclear power packs pulled such a punch. Nevertheless, check the area for any casualties before we light their fires.'

'That's some suit you are wearing, Commander!' Roseanne yelled.

'It was a present from our Grand Lord,' he replied, proudly. They knew he referred to George Peterson, Son of Destiny.

Although Andy was not truly aware of the true powers of his suit, they were designed for fighting Javols, which were the most invincible alien life-form in the universe, so any situation on Earth could have been considered a picnic by comparison. As they moved away from the area with those they rescued, Ebony fired three short plasma bursts at the pile of wood and the hell fire disappeared in a flash of intense heat.

'People, I haven't visited this town in quite a while, so I think we should pay them a visit and make our presence known. We can land our craft at the top of what remains of the White House.

'That should scare a few Infilates from the area?' his father, Mallory, replied.

Suddenly 12 glistening silvery ships appeared in the vicinity of the White House and several armed humans floated down in front of the ships as if from nowhere.

Many of the locals went for cover, but Andy and his group ignored them and floated through the walls towards the stairs.

A brave young nurse came forward.

'I am Catherine. I heard the distant explosion but didn't realize the Federation was involved,' she said.

'You are not from around here... Is there many like you assisting?' Andy asked.

'There is a small hidden portal at the top of this building, so we travel on a daily basis from Sol-Newtown.'

'Are you human or android?'

'Human, but some inside are androids. Most of these infilates are quite harmless you know. It's just that they have been neglected for such a long time. Like little hated kids they tend to bite the hands that feed them and lash out at anything if only to be noticed,' she said.

'I think we can learn a lot from people like you, Catherine,' he replied, and she smiled and decided to show them around the facility.

'You know, Catherine. I was once chief of security for President Gerald Fraser. That was over one hundred years ago, so I think I still know where most of the rooms are,' Mallory said. She was truly amazed by that statement, but even more when he dropped his visor and revealed the features of a man barely 25 years old.

While they were taken through the many remaining rooms of the White House, gangs of Infilates and rebel Fertilates found their way and congregated near the ships. They did it out of curiosity, but many appeared menacing with their strange multicoloured hair styles and filthy clothes. Many couldn't have had a bath in years. Some rode the vilest bikes on bio gas.

Ebony and her girls bravely move forward to subdue the mob.

'You guys haven't had a wash for quite a while, have you? I can smell you from here and I'm up wind. If I had my way I would place each of you on my knee and give you each a dam good spanking. Then I would rub you down with carbolic and throw you into the nearest swimming pool!' Ebony barked.

'I saw the damage you did to our pile and you took our hostages. You are not as tough as you think,' a young male Fertilate called Noel replied.

'They were not yours to take,' she replied, with both legs drawn apart and weapons in hand.

'Ok! Ok! Don't lose your drawers. Anyway, where are you girls from?' he inquired. He seemed to be in charge of the gang in that area.

'Presently, we are from Mars. But we have lived in many systems within this and other galaxies. Have you ever thought how rewarding life could be if instead of wasting away here in this pit-hole of ignorance and despair, you could be fighting great battles for your families and the rest of humanity. By so doing, you could all be living like kings in the most luxurious environments. So why waste your lives this way, when there is so much going for you!' she shouted at the crowd.

'It's the way we've been thought and the only one we know!' he said.

Then Andy, Mallory and others suddenly appeared before them as if from no where and they were scared out of their wits.

'Do not be afraid. We are not here to harm anyone. We are just here to help those who need our assistance. Many of you can be healed and all this area can be cleared free of all disease. So, all of you here have a great future if you so choose. The Son of Destiny has so declared and so shall it be written.'

'The Son of Destiny! Where is he now in our hour of need,' Noel complained.

'He is presently fighting our enemies in another galaxy, so you should all be assisting him in his efforts, by helping to take care of this world in his name,' Mallory said, and they were silent.

Before long the great federation battleship, Churchill, had arrived over that area and new buildings were being assembled by androids. That federation battleship was about two kilometres long and about half that in height, with massive weapons that could literally cut a world to pieces. There the all black and mighty ship stood as a pertinent reminder to everyone.

Their conversion plans had worked and once the word had got around, all the young renegade Fertilates were giving up their useless fight in droves and turning to the Empire. However there still remained a few stubborn Infilates set on a most spectacular suicide, to mark their painful time on Earth.

The rescued family had decided to assist in the rehabilitation program and had taken residence in Sol-Newtown Dome. They had forgiven the misguided for their near-death experience and were now among the helpers of Earth.

During the following decade there was much violence and uprising, stirred by the invidious Infilates, wanting to do their worst damage to society before their death, albeit of old age. As a result, many of Earth's cities had been left in ruin. One day several of the Federation ships parked in orbit above Earth and began to flatten all the major cities. The few remaining Infilates had become too much of a risk. During that time the revengeful fertilates had succeeded in damaging a few domes with minimal loss of life. Many of their occupants had been evacuated to others around the world. However Andy and his Imperial Warriors prevailed and set a caring example for all to follow. If not for those brave warriors, the cruel conflict driven by Infilates and rebel Fertilates would have lasted for many more decades.

Within that decade all Infilates had perished and Earth's population of just under 500 million had begun to rebuild the fragile planet. They were aided by several of the large Federation ships with the ability to transform worlds using the latest terra-forming technologies. Gone were the past political systems of Earth, its countries and their restrictive borders. Finally, there was just a new world called Solaria to be shared equally by all its inhabitants and most of it was slowly returning to jungle.

One day a signal was sent to Lodor and a massive Tetrion Mauler arrived in the solar system. Like one ginormous spider it wove a rectangular net many thousands of miles across between the Earth and the Sun. That net several thousand miles across in space would cast a shadow across the planet. Then the temperature on Earth dropped by 20 degrees centigrade. During just a few month the ice caps began to form again and the oceans subsided until most of the coastal cities were recovered from the waters. Then the web dissolved away with the Solar Wind.

At that time people moved and used the land freely, but no one was allowed to fence off areas to call their own. Earth had always belonged to all its life-forms and was meant to be shared by all. However fixed and permanent residence were allowed within domed cities.

At long last, mankind had been taken away and isolated within his domed environments from all natural planetary evolution, giving its many life-forms time enough to recover and replenish their sacred Mother Earth from the previous generations of uncaring Infilate mankind.

PART 3

A Changing World

CHAPTER 16

The chosen ones

With the crisis on Earth coming to a conclusion, the program of Earth's conversion into a paradise like Eden was left in the hands of the Lodorians and Polokans. They were the planet builders of Osmaron and could even move continents if so required.

During that time the warriors of Solaria were in Andromeda and Triangulum fighting their wars against the Javols. But Jull, the Supreme Patriarch which is also George Peterson, Son of Destiny, was currently based in Triangulum. That was the place where it all started and also the place where it was supposed to end. Nevertheless, he had the powers to visit any of the galaxies in the blink of an eye when he was required.

'Darling, you are very restless tonight,' George mumbled. He twisted his body around in a more comfortable position and placed his right hand gently about her waist, squeezing it with his fingers. In the past that ploy had always comforted her.

Cathy was two months pregnant and the biological process made her somewhat erratic and restless. However, tonight she was more erratic than usual.

'I don't know why, but I think it's to do with something Clair said at dinner,' she replied.

'What in all heavens did she say to make you so erratic?' he mumbled.

'It was... that she mentioned about funny looking reptilian dragons in federation uniforms, but I saw the sadder side of her humour. I knew she was referring to Ooh-Kaa and his people. I think she must have said it for a purpose... to get me going. She never ever says anything like that in jest you know. I think she sees purpose in our little stone age friends and wants us to visit them again. Darling! I think we should visit them as soon as possible. We could use the ship, Micol, for that trip and visit Earth on the way and observe the changes made to our world.

'What if we built Ooh-Kaa and his people a small domed city and placed them in charge of their planet and its moons. They could have schools, art, music and learn many new things. We could also introduce a few relevant industries and games like football, cricket and baseball. That way, they could enjoy their existence a lot more and also become responsible enough to guard our moon-base there and take some pride in their duties for the Federation. After all, it's our duty within the Greater Purpose to assist those that are being hindered in their progress,' she said.

'I know, Darling, you have given much to them already, by way of new hunting weapons and technology, but I still think they have a long way to go before they are capable of dealing with very complex matters. I mean... although Meradon is different, I think it's too much to put a species through at such short notice. One who didn't know how to light a simple fire a few decades ago, in charge of such crucial operations. If such programs are not implemented correctly there could be backlash and they could grow to resent us.'

'Not if we take it in correct stages, with mind boosters to the few responsible,' she replied.

'But mind boosters are not natural.'

'But you gave Meradon one?'

'Ok, Love, you win. I suppose you must have a plan, and if it's the only way I am going to get some sleep, you should let me hear it now instead of in the morning,' he said. She turned around, kissed him on the cheek and was instantly asleep.

During breakfast the following morning Cathy explained her simple plan to her husband, the Son of Destiny, and he had little choice but to agree. In any event, he knew from the start he could not reject her demands to assist those little reptilian dragons, the affection of whom she had unwittingly gained over the years. Her pregnancy also made her that way and she had become impatient for those she was concerned about.

The Supreme Council was informed of the operation and it gained their vote. George's mother, the Federation Empress, Sarah, sent the Great ships Venusa and Martia to complete that mission. They had built a large stadium for all types of competition, and the training of the many competing clans had begun in earnest on the world of intelligent reptiles.

Soon many hunters and others wandered towards that region to observe the great spectacle and marvelled at the beautiful structures and gardens provided by the Gods of the universe. Within less than 50 years their societies had change from primitive stone age to almost Class 1, technologically.

Instead of barbarous savages, fighting and eating each other, they were now competing on equal terms in the most savage of games. Yet, they were seldom hurt by such aggressive activity. How could anyone imagine such powerful dinosaur-like reptiles playing football with strong feet and flexible tails that were designed by evolution to lift an enemy of an equivalent mass off the ground with a single blow. However those scaly tails could spin a ball around and smash it into a net with incredible force. The competitiveness of those reptiles were beyond belief, with their grunts and hisses, that made even the ground ripple with their sounds.

The day of the main tournament was in one month's time. It was chosen by Ooh-Kaa's son, Meradon, the new chieftain of the southern tribes of the northern hemisphere. The occasion was to mark the day of their first meeting with Jull the Supreme Patriarch. He was the warlike and aggressive form of the Son of Destiny. The one they call their God, Jull. The one in whose name they had built many places of worship. But he was not the only one, for the females had chosen his wife, Cathy, as their Goddess and had build their own temples in her name. That famous day Jull had saved Ooh-Kaa's life, and irreversibly changed the ways of their tribes forever.

Meradon wondered whether his god would appear on that first commemorative day and didn't know how to send a message to such a powerful being, so he offered a sacrifice of his favourite hunting bow. He knew his god didn't like the killing of other animals unless necessary for survival, least of all for such sacrifices, so he swore he would never use the hunting bow again and had a special transparent case made for the artifact.

However, unbeknown to him, the Goddess Clair who was also

the ancient Matriarch Corra, knew everything and she had felt his emotions from afar. Therefore, she hinted at such matters to her brother Jull through his wife Cathy. Clair was always a most complex being and never made things too easy for anyone. In her opinion it was the journey that counted and not the destination, and she always made her journeys as intriguing and exciting as possible.

It was hoped that the large stadium and other facilities would be built and used for the final games after the better players were selected. That day had finally arrived with numerous visitors from all over their world.

There was a thunder in the skies above and two large ships of the realm suddenly appeared as if from nowhere. There they remained for a while, floating above the relatively new city, Tomara-akii. It was the first city to be built on Lori III by the Federation for its people. Presently most of the dragon-like reptiles of that hemisphere were being educated in the ways of the federation and they had taken well to the change.

Instead of their unpleasant muddy mound habitats, with their unpleasant smelly environments, they now constructed their homes out of bricks and mortar, with sanitary sewage systems and had adapted well to such life changes.

From the viewers on board Venusa's ship, Jerry could observe the strange but massive world beneath and remembered his first visit over a century before. At that time the planet stank to high heavens. He realized that the smell of ammonia and other noxious gases were mainly to do with a young world that hadn't yet fully evolved to replace them. It's large indigenous watery cacti and furry moss still proliferated her surfaces in abundance and were the primary food source within the limited food chain.

Nevertheless the flora and fauna of that world had changed. Since the introduction of wood-bearing plants and bees to assist pollination, those bio-engineered forms had virtually taken over the whole of that hemisphere. The honey bees had adopted well to the higher gravity and so did the trees. They had since become a major food source and the plants were invaluable for building and other requirements.

Since that time the planet had been altered drastically by the hands of mankind. It was an important example that demonstrated how bio-engineered plants could sometimes assist in the process of planetary evolution. Without hardwood plants on a world like Lori III, its diverse species were always at a disadvantage. Without hard and dry wood, how could her more advanced species light and control fire, make axe and spear handles, hunting bows, arrows, and other systems and equipment necessary for day-to-day survival. They would be permanently held in a stone-age prison with virtually no chance of moving forward technologically. An intuitive Cathy was the first to realize the problem, due to a lack of resources and involved her husband Jull in her caring efforts. From that time, he had taken them to his heart as his special project. Now the few introduced plants had fully circumnavigated that part of the Northern hemisphere. Jerry beheld the extensive green patches and was reminded that the Greater Purpose was present everywhere within the galaxy.

The patches of light green indicated the areas where they had been planted and the tribes found those areas the best for hunting, since they provided shelter for many of their favourite Uanas. They also had a rich supply of hardwood for their bows, arrows and spears. Jerry pondered the circumstances of his visit, remembering that all those changes were due to Meron, Lennox and their clever scientists, who had spared no effort in re-engineering a complete range of plants that had been specifically designed for Lori III's harsh planetary environment and more extreme gravity.

As he watched, he could observe marked differences in the flora and fauna of both planetary hemispheres. The purple moss in the north was contrasted by a deeper green in the south. It appeared as if the dead zone or desert band around the equator of that world had perfectly isolated its life-forms in both hemispheres.

'How strange a world!' he murmured.

'Now it's much more beautiful than before,' his wife Sharon commented and he nodded positively.

It was early spring in the northern hemisphere and the ground moss was now a deep purple. It's radiance signalled the time of birth for many of the herbivorous reptiles. Their natural predators were still tranquil from the colder conditions, giving their prey some vital time to grow and mature without too much intervention.

Only the most intelligent reptiles of a specific class had evolve to ignore such climatic changes. They had built their home enclosures in deep mounds which isolated them from the cold. On that world rain was never in abundance and could virtually be ignored. Nevertheless those were not like any reptiles found on Earth. They had evolved a hardy constitution to master their more weighty environment. An environment caused by a planet over twice as massive as Earth and with a much greater diameter.

Suddenly the ships glided along and began to descend towards the shows of the Maka-ai sea. A large depression now existed in the waters over which they hung, as their graviton fields switched into activity to support their massive weights. In another moment and large tubes extruded from their sides to span the show.

Jerry knew that the Shadite Lumak was on Martia's ship and that he had visited this world for a special purpose. A purpose, the implications of which he was not aware. He also realized that Grand Lord Gerra was always a part in such matters when Shadites were involved. Once he had a civilization in his sights he would soon choose them for conversion and Jerry wondered whether the reptiles were next on his list for conversion.

Jerry was never comfortable standing close to aggressive carnivores. But the Kanii-ai was not as fierce as the human-like cats of Tarran. They were, humble, respective, inquisitive and only hunted when they needed to eat. Nevertheless they had a vile sense of humour, backed by an almost human sense of fair play.

Most of all, they had a unique sense of knowing. That strange attitude of mind made them blend strategically as one during the hunt. That synchronicity of thought were doubtless an asset to the Federation. One that could be considered worth developing. Jerry wondered whether they were advanced and responsible enough to use Federation weapons and craft to guard their world against the Javols. Primarily, the Federation and its Grand Council wanted them to adapt to Federation methods and principles before they could progress along the relevant paths.

Although petrified by fright at the sight of such massive Federation ships, several brave male hunters came running towards the shore. They soon took position near the exits of the two doors. There they remained at attention like frozen statues, as if trained to play some part in a glorious epic.

The first to appear was Councilor Gerald Fraser called Jerry, by his friends. He was in human form and wore his silvery white cloak with wand in hand. This time he included a facial filter, just in case the smell was too much to overcome or overcame him. Either way, he didn't wish this meeting to be disastrous.

Suddenly, and without warning Lumak faded into appearance by his side in his black, hooded cloak.

'Good luck! Mister Ambassador!' he murmured.

'Thanks! But I don't think I need any,' Jerry replied, still nervous but courageous..

That single aberration was enough to make anyone bolt in the opposite direction , but those brave guards simply blinked their greenish eye lids and firmly stood their ground.

Over the years he had grown to love and admire the Kanii-ai because they were such a complex species. For those reasons Jerry did not wish to show any element of weakness, disorder or disrespect on this or any of his future missions to their world. He was always a perceptive ambassador and for that reason was always chosen for such missions. Yet, Lumak remained unimpressed by his side. Then in another instant Lumak had faded into nothing and was gone.

Jerry had within his brain implants thousands of languages. He could usually pronounce accurately most words while using his unique implants to activate vocal cords and facial muscles to the required format. Nevertheless if those methods failed, he also had a translation belt. The belt was only required when communicating with life-forms whose speech range was outside of the human's spectrum. In the case of large mammals and reptiles, all such voice patterns were audible and could usually be reproduced.

The strange looking guards stood as if out of balance, but for their powerful tails which constantly waved to altered their centres of gravity. Their almost yellow under-belly was hidden by what looked like an apron that was died by their tribal markings. Their sturdy and powerful arms extended into almost human-like hands with ten digits, but they were webbed and extended into sharp black claws. Their bodies were a dark green in colour and their large eyes, although white, displayed a yellow iris with vertical slit.

'Where is Ooh-Kaa or his son Meradon?' Jerry inquired in their language, but they remained unimpressed and silent. Suddenly they turned their heads around together and in the distance appeared both father and son, hastily moving in their direction. The band of comical dragon guards noddy their heads a few times in perfect sympathy and marched off in the opposite direction from whence they came.

'How on Earth do they do that,' Jerry said to himself, realizing there was a lot more to that species than met the eye.

'My Lord? I had no idea you were to visit us on this day, or I would have prepared a great celebration,' Meradon said nervously, while bowing and making a welcoming gesture with his right hand.

'I represent our lord in this matter. Because of the great deeds you and your father have accomplished in bringing the many tribes together, in educating them and in organizing the great games. Our lord has donated a large stadium for your games. It is to be built at a suitable area to be chosen by your people. For that purpose, we are to visit one of the great ships to discuss such matters,' Jerry said.

'A great ship, my Lord?' he replied with excitement in his voice.

'Yes, but first let me hand you your Federation Badges of honour,' he said. Then Jerry went forward and clipped the insignias to their garments.

Meradon's eyes glowed with excitement. For he had never been on board such a craft before. From where he stood both ships appeared the most daunting of war machines, yet his fright never got the best of him when involved in such adventures.

In an instant they were teleported to a special room that had been prepared for their meeting.

Jerry signalled and in another instant they were placed in a virtual world. It was the way that part of Lori III would have become after the stadium was built. He showed them the perspective sites for the building and took them to the many areas throughout the stadium and within its surroundings. Then there were refreshments of a kind the dragons never had before, but found delightful.

'This is all so incredible. I never thought there could be so much variety in our universe,' Meradon said and his overwhelmed father, Ooh-Kaa, shook his head and hissed in agreement.

'True variety comes from within our souls and imagination. That way, virtually anything, even the perceived impossible, may be revealed and realized,' Jerry said.

'With such technology, there is truly no limits to mind and its imaginations becoming reality,' a clever Meradon replied and Jerry nodded in agreement.

'Well, my friends, it's nice we all agree on the location. In that case, since no changes are required to the original plans, we shall commence construction from tomorrow at dawn. You can take along one of the plans for further study, if you so wish,' Jerry said, and handed him the 3D photo anyway, which he stared at in amazement but with sincere appreciation.

'Although we were unprepared for your visit. I have decided to commemorate this time with something of significance to our clan. Perhaps you might like to accompany us on a local hunt to catch some Spring Chocks at noon. Then we can have a feast in the evening,' Meradon said and Jerry, not quite knowing what it was about, agreed.

The following day Jerry went with them to a local hunt. They simply caught the young reptiles in nets and stored them in wire-meshed pens. Those reptiles were equivalent to chickens, but with scales instead of feathers. They used the name Chocks for all young reptiles of that type and Spring Chocks were the type they used for food. Those were very similar to the chickens on Earth and in some cases could be domesticated in a similar manner. Although Jerry didn't like the idea of hunting and eating other animal life-forms, he had little choice in the matter of diplomacy. He took a small piece and pretended he was on Eden and eating a type of synthetic meat.

The following morning Venusa's ship dropped off a pile of medical supplies along with android nurses and doctors. They were to teach the clans the subtler ways and practice of medical science. Those microid androids could change to virtually any form, including reptilian types.

Martia's ship had also released the heavy building materials, machinery and robots for the building project and the stadium was being constructed.

CHAPTER 17

The Games

'That is much too close for a proper target,' Lumak whispered and the dragon Meradon turned his head around to observe the image of someone that resembled a favourite ancestor that he knew when he was little. He was the exact image of an elder of good nature who had frequently taken care of him and his fellow siblings when his parents were away hunting and gathering.

'How far do you think is proper?,' Meradon responded, with surprise.

'Make it double, even triple,' Lumak replied, and a surprised Meradon stared again at the stranger, while blinking his most distinguished green eyelids to hide those most beautiful slitted yellow irises.

Then Meradon went forward and moved the bullseye from the cactus tree to one another hundred feet away.

'I have never tried that far before, not even for the most fatted Uana,' he replied.

'Only because you have been given the wrong impressions from others. We tend to lower our sights to the most common denominator, while we should always attempt to attain levels that are comparable with the order of the gods. You should test yourself to the limits without compromising others in the process, including yourself. It is by such extreme measures that advantage may be gained. Then one may become a model and set a unique example for others to follow,' Lumak said and Meradon saw the sense in his advise.

'How do you know so much on the subject,' a curious Meradon interjected.

'I have been around for a very long time. Even longer than you can ever imagine,' Lumak replied. Then Lumak selected one of the hunting bows, tested its structure and composition. Then he selected an arrow from the pile, which he patiently checked for balance and precision. He loaded the arrow, took a step back and let the arrow fly. It flew through the bullseye, then the cactus and went another fifty feet. Finally it stuck dead centre in another cactus tree. Meradon gasped with surprise and moved his long and almost forked town as if to moist his lips to ready himself for the greatest challenge of his life.

Then Meradon did likewise, carefully took aim and fired. His arrow flew straight through the target and Lumak's arrow, splitting it in two.

He couldn't believe the miracle he had just beheld, for he had always limited his capabilities to those set by his friends and clan. He also realized that he did it without trying as hard as he could and he enjoyed the competition.

Then they both walked forward to collect what was left of their bows.

'You know, Meradon, You could fulfill most of your dreams and desires if you were a Shadite like me.' Then Lumak transformed into his Shadite's form. Meradon was surprised, but didn't run away. He had seen too many miracles in his life.

'What do you mean, my lord? ' a curious Meradon asked.

'Shadites are servants of our lord. We travel throughout this vast universe assisting those in trouble and distress. We use the most advanced technologies, but are also allowed to excel spiritually. You will also be given the ability to live forever among other things,' Lumak replied. Then he changed into his adopted human form and faded into nothing. Finally, he faded back into the reptilian form.

'Sorry for the scare, but we also have the ability to adapt to different life-forms. This make it a lot easier to deal with others from different worlds.'

'I see the purpose in it. Although quite scary, it's incredible all the same. I know of the powers of the gods, but my people need me here at this time of change. Nonetheless I am very interested in your offer,' Meradon replied.

'In that case, I am sure you wouldn't mind if I assisted you in your program here and when the time is right, you may feel free to visit my world Eden for a vacation, and may be, we can discuss such matters further if you so wish,' Lumak said and slowly faded from view. Yet Lumak had planted the seed of adventure in Meradon's mind. A seed of curiosity that would grow until he had to follow that course to its ultimate end.

Soon the great spectacle of their new stadium loomed mightily on that part of the planet. It was designed for a great race of reptiles and was intended for all types of competitive games. However, football was the most suitable and was meant to be its main competitive sport. The vast grounds was split into two main sections for games and sports, each being visible to all its fifty-thousand spectators. Nevertheless, a few special seats were reserved for some of its special human types from Eden.

Many of its visitors had travelled far and wide to observe the great miracles of the gods. For they could not see how it was possible to construct such massive yet stable structures above ground.

There was no transport on that world, so many of its reptilian people, spectators and competitors alike, had been travelling for weeks to get to that area. The introduction of signalling mirrors had significantly improved communication between the clans, so messages could be sent and received almost immediately. That facility was used to send a constant report on progress to all.

Just outside the main stadium was a pavilion where the clans chiefs and their competitors were welcomed and given sustenance and uniforms. That area also included the most spectacular housing and other relevant utilities that were a constant surprise to all.

On the day of the games the air was humid and the atmosphere dense. All its people remained quiet and tense as if awaiting the arrival of their most important guest.

Amidst lightening and flames, the powerful figure of Jull the Supreme Patriarch glided on the air towards the stadium and everyone suddenly froze as if possessed by an uncontrollable fear, but completely filled with awe by the suddenly appearance of their god.

He landed in the centre of the stadium and slowly transformed into his more human form, better known to many as the Son of Destiny. With his golden wand in hand, he lifted both arms towards the sky and hailed.

'Let this day be used to commemorate and celebrate the unity of all our great tribes on this world, and may we constantly strive for greatness through the games. Such greatness will also include much better corporation and assistance amongst all the clans and tribes of these regions. For it is through such efforts that we can truly shine and show any real improvements as a unified race.

'If at any time there is a dispute that cannot be resolved through negotiation. It will then be solved before judges and through fair and honest competition in this arena.'

'With his last sentence, massive lightning bolts were emitted from his wand and fingers and he shouted into the stirring winds.

'Let the firmament be willing on this our first day of the games. I appeal to the heavens...' The dense mist immediately began to dissipate and very soon the sky was clear and blue and the sun shone as it had never shown before. Then he added with his arms outstretched:

'Now, let the games begin.'

Finally he floated towards his throne in the stadium and sat next to his wife Cathy.

'I think they got the message,' she whispered in his ear in English. He smiled and held her hand firmly.

Two groups of would-be footballers stood on either side of the small square on the green hissing, throwing insults and generally scaring each other. The situation was quite comical to watch. Those twelve, true and good, had been chosen from several clans, north and south of the stadium and represented opposing tribes. Yet, despite the temptation for taking the law into their own hands, they held their ground and waited patiently for the start of the shooters.

The first group to show their skills were on the other side of the green. They were the archers and javelin throwers.

Every clan had taken part in two of their most favourite sporting occupations, which was namely archery and the throwing of spears. However, the Federation bows, arrows and javelins were not the same as they had used before. Those were all identical and designed to take several impacts under extreme competition.

For that purpose each competitor had to experienced several practise sessions under android guidance.

On and about the archery range were over one hundred keen competitors and for fairness, everyone was given ten attempts at each bullseye setting. Each shot was recorded and precise comparisons made by independent Federation androids. That way there could be no arguments or disputes as to who was closest. At the end of each session many were given valuable presents for partaking in that particular sport along with a certificate with suggested methods for improvement. Those were then free to choose other sporting competitions and partake for more prises. Others preferred to visit the city with their new found wealth and witness the greatest adventures of their existence.

The Bullseye was gradually moved along rails from the first 100 feet in 50 feet intervals, until its new position remained at two-hundred feet. The three greatest archers remained. Not amazingly, they were the chieftains of the three largest tribes of the northern territories. There was Meradon, in his flashing silvery skirt and a diadem held firmly across his head by his large horse-like ear, but without fur or hair. Then there was Silanda. He was about twice the size of Meradon and even more spectacularly dressed in multicoloured rings. He also displayed a few golden bracelets and bangles. He was quite nervous in anticipation and kept hissing and shouting the strange wards, 'Sooloo, Sooloo.' Sarah asked George for an interpretation and he replied, 'Hot, Hot. He is feeling the heat of the competition a lot more than the others.'

'In that case, do you think we should anoint these chieftains and give them something special?' Cathy said.

'You mean something like a beautiful city and a large park to mark their homeland. But there can only be one Meradon and only one stadium for the great games,' he replied.

'What ever!' she replied, but was very pleased with the outcome of that conversation.

'I wager you a thousand hunting bows and arrows for the winner, half that amount for the runner up and quarter that amount for the third finest archer,' Cathy added, with that competitive gleam in her eyes.

'Ha! Ha! You are quite a piece of work, you know.'

'And you are not a Snow White, yourself.'

'And who do you wager for,' he inquired.

'Telidor of course.'

'In that case I double my wager on Meradon,' George replied.

'I don't know, but Silanda is quite impressive, despite his slight irritations due to the heat,' Professor Khan interjected.

'Dad, will you be placing a wager on Silanda?' Sarah inquired, forcibly.

'You are truly incorrigible. But, yes! I think I shall. Perhaps as much as my grandson's wager and five-hundred of each type as extra.'

'The gang of enthusiastic Edenians soon started a betting spree, but the only ones to gain from those wagers were the beautiful reptiles of that world.

Telidor was the one closest to the rails and she appeared to be the most relaxed. She carefully observed the field, wind speed and all other factors that could affect her aim and her arrow's flight. When she was happy with her measures she simply waited to be called by the judge. She took aim and fired as if without trying and the arrow found the bulls eye.

All three had hit the target in that session but Meradon was slightly out on that short. Nevertheless, their scores were more or less even.

The target was moved another fifty feet and there were just three bullseyes out of thirty shots. Finally the target's distance was doubled to four-hundred feet in order to end the competition. This time Telidor was frantic with her sensing and measuring. Moving about the field while sniffing the air even in the extreme, collecting some soil samples and crushing them in the palm of her hands. When she was satisfied, she had a final sniff. Then she said a small prayer and let her arrow fly. It actually hit the outer ring of the bullseye and she jumped for joy.

Meradon's attitude changed. He realized he was not performing at his best. The tension and stress of the moment had weakened his resolve. Seeing it was his last chance, he realigned his diadem and skirt in reverse manner to change his attitude. Sniffed the air currents, while rotating his ears about to discriminate the difference in sound waves due to the varying air currents. When he was happy with his stance he carefully aimed at an arbitrary position and fired. The arrow met its spot precisely in the centre of the target and the crowd rowed. Even the Grand Lord and his Edenian colleagues stood to cheer.

'Bravo! Bravo! Bravo! Meradon,' George shouted.

'This one is definitely not normal. It must be a fluke. No one can hit a distant target like that in this atmosphere. He could probably have done the same at 500 metres on Earth,' Cathy complained,

'So many sore losers!' George remarked and she was not pleased.

'But the competition is not yet at an end,' Professor Khan interjected.

Then Silanda took aim and fired, but missed and he was grossly displeased with that effort. He thumped his massive fist several times on the ground to make his point clear. Yet he was also cheered by all for trying. Finally the target was moved to five-hundred feet, which was the extent of the stadium along that side.

On that occasion all three failed to hit the target and the Grand Lord decided to visit and thank them personally for such an impressive contest.

'Mark my words, next year will be better. And you both will probably choose winners!' he jested. Then they followed him to the rostrum for presenting the prises.

'Meradon, Silanda and Telidor, you have truly proven your skills with the bow and arrow this day. Therefore, I have decided to give you Meradon sufficient of the finest Bows, arrows and spears to serve your people's needs for one of your generations plus a special gift of a new dome habitat for your tribe. Since the last shots were mainly chance events, I shall also do the same for you Silanda and you, Telidor. Further, to mark this day, I have under the pressure of my beloved wife, decided to give you both domed cities, similar in many respects to Meradon's. I have also decided to link all three cities of the plains with the latest transportation systems. So in future, when you visit the great games you may travel in style on those occasions,' he said and they humbly bowed in appreciation.

The great games went on for three more days, with their mad type of football, including their newly acquired abilities to curve the ball with their powerful tails directly into the nets. Meradon was soon hailed as the greatest archer in the land. However the clans and tribes were now much happier than they had ever been and looked forward to their next Olympian games with anticipation.

Part 4

The new Titans

CHAPTER 18

Starmaker

Volt, the Lodorian scientist, was presently occupying a more flexible type of human android that was the exact image of George Peterson. That one closely resembled the form his lord had taken on his first visit to their world. All senior Lodorians like himself utilized such mobile housing for safety and importance.

Their physical bodies were too small and fragile for direct exposure to many natural planetary environments, outside of the watery tank enclosures of their home world, Lodor.

Every android was built in the image of an important leader and included every facility for their comfort and existence. An android to a Lodorian was home, and remained that way until the Lodorian moved into another or returned to the sealed watery tanks of Lodor.

He sat on the expansive metallic balcony of the large mobile planetoid, overlooking the red dwarf, Triton. Triton was many times larger than the sun.

The planetary orbiting station on which he stood was christened, New York, after a human Earth city he and Bailor had visited decades before and that memorable experience had always remained vividly in his mind. Yet, he realized the once great bustling city was no more. The few parts left by the rising oceans had since been levelled for the greater good. Where it once stood was now a museum and park. How varied was the human species and how unlike his kind, and yet both species got on so well together, as if complementing each other. He transmitted a thought into the control Macron and his planetoid the size of Mars surged forward with great power, being propelled by its super-powerful stellar drives into a closer orbit about the giant star.

New York, the planetoid, was a converted dead planet like Mars that had since been re-enforced to withstand the incredible reverse forces of her stellar convertors. Four gigantic nozzles preceded the large sphere on either side and were focussed toward the centre of the giant star. For an efficient and balanced conversion its orbit was set to a precise distance and soon resumed an incredible orbiting rate about the star.

Its most central reflecting dish and focussed gravitron matter attractor were isolated from the body of the mobile planet by intense fields. They were themselves generated and maintained that way by the very same matter that was extracted from the star. All matter so collected would be projected at near light speed through the centre of the planet where it was sorted and modified before being propelled to the other side and out in space toward sub-stations billions of kilometres apart.

'Set initial neutralizers on and begin the matter conversion phase,' he thought within his implants and suddenly the area of the nozzles roared into activity.

The intense gravitational forces from the attractor and the focussing of plasma from the nozzles did two jobs. It cut large chunks from the star which floated towards the large dish in spiralling streamers. The clouds of super heated matter was soon converted into hydrogen and other elements down the periodic table.

The heavier elements including carbon was re-converted into more usable natural resources and hydrocarbons, while the hydrogen and other unwanted lighter gasses were turned into plasma and projected into space away from the star. In time that cloud of hydrogen and helium would eventually coalesce and condense to form a brand new star without planets . The planetoid, New York, had become a quasar-like object of immense power that stripped the massive star like an onion, removing layer by layer until there was nothing left within that area but low density super heated gas.

The cyclotronic power of the synchro-convertor units were so enormous, that within hours the complete star had been converted. In that area of gaseous space now stood a small globular cluster of a thousand solar size stars. The new children of a once great star soon began to twinkle as their gravitation forces took control over the tendency of the hot gases to expand outward in space. However during that short period the stations helped to contain them by applying a few special fields of its own.

The whole group of newly created stars rotated about a common centre in space that corresponded to the centre of the red dwarf star. They would rapidly condense to form a younger type, more suitable for transposition, which would replace dying stars within Osmaron. Thus saving inhabited worlds from sudden annihilation by unpredictable novae and supernovae.

That central part of the galaxy was like an old graveyard, filled with such dead and dying stars that had been transposed there in previous years by the Son of Destiny. Even with such recycling it would have taken several years to complete the task.

Volt realized that it was just a matter of time, in this case about 8 billion years, before the galaxy was completely consumed by the enormous black hole or cycler at its nucleus. Soon after that, the universe would begin another of its compression phases, when all matter would once again be compressed and renewed, like a ginormous tree shedding its leaves before winter. Then spring would come with a splash and flourish of a completely new set of galaxies in the making.

Volt observed the swiftness of the conversion process and was filled with admiration for the Son of Destiny and the technological prowess of his own people. George Peterson, the Son of Destiny, was now their eternal lord and saviour and they felt secured in that knowledge.

After all the years of war and struggle with Polok, they had finally found a solution to their problem of renewable resources. Now they had more than they could use and the stellar sources were inexhaustible.

'My dearest Lord, you are truly the greatest,' he murmured.

Using the local portal on planetoid, New York, he transmitted another thought through his brain implants and in an instant found himself within a portal in Lodor's main administration block. He left the star-making planetoid in that area of space until it was again required to convert another giant star.

'My lord, a thousand stars have been processed satisfactorily within specification. By so doing, we have synthesized five sentrillion tons of hydrocarbons and other elements for our Polok installations. However, the cooling process continues before core extraction can be initiated.

Within days the stellar cluster will be ready for the transposer,' Volt said and a glimmer of excitement shown in Bailors eyes.

'Our lord will be very satisfied with our humble efforts,' his android mouth replied. To them speaking with actual words was more sacred than using telepathic implants, so they used it to enhance meaning.

CHAPTER 19

Earth, no more

Place... The Metropolitan city of Croydon, England,   now the European capital and seat of power for planet Earth. Power was moved to Croydon when the Thames water levels rose and swamped London about half a century before.

Country... England, presently the place of the European capital and seat of power for planet Earth.

Macrons... Those very advanced super intelligent computers that rule the Earth under the guidance of its Lord Protectors.

Headrons... Super-Intelligent humanoid beings that control the Macrons and all other life throughout the known universe.

Osmaron... Our Milky-Way Galaxy.

Year... Earth-time 2145 CE.

At that time Croydon boasted a population of just over 1.5 million.

Since the turn of the twenty-second century, construction robots had built a new gigantic dome where once stood the suburban town. Its environment was carefully maintained within optimum limits for its many humans and other alien workers.

Most of the original City of London, once flooded and derelict, had been recently restored and its city area used as a planetary museum. Since the past decade Global Warming had reversed due to the massive Tetrion Maulers between Earth and the Sun. That large net or web in space reduced all solar radiation and ionized particles by about 40% causing planetary temperatures to reduce and polar ice to reform. During that time the Oceans gradually reduced by about 100 feet as thick ice reformed in the north and south polar caps. However it also covered Northern Canada, Northern Russia, areas of Scandinavia and Greenland.

As planned by the Solarians over a century before, over 10 billion Earth humans had perished leaving just the remnant survivors. The present population of Earth was 480 million and most of the planet had become semi-tropical. Large rain forests now spanned the globe with their many varieties of primal life. Those that had become extinct by the hands of the previously uncaring human population had been re-engineered and re-introduced by the Solarians. However not all were from Earth. Creatures like Unicorns, Centaurs and others had been introduced to add flavour to the variety. Many had been taken from Greek, Arabian and other ancient mythologies. Those had been bio-engineered from animals like horses and cows. Those caused no detrimental affect on the eco-sphere. They were referred to as mythical types.

There were many Earth-like planets throughout Osmaron and several alien life-forms could survive on Earth without detrimentally affecting its ecosystems and so they were. At that time virtually any creature could be grown to order by the bio-computers.

Large weather controlling satellites had been placed in geo-stationary orbit and those were assisted by powerful ground stations. They maintained a balanced climatic condition by heating and cooling specific regions of the globe, as and when required. Thus maintaining a balanced and predictable climatic condition throughout the planet.

Since the demise of the terminal disease decades before, the revival phase of the planet had taken just under twenty years to complete. During the first ten the large deserts like Sahara had been tropicalized. All those species that could only survive within its harsher regions were contained within an environmental dome by the same name. At current levels of technology virtually any type of environment could be created within such domes. They were completely shielded from external conditions and critically maintained by intelligent robots and androids.

With numerous transportation portals sited throughout the globe, vehicular transport were a thing of the past and those facilities also replaced air transport. However, for nostalgia and other reasons, many still used such outmoded methods of travel for holidays and fun, with special license granted where necessary to those involved. However all those were LPD driven and did not pollute the environment. LPD utilized nuclear fusion, the cleanest form of energy generation, and used hydrogen as fuel.

Since the reduction of Earth's human population from over ten billion to its present level of four hundred and eighty million, thanks to the terminal disease, its biosphere had almost returned to normal.

Gone were the separate countries with their political systems. Lord Protectors now ruled their territories on Earth for the greater good of all. Old established borders were no longer required and hence, were no more. Protectorate territories followed specific lines of latitude and longitude throughout its oceans and land masses, but were not considered separate countries for travel, recreation or work. Earth was finally free for all its life-forms, without predation and abuse from mankind. Now, every individual was considered an equal, except of course, where more security was needed. Then they would acquire the relevant security clearance.

Today is a special day in the history of Earth. It's the day of its renaming, when that once historical world will be given a name in accordance with its nature and purpose in the broader scheme of things. After all, the name Earth brought back too many bad memories of a sordid and degenerate past. A name more synonymous with death and dirt than a jewel of radiant beauty, reborn from the ashes of a ruined past. Perhaps the name Phoenix would have been more appropriate.

Nevertheless the Supreme Council on Eden had decided that the planet of birth be called Solaria. After all, Earth was the seat of power within the Solar System and now to be the future chosen capital of the Solarian Empire. Unbeknown to Earth's people, that empire had expanded in the previous decades to engulf the whole galaxy of Osmaron, once known as the Milky Way. Planet Eden could now fulfil her true purpose as a paradise planet for vacations, education, science, technology and philosophy. Henceforth, Planet Earth by its new name would handle all matters of politics and war, and bear the brunt of all such undertakings.

GONE FISHING

With angling tackle in hand, Michael (Mike to his close friends) walked across the bank from his cabin and continued along its stony shores. He carefully viewed the seemingly still waters for a suitable place to cast his line. There was a slight turbulence on the surface, so insignificant that only a super sensitive creature could detect its ripples. That small and insignificant variation signalled the presence of moving fish a small distance beneath the surface.

Today, the waters had acquired a tranquillity he had not observed before. It appeared more like a sheet of glass that reflected the banks and hills in fine detail. Perhaps he should have brought along his painters kit. That scene would have merited a great picture or so he thought.

At a mere one point seven metres tall, he looked majestic in the tall shiny leggings, with matching jacket and trousers. They were made of synthetic leather and a thin layer of microid which made them super resistant to the planet's raw environment.

He glanced towards the twin peaks in the distance, with its small cascading waterfall. There he stood for a moment, closely observing the undulations of Snaky Lake while pondering the future naming of Earth.

'Solaria! Solaria! You are so beautiful these days. Like a planetary gem.'

There were many strange happenings in outer-space that worried him. Then he reflected on his childhood days on planet Eden, with its diverse technologies and activities, not to mention his teenage friends. That world was the most beautiful gem of the whole empire, yet Solaria was not far behind. Then he thought of his newly founded pastime of fishing, or angling as it was more generally called in that part of the planet, and how relaxing it was. He had read about it in one of those old museum books. Yet, Earth was so different to Eden, and its harshness, turbulence and variations pleased him, for that was the true nature of the Cosmos. Not synthetic or man-made as on Eden, where everything was predictable and engineered to please. He also realized with all the present technological assistance, very soon Earth would be very much like Eden.

'Why don't these terra-forming engineers and their machines leave well alone,' he thought.

Nevertheless, he also realized that a few decades before all life on Earth was on the verge of extinction and it was those same engineers with their powerful machines that took her back from the brink.

Although a vegetarian, Michael enjoyed pitting his wits against the local trout, but always returned them to the safety of their watery world with as little discomfort as was possibly felt by their kind. Yet, with every catch they seemed to become more aware of his intentions and had found many ways to avoid his attempts. He enjoyed those subtle traits in an animal many thought was almost completely brainless.

Today was going to be a very important day in Earth's history and he awaited direct communication from the Supreme Council of Solaria, now based on Planet Eden, for their decision.

Suddenly he lost his footing on a slippery stone and stumbled, jarring his right arm on a sharp rock and he cried out in excruciating pain.

'Dam! Dam! Dam!'

Yet he realised he could control the pain centres of his brain. So he concentrated above the level of pain and it went away. The healing process would begin shortly and in minutes the damage would be repaired. After all, his superior body was designed to be efficient at all such biological processes. Yet he never liked pain, despite its uses in focussing one's attention to a biological problem.

He retrieved the hook and began to insert the synthetic bait, but instead the hook pierced his thumb.

'Not again!' he growled.

There was more pain and a drop of blood escaped from the wound. He realized if he felt such pain, how the trout would feel when biting the hook and even more so, when he jerked the line and lifted it out of the water. From that moment he swore he would never throw another line on that lake, at least not one with a hook that caused such pain and discomfort. However he could always figure out another less painful way to catch a fish using a special net.

'My lord, I have received important communication from Shadow Creek.' Came a sudden thought that cut his present trend, also removing the pain felt at that moment.

'What is it, Carl?'

'John O'Brian is on his way. An urgent matter he says. I am very sorry for the intrusion, but your implants are set to interrupt mode.'

'Tell him it's alright and give him my coordinates.' The communication ceased and his thoughts continued where they left off, but the pain had also disappeared.

He always came here when he needed time to think. That area in North America was well away from the many distractions of the new city while it was constructed and he could return at a moment's notice via his local cabin portal.

The silvery ship, Vogon II, glided through the air like an eagle and gracefully descended between the twin mountain peaks, to perch on its nearby shows. There the mighty ship stood briefly while casting a most spectacular rainbow effect across the lake. Silently, she glided across the still waters and came to an abrupt stop some ten metres away from where he stood. He retracted the fishing line with patient disappointment and awaited their presence. A small circular door suddenly appeared and three equally young figures walked on water towards him.

'Mike, this is a most incredible place you have here and quite difficult to find. I hope you don't mind our intrusion. Mac said we were to meet urgently,' David said showing a slight curtsy to be followed by a slight bow by his other companions.

John remained on board as pilot. Michael couldn't take his eyes off the antique ship, with its strange reflections. For at that moment of oneness, it had stirred and absorbed his very being to its innermost core as it had affected the waters of the lake.

'Dave, where did you find such a most pleasing artifact! She must be very old-world?'

'She is on loan to me by the museum. Apparently, I am the only engineer qualified to recondition her. I have also added a few extras and a small portal, just in case. I thought you would like her for a little fun while she is being refitted.'

'You mean lots of fun?'

'Sorry, you read my mind!' Dave replied.

'What are we waiting for! Lets climb on board!'

'By the way, she belonged to a friend of your dad. He used her a lot during the upheaval. When he had no further use for her type of transport he donated her to the museum.'

'Can you make an exact duplicate?' Michael inquired.

'I suppose so... but it might take a little while to duplicate some of the older parts.'

'In that case, make about ten, but with present technology and her surfaces and curves must be exact.'

After viewing the ship most thoroughly they decided to relax in a more homely place.

. Lets visit my cabin!' he communicated a thought to his apprentice, Carl, and a table was being prepared for him and his guests.

'We were informed by Mac to contact you immediately for orders,' David said, patiently awaiting Michael's input with curiosity, while enjoying the superbly fried synthetic chicken with a generous pouring of tomato ketchup on chips. Michael preferred the ancient and more natural ways of Earth before the upheaval, but couldn't tolerate the killing of other life-forms, nor the pain induced by such methods.

'Pirates have attacked one of our federation vessels off Mars. We can't be sure where they came from, but a general search has been implemented to locate their hidden base,' Michael said in an unhappy disposition.

'Is there a purpose in their methodology?' David asked.

'We have monitored such attacks over the years, but this particular one is different. Apparently, they tried to gain access to our main computer and not food and provisions as on previous occasions. However, for security reasons special codes are always required on such ships, before any information can be made available to an external source.'

'Could they be escaped criminals as before or just a few rogue miners?'

' We are not sure at this time. Nevertheless, I must update you on certain matters before I contact my father,' Michael replied, with a troubled expression.

Since Michael received the Macron's communication, several aspects worried him. He knew the Javols had several more decades to travel before their arrival in his part of Osmaron, however, what if they had discovered a faster means of travel. Special scouts could also have been bio-engineered to withstand intense fields that would normally cause death to others of their kind. There were many such possibilities which could have caused a group of Javols to enter that part of the galaxy a lot sooner than was predicted.

Any of those possibilities or a combination thereof, even mutated forms, could have caused special groups to arrive well in advance of the main ones and prepare the way for their invasion. Such an advanced or mutated form could have overtaken their main group decades ago and although few in number, could use their superior intelligence to infiltrate the Federation under the guise of pirates and others. After all, Terminus on Mars was still the seat of power for the Federation, until power was return to Earth after its inauguration.

While pondering those thoughts, he was once again interrupted by Mac, his Macron, who was the most advanced computer on Earth. The figure of a most beautiful woman appeared in front of him. Although through his implants, Virtual Images could be made to overlap those of the real world.

'Yes, Mac!'

'A secured communication from Lord Lumak.'

'Please connect him.'

'Son, the council has finally decided with you on the name, Solaria.'

'That's fantastic news, My Lord. Now we can initiate the program of conversion.'

'Relay our love to David and Joan, and please Visit us soon.' His communication was always precise and to the point.

As supreme lord of Earth at only twenty-three years old, Michael had many complex decisions to make. Being a super genius, he enjoyed his human pastimes, with a great admiration for nature and her many species and tried his best to be as basic and natural as they were. Only by so doing could he have learnt the true nature of primal life. To appreciate and feel its simplicities and complexities within the panorama of a constantly changing evolution; for within that greater survival plan lay true enlightenment and happiness.

Unlike the most advanced technologies, which in many ways worked against the natural order and did not enhance human feelings and emotions. He also realized that most technological evolution worked against the natural order and given its numerous worshippers, also a false sense of what was truly right and natural, cosmically. It had also created horrors like the Javols, albeit through accident. Yet, all technology was like a two edged sword, with its positives and negatives, each sometimes critically balancing the other. Further, when the true nature of the beast was unknown, any tampering in its modus operandi was akin to opening the proverbial Pandora's Box, with the resultant dire consequences.

Michael was a true visionary and had always pondered the true nature of the Cosmos. The one that would give the greatest fulfilment and happiness to its numerous life-forms, prey and predator alike. During that process he had also observed a bias created by technology that worked against the natural order, and in favour of its creators. Those almost insignificant few members of that particular club had further utilized its tentacles to enhance their self-indulgent needs above their more natural survival requirements.

His was a new type of human that had been bio-engineered and grown in a specially constructed incubator. In his case the complete foetal growth process had taken place outside of a mother's womb.

During the lengthy process of nine months he was educated from the moment the brain began to form, in such a manner as to use every aspect of that larger brain before birth. After birth and although a mere infant, he had the mental age of an eighteen year old and an IQ that exceeded five-hundred. However, intelligence wasn't everything and from a mere baby he had to learn human behaviour, coordination and social skills.

All such special children remained on planet Eden for schooling and usually went to Earth after their sixteenth birthday. Earth, with its rougher edges were considered an essential training ground for such incredible minds.

Discontinuing his disappointing fishing break, he asked Carl to pack and both returned to his apartment within the Croydon Dome in the Protectorate of England. He immediately arranged an urgent meeting with the inner chamber about Earth's new name and other important matters. He would keep any information about Javols within his own war council for now, until more was gained about their whereabouts.

He was now dressed in a white robe, with golden buttons and embroidery to match and with what appeared to be a white wand of office in his right hand. The wand was a symbol of power and status within the Solarian Empire. Golden-haired Michael entered the council chambers, with power in his stride. He boldly displayed the winged federation insignia on his left lapel. The moment he crossed the outer circle an announcement was made and everyone stood to attention.

'Please stand and be ready to receive the Chief Lord of Earth!' He made his way to his high chair and as he sat, so did they.

'My Lord Chancellor, Chair-Lord and fellow members, I have received final word from the Grand Council. They have as I, decided on the name, Solaria, for our planet Earth. May all our records be so changed. From henceforth, everyone within the known universe will refer to this world as Solaria. The former name of our world is no more and that name should not be mentioned in any future official documents, except in common language, within our museums and historical records.

'Our newly born world is soon to become the capital of Osmaron. From here on, all final decisions will be taken by its residing council of government for the general good of all. This places us at a significantly higher level of power within this galaxy.

'This inner chamber may now depart to consider these changes and discuss our new role and responsibilities towards the Greater Purpose and Osmaron. A further meeting of all council members will be convened in two days to discuss all implications resulting from our newly found status within Solaria. I now declare this gathering dissolved,' he said, stood up and left in a similar manner as he had entered.

They were surprised by his final statement but did not ask for clarity from the supreme lord. That information would be forthcoming at their next meeting, which would also carry their individual votes. They would however await communication from Mac, the central Macron. Mac was galactic in scope and would make decisions based on absolutes. However they sensed a change in the order of things and realised their existence would never be the same as of past. Suddenly, they had become the most important individuals in the known universe, and that knowledge was not accepted with joy and glee, as was expected but with bewilderment and candour.

'What are we going to do with all this power?' many grumbled between themselves and others, but the damage was already done. They were placed in the deepest of deep ends and hadn't any choices, or so they thought.

Within minutes their implants were updated with a myriad of new criteria and they realised how little their overall knowledge had been. Mac was always in direct communication with the Supreme Lord of Osmaron and would also have informed him of those relevant timely changes and events. Even so, they were not given information of the Javols preemptive invasion, nor essential plans for war preparations. Those aspects they had to work out themselves.

From henceforth, his strategy would be to wage a war of silence from within. His many trained spies and Specials would lead the way in locating the primary group of his enemy which could then be replaced by his own replicating drones. For he knew not where the Javol imposters were or whether they were within his grand council.

CHAPTER 20

Three Headrons meet

Those three were closest friends and took comfort from each other's company on a world not of their birth. Although free to make their own choices, they lacked the company of their senior members of family for comfort and advise. Not having had the normally close parental relationships, they had to adopt a way of life more suited to their respective needs and purpose.

Although not directly related, each considered themselves responsible for the others and a strong bond had been forged since their childhood years on Eden. At that time, Sarah, Empress of the Federation, had taken the place of their mother. Nevertheless, she was Michael's real grandmother, since he was George Peterson's biological son. Carl Fraser had been trained from birth to be Michael's apprentice and could take his place in emergencies. The name apprentice was given to personal assistants and they were more like a personal secretary.

David was the genetically engineered son of Jerry (Gerald Fraser Jr), the grandson of Donald Fraser. Donald Fraser was an old-world president of the United States of America, as was his father before him. That was towards the end of the previous century. His Apprentice was John O'Brian, who was the grandson of Andy Colman, on his daughters side. Unknown to Joan Colman, John was her nephew.

Joan Colman was the genetically engineered daughter of Mallory Colman. Her apprentice was Julia Lennox also the daughter of Clara Boden who was known to many as Ebony Blade. Julia was of mixed race.

None of the three incubated Headrons or Lord-masters knew who their real biological parents were. They had spent their childhood years on Eden where they were educated and trained in the ways of the federation. Every apprentice was of the same sex as their lord-master, whether male or female. Their duties included the day-to-day running of their apartments, security, travelling arrangements and appointments. They made sure their Lord-masters did not concern themselves with unimportant matters and were loyal unto death. Nevertheless they were treated with great respect by their Lord-masters. They would also be invited to partake in their many parties and social functions, but could also represent them on such social functions and other engagements during their absence.

Lord-masters had their apartments within the Metropolitan city of Croydon. From there they could visit their respective European protectorate states. With Mac linked to their many coordinators, they were seldom needed and spent most of their time on special projects or within the circle of thirty-two, initiating plans or passing new laws. The other half of the year they would be on holiday and experiencing nature in its many varied ways and forms.

The powers of everlasting life were only bestowed upon the few senior councillors. All others would have a natural lifetime of under 500 years if they so chose. However, all Edenians still possessed the privilege of an eternal existence. This was mainly due to the much lower population of that world when compared to Earth at its optimum. That world also favoured that way of life. Many of Earth's humans didn't mind sacrificing long life for a family and many would willingly pay the price of old age within two hundred years or so if it meant greater freedom.

Strict population control was essential if they were to maintain Earth's population under 500 million. Anyone braking the rules were obliged to take up residence away from Earth on one of the new worlds in Andromeda and elsewhere. That option was not acceptable to many.

Despite the new order, wherein everyone was to be maintained in a near perfect state of health, happiness and contentment, some still ached for old-world Earth, with its many varieties of intrigue. Those few enjoyed taking dangerous risks for thrill and excitement. Therefore, many dangerous games and activities had been revived, with the resultant accidents and self-cruelty, which led to pain, injury and death. Although some of those games were allowed, the truly dangerous ones were forbidden. However, that never stopped Earth's humans from taking undue advantage when the costs were higher. Dangerous competitions like car racing, mountain climbing and sky diving were allowed under license. Those few were given lifesavers.

Some of the more extreme elements went as far as lobbying the grand council to regain their ancestral homes and lands, most of which had since been ploughed over and replaced by forests. The new order was not democratic and could not allow such extreme views to grow and cause destabilisation of the planet and its environments, so many were arrested and dispatched as pioneers to distant worlds. However those few were given the option to return to their home planet on vacations after they had fulfilled certain contractual requirements. That option was more acceptable than mind-changing through the psyrotron.

Earth was presently in the hands of Solarians, many of whom were androids run by clever Macrons, and their ways were as different to normal Earth humans as butter was to cheese. They could see thousands of years into the future and cared more for the planet's long term survival and its other life-forms than Earth's humans, who to them were just flies in the ointment waiting for a time to revolt and return to their old ways of planetary abuse.

Mac interrupted an important thought.

'Master, your visitors have arrived. Shall I allow them in?

'Yes! please!'

'There was a brilliant flash and all four materialized close to a silvery partition in his apartment. They removed their outer garments which simply vanished into thin air.

'Come and make yourselves comfortable near the fireplace. Carl, some drinks and snacks, please!' Michael shouted, excitedly.

Carl also received the same instructions through his brain implants, but many liked to hear themselves talk. Conversation being an important part of social behaviour. Further, while on Earth they always tended to speak aloud, just in case their listeners hadn't the necessary brain implants installed to follow and respond in like manner. Nevertheless with their present brand of technology they could always hold their own private conversations in virtual space within their minds without anyone being the wiser.

Soon the android butler arrived pushing a trolley. Then it miraculously transformed into a small table. Several high cushions rose from the floor carpet and inflated themselves. Those they moved closer to the warmer artificial-log fireplace.

Joan removed her golden headband with its many jewels, then her earings and by a simple thought they disappeared in a gentle flash of light. Having no further use for them she had obviously transmitted them back to her apartment. They could be retrieved again at a moment's notice.

Carl transmitted a thought and relaxing music with tranquil scenes filled the room. It was what they called old-world beat, of the late twentieth century. Michael enjoyed the music and cinematics of that era, and had also become an ardent collector of its discs, CDs and other relevant electronic equipment. As first lord and an accomplished historian, he was also given first choice to any surplus equipment from the many museums in New London and elsewhere. By so doing he had created a sub-culture of collectors in artifacts of that period, which were numerous.

Joan pulled her cushion close to Michael's and they waited patiently to hear what he had to say.

'I wanted us to be together this evening for a very good reason. Nevertheless, it would please me greatly if you could remain here until morning. There is space, drink and food in quantity for everyone. We can also watch a few uncensored old-world videos or play some games. When we tire of those pursuits, there is always Mac and the virtual worlds like ancient Babylon, Egypt, Rome and others to play.

'Earth was renamed today and I would like to celebrate that major event with my dearest friends, in whatever manner they choose,' Michael said.

'Is it that important? I mean, naming Earth. After all a flower is still a flower by any other name,' David interjected.

'Perhaps not so much to Earth and its people, but it signifies a change of ownership and from now she will gain much more respect from Solarians throughout the galaxy. They will think she is the pivot of Osmaron, and their final home of empire. Also, it reminds the indigenous humans who are really in charge. Further, Earth will soon become the capital planet of the Osmaron Empire which includes the Federation of Worlds. Terminus on Mars still remains our military headquarters for now.'

'Wow! The seat of power for the whole of Osmaron? That's some status!' Joan exclaimed.

'Yes, it is! Coming back to my invitation, what do you say? Michael inquired.

'I would love to!' Joan responded, glancing at him in her usual seductive manner. She always liked teasing, but had always been very fond of him. Since her return from Eden two years ago, he had been responsible for showing her the ropes, and during that time they had become quite close. Many considered them a natural match and there was much gossip in many circles about wedding bells. However Michael was too involved in his official duties at this time to have considered any major changes in his life-style, least of all a matrimonial one.

The others confirmed their decision to remain with him via their apprentices, who were responsible for their safety and had the last word.

'Then we are all agreed. This is great!' A happy Michael walked towards the fireplace with glass in hand and gazed directly into the swirling flames, as if attempting to gather his thoughts. Without further ado he turned around.

'Have you heard of the Javols?'
They remained silent for a moment to search their minds for any reference.

'Are they one of the old-world group musicians,' Joan asked, innocently. He couldn't help but glance at her and smile. The smile soon changed to laughter and very soon everyone was splitting themselves, but still not any-the-wiser for who the Javols were.

'No, my lovely. They are not musicians.'

'If they are not musicians, they could be funny old-world

comedians?'

'No! Anyone with any better ideas?'

They looked bewildered. For their lord to have asked such a question meant the question was very important. Yet, no one knew the answer.

'I didn't expect you to know. After all, you are not trained historians. I am afraid, this one will be a very unpleasant injection, but I don't want you to be too disturbed by the information you are about to receive, so be prepared to use the necessary neuro-blockers in your implants. Personally, I received my dose from Mac when I was unprepared a few days ago and it knocked me for six. However, if we are all shaken together we can also console each other, together.'

'Let's have it! Nothing can be that dreadful,' David interrupted, and Michael linked his mind with everyone in that room and relayed all information on the Javols since the destruction of Caefon, over three thousand years ago.

After that episode most of the group and their apprentices rushed to the toilets to relieve themselves from whatever they had recently eaten. The others turned away in disgust while attempting to make sense of the deplorable and sadistic images that still flooded their minds.

Although they were young and reckless, they were unprepared for such carnage, even after playing the worst of old-world uncensored video games. Some of which were indeed bloody and violent. But nothing could have been as violent as the Javols invasion of Caefon.

David decided on a stiff vodka and poured it into his glass, nodding to the others for something stronger, to which they agreed. Tonic was not added as on previous occasions. Michael then poured two equally strong drinks for his female guests and handed it to them as they entered.

They still found difficulty in accepting what they had experienced in such vivid details. Those images were far too hideous and painful for reality, since they had never experienced violence of any kind before. Michael waited for the group to regain their composure before continuing.

'Just one more thing. This information can only remain with us for now. Never mention any of these details to anyone outside of present company,' Michael stressed.

'How can we! No one will believe us!' Joan replied, boldly.

He soon changed the topic within his implants, asking Mac to contact Chef for supper. Chef was an android that handled all food preparations. He wanted something special and most importantly, from an Earth's recipe. He informed Mac of his intentions and it was up to Mac to make a suitable choice.

'I would like you all over at the manor this Xmas. I know it's an old-world tradition, long dead, but I intend reviving many of our good traditions. It's to be celebrated on the 25th of December, you know. I have given Mac the necessary instructions, so from henceforth, let there be a season of pleasant thoughts, love and good will to all,' Michael added.

'You are about to revive one of Earth's ancient traditions. I think it's a brilliant idea!' Joan leant towards him and kissed him on the cheek.

'It's a most lovely thought, and we can shop for presents and such like as in the old days.' He accepted her advances, although slightly embarrassed at times.

'Those in favour of making Xmas a global holiday?' he asked and they shook their heads in agreement.

'So be it. But I shall have to inform the other members of the council, and it can't be linked in any way to religion, so we'll call it Goodwill Day. That way we won't offend those of other beliefs like Christianity. I have also decided to create a holiday for today's date, in memory of old Earth and all those gone before the renaming of this beautiful world. That one we can call Earth's Day, but I shall leave the final details to the council.'

Dinner was ready and Chef appeared, wheeling a large metallic trolley with his many dishes. When he entered the room the trolley transformed into a large circular table and six circular seats popped out of the floor equidistantly. This time they preferred to take their meals away, so they served themselves and returned to their more comfortable cushions close to the fireplace.

Chef waited until they were finished, then the table reformed into the trolley and he left in similar manner with the remains.

Although still shaken by images of death and destruction, they were willing to communicate on some aspects of the Javols.

A highly disturbed Joan remained silent. She, like the others, felt quite alone on a planet they still hadn't considered their home. Despite her brilliant and resourceful mind, her femininity made her wish she was even closer to Michael for protection.

Since Eden, she had always considered him her protector and now, more than any other time, she needed his closeness. As if by telepathy, he also glanced in her direction and observed her solemn features.

'Everyone, I have an important announcement to make. I have decided to make Joan my consort. I hope she accepts,' he said and everyone cheered and congratulated the couple. Joan's features suddenly brightened and she stood up to reply.

'I am very privileged and lovingly accepts my Lord's decision. May I always remain in his favour,' she said, bowed and sat.

Within the Empire, consorts were used by important individuals for visiting their many functions and were always unattached members of the opposite sex. At their young age, it was thought to be the first step towards marriage.

Michael soon resumed his conversation about the evil and rapacious Javols.

'When these monsters arrive here, it will be the end of civilization as we know it. What can we do to stop them?' a courageous Joan inquired.

'That's why I brought us all here, together. We have much to consider and perhaps we can engineer a plan... hopefully, not like the Ancients did with Caefon and Andromeda. Nevertheless, our technologies are now much more advanced, which gives us a better advantage. Even so, we have not been trained in the arts of warfare. Neither can we take pleasure from such activities of cruelty, death and destruction. We are not old-world Ancients or predatory humans, with an in-built aggressive nature. After all, we were conceived to preserve and procure life, and not to destroy it.'

'Yes, but we have to fight fire with fire.' David replied.

'I think you meant fire with water?' Then they began to laugh.

'Whatever, but if they are that nasty, we shall require some powerful weapons and shielding,' David responded.

'Perhaps my father can assist us in this matter. I've since learnt that he knew the Son of Destiny. The one destined to destroy the Javols sometime in the future. Apparently they were very close friends,' Michael said.

'How can one old-world individual destroy those almost indestructible microid monsters? Only a god can accomplish that feat, and there are no such beings,' Joan replied.

'My Dear, there is much we do not know of our past. All I am sure of, is that we cannot be weak. We as chosen ones have to face those painful images and get used to the idea of war. It is very obvious that since conception, most of our training has been selective,' Michael said.

'The Son of Destiny is very real... As a child on Polion, where I was born, my grandfather used to tell me of such a child. He was assigned to guard him for a while. He is now in his nineties and lived on Earth during the mid 21st century,' John said.

They all pulled their stools closer to him to hear more of his story.

'This sounds interesting. Please continue, John,' Michael encouraged.

'He told me never to repeat the story to outsiders. But I suppose we here cannot be considered outsiders. Anyway, from what he said, the Son of Destiny is immortal and is very much alive, but his true identity is unknown. His real name is Jull the Supreme Patriarch. He has the power to bend space and time and transform old stars into new ones and he is also a God ,' John said.

'Come on! come on! You are kidding us. Aren't you?' a sarcastic Joan remarked.

'No! I am not kidding you. Granddad was very serious when he told me the story and to this very day I believe his every word. Anyway, the story can be proved.'

'How can such a ridiculous story be proved?' a startled Michael interrupted.

'Several inhabited stellar systems were saved during that period.

One from a nova and another, just to flex his muscles. If you could get hold of the relevant historical records, that would be proof enough. Wouldn't it?' John said.

'Have you any idea how many populated systems there are in our galaxy alone. If the information is not available through Mac, such a search could take centuries,' Michael replied.

'We could work back in time and only search the records of the first few worlds of the federation. That will reduce our search to about ten worlds. The hall of records on Eden and the palace macron should still contain the information we require,' John said.

'Did anyone tell you, you have a most brilliant mind as a detective. I can search palace records from here through Mac,' he said and went silent for a moment.

'You are truly a genius, John. There were three search worlds. Tarran, the hostile planet of cats. One of the moons of Lori III and the Toral mining colony of Polok II. Their stars were transposed... No human could ever wield such incredible powers. Those records must have been kept from us for a purpose. But why?' an astonished Michael said.

'Perhaps they didn't want to burden our young minds with too many of those aspects of the past. After all, we were created to improve civilization, not to destroy it,' Joan replied.

'We are the foundation of modern civilization. If there are threats from outside, we should know and plan accordingly. After all, it's our responsibility. I think we are being tested by the masters. All this reflects our ability to discover the truth for ourselves and plan the future accordingly, hence the reason why it was left out of our education. If we are to be rulers of civilization, we are also to find and face the dangers. All six of us here, must search for his real abilities and use them for the good of civilization.

'From now on, our links with our apprentices will not be as limited as in past. They will also have their own missions. I know John is clever as a detective. Let him be our chief detective with the freedom of the Empire. We each will select a career of our choice for the good of civilization and to the detriment of our enemies. My task has always been in organising, so let that area be my career,' Michael said and sat down.

'Can I choose security. You will need my brand of technology in your quests for truth,' Carl said.

'Perhaps I can use my skills as a coordinator, to coordinate our military campaigns. I think I have a natural ability in that direction,' David said.

'I would prefer to remain a scientist with Julia as my assistant. Since childhood, we both had a natural gift for science,' Joan said.

'So be it. Officially, we become heads of our chosen careers along with our normal duties. We now know our destinies. Let all records be so updated. However, in secret we shall always remain the controlling pivots of the war council of Solaria,' he said and transmitted a thought to Central Macron or Mac.

CHAPTER 21

Summoned to Eden

'Madam, Lord Michael is on his way,' Mac interrupted.

'Please show him in,' a happy Joan replied and he appeared with a flash. However, it was more a point of light that expanded into his person.

'Your apartment has always appeared a lot more comfortably than mine. Perhaps mine lacks the feminine touch. Anyway, how are you these days?' Michael said, looking somewhat worried.

'What brings you to my humble abode, and why the unhappy disposition?' she replied, reading his every feeling like a book.

'I have been summoned to Eden for an unknown reason, and thought of taking you along.'

'Me? To Eden!' Joan exclaimed.

'Well, you are my consort, and I thought the break would do you good. Julia can take control in your absence.'

'I would love to, but only if you will join me for supper.'

'That was also my idea,' he replied, and both sat at the table.

'Have you any idea what it's about?' she probed.

'No. Not the slightest. It could have some bearing on our recent discoveries, but I'm not sure.'

'It can't be too important, then. Perhaps an upgrade with a new implant or more about the wars in Andromeda?' She said while dishing out the meals.

'I can hardly believe my eyes... recently you have become so beautiful and charming. Not the little immature girl I once knew. I suppose I must be falling for you. But it's not the right time, you know. We have so much to do and there could be dangers.' He turned towards her and for the first time they nervously kissed. Then they passionately kissed.

'You know. I have always loved you. Even during school days on Eden, and I always wanted us to be together,' she said, still embracing.

'We can get engaged, if you like. That way we'll know we are together and marry when the time is right. However, we must first check with Mac. I can do it from here,' he said.

Joan was worried and remained silent. She also had her fingers crossed, with both hands behind her back, just in case the answer was negative. Michael then searched the records through his implants to ensure they were not closely related genetically. Such weddings were not allowed by the Supreme Council. If adopted, they could unknowingly have been brother and sister. But that was not all. They had to be genetically compatible.

The information he received was quite vague, but indicated they were not closely related and their genetic groupings were different enough to make them a suitable match. With a sigh of relief, both smiled and embraced each other again, thinking how fortunate they were.

'Thank God! I don't know what I would have done if the answer was no. Yet, they are correct in such matters and always have the final say,' he said and kissed her again.

Michael's interstellar link was situated at the Hearst Mansion, just outside the old city of New York. That once great city had since been demolished. Nevertheless, as in most old-world cities, a small and most central part of New York had been kept as a museum. During the previous century most coastal cities were covered by rising waters due to global warming. Those few that were walled remained for a while. However, in later days those main cities were primarily occupied by Infilates. They were those that had been infected with the Terminal disease. Because of that reason they were unable to have children and were treated as outcasts.

After the turbulence of that period and the subsequent demise of their populations, those innermost city areas were demolished and covered over with large environmental domes of the same name. Such well guarded domes had been built as a depository for antiques and other cultural items. However, large areas had been set aside for the military Specials, Fertilate families and animals at risk. That was during the rampant spread of violence and disease.

For reasons of security, interstellar links on Earth could only be used by Lord Protectors, and only a few councillors with Grade 1 clearance. Those few could only gain access through special codes within their brain implants and via Central Macron. Therefore, no external controls were visible. Further, all normal passenger transport away from Earth was via Terminus City on Mars.

The old Hearst Manor or mansion, once the residence of George Peterson, was still guarded by his two large Primorphs called Hercules and Ulysses. They resembled bronze statues and could transform themselves into any life-form of an equivalent mass. They were once the guardians of the Son of Destiny and no one could enter the mansion without their permission. They had been created with microids and were specifically designed as hunter-killers at a time when that type of guardian was necessary.

Over the decades they had been regularly serviced and left to guard the manor and its associated grounds. But those two had become living entities by virtue of blessings bestowed upon them by their lord and master. Nevertheless, such Primorphs were exceedingly dangerous with supreme powers and a willingness to kill and destroy their enemies. Presently they spent most of their days playing golf within the most favoured mansion grounds.

Michael and Joan transposed to the mansion and materialized in one of the cubicles sited in the basement. Having a detailed plan of the house in his implant, he held her hand firmly and escorted her to the main floor at ground level. Hercules was already there to welcome him.

'Hello, Hercules! It's my first time, so please show us around.'

'Yes, my lord. Please follow me for the grand tour,' he replied, with a keen smile.

Although Michael had transferred telepathically most relevant information to Joan about the manor and its Primorphs, she still couldn't believe such a handsome male wasn't made of flesh and blood.

'This place was given to me on my twenty-first birthday, when I took on the responsibility of First Lord. It's the size of a palace and so... regal. I wonder about her past,' he said to Joan, but something in the distance took her eye.

'What can you see in that painting, over there?' she said, pulling him along to get a closer look.

'Why! He looks almost exactly like me. Except for brown eyes and hair... and old-world clothes. He could quite easily be one of my ancestors,' he said, utterly surprised by the discovery.

'I think it's too close a likeness for mere coincidence. Don't you?' she advised.

Hercules took them to the upper floors where he introduced them to Ulysses, who was scanning the grounds via the roof cameras.

'I think I should upgrade the security of this place before we take residence. A simple satellite link could give much better coverage of the area,' he said and Joan nodded in agreement.

Having time to spare, they ventured into the grounds, workshop and stables, which had not been used for sometime. There was also a large hanger and a workshop cum laboratory

'Apparently, the manor had been deserted for decades, but maintained in its original condition. It had been kept that way over the years by several robots. During that period of Earth's history many of the local towns had been demolished. During the upheaval it was said: neighbours turned against neighbours and friends against friends. Those riots and the general unrest of that time was caused by the terminal plague which infected the whole planet.

'That must have been a terrible time for its inhabitants?' she responded.

'It is said, the disease was genetically engineered to control the growth of the human population, but mutated into an uncontrollable form, turning many humans into insane animals. Within decades the population of over ten billion had dwindled to a mere five hundred million. Only those few with extreme resistance to the virus survived,' he said.

'I have also been given that sad tale.'

'Why! Don't you believe it happened that way?' he remarked, sensing disbelief in her manner.

'I have never accepted such stories as factual, and can never without real evidence or genuine proof. It does not bear the stamp of historical evidence or scientific knowledge,' the scientist, Joan, spoke and he respected her clear-mindedness.

'Darling, I think it's time,' he interrupted, giving her a gentle hug and they were on their way to the basement.

They entered one of the larger concealed portal cubicles that linked with Terminus City on Mars and in an instant found themselves at one of the main stations in Eden City. That planet Eden was within another stellar system within 50 light years. From there, they entered another code and arrived in one of the palace portals. That one was situated in a small out-station for security reasons.

They were greeted informally by the Solarian Empress, Sarah, her husband, Lumak, and their many friends and relatives.

'You both appear to be quite healthy and happy,' Sarah remarked, observing their every expression.

'Thank you, Mum. Things are very kind on Earth, or should I say Solaria, at this time,' Joan replied and bowed. They always called her Mum out of affection and respect.

They approached their other friends whom they hadn't seen for the better part of two years and embraced them all.

Sarah and Lumak accompanied them through one of the palace gardens where they chatted about the situation on Earth, now Solaria.

It was near noon on Eden and its sun poured its bright rays on that most beautiful part of a paradise world. The perfume fragrance from its many giant flowers made the Earth humans feel intoxicated. Having been away for so long, it affected them like strong liquor and they began to feel strongly romantic towards each other. Such emotions they had never felt in such strength while on Earth.

That world was truly enchanting, with its little butterfly fairies, darting too and fro while collecting the rich nectar for their families and stores. Once more, the two felt at home and wished never to return to the stresses of Earth. Yet, Earth, despite its rougher edges were now their responsibility and home.

Sarah took them through the main hall with its many young palace guards who assisted at her every request. Finally they entered a reception room where the main party awaited their arrival. Michael was reacquainted to everyone.

Soon the party dispersed and lunch was served. They had a keen appetite and filled themselves to the brim.

'Mum I have great news. I've chosen Joan as my consort,' he said.

'I'm so happy for you both. I think it was always meant to be. Anyway, tell us what your plans are and we shall assist in whatever way possible,' Sarah said, but she was not too excited and that worried the couple.

'Don't you like the idea of us getting together?' Joan inquired.

'It's not the reason, my loves, and I wish I could tell you, but I can't. Anyway, you'll find out soon enough,' Sarah replied and changed the topic.

'Your old rooms have been prepared. You should have some rest and get dressed in more suitable attire before joining us for supper. Pamela will accompany you to your rooms,' Sarah added and Pamela stood up and they both did likewise and followed her to the upper level.

'I wish I knew what she meant. Now I'm worried,' he said, but she changed the topic as if it was not important.

'Mum has not changed her physical appearance since we were last together,' Joan remarked.

'These days she tends to wear her original form more than any other. Only when visiting certain unimportant functions and while shopping will she transform to another unknown body format. Anyway, I think it's much better when you know the person you are speaking to,' Pamela said.

While at supper that evening, Lumak officially welcomed them.

'We are very happy to have two very important family members here again with us. I sincerely hope their brief stay will be a very happy one. From their recent successes on Earth, now Solaria, I am sure they are the right ones for the job. So let us welcome Joan and Michael and may their successes continue unabated,' he said and they lifted their glasses. Michael then got up to speak.

'Firstly, I must thank Mum and Dad for their kind words and fantastic welcome and add, that we shall do our utmost best in securing Solaria. Furthermore, I would like to take this opportunity to invite you all on holiday with us at the Hearst Mansion on Earth, after its refurbishment.

'We happily accept!' Sarah shouted.

'Secondly, I would like to announce my future engagement to Joan Colman. With your permission, I would like to celebrate that ceremony here with family and friends. Don't worry, we are also going to hold a similar celebration in Solaria on our return.

'That's fantastic news!' Lumak cheered, followed by the others.

'Thank you all for having us,' he said and they cheered some more.

An agreeable Sarah stood up to say a few words of her own.

'May I congratulate you both on your future engagement and when you are ready for the wedding, just let us know.'

CHAPTER 22

A powerful transformation

The following day Lumak took them to their central Macron called Mac. She was the one responsible for all life on Eden and most of all, her special bio-engineered children. That Mac was a conscious super intelligent AI computer that presently ran the whole galaxy, and she and her humanoid androids were at equal status with humans. However in such a hybrid system all were dependent on each other for survival.

'Dad, I didn't realize I was due for a complete checkup?' an unhappy Michael said.

'Son, although Earth is an improved environment, you have great things to accomplish in the future and a good overhaul is necessary at this time. The same applies to Joan.' Michael decided not to argue with his adopted father and opted for his advice in such matters..

After security clearance they were taken to the most central building in the central part of Eden City. Lumak handed them over to an android receptionist who took them through.

'Ah, Lord Michael and Lady Joan. I see you have arrived for your timely changes. Please wait here while an attendant take you to the labs,' another more senior android said. Then Joan was taken away by an assistant.

'You have been brought here for a very important reason... of which you will be informed in due course. In the mean time, you are to receive your well overdue medical checks and new advanced programming,' the female android said.

'I see!' Michael replied, accepting as she advised.

She was dressed in white and boldly displayed the federation insignia and badge of superiority over her left lapel.

'First of all, let me introduce you to your new portable Macron. She is the most advanced of her generation and will enhance your pool of knowledge on all relevant subjects. Her simulacrum is a most attractive human female with the most pleasant disposition. You will both be programmed together as one. That way, she will be tuned and synchronized to your personality. From that moment she can be considered the female side of your being. Don't worry, she will not be jealous of any future female partner, because she is the female side of you,' she added.

'Thanks for that minor observation and advise,' he mumbled to himself, with his mind elsewhere, contemplating Joan's faith. Assuming she was undergoing the same procedure with a male simulacrum.

'Please follow me to the chambers. Your body must be thoroughly checked before transformation.'

'What exactly do you mean?' a very nervous Michael inquired. He had no idea that there was going to be a change in body as well. Or perhaps they were just giving him new and more powerful brain implants. She placed a device close to his neck pressed a button and he fell limp onto the couch. Although he could hear her words, most of his body was paralysed and he could take no steps to resist her attention.

'You are to be transformed from an ugly caterpillar into a most beautiful butterfly. You will soon be changed into your final form. Your present body has outlived its usefulness and is no longer required. It was only needed while you were growing. The growth process is now at an end, so it's time for the next phase of your development.'

'What will my Joan think if I am transformed into an alien monster beyond all recognition. What if she was...' he thought not wanting to consider that horrible thought.

Despite his overwhelming fears, a very worried Michael muttered words to himself, trying his best not to aggravate the situation while searching for the nearest exit. But then, although he could move his head and eyes, his hands and feet were useless. Then he realised he was a product of their experiments and had little choice when it came to such decisions, and so did his beloved Joan.

He realised he was cunningly tricked into a most bizarre operation. Whatever it was, it sounded alien and very painful, and he didn't relish pain to any degree. Nevertheless his foster parents had permitted those changes and he had second thoughts about bad things happening to his body.

'No wonder Mum was not too excited when he told her of their future marriage. She must have realized something dire was going to happen to both of us, to make our marriage irrelevant, but what could be so horrible,' he contemplated.

More androids came and took his body away to a larger room with many devices. He was undressed and made to lie in a horizontal cubicle. His body was then clamped into position. After being thoroughly scanned, a band was placed around his head and he was injected with a pink substance.

A mechanical arm descended from the ceiling towards his head and he felt his mind being drained of all knowledge and emotion, until he was a blank slate and no more.

When he awoke from the dreamlike state, he was standing in another cubicle and being checked from head to toe by another senior android.

'Lift your left hand. Now your right.

'Lift your right leg. Now your left.

'Do you feel this... and that?

'Good! Good!

'Again!

'Do you feel this... and that.

'Very good.' The android continued pricking and prodding every part of his new body until she was fully satisfied.

'You are a most delightful specimen. Would you like to say farewell to your old body?' she asked and he nodded in disbelief and utter bewilderment, not realizing what she really meant.

His metal straps were released and he glanced at his reflection on the half opened lid of his cubicle. Although there were some facial resemblance, the body was not his original. From a previous height of one point seven metres, he had grown to over two metres, with a corresponding increase in weight and he looked more like a hardened warrior in a tight fitting black garment, than his former shy and timid self. Even his voice sounded more boisterous. His golden hair and sea-blue eyes had been replaced by jet black and light brown eyes.

'Come and say farewell to your old body before it is incinerated,' she said and he followed her in disbelief.

'Oh no! What have you done!' he broke into tears and began fondling his former self, but there was no response. The body remained lifeless and in the same position but still wearing the headband.

'It is in a state of suspension. After all, you are not there any more. Are you?

'Like an ugly caterpillar, you have surrendered your old for a much better one.'

He could not accept the fact of his own death and tears continued down his cheeks. At lease, his new body had the same emotions as his old, with all its peculiarities, or so he thought. Yet, suddenly he realized he was still alive.

'Forgive me for letting you down my old and loving friend,' he whispered and kissed the cheek of his former self. He turned away in sorrow, and became desperately worried for Joan. He knew she would have undergone a similar transformation, and how would she accept the death of her former self.

He was utterly disgusted with the superior androids and their uncaring brand of technology. He was subsequently taken back to the training room where the supervisor waited patiently for his return.

'Now, you will be trained to use your new implants and afterwards, your body,' she ordered. He realized he had no choice in her plans and decided to follow.

He was sat in a special chair and a band placed around his head. The process took a few seconds, during which time he was able to configure his mind in a similar way to his original. But the present one was infinitely more powerful than his former.

He was assisted by his new Macron, who could now have been considered the other half of himself. During that time billions of new pathways and connections were made in his mind.

His mind now contained superior elements and knowledge of things he hadn't even considered. When it was over, he was taken to a large engineering facility and bound to a wall.

'Don't be alarmed. It's completely safe. Your body will now be tested for strength and resilience. Under no circumstances should you attempt to escape,' she ordered again.

A large metallic object accelerated on rails towards him. Judging from its mass he knew he would be pulverized and flattened like a pancake, but on impact the metal could not affect him and melted into his shape.

'Wow! You are virtually indestructible! You may have realized that your body, although of human form, is made of much sterner stuff. Now we can proceed to your final tests,' she advised in her usual sarcastic tone. Like some sadistic Frankenstein monster creator, wielding the scalpel of advanced technology, she seemed to relish in his discomfort. Yet, there was no physical damage, pain or discomfort.

He was utterly shocked by his ordeal. It was like playing Russian roulette with God and he prayed he would come out of the experiments alive. But even now he could feel no muscle power under his control It was all under the control of the operator..

'Now I shall attempt to cut through your body with a high energy laser.' She tried it on a thick metallic bar and it cut through like a hot knife through butter. She then focussed the beam towards his chest and that part of his body absorbed all its energies and remained at its original temperature with not even the slightest damage.

Finally, he was made to kneel in a finely meshed cage which was thoroughly secured from the outside.

'Promise me that whatever transpires you will not try to behave violently,' she stressed. He knew that sooner he was through with her experiments, the sooner the whole episode would be over, one way or the other, so he obliged.

'I promise. No violence!'

In any event, his old self was never violent, but he was unsure of his newer and more sinister form. From previous observations, he concluded it could easily have taken the laboratory apart along with a large part of planet Eden. So he was also worried for the safety of his friends and most of all his beloved Joan. Again he tried to move his arms but they were dead.

'Within twenty seconds you must escape without damaging a single strand of the mesh on this cage,' she ordered. Try as he may he couldn't escape without damaging the cage.

'Try harder! Use your inner mind for a solution!' she shouted. Suddenly his body transformed into a substance resembling syrup and it began to pour through the thin slits in the mesh. It formed into a blob on the floor where it began to reform into his former self. The one he had always preferred. During the whole episode he was overpowered by the strangest feeling of detachment, yet he could control the process to attain any desired form. So he selected his original body.

'There is much more. However, this is just your initial training and you are now ready to face the harsher universe. You will be returned to the outer waiting room where you will meet your fiancee. From henceforth, you must remember your secret code name is Aron. That name will cause your matrix to change into your warlike form. You are now back to your original body, but made of much sterner stuff, so go in peace, Lord Michael... or Grand Lord Aron, the Supreme Patriarch... and may Grand Lord Gerra guide your every move,' she said and smiled.

He recognized Joan sitting close to a desk and ran towards her. Suddenly he realized he had regained all his bodily functions and feelings.

'Darling, is everything ok?'

She stood and he was amazed. She hadn't changed an iota. Neither did she consider him strange when she kissed him.

Then he glanced at his reflection against a panel and realised he was back to his original body. Even his clothes were the same. It was like awaking from a nightmare.

'Thank God! I am myself again!... I am me!' he shouted joyously, lifting Joan off the floor several times in the process.

'Is everything alright?' he again inquired.

'Everything is alright, Darling. I am just made of sterner stuff than before,' she replied and he went cold.

CHAPTER 23

Within the bowels of Eden

When they arrived at the imperial palace that day, Sarah smiled with happiness.

'You are both ok!' she cried and ran to them.

'Yes Mum, It went much better than I thought,' he replied.

'I was quite worried for you both. But thank goodness you are the same people as before,' she said and they followed her in for lunch. Although she didn't like such drastic changes to her children, she had accepted them as necessary for the survival of the Empire in the face of the Javols threat.

'Your new wardrobes are ready. Perhaps we could check the garments after supper?' Sarah said, appearing little disturbed by their recent ordeal.

As empress, she knew of the awful decisions and sacrifices that had to be made by all. She had little choice during their enactment, even with the ones she dearly loved. During those unpleasant moments she tended to focus her mind on triviality and irrelevance. That was the only way she could cope, by taking her mind away from such issues in order to reduce the pain.

Nevertheless, Michael and the others always had their clothes made on Eden. Somehow, those fabrics appeared more elegant than when worn on Earth and were more hard wearing.

Later that day they followed Lumak to one of the local citadels. They were places of prayer for many of those from Caefon in Andromeda, including the Ancients. Most people on Eden were Senots who followed the words of their great profit Siend Seno of Mond. Nevertheless, many chapters had been added to their great book which included passages about the Son of Destiny and the Ancient Patriarchs or Demigods like, Jull, Aron and others.

Unlike churches, citadels reminded the couple of old-world buildings in the far east, with their many circular spires that pointed to the heavens. However those were of pure gold and with many rooms for private prayer and the accommodation of a spiritual caretaker. Caretakers were like monks, and had given their existence to the cause of caring for all life within their fief and the Greater Purpose, and they were assisted by religious androids.

They followed Lumak through an underground passage and with a flash, they found themselves in the centre of a vault of immense proportions. There were racks of numerous weapons everywhere.

'There are several of such caches here, on Mars and on Earth. We have been stockpiling such weapons for many decades. Now we have more than enough to defend our galaxy against all invaders.

'We also have factories in Andromeda for producing their own weapons,' Lumak said and they were astonished.

'Is there a war in Andromeda... ?' Michael asked, holding back out of respect.

'Yes! I am pleased to say, and we are gaining on the enemy with very little losses on our side. That's mainly because of our advanced technologies.'

'There must be many sacrifices?' Joan asked.

'You should not be unduly concerned about the loss of your original frail human bodies. In time you will accept those losses and thank the Greater Purpose that you have been so chosen to fulfill a greater purpose. We are all on one side, you know. It is the side of our families and friends against a most disgusting and deplorable fore.

'They see us only as food.

'They appreciate nothing. Not art, culture, love, music, science, absolutely nothing. They only crave cruelty, sadism and feed on all primal life, getting greatest pleasure from the painful screams of the more advanced species like ourselves. The sooner we rid the universe of these hideous monsters the infinitely better we shall all be,' Lumak said. He couldn't help letting out some rage against those that threatened civilization.

'I am afraid, you are now an important part of the Greater Purpose in defeating the Javols. Nevertheless, we are all servants in the scheme of things,' he continued with a more calmer voice.

'Have you met with the Javols?' Joan inquired, innocently.

'I have been with others on campaigns to Andromeda and elsewhere. You will be on your first in due course, after David's transformation. However, you must not mention about your changes to anyone, including David, at this time. Always try not to preempt future events, unless you see a greater danger and the need arise to warn others. On your first real adventure you will meet the Son of Destiny. He is also your father,' Lumak said.

'My father?' A surprised Michael inquired, taking several steps away.

'You all have real parents, you know. They are at the highest levels of power within Osmaron. Since they are actively fighting the enemy, they are always away on campaigns, so we voted to take their places here and be your guardians for a while. Now, you are of age and are being given the facts. Your new implants have also been updated with all relevant details.'

'And no one told me!' he griped with sadness.

'These painful decisions were taken by the council for the benefit of all. There are many things I find distasteful in our struggle against the Javols, and I hope that very soon our lives will return to a semblance of normality. But alas, not until the dreadful monsters are destroyed.

'When you learn of your parents' past and the many sacrifices they had made, you will become very happy and be focussed individuals with a single purpose; namely to follow in their footsteps,' he said, proudly.

'Is he as powerful as they say?' Michael stuttered, with tears running down his cheeks.

'He is much more than they say, believe me, and so is your father, Mallory Colman,' he replied, turning his attention to Joan. She also was reduced to tears and began to sob.

David's father is Donald Fraser's son. I am your real grandfather and Sarah your real grandmother, my son,' he added. Michael ran towards him and they embraced.

'I never knew. If only I knew... all these years...' he sobbed. Wiping his eyes and glanced at Joan. Michael asked another question.

'Dad, what are we now? I know we are not flesh, and normal blood do not flow through our veins?' He patiently awaiting a reply.

He was still disappointed by the loss of his frail human body, with its many weaknesses and pains. Yet, after some reflection, he felt just as good with his more recent one. Only the shell was removed, like a serpent shedding its old skin for a newer one.

'You are made of sterner stuff than anyone I know. It is not microid technology. A new type of matter that can also exist within our universe. Each of your primary cells can individually communicate with every other and with your extremely complex brain. They can also be phased differently to normally vectored matter, making you virtually indestructible. If you were blown apart into a billion fragments, they would come together again to reform your original body. The reverse is also possible. Your body can be transposed into millions of small insects in any shape or form.

'Several blueprints and templates of life-forms including alien have been installed within your implants to save time in computing vague forms. You can transform into any one of those templates almost instantly. You are truly unique among humans, and your natural children will be exactly like you.'

'Really? We are like the supreme warrior!' Michael was utterly surprised.

'You are the supreme warrior and patriarch, Aron. When the time is right, Joan will melt down and a small part of her will form the child. The infant will imprint on the features of its parent and by so doing the infant can become a human child or for that matter, any other life-form. It will depend on whatever form you adapt at the time of its birth.'

'Stranger and stranger!' she replied.

'You can only conceive human children with very advanced technology, but that path is unlikely for now. One more thing. With your kind, sex in terms of maleness and femaleness is purely a mental concept. This is because you can transform into any type, male or female. However, you have chosen maleness, because it's from your previous form. In a similar manner, in order for any of your children to be of a particular sex, he or she must imprint on a suitable male or female.

'You are truly unique among humans and as far as I know, all other life-forms within the known universe. Not even the Javols can harm you,' he said, full of pride and satisfaction.

'Dad. How long are we made to last?'

'I am not sure, Son. But I think forever. Mac will send you the specifications in due course.

Despite everything that had occurred, it was as if a giant weight was lifted from their shoulders. They realized for the first time that they had real parents and families in Osmaron and elsewhere. At least, those were the real parents of their former selves and that must count for something. They also realized that sacrifices had to be made and the donation of their human bodies were their first real one.

They contemplated the raging wars in Andromeda and elsewhere, and pondered the sacrifices made by their brave and loving parents against a most devilish of fores.

'Now, let's return and have some sustenance,' Lumak said and they patiently followed.

CHAPTER 24

Summoned to Little Osmaron

'You both have been invited to Little Osmaron by the Grand Lord himself. It is a very great honour, so be at your best behaviour and show humility and reverence always while in his presence.' Sarah said.

'That's truly the greatest honour,' Joan replied.

'I have chosen your garments for the special occasion. Pamela and John will help you both to get ready,' Sarah continued, playing her motherly part to the last. She felt important in the fact that her grandson had been chosen for greatness like his father before him.

Little Osmaron, so named by Grand Lord Gerra, lord of the seventh part of the universe, was one of the artificial satellites of planet Eden and also his residence.

The satellite was like a giant diamond mountain with not a single entrance and glittered like an enormous jewel in Eden's sky. At night a strange blueish haze emanated from its base to fill that part of Eden's atmosphere and surface, barely visible by the naked human eye.

The Grand Lord was not human, neither was he primal and many thought he had come from an older universe within another space-time continuum. Since his arrival on Eden he had adopted the human form for convenience. He was probably the oldest living entity in the known universe and with incredible powers.

A large and most beautiful bee-like creature, the size of a small man, escorted them from their point of arrival and walked through the solid wall of the gigantic diamond. Hesitantly, they followed and were not inhibited by its super denseness. Within the inner sanctum could be seen many fairy-like creatures of light that travelled forward and backward through the bluish haze of unbounded space, which appeared to expand to infinity.

That part was truly inter-dimensional and those messengers,

called Luminites, carried information to the furthest reaches of the universe and to other dimensions. That way, his purpose could be felt and followed.

He formed the Greater Purpose of all life within that part of the universe and loved and respected all of its many life-forms. However he would not use his powers in any way to alter the natural order and evolution of those creatures. Only when life was severely threatened would he, through his servants the Shadites, inform and organize civilization against such dangers.

Suddenly, the incredible scene faded into a more human one. They found themselves standing in a large room that was mainly white with furniture and a large table. The figure of a most handsome young man now faced them and he walked forward to shake their hands. He was radiant and wore a white tunic with a winged insignia pinned to his broad lapel, but it was not the one of the federation.

'It is strange how often history repeats itself. You must not be nervous. Please join and seat with me in comfort,' he said, and they wondered whether he was the supreme being that everyone on Eden spoke so much about. The one with many names that had existed since the beginning of time and was well over thirteen billion years old.

'How do you like my little Osmaron?' he joyfully inquired, making them feel more at ease. By those words they realized he was the one, but he looked so young.

'Battles raged and souls perished.
Many of those were friends, cherished.
With great sadness I turned the page.
A new chapter begins, and a newer age.

'I welcome you to my fold of friends,' he said in a most enchanting manner.

They gazed at him but did not answer. The figure was too powerful. His power overwhelmed every atom of their bodies and to the very core of their being. Yet, it was not evil. It was of intense order and purpose.

'Was it in Andromeda...' a brave Michael replied, with

reference to his short poem, while trying his utmost to overcome all his weaknesses. He felt like an inadequate gnat in his presence as he somehow forced those words out of his mouth, or was it through his mind. Yet he realized that poem was said for a purpose.

'They are also here, but not for long. From now, your father will guide your hand and assist you along your way with my blessings. May your light in future shine brightly among the Stars of Osmaron, as it had done in previous times, when the universe was younger,' he said.

An image formed within their minds, of battles lost and won since the beginning of time, of the ancient Patriarchs of Osmaron and he realized he once lived in that distant past aeons before as another by the name of Aron. Then the images changed to the recent past, the present and the future for almost a thousand years. They realized that the Greater Purpose was a body of intense intelligence and with the ability to plan the future of all life for thousands if not millions of years.

Now they knew the way and while they observed the myriad of images that flooded their minds, they realized their purpose was clear, but crucial to the survival of Osmaron. It was one for which they had been specially chosen.

Suddenly the room changed back into the unbounded bluish space, with its many Luminites darting too and fro.

The same bee-like creature appeared and escorted them out of the inner sanctum. Then as if by magic they were in the palace hall-way. Joan stared at Michael for a while and felt his hand, to make sure she wasn't having another dream.

With such advanced technologies it was sometimes difficult to know whether one was real, where they were and with whom. Nevertheless they now had a clearer view of the past and their future and would follow that course or destiny to eternity.

Part 5

Battles Rage

CHAPTER 25

Beyond enemy lines

Somewhere within Andromeda on one of its habitable moons, within the Santoran System, another battle begins.

'My lord, I have received report from Santora III. The planet has been mined and concealed portals positioned for a speedy retreat,' Captain Perry said through his communicator.

'Get the men ready!' Andy barked.

Commander Andy Colman lifted his special utility belt and fitted it about his waist, then he walked out of the tent towards his troops. He realized that his previous efforts on Earth with rebellious Infilates would be a treat compared to his present command.

Trivan was a ghastly world that time of the year, with its constant rains and blood-sucking insects that made him very irritable and uncomfortable. His specials, tough as they may, were also quite irritated by the long wait and were getting impatient. He worried for his troops morale if their waiting was much longer.

Since their arrival three months ago, they had the worst weather they had ever experienced during morning, noon and night, on a satellite world only a little smaller than his mother planet, Earth. Here, they waited within the enemy's stronghold, concealed until they were ready to act.

All the necessary equipment had been planted by remotes, including the special drones that would take the place of the enemy just before they were destroyed.

Several of the enemy's H-wave transmissions had already been intercepted and deciphered, and identification codes installed. Now remained the more difficult task of acquiring personal ones from their superiors. That had to be done before they began infiltration.

The Javols' Master Mind would always ask for the

identification of the sender and that privilege was allotted to many in the Javols' hierarchy.

Several undetectable surveillance satellites had been placed in orbit and were searching every small area of the massive planet below, but nothing unusual had so far been detected, other than the unusual scarcity of Javols.

Javols always installed their food caches and operations underground in large caverns. The entrances of which were usually filled with activity.

So far no such activity had been observed and Andy thought something was seriously amiss.

Once the Javols' command centres had been detected, his troops would use the closest portals to gain access to the surface above, before entering their underground dens. It was a very risky business and the whole purpose of the operation was one of surprise.

The soldiers would initially gain access to the first underground level and slowly descend and infiltrate the lower levels, replacing Javols with drones as they went. That way, many Javols would be non-the-wiser until it was too late.

With thousands of Javols in such facilities, it would have been an unimaginable nightmare if they were prepared and waiting. There were many dark lairs and caves in which they could hide and they had the ability to transform into all types of shapes, including pillars, boulders, rock projections and such like.

Every Javol had to be destroyed and every inch had to be searched and cleansed. Furthermore, booby-traps were not uncommon when they were expecting their unwelcomed guests.

Javols were very resourceful and could quickly organize themselves into a formidable force. They never took prisoners unless for food and cruel entertainment. Any mistakes on the part of Andy would have led to a major tragedy for his fragile men who also made enjoyable food for Javols.

All those factors worried Andy and he would never risk his soldiers without first knowing the strength and weakness of his fore.

'We are unable to locate their control centre, Sire. Exhaustive satellite scans have not detected anything out of the ordinary. They must be well hidden underground, since there is little surface activity,' the impatient voice said.

'In that case, we'll have to flush them out. Arrange to shower them with our meteorite drones and a few incendiaries and gas capsules. If anything, that should wake them up and they will be none the wiser of our presence. First, make another thorough sweep of the surface,' Andy ordered.

The fatigue of that particular operation was very apparent in his features. When they first arrived he thought it was an easy take. Now he was having serious doubts and his feelings seldom lied.

All previous intelligence reports and long range probes had pinpointed that world as the major centre of operations for the ninth sector. But since his arrival they could only observe a few Timit farmers without their Javol overseers cracking the whip. He wasn't sure whether Javols celebrated national holidays. Such changes in their routines could only have occurred if they had been forewarned by a Mut in the form of a Fed's traitor. Then they would occupy every rat hole and be waiting to make a feast out of his unsuspecting soldiers. It also worried him that not a single one of their mother ships could be observed in the area, even with his most sensitive scanners.

Such situations had occurred in the past; they had once used one of their engineered mutants to penetrate security posing as an operator. Luckily, they found the imposter in time. Even while he dissolved away, he swore blindly he was nothing to do with them.

'Those Muts can be so damn convincing,' Andy thought while considering those possibilities.

All Javols carried with them a smell of rotting flesh. Although a most natural and acceptable smell to them, it was most repugnant to humans and usually gave them away before they could act. That particular smell could not be suppressed by even the most fragrant perfume. It reminded us humans of death and aroused something primal in our subconscious of utter evil.

'Lucien, call central again. Check to see what the delay is all about and whether our orders have changed,' he barked. Lucien soon came running out of the tent.

Sire, our orders still stand. Central wants us to wait until more information becomes available.' Then she left briskly for their main operations console.

'That could mean their Muts might have gained access to our main operations computer. I wonder if they also know about the Hexotron? If they know, that could set our war effort back by decades,' he mumbled.

Andy, while taking a major risk, transmitted a coded message to Martia's ship now docked on Caefon.

'I think we might need some major assistance. Our enemies appear to be dug in. Can you help?'

'We have just arrived from Earth and will be free for a day or so. Anyway, we are on our way to your present location.' He was less stressed, knowing he now had an imperial war machine to watch his back. Also, his men could have a break on one of the largest federation battleships.

Then he explained the situation to his warriors and handed them double rations to raise morale. They would need that much in a prolonged fight. This one he knew would be the mother of all battles. He only wished he would have enough help before he and his men were sacrificed.

CHAPTER 26

A major disappointment

'How could the long range surveillance probes have been so wrong in their interpretation of this system and local H-Wave traffic,' an unhappy Andy thought while glancing at one of the rougher surface areas on the world beneath, now displayed on one of the observation screens.'

'It's a trap, Commander. I can feel it in my bones,' Lucien interrupted his thoughts. But he ignored her comments.

'Send message to Base Central about our situation here, Lucien, and stress the conditions in this swamp infested hell hole.' Lucien, his personal secretary left immediately to relay the important message.

The H-wave message was sent on a tight beam to avoid interception by the enemy and she awaited confirmation, which was not long in coming.

'Be on alert! We have since found out that security at Central has been compromised by Muts. We are now running checks to verify to what extent. You will be informed in due course. Take whatever measures necessary to hold your present position,' the female voice said and the communication snapped five times. She also realised it had been relayed that many number of times to avoid detection and tracing.

The name Muts brought shivers down her spine and reminded her of an experience she once had with those Javol mutants. She barely escaped that one, but it left her with many psychological scars and recurring nightmares. From that moment on she swore she would spend her remaining life fighting the monsters who killed her parents and younger brother.

An exhausted Lucien came running. She was almost out of breath and gasping.

'Co... Commander, security at central has been compromised... infiltrated by Muts. They are not sure to what extent. They may even have had time to transmit details to their MasterMind. They want us to take whatever steps necessary to hold our present position!'

'What are we meant to do in a bug infested swamp like this... and what about all our other people throughout this confounded galaxy!'

'We have to be patient, Commander!' Her advice was accepted and Andy became less furious.

'If their MasterMind knows of our efforts and have warned them, our task of taking this galaxy will be a thousand fold more difficult, even with our advanced technologies.'

'But, Commander, there is the Son of Destiny and others with great power, so we always have a good chance of beating those bastards!' she yelled.

'I know how you feel, but I am afraid it's only a matter of time before they are able to pursue us in great numbers. During that time they will absorb and copy our own technologies and use them against us.'

'That's easier said than done. First they have to pass me!' she replied and he was amused by her persistent nature. He loved that attitude in a woman.

'When the time comes, you be very careful. As for now, we can only take our best shot and pray we come out alive,' he said and left to inform his specials of yet another problem. They would now have to formulate a tighter plan.

As always, his specials were given the choice of fighting when danger was far beyond the call of duty, and as always, they preferred fighting the enemy to the death.

Now, he was sure the Javols were prepared and waiting for them in their many underground traps and snares. Nevertheless he had not come unprepared for such an eventuality.

Thanks to Martia, he had taken along six experimental suits. She said they would protect them from the Javols' poisonous breath and had the power to penetrate deep within rock. However, their users had just six hours of oxygen during the phasure mode. His phaser cloak was not available to him at that time.

There were sixteen captains and only five suits remained. As commander he had taken the first and there were no life-savers.

Andy summoned his captains into his tent.

'There are only five of those special suits left, so we'll have to draw lots. Lucien, get us their numbers,' he shouted and left to speak with one of his captains. Soon she returned with a small container that resembled a paper bin.

'Commander, can I also draw?' she asked and took a number from the small bin. It was number fifty-six which was her own personal number. She had obviously stuck it to the side of the container. Seeing the fight in her eyes he spoke quietly in her direction.

'One gutsy little lady, eh!'

'Just want some payback, Commander!'

'I know what you are up to, but someone will have to remain here to coordinate our efforts below, so see to it, Sergeant,' he said, taking the container from her. An overjoyed Lucien instantly retrieved her communicator.

'Operator, Cathy Friedman!

'Commander's tent at the double!'

Andy began to ceremoniously retrieve their numbers from the bin, calling them out as he did. Number twenty-five, Captain John Roche... thirty three, Captain Anthony Weever... forty-one, Captain Joe Sinclair... forty nine, Captain Tricia Munroe... fifty-six, Sergeant Lucien Lopez, etc

For a brief moment of disbelief they shifted their gaze to the little fiery woman, who was just a senior operator-com-secretary and shifted them back to their commander. They never argued with his choices.

'I know guys, this one is going to be hell and I don't give much odds for any of us coming back. Let's go into it like soldiers from hell. Perhaps that way even hell might refuse to have us.'

'Yeh! Yeh!' Lucien yelled, as if she was about to leave for a most delightful holiday.

'Here is the plan... We the chosen few, break up into three groups. Each visit the three red spots on our map. Their main one has got to be in one of them. When we find what we are looking for, we call our regiments, transfer the location and give em the works. I don't want to loose any of you, so everyone will be issued with the special masks and inhalers. Load yourselves with as much shielding and fire-power as you can carry. We are going to turn that world below into an inferno.'

'Any action is better than remaining in this confounded swamp,' one of his captains commented and he nodded in agreement.

'Tell your men they are to get ready by twelve and keep yourselves concealed until then.'

'Yes, Sir!' they saluted.

'One more thing, nothing must be left behind in this place, so burn the tents before you leave. Until we meet again,' Andy advised his comrades as best he could in the circumstances and with sadness embraced each one as they left. He had known that particular group of troopers for more than a year.

That gang of his Specials had left Caefon two years ago with fifty-two captains and over eight-hundred fighting men. During that time they had taken over one hundred of the Javols' strongholds. However their operations were not without loss, and during that time their numbers had dwindled to a remainder of just over three hundred with a mere sixteen captains, twelve from his original bunch. Many of those departed were close friends and he cursed the Javols with every breath of air. Without the great ships there could be no life-savers, so those were lost for good.

'Lucien!'

'Yes, Commander!'

'I have decided to have you as my second. That way I can keep one eye on you. Get the special cloaks from my ship and check them out. Also double check the new communicators. I want no mistakes today!'

'Yes, Commander!'

'One more thing. Get used to calling me by code. The enemy might know the meaning of "commander". That's all for now, Sergeant,' he said and she saluted and left. He smiled as she went and realized she had what he called "true grit". He just hoped she didn't crack at first sight of the enemy.

From a local portal she transposed into a ship and recovered a trunk with the usual coded signals to identify its contents. She opened it to make sure they were all there and were intrigued by the thick metallic cloaks from which emanated a strange kind of irradiance.

In the second trunk was six large portable weapons, the sight of which she had never seen before. Pulling them into the ship's portal she transmitted them to her tent.

'He said I could test them,' she thought, and began to put one on. It was a bit awkward at first and much larger than her size, but she persevered. Then she clipped the winged buckle in place and the suit began to shrink to her size. Large shoulder flaps stood out to compensate.

The utility belt contained first aid and her oxygen mask became a natural extension of her nose. She immediately viewed herself through her implants and was very pleased with what she saw.

'Wow! This is one great fashion. I wonder if there is a helmet or head protection,' she thought and the shoulder flaps became vertical and covered her head. A veil formed in front of her face. Apparently its functions linked directly to her brain implants.

'Now to really test you!' Lucien murmured. She was lifted off the ground and began to float in mid air without any type of propulsion. She was suddenly fearful and grabbed hold of one of the tent poles. Her body stopped abruptly and she realized she had close to zero mass.

Lucien soon got her nerves back and floated through the tent, gliding through a large rock as if it wasn't there.

'What a bloody garment! How do I turn you around?' she thought and it rotated itself to retrace all her moves.

The strange cloak was unbelievable in the way it formed a mental connection with its wearer, making both as one through thought. She also realized her implants had a lot more than she had realized.

Lucien knew that with such a cloak they could infiltrate the Javols stronghold without being observed and relay invaluable data to their specials. Now they had a much better chance of survival.

There was only one snag however, they could not blast the enemy while the suits remained in phasure mode. They had to become visible first and be as susceptible to the enemy's weapons as the other specials.

'Co... Commander. I mean... S-five-three. This is Lucien. I found an advantage,' she said through her implants and Andy left the men and horridly returned to his tent. There she stood like a small silvery angel, less wings. He could not believe his eyes and slowly progressed towards her.

'Lucien! Is that you?'

'Yes, Commander. It's me, I mean S.. five-three.'

'These things are marvellous, Sir. Now I know how we can have an advantage.'

She linked implants and down-loaded her experiences of the hour to him and he was fascinated.

Andy assigned her as chief coordinator for all training of the cloak wearers, including himself.

He explained the new plan to his men, who immediately regained their lost morale and cheered. At least, now they were not fighting blindly.

They would retain a base on the near Earth-size moon and with the aid of the chosen six, locate every Javol in the world below before the soldiers-from-hell were dispatched. Yet, the gravity on the enemy's world was almost twice that of Earth and they worried it might give them a disadvantage against the enemy.

CHAPTER 27

An important discovery

Turning his attention to the operations map, he glanced at his captains. Then he turned his head towards Lucien.

'Where do you think they are hidden?'

'Since our last long range, I have given the situation much study and have come to just a single conclusion,' she replied.

'And what is that?'

'I think there are three centres, which are linked underneath by passages.'

'Passages... over one-thousand miles long in some places?'

'I know. It sounds ridiculous, but that's what the data adds up to... and what I think. They could be using that world for some other purpose, like mining, perhaps. It's also very rich in metals,' she replied.

'If it was for mining, wouldn't there be large freight-liners to transport the stuff off world?'

'What about interstellar portals?' John Roche interjected.

'They tend to fall apart when they are transported that way. Something to do with the involuntary trauma after the process is completed. We all know what it's like the first time we get transmitted. Like your knees want to pop from under you and you almost fall to the floor. However, after a few times our brain gets used to it and compensates. Some reckons Javols respond to those changes by turning into an uncontrollable pile from which they are too disorientated to reform. Anyway, all our portals can sense Javols and are programmed to destroy them.'

'Yes, I agree. Nowadays our implants have special circuits to remove ill effects due to portal travel. While Javols cannot tolerate changes that are not under their full control. Call it a phobia if you wish. As a matter of fact, they detest all portals,' Andy replied.

'Couldn't they use other life-forms, or even remotes?' Lucien asked.

'That is not the way Javols work. There is no compromise in their nature and they will not trust another life-form to any degree. Anyway, by nature they detest all others. Except of course their slaves, which they detest even more,' he replied and they were dumbfounded.

Andy and Lucien arrived at the centre of the star delta of tunnels as indicated on their map.

Despite an extensive search of the surface, they could not locate an entrance, neither were there ventilation shafts as were common in all such places. Those were mainly for the benefit of other life-forms and food storage.

On arrival they vectored their cloaks and were floating through the dense layers of rock. It took a little while to get the settings just right. It was like swimming in an ocean of matter using similar hand and leg movements to propel oneself.

The suits could also move on their own while using their implants, but it was more unnatural for beginners.

It was not long before they found themselves in a gigantic underground complex, with all forms of fabrication and assembly robots.

As usual in such complexes there were no stairs or elevators, which always tended to make the task of his Specials more difficult.

Javols were fully mobile life-forms and didn't require such means of access, as required by bipeds and quadrupeds. Those facilities were unnecessary, unless there were human-like slaves about, which was seldom the case in such environments.

They could observe many Javols. Those were the orange-brown variety that specialized in science and technology. The soldiers were in grey, black and blue, depending on rank. However they could change their basic forms at a moment's notice to any of their standard types.

Their superiors were usually of a different form altogether and a lot more massive. Those spent most of their days feasting, when not being entertained by their many slaves. One in every ten Timit slaves were sacrificed frequently for that purpose.

Communicating with his other four captains, he soon realized the complex was almost as Lucien had imagined. It formed a star-delta tunnel array with one large central area which connected to the three outer nodes through large tunnels. The outer nodes formed a triangle and were each over one thousand miles apart.

The many tunnels were straddled by many holding bays which were covered. One such bay had its cover removed and displayed several strange craft.

'Those must be thoroughly investigated after this complex is captured, providing the Javols hasn't already set the whole place to self-destruct,' Andy thought.

Through the many tunnels could be observed many heavily armed Javols moving in their thousands, but those were mainly guards that had been recalled from the planet's surface since the base went on alert.

Having investigated the nodes within their many levels, the information was coded and transmitted on tight electromagnetic beam to their moon base, where they would be studied in more detail.

Once again Andy decided to explore the central complex in greater detail. This time he took the others along and assigned each a separate part of the expansive facility.

To avoid tripping the enemy's sensors, they vectored their cloaks to full phasure. At that setting even the densest metal would appear as a vacuum, but they could only control their movements via their brain implants.

A large metallic pyramid caught Andy's eye and he took Lucien along to investigate. They entered through its southernmost face and settled on its lowest surface, which corresponded to the interior ground level. The room was brightly lit and above their heads could be observed many grids, panels and rods, forming some type of accelerator array that extended towards the apex. It resembled one immense cathedral with a large array of organ pipes, but unlike a real organ the pipes were pointing downwards from a high dome-like ceiling.

The floor contained many rings and insulating circles.

'It's truly massive. We can build a multistory office block in here and still have room for more. I wonder what it's for? It seems to be completely isolated from the outside,' Andy said, gazing at the powerful grids that extended several hundred feet above his head.

'It's some form of amplifier. You know something? It reminds me of portal technology. It must be a gigantic portal, perhaps even galactic in range, and thoroughly screened from everything external. Why would they want the use of such a powerful portal?' Lucien inquired.

'I told you before, Javols don't use portals! Anyway, lets relay all this information to the guys above. We can send a top priority coded message to Caefon. Now it's time we left this place,' Andy said and they travelled straight through the walls and upwards through its dense atmosphere.

They soon arrived back on the moon and he called all his specials together.

'We've had a close look at their facility and it's full of Javols. The reasons why we were unable to detect them is because they all moved to the lower levels. There is also a lot of stuff down there that we don't understand and have to relay to Central for analysis before we can press forward,' he said and they were not amused for another lengthy wait.

CHAPTER 28

A friend in need

Then Andy brought all his officers together in his large tent. He had several bottles of Scottish whisky which had been saved for their victory celebrations. But this time he was not sure any would survive. Furthermore, their discoveries of that day gave them much to celebrate. Despite the great odds against their survival, they could now plan a better strategy.

A very pleased Lucien had collected the glasses and two bottles were poured.

'Guys, I think they must know everything about us. That also goes for their MasterMind, and that knowledge isn't recent. They may have been planning such counter measures for decades,' he said and they were utterly surprised and disappointed by those recent developments.

During debriefing, Andy explained the details of their findings and asked Lucien to despatch a coded message to Martia's ship. Martia ship's computer would know exactly what their findings were and reply within the hour.

A reply was not long in coming.

'Do absolutely nothing. Hold your present position. We are on our way.' Martia ship's transmission said and overjoyed Lucien immediately relayed the information to Andy.

'Commander... I mean, S-five-three! Ma...artia's ship is soon to arrive!'

'That's great news!' he complemented her. She saluted and left.

Martia's ship, which was one of the main flagships of the federation had also been recently fitted with some of the deadliest weapons in the universe.

From a once most beautiful cruiser at over 2 kilometres long, her colour had changed to mat black and she had increased to over twice her original length. Her many beam weapons had been designed to rotate and vaporize Javols' spheres, which usually contained thousands of Javols, and gave her the look of a fearful monster with sharp forbidding spikes.

She used the most advanced form of inter-dimensional drive, which could transposed her extreme mass across the galaxy in under fifteen minutes.

Her present journey from Caefon would barely have taken ten minutes, Earth-time. However, it would also have signalled many Javols within the inner half of Andromeda. That volume of space was still a part of the Javols' territory, previously left to the slow moving infiltration of federation soldiers and Specials.

Presently there was little need or desire to keep Federation presence a secret. The Federation now had control of the outer half of Andromeda, within their numerous underground bases. Most of which had been taken from the Javols in previous decades even without their knowledge. Most of those bases had been duplicated with Solarian Drones and microid mines that could duplicate Javols.

Soon, security would be tightened throughout their dominions. At that time they would be refitted with even more powerful weapons.

The pretence was finally at an end. Now, they were at phase three of the master plan. During this period Andromeda would be finally cleansed of all Javols. Nevertheless, that phase would be the most bloody for its mainly human soldiers until the Primorphs were released to clean up the mess. They had planned their advances in such a manner to minimize the Javols copying their technologies. That was the main reason why human soldier's were sacrificed during the initial phase.

To avoid immediate detection, Martia's ship materialized at the other side of the large moon. From there she communicated with Andy's base using H-wave.

All his officers and soldiers were immediately taken aboard via portals. While on board and away from the swamp insects, they would have a well deserved, but temporary break from the unpleasant climate of their base.

They were called to the main reception hall that evening for an extensive dinner. That area was filled with hundreds of veterans from Caefon and elsewhere.

Andy and his remaining specials proudly marched down the isle of the main auditorium in single file and everyone cheered the bravest of Osmaron. They wore their clean grey uniforms that had been saved for such an occasion. Their federation insignias showed boldly on their broad lapels. They sat in the central area near the large stage. It was an section specifically reserved for them.

Martia, the human part of Martia's ship and also a joint minister of the War Council, walked towards the podium to address them all and welcome Andy and his men aboard.

She was a truly beautiful and most desirable woman and resembled a Greek goddess with her period hairstyle and jewelled headband. Her turquoise tunic appeared to be of the finest silk and behind her shoulder dangled a cape of similar colour that was fastened to her upper garment with thick golden rings. Her long earrings were of gold and bluish pearls.

'Brothers and sisters of Osmaron, let us welcome Commander Colman, one of our bravest and dearest brothers, and his fighting Specials to our fighting ship!' she yelled and everyone stood up to cheer. Then Andy and his officers stood up and bowed their heads in respect.

'We had our doubts for sometime... that they also had a master plan. It was probably put together by other more advanced minds, who have been using the Javols from the beginning.

'Information collected form our drones over several decades had led us to the conclusion that it was the case. However, we could not gain easy access to their MasterMind, which is located close to the nucleus of this galaxy. It was too well guarded and had most likely been set to self-destruct. Further, we did not wish to disturb our own master plan in any way. Now, and finally, we know what that plan is.

'The Supreme Lord is very interested in our recent findings and will be with us shortly. He needs to investigate the world in greater detail before the attack,' she said.

'Will my lord be coming here?' an impatient Lucien shouted, for he was also her idol.

'Why, yes, Madam Lucien. He will be visiting us in person.'

Lucien could not believe her luck. For her greatest wish was always to meet the Son of Destiny.

She had always prayed to meet him before she died in battle and now her prayers had been answered, but she also wondered how Lady Martia knew her name.

After dinner that evening and while they were being entertained, the musicians stopped and two very strange life-forms entered and took their places on either side of the podium. Those two were like black statues and their garments appeared to be part of their bodies. Their hands were clawed, eyes were glowing and they gave the impression of fiery demons from hell. One of the demons eyes glowed red and the other an intense blue.

The Supreme Lord in the form of George Peterson followed them. He wore a princely gown and appeared like a master of ceremonies. They cheered him like a pop star and Lucien couldn't stop her clapping, even when the others had stopped. Then he waved his hand and she stopped.

'For reasons I am unable to explain at this time, this will be the last major battle within Andromeda. The Javols empire will be crushed from this galaxy in just ten days. All that will be left thereafter, are their few populated worlds at the centre, and those will be destroyed by the Primorphs and Hexotrons. I estimate the cleansing of this galaxy to be completed within a single decade.

'Never again will their disgusting kind haunt us within Andromeda.

'Never again will they be allowed to overrun this galaxy and destroy primal life in such numbers. Nevertheless, we still have numerous quantities entering Triangulum and Osmaron. Those will take longer to eliminate.

'All our attention will in future be focussed toward Triangulum and Osmaron. Because, numerous quantities are also on their way to those galaxies and many have already arrived.

'This is the beginning of a new year on Earth, now Solaria. Let this time also mark the end of all Javols within this galaxy.

'To save you, my comrades, from further death, my two

friends here will search the world beneath and deactivate any traps and self-destruct devices.

'Finally, you will be given new life-savers for this final mission, so that you and your children may remember it in perpetuity.

'I must return to Triangulum immediately, however, but three of the chosen ones will assist you here and in Osmaron. Neramon and Felspar, we are to search that world and inform of dangers,' he said.

'Yes, my Lord!' the demons replied in a most powerful voice.

Suddenly, all three figures became points of dazzling light and floated through the walls of the ship as if it wasn't there and darted off towards the world below.

Part 6

New Titans on the war path

CHAPTER 29

A Secret Mission

DEEP WITHIN ANDROMEDA

The Ploran, Lord Vektron, in his preferred material form of a large floating sphere of black, bobbed up and down along the warm but subtle air currents above his circular desk. To him it was like having a Jacuzzi. The stimulation helped him to meditate and focus on important matters.

A timed communication broke his concentration and the air currents died. He floated downwards towards his exalted position behind the large circular desk. The federation insignia could be clearly seen on his featureless spherical form. It was the only distinguishing mark that indicated his forward position. However, being multi-dimensional, direction or orientation didn't matter in his case.

Several important human figures entered, including Lord Meron of the Andromedan Ancients.

'We have finally arrived at our destination. It's time we anchored our Hex in place and ensured the other five are similarly positioned about the galactic nucleus. When they are all in place the charging process can commence,' Meron said.

'We can now mount our defensive weapons and traps, and be ready to leave at short notice. The first Javol that finds this place will be the one to initiate their final destruction.'

'Yes, My Lord! So be it!' Lord Hamil said and bowed.

'You have all done extremely well since we left Caefon's moons a decade ago. Soon, most of us will return to our homes in Osmaron. Therefore, let us rejoice in this incredible undertaking and achievement!' Lord Vektron barked in his metallic voice as if eating his words.

Meron and the other scientists, technicians and officers, cheered with joy, realizing their dangerous mission was almost at an end. Those few security guards that remained would sacrifice their lives if necessary for the survival of civilization.

Within a week the large matter converters pointed towards the large black hole within Andromeda's nucleus. They would soon initiate a process of utter destruction of immense proportions.

Several giant probes would first be sent just within its event horizon to initiate a destructive sequence. By so doing, all matter would be amplified and transposed in such a manner as to cause catastrophic disruption of all heavy nuclei within that region of the galaxy.

The disruption waves would proceed outwards only to be stopped by generated fields from the massive Hexotron stations. Then they would reflect those intense waves back towards the galactic centre over and over again. Such synchronous pulsating waves of space-time tended to neutralize all strong bonds within nuclei, leaving behind raw ionized hydrogen gas. It was meltdown on a galactic scale. In time, the excited gas would cool, then condense to form new stars and planets. During this time the Javols Mind and over fifty percent of all Javols in that galaxy would be obliterated.

Suddenly red lights began to flash throughout the Hex and sirens sounded.

'A large carrier and 5 large spheres are approaching. We estimate about 50,000 Javols.' The forward observers had relayed the data through their implants. Then Lord Meron gave an order.

'Release 50 Vipers and set protective screens to maximum. Standby plasma cannons and Gravitrons in case they get too close. I was looking forward to some action, now finally it's here!' his communication snapped within their implants, but they were already ready.

As they got within range all the Javols' spheres unwounded their load of Javols who dived en mass towards the main installations.

They could not destroy all the thousands of Javols in one go and several punctured through their screens and blasted through the installations.

The Javols in the installation began to create as much damage possible by taking the whole installation apart. Apparently to stop their weapons, but they still kept firing. Several Specials contained them in that area and kill several, but over a thousand still remained. Then to their further surprise the Javols began to link together to form a massive demolition giant. To their further dismay the giant began eating every bit of metal in that area. Their small plasma weapons were useless at that monster. Then Lord Meron gave an order,

'Everyone move out of that installation immediately, if you don't want to end up in deep space with our friends!' he yelled and they complied. As they left the main door shut, there was a blinding light and perfect silence.

'It's a very sad thing our enemies don't know all our surface installations are dummies and each room is a live portal ready to take them to oblivion!' he yelled and they were amused.

The Vipers had reaped much damage to the Javols carrier, but it was still coming and ready to discharge its bombs and beam weapons.

'Number 5 and 12, knock out their main thrusters, then we can do the rest from here,' their commander said and it was done.

There was a blinding flash and the roar of a thousand cannons and the Javols ship simply evaporated away in a ball of cosmic dust.

'Those are not going to bother us again!' Meron exclaimed with glee,

Plasma combined with intense gravity waves were not the kindest of weapons and tended to disrupt all forms of matter and transform them into their most basic constituent parts.

Once more the station was peaceful. This time with no loss of life and the specials found time to celebrate until the next encounter.

Lord Meron realized that despite the many Javols they had encountered during the journey, they had always managed to either destroy or misguide them. However out of the original nine-hundred and fifty humans, only four-hundred and twenty-five remained, and hopefully, their MasterMind were none-the-wiser.

They had designed all their stations and craft to look exactly like those used by Javols, including ID codes and concealed chambers for humans and stores. The Hexes themselves were like six large Javol spheres surrounded by drones.

Only when extreme need arose, did the human warriors take to their fighting ships.

The large spheres had been constructed on Caefon's smallest moon.

Those six massive black stations, the size of small moons themselves were completely screened from all long-range scanners and could only be visibly observed. Despite their enormous size and the numerous Javols in that part of the galaxy, the chance of confrontation along their chosen paths were minuscule. However they could still be detected and identified as foe.

Once all Hexes were in place at the perimeter of the galactic nucleus, they became like large portals that intercepted all matter along the hexagon formed by their inter-spatial connection.

For optimum effect, they were focussed to large probes at the event horizon, thus forming an immense gravitational amplifier, among other things. By so doing the outer parts of the galaxy would be partially shielded from all dangerous energies.

Despite great risks to all life within the galaxy, they could not warn them. Neither could they evacuate their friends and families to Osmaron, without arousing their suspicions, including those of the Javols.

Anyway, if disaster occurred it would not have been felt by humans outside of the hex for several thousand years. This gave them time enough to evacuate everyone from Andromeda.

Each hex required seven Earth days to charge, until it reached maximum level, then it would remain that way until the final process was initiated by curious Javols tripping one of the numerous sensors.

The aftershock would take several millennia to reach Caefon. By that time it would be greatly weakened and just an undercurrent felt by the most sensitive equipment.

They were each placed in orbit about cold and barren worlds and their energy collectors initiated, but their shields remained on.

Sixty human soldiers, ten per sphere, would remain behind to communicate or sacrifice their lives if necessary in the defence of their territory.

After the spheres were fully charged, the soldiers would leave via the long-range interstellar portals. But they could also call for help from their colleagues on the other stations or from within local stellar systems if the need arose. All their bases utilized the latest H-wave technology which was an immediate form of inter-galactic communication.

CHAPTER 30

Back on Earth

The Headrons Michael and Joan arrived back on Earth from their time on Eden two days before the new year. While at his flat they contacted the others and dinner was arranged for the very same evening. A very excited Julia was the first to arrived.

'You both look so fab!' she exclaimed, while scanning their well toned bodies with what appeared to be a tropical tan.

'Need I ask... how was your brief vacation... and Eden?'

'It was fantastic and Eden is as beautiful as always. I could also observe a few more horses and children,' Joan replied. Then there was a flash and David and John arrived almost simultaneously.

Carl had previously arranged the drinks. It was one of those occupations that he enjoyed and continued out of gratitude for his Lord-master. He was also very pleased to be regarded as an equal and quite keen in pursuing his own independent career for the sake of the common good.

Carl wondered about what the couple had learnt on their brief visit to Eden and had an inkling it wasn't all to do with fun.

'Madam Dragon was spewing and spurting fire and brimstone like Mount Saint Hellenes today. The same old gripe about a fog on her plantation. She even threatened to take the matter to a higher court.'

'Wow! Who got her so pissed off?'

'You, I think! She also made it clear that your presence was always needed during session, and you should not have been away during this critical time. However, I think she missed you both. I also thing she was a bit jealous you two had taken an unannounced holiday to Eden without her knowledge. She never liked our powers and privileges, and I think she is after your chair,' David said Jovially and embraced Michael, then Joan.

'In that case, I shall have to pay her a visit after we return from Andromeda. We have an urgent mission to that galaxy.'

'When are you going?'

'As soon as we do some training and are battle ready!'

'It sounds exciting!' David yelled.

'War is never exciting! Anyway, not as exciting as Madam Dragon. Nevertheless, I understand her fears. Her home is close to one of our ground weather stations. It creates high humidity levels which accounts for the local fog. It's a long story and not all pleasant,' Michael replied.

'You guys look so different. Like you had a complete refit,' John greeted and immediately parked himself in front of the Vidicom. It was like a flat screen television, used mainly for watching old-world videos and films. Its thickness was of a picture frame and one could increase the image width by a simple command. Then it would appear to divide into 4 equal parts to form a screen of four times its previous area. At other times it could imitate a window frame with beautiful outside views in virtual 3D.

He had a quaint fascination for that type of entertainment and was already building one for his flat. They tended to follow Michael's taste in such matters, but such hobbies were also very fashionable at higher circles among the young. It was akin to the Old-world hobbies of collecting antiques.

'David, Mum wants you to visit as soon as possible. Therefore, I would like you to take your brief vacation to Eden immediately, so please leave first thing tomorrow,' Michael said and David was surprised.

'That is fantastic! Can John come along too?'

'Yes!

'Carl and Lucia... you must go along as well, but not all at once. Now I don't wish to talk anymore shop,' Michael said and pulled Joan towards a nearby settee.

'By the way, Mum and Dad sends their love to you all. We've also brought you some presents, which we shall open after dinner,' Joan said and they lifted their glasses.

'Tell us more. Has it changed?

'Is it as fantastic as ever and did you play any VR games,' an excited Julia asked.

She had always enjoyed the Virtual Reality games in which one could play the part of anyone and even feel pain and suffering to such an extent that it was not always possible to tell the difference.

One could select almost any period of Earth's history. But they always preferred the ancient worlds, from ancient Babylon to Greek, Rome and Egypt. There were also several programs on planets Caefon, Polok and Lodor, including fighting Javols.

Lucia wished she could gain access to such a Games Macron, but realized Earth was still in the dark ages compared to Eden. It was also one of the reasons why her other friends had not visited before.

In the past, Earth had always been regarded as the troubled world by Edenians. Yet, most had never visited Earth and neither could they ever without the special imperial permits, since she was then declared a no-go world. However since her re-naming to Solaria and promotion everyone hoped Earth's general status would also be reviewed and upgraded to full technological.

Julia realized how biassed people were and decided to take a stand to improve the image of her adopted mother planet in the eyes of every member of the Federation.

The changing of Earth's name to Solaria was the first and most important step in that direction. Then there would be interstellar trade fairs, conventions and conferences.

The old Solarian Bank could be revived for just such a purpose.

'Our beautiful world, Eden, is still the same, but it's also very quiet. Many of our dearest friends have left for Andromeda. I reckon the war over there is now in its final phase,' Joan replied.

'Oh, my God! Are they in grave danger? I wish I was there to help,' an unhappy Julia inquired.

'Don't worry, you will be there soon enough,' Michael replied.

'What can we do?' Julia asked and began to sob.

'Don't you begin to go all soft on me. Anyway, after you guys return from Eden we are to visit Andromeda. However, you must first be trained to become competent warriors. As you may have already realized, our holiday wasn't all fun. We underwent some very stringent training. Now we can take on virtually anything and win, because we are made of much sterner stuff and so will you. And it's not all physical. You have to be conditioned as well. So you will be going there for a proper course in all relevant fields. That is... if you want to give your best in the war against our enemies,' Michael said.

'Of course we do! After all, you have had the treatment and you look a lot better for it,' David replied, not quite knowing what the treatment was..

After dinner that evening they enthusiastically gathered around the large casket for their presents.

Joan opened the casket and withdrew the first gift which she handed to Lucia. Lucia removed the silver wrapping and opened the bio-degrade-able plastic box. Then she removed what appeared to be a large ring with many orifices and several separate attachments. Its box also contained many packets and tubes of chemicals.

'What on Earth is it?' she inquired.

'You mean Solaria, don't you?' A happy Joan scolded, but Lucia's mind was more on her presents, so she ignored the correction.

'It's an automatic hair styler, silly!'

'Wow! Like an alien piece of gear!' Michael said.

'You place it on your head and concentrate on a suitable hairstyle. Then you force your imagination upon it. You must first read the instructions through your implants. Once you have the programs downloaded into your implants, you simply select a suitable style from the new menu.'

'That's incredible!' Lucia replied and went over to kiss them.

'Thanks for such a lovely present!'

'Anyway, it can only be used with implants. It's one of the latest gadgets on Eden and also very novel,' Joan said.

'Isn't that truly incredible!' an excited Julia exclaimed and immediately left with her toy for the bathroom.

Joan retrieved another present. This time she passed it on to Carl. He also couldn't make heads or tails of the strange device.

'It's... I think it's an electronic device of some kind,' he said, doubtfully.

'It's an electronic assembler. You can use it through your

implants to produce small units. It is ideal for fabricating old-world equipment. It also has the means to test and repair them. In fact, it can test and repair almost all types of old-world and modern circuitry, with built-in test equipment that can be controlled through your implants. Part of it is robotic. Micro robotic with copying skills,' Joan said as she downloaded the information from her implants.

'I always needed one. Now I can do some real work refurbishing some antique electronics.'

'It is also fully mobile and can move within large main-frames with search-and-find. It is an invaluable kit with a full human lifetime guarantee,' she continued. Carl kissed her, still not quite believing the incredible gift had all those features.

The other item was a very large cylindrical container.

Joan, with little effort lifted it out of the casket and placed it to one side.

'This one is for you, John,' she said and he went over to remove the lid. All he could observe were bluish crystals that tended to change colour in the light. Then thinking it to be some form of soft wrapping, he began to lower his hand into the container but was immediately stopped by Joan.

'It's the latest in cross Primorphs (CPMs for short). It's an advanced form of microid.

'Once programmed by you, it can accomplish virtually any task. But during the forming process it must imprint upon its master's features. From that moment on it will be obedient to that master.'

'You don't mean a real Primorph with shape-shifting ability?'

'Yes, I do! It can change its form to almost anything, so it will be very handy for making things and assisting about the home,' she said. He was completely overwhelmed. He had always dreamt of having a pet robot about his flat but never in his wildest did he expect a Primorph of the latest design. He kissed her and returned to his seat.

'Thanks, it's the best present I've ever received!'

She removed another and handed it to David.

'We didn't get you anything major. Just a token of our affection,' she said and he took the small box from her hand and opened it.

'Just what I wanted, a talking... computerized pen?' he said and kissed her.

'That's not all. It can also write. Just point it at a white surface or sheet of paper and think of a sentence,' Joan advised.

He did as she asked and letters began to form on the blank sheet several inches away. He thought of removing the writing and it disappeared. It could also communicate with central macron and display information in that media, but it could also speak. Although not essential for those with implants, many on Earth didn't use implants, so it was a useful interface.

Later on that evening, when they were ready to leave, John decided to move his large container of microid crystals towards the departure point but couldn't shift it. It could have weighed several tons.

Joan gracefully went to his assistance and to the amazement of all, moved it as if it was a feather.

'What did you take on Eden, Superwoman!' an astonished John jeered, but the others remained utterly shocked by her new powers.

CHAPTER 31

Two universal beings

The following day Michael and Joan saw their friends off to planet Eden and they both disappeared to the quiet cabin at Snaky Lake.

They wanted to learn more about their new bodies and in the process, attempt some of its stranger attributes. Those dangerous experiments could only be carried out in a remote place that was well away from human populations, in case something went wrong. Even so, they didn't want anyone to observe their strange powers in action and it was essential that any out-of-doors transformations were kept well away from prying eyes.

When they arrived the area was covered in snow and most of the lake was frozen over.

They visually scanned the area and found there wasn't a single human in sight. But that was not all, they soon found their vision could be adjusted to any part of the spectrum, which included infrared, visible, ultraviolet and x-rays. Frequencies could be tuned in or out in different proportions to enhance an image. That vision was also panoramic and telescopic. Those changes and enhancements were realized by a simple desire of wanting.

It was like being in a completely new universe. Even the fish in the lake could be clearly observed under the ice.

For the first time since they left Eden they realised they were not human, but a life-form thousands of times improved, even alien to the universe. Yet, they felt all their original emotions and passions to be exactly the same. In that way they realized they were human through and through. For humanity had little to do with form and more to do with attitude, emotions and mind.

They stared into the cold black moonlit night. At that time of winter it was extremely clear, with a bright full moon and several stars.

While they watched the immensity of the heavens their spirits lifted and they felt a strange sensation come over them. It overwhelmed to such an extent they couldn't stop repeating a name. It was the name the operator gave them after their conversion.

'Aron! Aron! Aron!' Michael shouted to the heavens with arms outstretched. It was as if the universe was calling.

'Bella! Bella! Bella!' Joan shouted, in similar posture.

Slowly at first their bodies began to change into the powerful figures they were given on Eden. Then they realized they would have to take that course of action to wherever it led. The forces were much too great to resist or reverse.

'Look up! What do you see?' Joan asked.

'Why? I see a moon in all its glory!' he replied, joyfully.

'Concentrate on its surface features.

'Now what do you see?' she again asked.

'I see a much larger moon. I do believe it's getting even larger. Now it's swallowing me. The more I ask for surface features, the larger it becomes. I suppose this process will continue down to the very atom and beyond. Can my eyes really magnify that well and to that extent?' he replied.

'Now think you are there... on its surface and see what happens,' she said.

'I think I am now in a small crater. Where are you, my love?'

'I am here! Joan shouted.

'Turn around!' she said and they were both standing on the moon watching Earth as a distant world one quarter of a million miles away.

'There is no oxygen or atmosphere in this place, so why are we still alive... and we communicate without air and implants?' his original thoughts questioned, only to be overridden by another more powerful consciousness.

'Our bodies can convert matter into energy by any part in contact with the environment. We are now collecting energy through the soles of our feet and can absorb and channel it to any degree.

'We use an inter-dimensional form of communication that can traverse any distance within this universe almost immediately,' she said.

'This is truly incredible! We are like gods!' he said, full of utter excitement.

'We are Gods. We are the new Titans of the universe! I wonder if we can fly or float across its surface for surveillance purposes?' she asked, in a similar state of utter well-being.

'Soon they were hovering across the moons surface and through its high mountains as if they were not there.

'They began playing hide-and-seek with each other until they were bored.

Then they were going to embrace but Michael held back. He was worried that he would absorb Joan's energies if they touched, but she went towards him instead.

Then they embraced each other and kissed like gods of the heavens unimpeded by anyone or anything.

'You see, we have nothing to worry about. Our type of matter is quite normal to us, since our bodies are made of the same stuff, but somewhat different from that of the natural universe,' she said and he was happy in that knowledge.

'Darling, if we can convert matter into energy for sustenance in such environments, how much reserves do we carry and how often do we refill?' she asked.

'That's very easy to answer. Since our conversion on Eden, all our food and water intake has amounted to a figure well in excess of several billion kilojoules of energy, equivalent to Earth's total output over several months. Obviously, our bodies needs much less than that conversion mass in order to survive. Remember, we convert matter directly into energy with virtually zero loss. When energy levels dip below our reserves, we will become hungry and begin to consume our surroundings if normal food is not available,' he said.

'What happens if we continue to absorb energy in that manner? Can we be starved to death?' she asked.

'I suppose when we have enough the process of absorption will slow down and stop. It's a process akin to being satisfied after a large meal.'

'Oh!'

'As for being starved to death, I think we are much too powerful for that and normal matter can't imprison us. Anyway, the starvation process will take months, if not years and during that time we will find something to absorb. If the worst happened, we might just go into a form of hibernation for a while,' he replied.

'So we are truly indestructible and eternal?'

'Yes, we are!'

From the questions they asked each other, they soon realised he was the scientist.

She was the astronomer and navigator, but also knew a lot about his implants, so she could also have been a psychologist or medical doctor of some kind.

'Love, let's return to the cabin. Tomorrow we can experience form-changing and shape-shifting,' he said and they departed in a similar manner to when they arrived.

Michael always enjoyed a peaceful walk around the lake. The tranquillity of the surroundings assisted his understanding of life and nature and today, most of all, with his beloved and their newly found powers.

He also wondered what had happened to his original flesh-and-blood body, but soon realized Eden's technology could quite easily have built him an exact copy if he so desired. After all, that body was just a shell of flesh, blood and bones that had been previously scanned.

He also wondered what would happen when they had sex together. Although not essential for having babies, he enjoyed the closeness and satisfaction it offered. He wanted himself and his future bride to be at one with each other and that was the only way to fully cement their relationship.

Then the Javols came to mind and he realized how fragile all primal life was in the universe. The natural order was borne out of evolution and carried that process onward. But that process was not an end in itself. It gave birth to superior minds who could create systems that were not even within the natural order and those very same systems, like himself, could alter that order. They could even mislead it to attain their purpose, which led to newer forms of evolution, ad infinitum. Then he thought again.

There must be a greater consciousness in all this, to allow such diverse changes to occur, even when they were not of the natural order. That must be the Greater Purpose.

'What an incredible universe it is, to allow such possibilities, and it only placed the most advanced possibilities, in the form of advanced technologies, in the hands of higher intelligence. Was that what was meant by The Greater Purpose?' he thought aloud.

'Darling, breakfast is ready!' Joan shouted in her natural human voice and he felt more comfortable than he had ever been. He did not wish to use any strange telepathy today. He wanted to just be his original normal self with all its usual rough edges.

'I am on my way!' he shouted back, but he had completed the route and was now close to the cabin anyway.

'Love, we have much to do before we leave for Andromeda, so I thought while the others were away, we could use this time to learn more about each other and our new bodies,' Michael said, while enjoying a most tasty old-world American breakfast with coffee just the way he liked it.'

'You read my mind!' she replied.

'This is absolutely delicious!'

'I'm pleased you like my cooking!'

'Where on Earth did you learn to cook like this?'

'I don't quite know. I find it quite natural. It must be another one of my special gifts,' she said and he got up and kissed her on the cheek.

That morning they found they could change into virtually any object of an equivalent size, but not of equivalent mass. For some reason their quantity of matter remained the same per unit volume. That aspect could only have been altered by a massive intake of energy.

Changing into normal objects were easy, but heavier elements like gold and led weighed the same as an equivalent volume of their bodies.

However, they could also form into many small animals of the same kind.

Using more imagination and concentration it was possible to become obstacles like wooden beams, stones and so fourth. Such obstacles could coexist with smaller animals also formed from their original bodies. Therefore, items like flowerpots with flowers, stones and trees were quite natural to become once a few cells of the material had been absorbed and analysed. That way, any life-form or object could be replicated. Then the transformation would become part of a database within their implants for instant transformation.

They soon realized they had a large list of objects and numerous life-forms had already been programmed in their subconscious, including all known forms of Javols.

'You know, since that recent report about the operation of pirates close to Mars, I've been worried that it could be due to Mut infiltrators. Our enemies could know a lot more about us than we realize.

'Are you sure?'

'Not 100 percent, but I have an idea.' he replied.

'I hope it's an adventurous one.'

'Before the others return, why don't we do a bit of snooping around a few local worlds and search for some pirate look-a-likes. They could be using one of the outer worlds or moons for shelter,' Michael said and Joan concentrated for a moment.

'We have lists of all federation bases, stations, ships and mining colonies in the vicinity of the Solar System and nearby stars. I am sure we could detect their presence by a simple process of elimination,' she replied.

'One more thing, Love. Under no circumstances can we show anyone our new powers, or act in such a manner as to attract attention to ourselves. Such behaviour would arouse the attention of infiltrators and could cause them to change their existing plans.' Michael stressed.

'I know!'

'We must give everyone the impression we are soft imperials. In the mean time, through subterfuge and disguise, we uncover our enemies plans. Not even Central Macron should be informed of our present campaign.'

'Then we do a bit of shape-shifting!'

'You got it! At this moment in time, we do not know how far

they have infiltrated our security systems and we must take
nothing for granted,' Michael replied.

'If as they say, the pirates are sons and daughters of miners.
Don't you think it might be advantageous for us to begin with
Terminus City on Mars?' Joan said and Michael nodded his head
in agreement.

'That's a great idea, Love!'

They had decided to visit the Martian Capital, Terminus City
incognito to further their investigations. Since it still contained a
few space miners and pirates, it was also the most likely place for
the unobserved arrival of Muts.

CHAPTER 32

Martian miners

Due to an old agreement between Solarian Banking and the US Senate about a century before, all Miners were given a small share in Solarian Banking. As a result, during that time they could only sell their ores through that bank. That agreement also gave their children certain rights along with Earth status irrespective of where they were born, but they had to visit Earth for registration.

In old-world times, George Peterson, who was then president of Solarian Banking, stood up and fought for the rights of their Martian ancestors. They were at that time cut off from Earth with no legitimate rights. During the intervening turmoil on Earth and hard times that followed, many of those isolated miners began to starve. Thanks to George's intervention and support they survived and made him their president.

Because of their harsh way of life, Miners had always been very religious and superstitious. They followed the Miners religion, which was in the Christian Baptist traditions, but with one exception. They had since accepted George Peterson, Son of Destiny, as their Saviour and the one foretold in the bible as the true Messiah. Nevertheless, many in Terminus City were of the newer Senot faith, which revered all life and that religion was spreading far and wide.

In the intervening years that followed, they had been given control of Terminus City and had kept it for their lord in the most immaculate condition. Now, with direct portal links to many main stations on Earth, they could visit whenever they pleased. However, they always preferred their Terminus City to anywhere else in the universe. After all, it was miners' home and paradise, with miners' attitudes, culture and laws. Nevertheless many yearned for real blue skies, oceans and green forests.

Even so, Mars was gradually being transformed into a more suitable environment for life. The numerous robot ships were constantly extracting suitable gasses from Venus which they would dump within the Martian atmosphere. That way both worlds were being reformed at the same time. However that process would have taken several hundred years.

Michael and Joan decided to visit Terminus City incognito, pretending to be husband and wife on their honeymoon. That way they could avoid the press and not attract too much attention from others and be tied down with ceremonious duties. After all, they were the most important people in the Solar System.

As visiting tourists with keen ears, there was the slimmest chance they would find some clues. With the advent of ship-to-ship and ship-to-base portals, every miner tended to returned to base sooner rather than later. Martians were a lot freer in the use of portals than on Earth, with its many levels of security codes. While on Earth, inter-planetary portals were inaccessible to its populations, with the exception of those with brain implants. On Mars, they were freely available as normal transport. However, strict security was used in homes and buildings.

Martian miners tended to be very talkative. That tendency was due to a basic psychological need. They alleviated the stresses and loneliness of outer-space by chatting and cracking jokes. But they, like most miners, enjoyed taking the mickey.

Miners worked four days on and three days off. That way the dangers were more evenly spread and they had longer periods with their families. Tired miners led to accidents which usually led to the detriment of other miners, so they made sure they were well rested.

Drug penalties were high and a drunken miner if found guilty could be banished to Earth for life. To every miner such punishment was equivalent to life imprisonment with little or no access to their families in Terminus.

The couple under the disguise of George and Brenda Collingsworth took residence at the Metropol Hotel in Central Terminus.

When they arrived there was much commotion in the hotel's lobby and they wondered what the excitement was about. They were hoping their cover hadn't been blown. But they were not the celebrity of the moment. Councillor Lady Lia Chiang arrived several minutes earlier for her annual vacation and had generously tipped many of the hotel's staff.

Being the president of The Confederation of Inter-Planetary Miners, which was one of the largest mining groups, Lady Lia Chiang always visited to voice one of her complementary new years speeches. It was also her role to acknowledge and hand out presents to the high achievers of the previous year. Miners always looked forward to their traditional new year's celebrations that was held in the main hall of the Civic Centre.

However, that was not the only reason for her visit. Her father was also a miner and had lost his life in one of the frequent accidents on one of the asteroids. He had since been buried in Terminus City and she visited his place of rest each year to say a prayer.

Michael's suspicions were aroused and he immediately contacted his personal macron, which he called Joanna to make a few checks through Central Macron or Mac.

The information on Lady Lia Chiang was not long in coming.

To all intents and purpose, she was a respectably and trusted lady in proper control of a small protectorate state on Earth. Her long record with the miners and other business associates was also honest and above board and her standing at council was unblemished.

However he soon realized that if anyone intended to infiltrate Earth's supreme council, she was going to be the perfect target and new-year's celebrations would offer the best cover for such an operation.

A Javols Mut could quite easily absorb her body, take over her duties and carry on the pretence for several days or weeks until found out. By that time security would have been severely compromised and Lady Lia Chiang would be no more.

'They must have found a way to mask their awful smell,' he thought. Realizing all Javols, including their Muts always smelled like decaying flesh.

'Love! I think we have a major problem,' Michael said and

transmitted his thoughts to Joan.

'Why are you so sure it's this time? They had good opportunity last year and the year before that,' she replied.

'The recent pirate problems. I think it was done for a reason. Perhaps for Muts to take over some of our chaps in that federation cruiser. It would then be a simple matter to pass through federation base security here in Terminus City. They could have masked their smell by a chemical substance and special clothes.

'And by the way, the ship is also here in Terminus Base,' he replied.

'In that case, we shall have to transform again to two security officers with all necessary ID. Central Macron must have a list of such operatives and their schedules. Let me try my macron this time,' she said.

They had the personality profiles they required and immediately changed into them, including cards, sex and clothes.

Michael was Brody Matloc and Joan into the man, Mike Weaver. They were both undercover agents for the Supreme Lord Protector and with a license to kill.

While Lady Lia Chiang was out, they entered her room and hid several small scanners no larger than the small spiders indigenous to Terminus City. Those bugs would remain concealed and inform them if she had become a Javols' Mutant or Mut. Muts tended to exude a most unsavoury odour, like a dead rat and the bugs had such smell sensors.

If she had been replaced, then her original would have been terminated at about the same time of her capture. If not, she would be informed of the threat and be guarded during her stay on Mars. Extra security could easily be arranged through Central Macron, but they would take several hours to arrive from Earth through the usual channels. In the mean time, they would have to carry on the pretence game until the infiltrators were discovered.

On all her previous visits to Mars, Lady Lia never concerned herself with security. She was held in high regard, well loved and respected by the community. After all, planet Earth and Mars were not existing in the times of old-world violence.

The only people she travelled with were her press agent, secretary and page. Local security could always be arranged by the hotel at short notice. Furthermore, she could always communicate to Central Macron via her implants in an emergency. Although not the most ideal method, Central Macron always had a few special security people in Terminus. However there was always a delay of several minutes before they were present at the scene.

Lady Lia arrived back at her hotel suite at about 8 pm. Time within Terminus City was synchronized with Martian time and was not the same as on Earth. She intended to make a few final changes to her speech and take a small snack before leaving for the central auditorium, where the miners' dinner celebrations were to be held.

After a short time her suite was thoroughly scanned remotely. There were no disgusting smells or suspicious behaviour from her or members of her staff. Michael and Joan came to the conclusion that no one in the group had so far been replaced. However they were to make their move before she left the hotel.

From their ordinary detective outfit, they had suddenly changed their disguise to the black leathery uniforms of the deadly Imperial Specials, dangling plasma weapons and others on their thick utility belts.

There was just a single guard standing outside of her main door when they approached.

'Imperial Security! Stand where you are and do not move!' Joan, now Mike Weaver shouted and the guard simply dropped his weapon.

Michael bent down and checked the guard's weapon and then he checked him over, but he was just armed hotel security. Then he handed the weapon back to him.

'Make sure no one enters or leaves until I say so!' Michael, now Brody ordered. The somewhat shaken guard nervously saluted and continued his watch.

Everyone in the federation were scared of Imperial Specials as they were legendary fighters with license to kill on sight.

Michael transmitted a code to the lock, the door opened and

they walked straight through.

'We apologize for this untimely intrusion!'

'What the hell!' Lady Lia complained, annoyed by their untimely visit.

'We are imperial security! So keep your places!' they yelled.

'You are? Well I haven't asked for any security!' she barked, with concern.

'I am Captain Brody Matloc and my colleague is Captain Mike Weaver,' Michael said and handed them a coded security badge.

Lady Lia was utterly shocked by the intrusion and almost had a fit, but her page quickly went to her assistance.

'How can you... have the audacity to enter my apartment uninvited and unannounced. Do you know who I am?' she barked again with utter fury.

'There could be dangerous infiltrators and extremists about. So you must be extra vigilant!'

'Someone... someone will pay dearly for this!' she growled.

'I have transmitted your codes to Central. I just hope you are who you say you are!'

Michael and Joan could only admire the slender woman dressed in the red and blue costume. Where many warlords would have surrendered, she stood and fought her ground like a panther. She had no weapons, yet her words and bravery carried so much weight.

Having checked their ID's, her apparently shocked appearance changed into a milder one.

'We must talk in private. I want all your staff in the other room behind locked doors!' Joan shouted. She gestured with her head and they left.

'I was not aware of a breach in security?' she said.

'There has been a major one. Our intelligence indicate certain pirates of a political persuasion have infiltrated Terminus City. They are also intent on infiltrating the council. Someone in your position would make an ideal subject for kidnapping and reconditioning. If you did not accept their terms you would quickly become a dead councillor and they would try again with someone else. Accidents are easily arranged by such cutthroats on a world like this.'

'That bad? I've been coming here for years, why now?'

'It's probably just random. Anyway, it's our responsibility to take good care of our senior councillors, so we had to take those measures and warn you. You are to follow your normal schedules, but be aware that we'll always be close at hand. You must tell no one about us, or of your future plans and do not visibly alter your security arrangements,' Michael said.

'In that case, I must thank you for your concern for my safety and formally invite you to our miners dinner,' she said and they accepted.

Lady Lia Chiang had become as quiet as a lamb. She suddenly changed her resolve to finding whoever was involved in such criminal activities. She had many contacts in high places and soon sent a message through the miner's grapevine to locate the culprits.

CHAPTER 33

An unexpected visit

The couple changed back into their original forms at the bridal suite and decided to observe the more historical parts of the city.

Terminus City was built at about the beginning of the 22nd century, with technologies from Eden, so it was more advanced than any city on Earth.

Being also the site of the main Federation base in the Solar System, made it quite popular for military types and those with a yearning for space exploration.

Despite its many advanced features, the builders had also constructed an underground tube transport system with many old-world type fun-fairs and entertainment venues along its dual pathways that straddled the lines. There were also moving walkways, pedestrian walkways and cycle paths for those needing that type of recreation and pastime.

That part of the underworld glittered with every conceivable tradesman and venues at miners rates, which were affordable by all. Due to the Son of Destiny, official miners had always been greatly subsidised.

They soon realized how friendly and communicative its people were and despite their apparently hard exterior, were very warm and kind. He also understood why his father, the Son of Destiny, had taken so well to its people and vice-versa. The homeliness felt in Terminus City bore no comparison to any present-day city on Earth.   However, Earth was still undergoing a major transformation, while with the exception of the constant changes in the Martian atmosphere, Terminus was not.

Half an hour later they entered the main square and shopping precinct with its many stores.

Being a national holiday, all the main centres were closed and few people could be seen within the commercial centre of the bustling city. They made their way towards the central area attracted by the many worshippers. Such religious dedication was an attitude they had not observed on Earth.

Seven equidistantly spaced walkways radiated from the central temple to the seven almost equal parts or sectors of the city, all within one massive sealed dome structure. On either side of the temple were three large bronze statues.

The whole area was flooded with bright light from an expansive and continuous high ceiling.

The largest statue was that of his father, George Peterson. There he stood in a white robe with sandals and outstretched arms, as if calling his multitudes for prayer.

Next to him was the little girl, Clair, and on his other side Sarah, his mother. She was also portrayed in other statues about the square as the reverend mother with George as a baby.

There were also statues of Cathy, Michael's real mother, Clair as chief priestess, and others which they referred to as the immortal saints.

The inner temple was filled with flowers and candles which were kept constantly burning day and night.

The scene reminded Michael of old-world religions like Christianity and Buddhism, but all jumbled into one. However, since many in Terminus were of mixed race, including Japanese and Chinese, such religions were a natural evolution. Then he realized a better comparison with the miners religion, Pa-Baptist, was a mixture of Christianity-Baptist, Senoism and Buddhism. However, they had chosen George as their saviour and the others as their revered saints.

Suddenly a strange loneliness came over him as he thought of his father and the others in constant struggle against a devilish fore in a distant galaxy. He wondered if they were all safe and when they would return to fill the vacuum created by their absence.

Grabbing Joan by the hand he took her from the square and they continued towards the civic building where the miner's dinner was to be held.

Terminus City was an incredible place, but it was lacking all its mighty people and saints. Their absence had given their enemies a chance to take a foothold.

Perhaps that too was part of the master plan, to give the enemy a false sense of security in order to entice them into a trap to flush them out.

They had to be careful not to interfere with or disturb such a plan until they became part of it. However, any involvement in locating the Javols' Muts and stopping an assassination would have made them a major part of the plan anyway.

Since the miner's depression, at the end of the previous century, many mining families had become self-employed.

Caefon Dome, once their Martian home, had since been converted into a large vegetable farm. Many of the Solarian Domes had also been similarly converted or changed into arenas for competitive sports like football, tennis, baseball and others. Each was linked to Terminus City with sealed underground tubes and portals.

George Peterson, then President of Solarian Banking, the largest financial organization on Earth, gave them many concessions including loans for spacecraft, conveyers, drilling and cutting equipment.

He also ensured they had shares in its many other undertakings. As a result, from the very poor and starving, they had become extremely wealthy and independent. Because of their new self-reliant attitude, competition for contracts was rife among the few main families. Once those contracts had been issued, it was up to the contractors to issue sub-contracts or employ their fellow miners, not necessarily from their own family. Because of the limited contracts available and the need for work, every miner respected the heads of each family and so did their family heads. Although present mining in the Federation relied mainly on robots and androids, miners had an agreement with the federation which made their careers secure.

Then, many of those mining contractors and subcontractors were also involved in the terra-forming program on Earth. Presently they were the ones doing the demolition and reclamation of metals for Solarian Banking.

The main hall was filled with 3D holographic displays of the main families, of which Lady Lia Chiang and her father's clan was boldly represented. Her father's crew was one of the bravest and had always exceeded yearly quotas.

Next came David Anderson's family, then Mayor Sampson Richmond's and so it went on. They glanced at each lifelike hologram in turn, displaying their most important family members, including their mining dogs in little spacesuits and realized how proud and caring Martian miners were.

Finally they came to the bottom of the hall and were surprised to find the complete images of Mallory Colman, his wife Roseanne, son Andy and his wife Joan with the six female warrior specials or Amazonians as they were called.

They had once saved the lives of several miners somewhere in the asteroid belt and had been given the freedom of Caefon Dome. They had also been made miners and given the miners badges of membership.

Joan viewed the lifelike figures of her parents and grandparents in utter disbelief. She had never met them in the sculptured flesh before and certain emotions and instincts came home to her.

'I can see a family resemblance. You have your fathers eyes, but your mother's features,' Michael said and hugged her. He felt she needed to be consoled at that moment.

'Do you realized I was named after my own mother,' she said and shed a single tear.

'I hope you won't mind me calling you Junior when we are all together,' he said, with a smile and she grabbed his hand and they both continued their pressing business.

Transforming back into Imperial Specials, with all necessary identification, they quickly gained access to every part of the building. Within Terminus City the people never said no to uniformed Specials and treated anyone imperial with tremendous respect and admiration.

They decided to quickly survey the complete building for explosives and other deadly devices through its own security scanners. When they found everything was in order and all items accounted for, they decided to limit access to the building.

The many workers throughout the building were individually checked and sniffed for poisons. Once cleared, they were temporarily restricted to certain areas of the building. Then all portals above ground level were sealed off. At ground level, one of the two main portals were sealed off and so was the main exit.

Now, everyone were expected to enter and leave from a single entrance. The fire risk was minimal and Michael assumed the Muts would not be aware of those changes and alter their plans to any degree.

The main hall was designed to seat about three-thousand people, so only senior family members were invited.

The novices and unimportant families sat toward the rear on the seats coloured green, then there was orange, and red toward the front. Those at the rear always dreamt of moving towards the front, because it gained them higher status with greater respect and more sub-contracts from the seven most senior families.

However it was also possible for a family to be relegated as a result of crime, incompetence or low quotas. But that was seldom the case with hardy and very proud miners. Nevertheless there were great incentives and competition was rife.

After they had completed their plans, the couple changed into the identities of Aron and Bella, with brown hair and eyes. Those colours more closely resembled those of their real families, although infinitely more powerful.

Their original personalities of Michael and Joan was different, and fairer. Michael had golden hair and bluish eyes while Joan was mildly tanned with grey eyes, and could easily be recognized by members of higher status and councillors, including Lady Lia, so it had to be a more drastic transformation.

Their new features bore a closer resemblance to their real biological parents. Bella closely resembled her mother and Aron his father with different hair and eyes.

Although they called themselves Aron and Bella, they had not transformed into their warlike counterparts, they just used their names.

As Bella, Joan wore a most spectacular white dress with

sequins. On her head was a jewelled band with pearl choker and earrings to match.

As Aron, Michael wore black with the pink and blue sash of the miners flag about his waist. He looked the very image of George Peterson, the Son of Destiny.

Both wore the winged insignia of the Shadites. It was the ones given to them by the Grand Lord himself, for they were also Shadites.

By eleven p.m. the rear of the hall was full. Then came the more important families. As they entered they handed their cards to the usher and were announced and guided to their reserved seats.

Ten seats were always left unoccupied at the very front for special guests.

They waited for the last moment before showing themselves and handed their personal celebrity cards with the imperial seal to the usher. He stuttered with words of astonishment at the likenesses he beheld.

'Lord Aron and Lady Bella of the Imperial Houses of Peterson and Colman!' he announced and the complete house went silent with amazement and disbelief.

Most of the young generation of Terminus had never seen a member of the imperial household before and could never have dreamt of meeting the son of George Peterson, the Son of Destiny or Andy Colman's granddaughter.

As far as many were concerned, the Son of Destiny was just folklore, images made up by painters, sculptors, priest and priestesses to keep them on the straight-and-narrow.

However, as if by miracle there they were in the flesh and in their midst. The miners were confronted by an unbelievable reality. Yet they both appeared to be so like their parents statues and holograms.

Michael and Joan were guided to their seats and made themselves as comfortable as possible for the new-year that followed.

The whole incident had been carefully planned by the couple to divert attention to themselves and away from Lady Lia, and also to confuse the Muts and their subordinates. However they still hadn't any idea of the Muts identity and neither had they been able to sniff them out, so they were assumed to be outside the building.

CHAPTER 34

Miners' dinner

Finally Lady Lia was cheered unto the rostrum and took suitable stance to deliver her encouraging speech.

Before she began she took curtsy to the supposed royal couple and they gracefully shook their heads in response.

'Your Imperial Highness, Mr Mayor, fellow miners. I consider it a great honour to be here and even more so in the presence of our honoured guests.

'We have achieved much over the preceding years, breaking all our production target quotas well before their due dates. As a result, our order books are full for the following years. During this period of the rebuilding of our home world, Earth, all such supplies are in great demand, so I can only emphasize the need for a higher throughput.

'Further, we have received more and larger orders from Central to manufacture fixtures and fittings for several Federation ships. Hopefully, we might even receive contracts to build the larger frigates when our new space docks are ready,' she said and went on to discuss specifics, with a few encouraging words to the bravery and persistent hard work of the younger miners and novice groups.

After she had completed her lengthy speech the mayor went to the rostrum and said a few encouraging words of his own. Then trophies and presents were handed out to all groups.

It was a time of celebration and many of the young had preempted the celebrations and were merrily intoxicated.

Prepacked meals and snacks were available in the small microwave tables in front of each seat, but on this special occasion there was wine and champaign.

Finally the Mayor went over to the royal couple and thanked them for coming. Then he asked Michael to say a few words and he agreed.

As usual everyone waited to receive their trophies and gifts before settling down to dinner.

Michael was never a nervous type and saw the opportunity for more anti-Javols and pro-imperial propaganda. He also wanted to create a good impression with the young.

He had previously made his choice to adopt them for his own fighting force. After all, they were brave, hardy and tough and would serve him well in the struggle ahead. Further, he was much too close to the Imperial Senate on Earth to use locals.

'Mr Mayor, fellow friends and miners of our esteemed federation.

'My fiancee and I are greatly honoured to be here on the eve of a very important new-year and for your important celebrations.

'Many years ago, just after my father built this beautiful city, he and your great saints left our galaxy for the greatest crusade of all. It was to defend other races in this galaxy against a most deadly and devilish fore.

'My trip through your city today made me realize that you had not forgotten them. However, I would like to revive their memories and place them more firmly in the thoughts of the young, particularly those of you who do not believe in the saints and their incredible powers.

'It has been brought to my knowledge that for many of you, the Imperials on Eden are just folklore. I therefore consider it my duty to further assure you that I am from that heavenly world of immortality where virtually anything is possible.

'Very soon, many important opportunities will be offered to you, but at this moment let us drink a toast to absent relatives and friends, the immortals and those on the front lines of great battles fought and won in distant galaxies!' he said and they stood and cheered.

He attained the stance of a great leader. A figure lacking in the lives of all brave and courageous miners.

'More! More! More!' shouted the excited young at the rear of the hall.

'Let the immortal prince speak!' a senior member shouted, enthusiastically.

Then they lifted their glasses and toasted all absent friends and

Michael continued.

'The crusade is reaching its end in Andromeda and very soon the Great Lords and faithful will return.

'Let us prepare a grand welcome for their reunion and plan for the utter destruction of all infidels that have since entered our galaxy with plans to destroy us.

'Because of those immediate dangers, we must triple our security throughout our cities and within our remote isolated communities, mines and ships. We must also realize our enemies are aliens. So they are very clever at disguises and can exist in most environments.' He was soon interrupted by a young female miner.

'If you are truly an immortal, show us a sign!' she shouted and was joined by her unruly colleagues at the rear of the hall. Michael accepted her challenge.

'What would you like me do?' he shouted back.

'Turn my silver trophy into solid gold, without altering the quantity or taste of the champaign it contains,' she said and brought the object to the stage assisted by her many inebriated friends.

The mayor and Lady Lia stood up to put a stop to the youths exuberance, but Michael signalled them to remain seated.

Michael had also realized the young miner involved, was a brave and hardy individual who had on occasion rescued many of her colleagues. Furthermore, it was not the first trophy she had received on behalf of her family and mining group.

In a split second he had scanned his Macron records and found the girl's name. Although he could have scanned her mind while she was in his presence, he would not invade a person's mind without their express permission.

'Diana, you must hold on tightly to your cup. We don't want anyone to think it was replaced, and there is little chance of you becoming a most beautiful golden statue in the process,' he said. The audience laughed, but nervous wrinkles began to show on her face.

At that moment she would have given anything to lose that cup. However she couldn't lose face in the midst of so many, so she took courage.

'By the powers invested in me, let this silver cup be changed into pure gold. Let it remain that way as a constant reminder to those of little faith, and may the Greater Purpose guide your hand, Diana, so that you will one day become a great child and follower of the Sword,' he commanded.

Then he touched the silver cup and it slowly changed into gold in front of her eyes. The process was not immediate but quite visible, and in such a manner that she changed hands several times, thinking that method would prevent her from becoming a golden statue. The audience remained silent and amazed. Afterwards, Diana boldly drank the contents of the cup.

'It's much better champagne!' she shouted to the audience and knelt in front of Michael to ask forgiveness for her and her ignorant group. He smiled, lifted her to her feet and shook her hand.

'There goes a beautiful child of Osmaron!' he shouted and they cheered.

'We, the sons and daughters of Osmaron, by our very efforts can each attain power and greatness. No one is too lowly to become an immortal.

'Our powers are for the enhancement and procurement of love, order and life within their many habitats. By respecting all life and carrying out our responsibilities, we the faithful, will be made powerful.

'Terminus City has always been an important home for the faithful and will continue that way in its own independent manner. That's the way my father intended and that is the way it shall continue to be,' he said, and the audience stood up to cheer.

'After many years, finally we have a great one in our midst, with knowledge of advanced sciences and battles afar. Let him instruct us and tell us what to do to assist and we shall follow,' Diana said and Michael stood up to answer.

'This night marks the beginning of a new age within our galaxy. It also marks the fall of our enemies within the galaxy of Andromeda. You must be ready when called and be trained as my loyal warriors. Like Imperial Specials, so will you be feared and respected by all within the known universe!' he yelled.

Suddenly there was an uproar in the centre of the hall, to be followed by several external explosions and some older miners stood up from the area of the orange seats, brandishing small firearms.

The two main entrances were forced open and two powerful figures walked in welding large plasma projectors. Michael and Joan could now smell the stench they had missed during their careful search of the building.

'Don't you listen to such imperial nonsense. These so-called imperial princes and princesses are all con-men, con-women, liars, tricksters and half-baked magicians.

'Let's see how well they take a dose of hot plasma. Perhaps turn themselves into two little hot stars,' the largest antagonist said and laughed sarcastically.

The others encircled the small area where the main families sat, clearing all the seats nearby. Then the tallest of the two walked over to the rostrum and took the microphone.

'Your important families are being collected for ransom. Pirates ransom. That also includes your royal prince and his woman, who I am sure will get us a much better price. So remain seated, everyone, or you will be blasted to atoms!' he shouted in no uncertain terms, pulling the microphone out of the holding socket and throwing it into those few standing that had lost their seats in the previous commotion.

They realized he meant business and quickly sat in the nearest passageway.

Michael realized the kidnappers had to take them away from the building and work on Lady Lia who was their primary target.

They would use drugs and drain her of most of her knowledge before her body was disposed and the imposter created. He played along while concocting a safe plan that would not endanger the lives of innocent bystanders.

During his previous speeches, his words had been carefully chosen to bring out the worst in his enemies, who he assumed would be listening. Realizing he knew too much, they had to move in the most obvious manner, because their more subtler plans had been blown.

Michael and Joan soon realized the two powerful pirates were

Muts, pretending to be their original leaders. He couldn't use an explosive or fiery weapon against them, but he had another even more deadlier one in his armoury which would also show his audience who they really were.

'There is presently a stench of rotting flesh in this place. I think our visitors need a wash or perhaps they are alien mutants commonly known as Muts,' he said.

The tall one lost his nerve and blasted Michael in the chest, but the hot plasma was reflected off his body and vaporized part of one of the chairs. Suddenly fear came over them, but they remained close to their more fragile human victims.

'I can assure you both, that my breath is much worst than your stench!' Michael yelled.

Taking two deep breaths the couple blew a reddish beam in their direction and billions of strange molecules touched their bodies.

'It was a type of virus that had an effect equivalent to bubonic plague on Javols. Once within its host it multiplied extremely quickly. But that was not all, they accumulated like a swam of red flaming fireflies about their victims.

Their clothes began to disintegrate and their human forms began to change into all types of hideous monsters, even some with many arms and legs.

Both changed colour from normal to blue in seconds and began to shake violently. Then they became super heated as matter ejected from their bodies. Then their smoldering remains fell to the floor. Both forms struggled until they were unable to sustain the heat generated by the infection, then parts of their bodies exploded. Even then, smaller sections were trying to rejoin the main parts to reform, but the virus spread too quickly and without the support of the larger parts, they simply melted into something resembling hot mud. Then the swam of virus elements or whatever they were returned to Michael and Joan and were absorbed through their fingertips.

The stench was unbearable and many had to place their hands over their faces and hold their breath.

They had never witnessed such a revolting performance in all their lives. It was a thousand times more dramatic than watching an old-world movie, where the antagonist, Dracula, had been given too generous a dose of sunlight.

The scene was so bizarre that their human accomplishes dropped their weapons and surrendered.

A very brave Lady Lia went to the rostrum to calm them, shouting at the top of her voice.

'Please! Please! Please! Be seated!'

Then Michael stood up and everyone sat down and remained calm.

'Please remain in your seats, everyone. The danger is now passed,' he said and signalled the guards to take the pirates away for questioning.

'You have seen the enemy we wage war against. They are not human and are extremely difficult to kill. They can take the form of virtually any animal of an equivalent size.

'First they learn everything about their victim with drugs and other bizarre methods. Then they change into their form after they have disposed of their victim's body. That way, they are able to infiltrate our organizations and take control. Now you know the reason why you must be extra vigilant. You will be supplied with more information in due course and suitable detectors. Dogs can also be trained to assist in detecting those that are already here,' he said.

'How did they die like that?' ask Mayor Simpson's wife.

'We have the powers within ourselves to alter the very state of matter. By so doing, we can also change the air you breathe into a virus deadly to Javols. That is what we did when we blew contaminated air in their direction.

'We have had enough theatre for tonight. Let's continue with dinner and celebrations. I want us all to enjoy ourselves on this important new-year.

'Let there be celebrations in the streets today. Yes, let us forever celebrate the defeat of our enemies on this new-years day,' he said and the hall roared and cheered.

After many more celebrations and speeches, they were given the freedom of the city and made miners like their parents before them. That was the greatest honour bestowed on outsiders.

After many more security checks through Terminus city, Michael and Joan changed into their original bodies, with golden hair, light blue eyes and her slightly tanned complexion with grey eyes. Then they left for Earth. However, they knew they would soon be back as the royal couple.

CHAPTER 35

Venusa's ship arrives on Earth

The massive battleship, Venusa, suddenly materialized above the newly constructed military spaceport of Gatwick, in the protectorate of England.

Gatwick was once a large passenger airport in old-world Earth, but had since declined to bulk cargo transport when portals were introduced. She was presently the main Solarian space port on Earth and was use mainly by the military.

During recent times that space port had been used as a secret military base for training imperial soldiers for the Federation. It relieved the Martian bases in Terminus and eased military transport between both worlds. Once so trained they could be transferred directly to other worlds within the Federation.

The air displaced by Venusa's immense volume created a mild breeze and its form temporarily eclipsed the sun over that area of Sussex.

Its many local inhabitants stared in awe and dread at its immensity, spiky blackness and destructive potential. She was presently over 3 kilometres long and close to 1 kilometre across her widest parts.

Since the creation of the giant ships, Martia and Venusa, during the previous century, they had never landed on Earth.

During that period, Earth's inhabitants knew nothing of the planet of Eden or of the superior intelligence of those evacuees from Andromeda and elsewhere. Neither did they know of the Andromedans intricately planned escape from Andromeda or of the Shadite Lumak, who was then on Earth as one Doctor Jeffery Longhurst. That knowledge was kept a secret until Earth's conversion was complete and its population reduced from over ten billion to a mere five-hundred million. That population reduction was caused by the introduction of the Terminal Virus in its atmosphere.

Thereafter, only those few chosen could have conceived offspring. Within a century most of Earth's population had died of natural aging, leaving behind the few genetically purer Fertilates who would take control of the newer order.

That survival order was chosen by the Son of Destiny who was also the chosen one.

All remaining Infilates were sent off to Andromeda to farm and help fight the wars there. For their efforts they were given the Ancient's planet of Caefon to start their new civilization and also a chance to have their own children again.

However many of Earth's children on Caefon in Andromeda still yearned for many things from Earth. Some as basic as vegetables and fruit, many of which hadn't taken so well to Caefon's soil and climate. Further, they had to maintain a low profile during the period of siege, so genetic modification was not high on their list of priorities.

The ship slowly descended towards a large area reserved for the larger space carriers and extended its massive shock absorbers that extended into four gigantic legs.

During the docking procedure she had to initiate the powerful gravity neutralizers. They would make her more than ten times lighter and prevent her from sinking into the ground. That way she would be maintained at minimum weight for the duration of her stay.

There she stood majestic in the sunlight, most of her outer shell intricately covered by numerous types of screen generators, weapons and plasma projectors.

She had returned to Osmaron to take on supplies of every kind, including vegetables, fruit, spices, herbs and toys for the people on Caefon. They would be replaced by an equivalent amount of bio-products and chemicals when they returned from Andromeda.

Federation law only permitted the exchange of an equivalent amount of elements from the different worlds, so all elements taken had to be listed and would be returned to the donor world within a period of one-hundred Earth years. It was imperative that there was never a constant drain on essential planetary resources, since such deficiencies could build over several millennia to cause destabilisation within ecosystems and weather patterns, to the detriment of all.

Michael and Joan arrived back on Earth a day before their friends return from Eden. Since the episode in Terminus City, they had discussed the matter and had come to the conclusion that they would have handled the situation in similar manner again.

It was the first time they had terminated lives and that aspect worried them for a while. It also made them aware of the fragility of normal humans like Carl, John and Lucia. Despite the fact they were also immortals, they were the types that suffered pain and damage. Therefore, from now on they would keep a closer eye and guard them against such dangers.

However, they would not let them know of their superior bodies, incase it gave them an inferiority complex. That aspect would be revealed to them when the time was right.

They preferred their recent identities as Prince Aron and Princess Bella. It gave them a closer resemblance to their real parents, but also enhanced their looks. Instead of his freakish golden hair and light blue eyes, his complexion was more natural with light brown hair and eyes like his father.

Even if they could change, everyone in the Senate and Inner Circle knew them as their previous selves, but many also knew of the advanced technologies on Eden that could give anyone a newer or even different body.

They discussed those ideas and decided to postpone any more permanent changes until a more general solution was found.

Their four happy and enthusiastic friends arrived at Michael's flat later that day for lunch. They were full of excitement and carried on in much the same way as they had on previous occasions.

The couple could observe changes in the personalities of their apprentices, that could not only be attributed to a restful holiday on Eden and assumed they had been given more powerful brain implants.

David remained slightly disoriented and quiet, and they knew he had undergone the body transformation. He was still undergoing the grieving process for the loss of his original body. Pity he hadn't a girlfriend to take his mind away from those images, Michael and Joan thought.

They would have to separate him from the others for a very serious chat without arousing their suspicions. They also wondered whether he would choose a human wife and whether such a bizarre relationship could result in offspring.

Michael couldn't stop thinking about the trouble the Masters had gone through in order to ensure their survival against the Javols and fulfil their part in the defence of Osmaron.

They were the latest generation, with a newer approach than their predecessors and had been specifically engineered to take a lead against the newer and more deadlier forms of Javols, namely Muts.

Carl, John and Lucia had not been selected and would always remain their human assistants, but with much more powerful minds. However it didn't mean they wouldn't live forever or could be easily destroyed. They would be aided by armoured suits and cloaks, and there was always the Lifesaver. The only problem with bringing someone back to life that way was that they lost all previous experiences and memories since their last body scan by the Megotrons and psyrotrons.

After their joyful reunion, they settled down to more serious conversation.

'Guys, with the exception of David, you all appear to have had a great time on Eden.

'We went over to Terminus City during your absence and spent new-year's holiday with the miners.' Michael said.

'What was it like?' Carl inquired.

'That place I can really recommend for real fun. Mind you, with the excitement goes a little danger. But the intrigue is what makes it so exciting.' Joan replied.

'Anyway, while you guys are relaxed, I would like to have a few words with David in private. If you don't mind?' Michael said and he and Joan took David into another room.

'So, Pal. You had the changes?' Michael asked, with concern.

'Yes, Brother, and I had no choice in the matter. In all my life I have always been given choices. Can you imagine how I felt when I saw my real body lying dead next to me in that laboratory. And the operator treated me like a little mouse in one of her sadistic experiments.'

'Yes, I know how you feel.'

'I feel like... I feel like property. Like a piece of equipment, and I don't even know who I am any more,' he said, overwhelmed by sadness.

'We both also,' Michael replied.

'You mean you and Joan?'

'We think it's fantastic. We went over to the moon recently to practice and you can't even imagine our powers. Anyway, why worry. They can always give you back the original if you really wanted it,' Michael replied.

'Can they?'

'I'm sure they can. They have all our coding in records,' Michael replied.

'Tell you what. Tomorrow we teach you a few tricks and take you to the moon to try them out. In the mean time, don't tell anyone that you are any different to them. Let that knowledge remain between us three for now,' Joan said.

Once he had company, David soon recovered from his melancholy and was once again his normal happy self. He was given the entity of Melka, one of the ancient demon patriarchs.

Suddenly, Michael's personal macron interrupted his thoughts.

'Master, the battleship Councillor Venusa has arrived at Gatwick Space Port. Venusa's person would like to join you.'

'We are to expect another guest for lunch. Venusa's ship has just arrived at Gatwick. That's fantastic news, now we can have some information about the wars in Andromeda and elsewhere!' he yelled at his colleagues and they went numb in anticipation.

Lady Venusa was the human part of the great inter-dimensional ship also called by the same name. Her twin counterpart was Martia, who was the human part of Martia's ship, now somewhere within Andromeda.

Both ships had been named after the planets Mars and Venus.

CHAPTER 36

Michael visits Lady Lia

A point of light appeared near the wide screen in Michael's flat and slowly expanded into the figure of a beautiful woman. She was dressed in a white gown and wearing the imperial headband, but with a small diamond cluster that dangled just above her forehead. On her feet were golden sandals but her toes were not visible.

'I have been commanded by the Grand Lord to take you and your gang to Andromeda. Your assistance will be needed and you are also required to witness their destruction,' she said and walked towards the group to be introduced.

That was just a formality. She would have digested their individual records from the time they had been conceived. Lady Venusa was always interested in the children of Osmaron and had always observed their progress.

'Lady Venusa, please join us for lunch,' Michael said and showed her to a seat next to him.

'How long is your port of call?' Joan asked, trying to make conversation.

'We are to take on provisions for Caefon. This should take us two days maximum. Then we are to have some dangerous fun with Javols!'

'Fun with Javols! I don't think those monsters are much fun and they have the most bizarre eating habits,' Joan replied.

'These Javols are beginning to enter the rim of our galaxy, so very soon we shall have a fight on our hands,' she said, but the three Titans were not worried..

'In the mean time, would you like us to show you around our small city centre? Perhaps we can also collect some presents for friends and family on Caefon?' Joan replied. Although wanting to ask about the situation in Andromeda, they considered it to be in bad taste.

'Perhaps some of your people would also like to look around an important ship of the realm, and get more acquainted with our war machinery,' Venusa replied, while observing some of the old-world equipment.'

'We would love that, Mam,' Michael replied.

'Have you much of such equipment here?' Venusa asked about old-world antiques with curiosity.

'It's one of my favourite hobbies. I collect almost everything to do with old-world music, films and videos. I find them very entertaining.'

'That's very novel. I remember some of this equipment, when I lived on Earth before the upheaval.'

'Would you like to watch an old movie?' Michael asked.

'Perhaps a little later. I have friends that would also find them very entertaining. Perhaps you could lend us some for duplication.

'I remember the old-world times well and have spent many hours at Sarah's manor and your father's Hearst Mansion. At that time we were also a young gang like yourselves seeking adventure.

'I sometimes wish history could repeat itself. Yet, it does, but never with the same people and systems. However, I will give you a list of the movies I prefer, and as a reward, I will take you to a few lovely worlds and introduce you to some lovely friends of my past,' Venusa said.

In all his time on Eden, George had never known of his grandparent's manor on Earth and wondered whether it was still standing. If it was, he would possess it immediately and have the whole building brought back to the way it was during that period. If it wasn't, he would have it completely rebuilt.

'Is the manor still there?' Joan asked with utter curiosity.

'Yes, It was, last time I looked,' Venusa replied.

'I would love to visit that place just to feel the past and be at one with its history,' Joan replied.

'It's very nice to know you also have a keen interest in the past. Perhaps we can rebuild some of the better aspects of that period in an attempt to relive it,' Michael replied.

They chatted well into the night, while they were taken on an interesting trip of nostalgia. The young knew so little of that period outside of the history books and hearing it first-hand from Venusa made them appreciate their parents even more and brought tears to their eyes.

Later that night Michael realized he had to visit Lady Lia Chiang's home before they left for Andromeda.

'There is one invitation I must deliver personally and in the process sort out Lady Lia's property concessions before there is any more hard feelings between us. The so-called Dragon Lady is not as dreadful as we first thought.'

'That's only because she hasn't decided to eat us yet. But I think she handled herself most graciously on Mars. Now I have the greatest respect for that lady,' Joan said.

'I think Carl and myself should visit her first thing tomorrow, while you and the others show Lady Venusa about the city. We can all meet up here later for lunch or afternoon tea. I hope she has recovered from her Martian shock by now?' Michael said in humble tone to Joan, who was agreeable.

'That lady is a tough cookie. I'm sure it's all like a piece of dirt she would have flicked off her coat in a split second,' she replied.

'The Supreme Lord of Earth visits, Mam,' her chief maid said.

'When is he expected?'

'Tomorrow morning at ten, Mam!'

'Tell Martin and your staff to be prepared, and I want this whole building cleaned and dusted from top to bottom. Tell kitchen to use their best utensils, in case he decides to remain for lunch, and cancel all appointments for tomorrow morning,' Lady Lia said, full of excitement and anticipation.

Despite her many years in Senate, it was the first time she had been visited by a member of the Inner Circle, and not just any member, it was the Supreme Lord himself. To her that was the greatest honour of her whole political career. However, she also considered it a great pity that the appointment was not arranged for the afternoon or evening. The morning period was always the worst time of the day for her and she wouldn't have had enough time to make proper arrangements.

Michael took Carl along as his aide and informed him of his

intentions. When he was away, his personal macron always took control and being like a second half of himself could make important decisions without his authority. However his macron's body was just a hologram and did not physically interface with the real world. It could only give instructions and receive information.

It was a most pleasant and sunny spring day on Earth and the birds and animals seemed to have been completely revitalized. With virtually zero pollution on the planet, they were once more free to roam and take advantage of the planet's every resource and intrigue.

Cattle, sheep and others were no more reared for food and free to roam wildly throughout their habitats and that was not all. Unicorns and mythical creatures could be observed in those green fields and in households following their unique patterns of existence. Although many such creatures were used for show and entertainment, they were mild-tempered and useful in maintaining a better world. Further, the many android vets ensured they were well cared for and maintained within survivable population levels.

Every human throughout the federation were vegetarians. Humans now lived in a period when virtually any food could be synthesized in substance, taste, smell and form. All such food was plentiful so there was no requirement to butcher the innocent life-forms. Anyway, the punishment for such conduct was banishment from Earth, now Solaria.

Michael and Carl did not take the portal directly to Lady Lia's house, but used the imperial coaches and walked from the local station, admiring the flora and fauna on the way. Those coaches ran on ancient rails, but were driven by LPDs.

In the distance, towards the hills, he could observe the massive weather control station with its surrounding fog and realized why Lady Lia had complained so frequently for its reciting.

Michael wore a tight fitting ribbed suite resembling a divers costume. It was made from a thick foam material and extremely comfortable in the cold climate of that part of North America during late spring. Not that the weather could ever bother him.

It was all in one, blue and with extended shoulder pads. Around his waist was a broad utility belt to match.

As official apprentice, only Carl carried a weapon and would come to his defence at a moments notice. But with his new powers such protection was not required. It was only used to maintain the status quo.

Lords and Ladies of the realm were always accompanied by their aides and other members of staff when on important business.

They approached the mansion's gate and were greeted by its many ferocious looking dogs. They began to bark furiously, but suddenly went silent when the word 'friends' were uttered by one of the male staff. Then one of the maids ran outside to greet them.

'We were expecting you from within, my lord,' she curtsied and guided them towards the sitting room where Lady Lia and her chief maid was sitting.

'To what do we owe this great honour!' she greeted and lowered her head as a matter of respect.

'For your trustworthy and unflinching services to the realm,' Michael replied and her features brightened with delight as she invited them both to seat on the adjacent couch.

'My superiors on Eden have decided to make amends for the problems created by one of our local weather stations at the northern end of your fief. We would also like a more permanent link between Earth and Terminus. For those and other reasons, we have decided to make you Protector of the Protectorate State of Sahara. It's at the northern tropical regions of Africa.'

'Really? That's fantastic, My Lord!' she replied.

'As you may appreciate, it's at least twenty times the size of your present responsibilities. However, Terminus City will be its capital, giving full freedom of access to all Martians, but with the usual security checks. You will also be reimbursed in full for all expenses incurred during the move,' he said and handed her a folder with all relevant documents.

'Do I still keep father's lands?' she asked.

'This agreement will in no way affect your current properties, but regrettably the weather station remains,' he replied and she smiled and handed the papers to her chief maid for safe keeping.

'I must say, I like the idea very much. Sahara is now one of the most beautiful parts of Africa and the miners have always yearned for a place of adventure with forests, meadows and wild life. Not to mention a real blue sky above and natural air to breathe. Now, thanks to you, they can forego those experiences when they choose.'

'Yes, that was one of the main reasons for my decision in this matter,' he replied.

'I would like to accept those new responsibilities, even at the expense of the weather station.'

'I thought you would also like some more responsibilities and seniority in the Senate. Because from now on, you can also represent and defend the miners position, politically.'

'Really, My Lord?'

'Yes, and Finally, you have been officially invited to Venusa's ship for tomorrow evening's dinner. You may also bring along some members of your staff, if you so choose,' he said.

Lady Lia Chiang was surprised by the extent of her promotion and new status. She had always thought she was disliked by her superiors in council because of her abrasive manner and fiery attitude. But never in her wildest dreams did she ever consider such an acknowledgement by the Grand Council.

After all, most of her peers had always jeered and slanged her off as the Dragon lady, Madam Dragon, Lady Draco and such like insults. Not only because she was half Chinese, but mainly because of her fighting spirit for justice. Now she was finally being recognized for what she really was and all of her opponents would have to eat their words from now on and give respect where it was due.

Then she realized her present position could also have been because of a few words from a noble prince and princess after their brief visit to Terminus City.

'They had saved my life in the strangest of circumstances. I shall have to send them a most appropriate present, but to where shall I mail it?' she thought for a moment until interrupted by

Michael. This time one of her household staff entered with refreshment and handed it around.

'By the way, Prince Aron and Princess Bella ask me to convey their thanks and appreciation for the manner in which you handled the situation in Terminus City,' Michael said.

'But I hardly did a thing. Their royal high-nesses did everything, to the extent of saving my life,' she replied.

'Anyway, they are very grateful and would like you to keep the incident a secret for now because of security reasons. That rule also applies to your family and staff,' he said.

'Don't worry. No one will know,' she replied.

'The political scene here on Earth is changing quickly and so is our expectations for a more favourable and enjoyable existence modelled on Eden. Since the name of this world was changed to Solaria, it had become the capital of the Federation and in future we must take the role and behave like imperials, each and everyone of us.'

'Perhaps we should change our garments of office, for the new Solarian governing council,' she said.

'Perhaps we should. Perhaps you have ideas on that particular topic. Put something together and we can bring before council at our next session. Since our planet's conversion, there has not been much social activity among us. However, that aspect is soon to change after my return from Andromeda. Very soon I intend to link Eden with Earth, so that we may live as one.'

'What about security?' she inquired.

'Javols cannot enter our portals and live. In the mean time, you must follow your heart as you have done in the past and always be your caring self while standing for what is right. Strict standards must always be maintained and I am on your side.'

'Thanks, My Lord for the vote of confidence,' she said.

'Most finally, I am afraid I must leave you now. I have a prior luncheon engagement with Lady Venusa, but we shall meet again soon,' he said and Carl immediately stood up, signalling it was time to say goodbye.

CHAPTER 37

An incredible ship

Venusa's ship retained her original portals from the previous century. They were the rotating type and made to last several thousand years. Presently there were three forms of technologies used for such types of transport, rotating, stationary direct cubicles and the latest, which were point to point using focussing satellites.

The latter type could only be used on worlds like Eden and relied on accurate positional information. For that method to work the completed planet had to be precisely scanned, with knowledge of every square centimetre of surface area. That was essential when transposing from surface to surface, if one was to avoid materializing within rocks or solid parts of buildings. Therefore, satellites constantly scanned the surface area and updated their data banks with any surface changes in virtual 3D. The more recent types did not rely on surface changes when the target was wearing special Federation insignias. Those special insignias always relayed precise location parameters to the relevant stations and satellites.

The larger Portals currently used by the Federation were the stationery type with two fixed cubicles. One for sending and the other for receiving. Although programmable for reverse operation, a single unit could not operate in different directions at the same time or handle queued operations.

However, rotating portals could each act as duplex transposers and transmit or receive several operations in sequence and in different directions. They were ideal for military use where soldiers could immediately change destination even during transit, without first having to get out and change cubicles.

All visitors, including crew members, arrived at the main reception area of the ship where they were issued with their on-board destination passes.

Although many small passages existed on board ship, those

were only included for the service robots and access to on-board places which were via portals.

All touring visitors were accompanied by specially programmed android guides who would take them to the correct places and explain their varying functions.

All androids were recognizable as normal Earth type humans and could communicate in every conceivable language.

The ship itself was made from billions of microids, each no larger than a living cell, and every individual micro robot could communicate with its neighbours and the intelligent mind of the ship.

Being constructed from heavy metals they were exceedingly tough and could quickly repair themselves in an emergency. However, such repairs needed large amounts of energy which was usually supplied during inter-dimensional transposition.

There were many comfortable rooms and cabins reserved for passengers and guests. Every aspect of their interiors from wallpaper to furnishings could be altered by a simple command.

Despite her many advanced technologies and weaponry, she could not directly transform matter into energy without the aid of specific devices. Only the Son of Destiny and the three Headrons like Michael, Joan and David had those incredible powers. They could also create nuclear viruses, which could changed an element like iron into another like silicon. A hydrogen based virus could transform a dwarf star from its heavier elements back to hydrogen giving it a new lease of life.

The dinner party included many senior government officials, including Councillor Lia Chiang who was dressed most spectacularly. Their arrival was marked by enthusiasm and curiosity.

Although a few had been to Eden for special training, thoughts of the Federation and intergalactic wars were very remote from Earth's organizations. Many who had been told those bedtime stories by their parents, considered such belief akin to fairy tales and religious nonsense.

However the presence of the massive warship over three kilometres long brought home a feeling of a tremendous power outside of Earth. One even capable of obliterating Earth at a moment's notice.

They viewed the many reception androids going about their many duties with an efficiency to exceed by far any human and wondered why they hadn't been informed of their presence before now.

For reasons of security and safety, the population of Earth had always been kept ignorant of their alien masters on Eden until now. They soon realized that Earth had been acknowledged and her status changed since her renaming to Solaria.

Venusa took the evening party to her Mind Room which had been specially prepared for the occasion. The place reminded her many guests of ancient royalty, with its large white table inlaid with gold and several ornate chairs to match. Around the expansive room were many clusters of settees, chairs, stools and smaller tables of the same suit.

That area of the ship could be transformed at will by the ship's mind and may have reflected her mood on that occasion.

Firstly, they were made to relax with their favourite drinks and hors d'oeuvres. During that time they were taken through the ship's many departments by virtual reality via their implants and were amazed by its capabilities.

From her original status as a peaceful federation passenger cruiser, she had been completely refitted for war. Those changes facilitated her use as a troop carrier and for the manufacturing of the special weapons needed to defeat the Javols.

She could use the raw resources of any world for their production and being mobile, those features made her a very important asset within Andromeda and elsewhere.

Michael could sense a lack of enthusiasm within her mind's consciousness and wondered whether it was to do with her conversion or her temporary separation from Martia, her twin sister, now in the midst of battle within Andromeda.

Yet, he realized only a very few in the Federation knew of him and his Hadron companions and those few didn't include the ship. He also realized he was not created by anyone within the federation, but by Grand Lord Gerra himself and that he was the real incarnation of Aron the most ancient Patriarch. Only Shadite Lumak, Sarah and the Federation Macron knew of their existence, but in the interest of everyone, that secret would not be kept for much longer.

As Supreme Lord of Earth, Michael stood up to address the many ministerial guests sat at the many tables and other areas of the room.

'My dearest friends, this is the beginning of the new year that also marks the beginning of a new era on Earth. You are all to be taken into the fold of the federation and become a truly intergalactic breed.

'From henceforth, our great planet Earth, now with its new name, Solaria, will be modelled on the laws and concepts of the paradise world, Eden. Therefore, let us lift our glasses to a new era in the history of Earth, presently Solaria and in an immediate victory over our enemies in Andromeda and elsewhere.

'Solaria also becomes the capital world of the federation. That means, our world will also take the lead in interstellar government and in all intergalactic wars against our enemies, the Javols. Very soon our administration will expand throughout this protectorate state and other worlds within the Solar system as we take over our new position in the scheme of things.

'I have been among you for several years, since my education on Eden. Therefore, I must be honest and tell you now, that I am an Headron and what you may call the culmination of human evolution.

'The form you see before you will naturally occur eons of years from now. At that time we shall become too powerful for this universe and leave for another or create our own in which to exist.

'Don't worry, I am not about to leave you yet on a permanent basis.

'During my duties as Supreme Lord of Earth, many of you were not aware of my real purpose or true nature,' he said. Then he thought of the word Aron in a particular way and he began to change before them into a brilliant light which slowly dimmed into a different figure. It was the ancient warrior patriarch Aron.

'In this form my powers are infinite. My mind insurmountable. My life eternal and my true purpose is to rid the universe of all predator species that corrupt and prey on the innocent. Therefore with our presence you will have nothing to fair from any invaders,'

Once again and to the utter surprise of his audience, his image melted into the brilliant light and he changed back into his normal form.

'We three are of the same nature and disposition and are here, within this universe, to maintain a better survival order among its many life-forms.

'All plans within the Greater Purpose are universal in scope and must be observed by all its citizens for the mutual good and happiness of all.

'Over the years Earth has been transformed into a better planet for all. Now the time has come for its people to become aware of the greater plan and partake in its every implementation.

'You have always been close to our hearts and we shall always ensure your freedom and happiness. That is also the reason why my friends and I will be leaving you soon for Andromeda, to finish the war in that galaxy.

'However, it is time you were given more specific knowledge of our mutual enemies,' he said and the ship transmitted the images of the destruction of ancient Caefon, during the first attack of the Javols.

They observed in gory detail as its almost complete population were systematically slaughtered and eaten by the monstrous Javols. Most of those that survived the falling buildings were summarily decapitated and absorbed. Others were taken away to be flayed and skinned alive as entertainment for their troops.

The experience was too extreme for many, particularly at dinner, and they rushed to the nearest toilets to relieve themselves.

Michael wanted it to be an experience they would never forget for as long as they lived. He waited for everyone to return to their seats before continuing.

'Finally, and most importantly, you must all be on your guard from this day on. Many of their kind are soon to arrive within our

galaxy and some can even take the place of humans.

'*More information will be made available to you by Central Macron in due course. I have already implemented many plans to be executed during my absence. Those plans, each of you must carry out to the letter and without question. The survival of our world may depend on it,*' he said and sat down.

His audience was shocked, astounded and completely silent.

They had no idea such a major threat existed, and of all things, aliens that were not even made of flesh and blood. Creatures that could change parts of their bodies into dangerous weapons at will and not even be scratched by a bullet or explosives.

The mutant, Muts, were even more deadlier, with the ability to transform into a human lookalike and even travel through the more basic types of portals which was not possible with their original ancestors. Luckily, they were not able to procreate like their parents or the universe would soon be overrun by their more advanced kind.

'My lord, do you think such dangerous creatures could be on earth at this time,' a worried Lady Lia shouted. She wanted to make sure she didn't face a similar experience as on Mars. She was also worried that she might have been marked by the Muts for future conversions.

'I wouldn't worry too much if I were you. Although they will attempt to mask their smell from us, their smell senses are quite crude and they are unable to remove it altogether. Very soon we shall have trained dogs within our streets and offices that will sniff the infidels out well before they take root. In future every councillor will be assigned a trained guard with a sniffer dog,' he replied and she was pleased with that answer.

That evening many uncomfortable politicians left Venusa's ship to consider the new situation in which they had found themselves. With a firm resolve they were going to do whatever was required of them to rid the universe of those detestable pests.

CHAPTER 38

Interrupted Journey

The following morning Michael and his group met together to discuss their roles and capabilities. Then their implants were updated with all relevant information for their mutual survival. Carl, John and Lucia were then sent off to Venusa's ship to prepare for their departure in the evening.

Later, Michael and Joan took David to the Lunar Landscape to practice some of their more powerful moves. From there they could easily have entered the core of the sun for greater energy reserves or even transpose directly to the Andromeda Galaxy by themselves, but that option would have let Venusa and their friends down. Although powerful beings, they had to tour the line and respect the plans and expectations of others.

After the many politicians and nobility had come to terms with the dangers that lay ahead, they realized how important Michael and his group were for their mutual survival.

They began to consider them as supernatural entities and word of their powers soon travelled throughout the globe and in its many populated satellites.

Many thought the information to be ridiculous at first, but visual evidence was also relayed over the mass media. There was also some information of a battle in Andromeda against flesh eating monsters. Therefore, there was a great need for more security and vigilance during their forthcoming departure to Andromeda.

With such little time remaining, they quickly arranged a sending-off parade for Venusa and the three Titans.

That day every school took time off lessons to prepare for the pageantry. Although it was a rushed effort, the many school children had collected whatever useful items they could find for the people on Caefon and elsewhere in Andromeda.

Venusa's ship was informed of the preparations and delayed her departure for several hours.

Michael and his group wore the light grey federation uniforms and displayed the insignia of the Shadites on their left lapels.

They left the ship to greet the many uniformed groups of children, cadets and soldiers, all standing politely at attention in the afternoon sunlight.

While he walked along the many rows of children he could observe a change in their resolve. It was one with an attitude to participate in whatever perilous course that would be undertaken to defeat the Javols.

When he had finished the tour, he stood among them for a while and lifted his voice.

'You are all beautiful Solarians. I love you all and will return within the year. During my absence follow the plan. Do not worry and be happy!' he said.

The children shouted back, 'We love you. Lord.'

They all began to clap and cheer while he and his friends boarded Venusa's ship via one of its external tubular portals. Like transparent elevators, they could be extended from below her undercarriage to the tarmac surface beneath.

They slowly ascended into the black ship, still waving to the uniformed multitude.

While they watched, the ship vanished from before their eyes, leaving behind a gust of air that rushed in to fill the vacuum left behind.

Not long after, the ship arrived on Planet Eden to collect a single passenger.

Lumak was the only one to board and he was wearing his black Shadites' cloak with its large belt and buckle. He displayed a similar insignia like with Michael's group.

'We are soon to arrive at Polok II and will remain for a short while to receive more supplies,' Venusa said.

The six were surprised to see Lumak dressed in the strange cloak that never reflected any light. It absorbed all radiation and could shield him from almost any danger. It also indicated to them he was on special duty for his Grand Lord Gerra.

'I heard you were going to the front line and thought I would tag along to keep an eye on you. We will also be joined by many others on the way,' Lumak said. Michael soon realized that he was none other than his grandfather, Dr Jeffery Longhurst. Then Michael went up to him and hugged him.

The ship landed in one of the massive docks outside of Mira's City on Polok II called Miran and were greeted by many.

King Malik had only recently returned from the battle front on a brief leave and was to return with Venusa's ship.

Then the ship visited Lodor III to collect councillor Bailor. He insisted he would not be left out of the final assault in Andromeda. He had left Volt and others in charge during his absence.

Finally, it followed the quickest route to Tarran and collected Princess Bawaki. She was also wearing her Shadite's cloak, but was in her most ferocious cat form.

As usual, Venusa got up to greet her guests in a more comfortable Mind Room, with red carpet and upholstery throughout.

'Greetings, friends. Let me introduce you to our newcomers, Grand Lord Aron, Grand Lady Bella, Grand Lord Melka, Lord Carl, Lord John and Lady Lucia. I am sure there will not be a requirement for second names in our gang,' she said and they all cheered and introduced each other.

As far as Bawaki was concerned there was only two Grand Lords in her universe, which included The Son of Destiny. Now she was introduced to three more and she wondered whether she should bow or kneel.

'Noble friends, during our presence in Andromeda, please do not show us any special treatment. We are all of the Greater Purpose and for that same purpose we fight together as one against a common foe,' Michael said, and bowed his head showing them even greater respect for the great work they had accomplished in the past.

'Our route to Andromeda will take us close to one of our main defence stations. That one is just outside our galaxy and is used for the detection of invasion fleets. It is well hidden and is also available to our large fleet in that area. There are thousands of such stations between the rim of Osmaron and its two neighbouring sister galaxies. They act as early warning and deploy interception.

'However, the space is very extensive and many of our enemies have already slipped through the net,' Venusa said.

'Can we visit for a short while. I would like to observe their methods?' Michael asked.

'I see no reason why we can't, but we shall have to maintain some distance when we materialize. There may be many Javols in the vicinity and we wouldn't like to draw undue attention to the station or ourselves. We can transmit you there by portal,' she said.

'That will not be necessary. Carl and John, get your special suits. Lucia, you stay behind to coordinate with our group here. Joan and David follow me!' he ordered.

Before long they were ready and waiting to take the leap into deep space.

In full view of Lumak and the others they simply walked through the wall of the ship. Then Michael curved space using his magnification method and they were suddenly in the massive station.

When they materialized the warnings sounded and many android soldiers appeared, ready to fire on the intruders. Venusa's ship immediately communicated their presence and they were welcomed aboard.

'We thought you were Muts, but you do not carry their scent,' said a young female soldier. Michael and the others were surprised to find any member of humanity on such a remote outpost and in the midst of such danger.

'We are on a special mission and are journeying from Earth to Andromeda. However, we were curious about the operations of such remote stations,' he replied.

'You are from my home world, Earth. Aren't you?

'Yes, we are,' Joan replied.

'My first name is Jane but my middle one is Kazok. I am the captain of this station. You, like everyone here, can call me Kazok. It sounds more masculine and I use it as my military name.'

'Ok, Captain Kazok!' Michael said in jest.

'I have not been back since I left for Polion, five years ago. Are you all fully human?' she said, suspiciously.

'I am Grand Lord Aron and these are my friends. We are also warriors like yourself and are on our way to defeat the Javols in Andromeda. We journey to assist in the final assault,' Michael said.

'You are truly a Grand Lord, my Lord?' she queried. But Joan gave her a stare and nodded her head in the positive. Then Kazok knelt before them.

'I am sorry, my Lord, for doubting you,' she said.

Then Michael lifted her to her feet.

'I am astonished by the way you entered our station and hope our enemies have not devised such advanced methods,' she replied, nervously, but realized by their insignia they were not the enemy and were very important people.

'How many humans like you are on these stations?' he inquired.

'Only one human and other primal entities are allowed per station, but most stations have a single human. That is a requirement of the Federation. That restriction is to minimize the loss of human life in case such places are overwhelmed by Javols. There are no portals or other means of escape from such places, you know. Only the means to transpose to a sister parallel universe and that process is not immediate..

'We have been specifically trained to run such stations including the war computers through our implants,' she said.

'Then why are there other human life signs aboard. I detected thirty such life signs on my arrival,' Michael said.

'I am very sorry, my Lord, but I couldn't leave them behind. My father is also away fighting the wars in Andromeda and they would have been left all alone on Earth. Anyway, they begged me to take them along and I couldn't refuse.. But they are not fully human,' Kazok said, with a worried expression.

'Bellerophon and Chiron! Bring your company along!' She cried. There was a noise of many hooves coming from the higher gangway above head level, and there they stood, with bows in hand and waiting to fire what appeared to be ancient arrows. They were mythical Centaurs, with a human-like body from the waist upwards, but their bottom part was of a powerful horse.

'Good God! They are the most magnificent and beautiful specimens and fighters I have ever seen. They belonged to your father?' Michael queried, with that expression of utter astonishment and amazement written throughout his features.

'They belong to no one. My father gave them their independent papers years ago. They remain because we are all family and I consider it my duty to be responsible for them in a world of humans,' she said.

'Chiron, where is Bellerophon?' she asked. But not far away a much larger creature showed his face. Well, it was not a human face. It was the head of a mighty bull with a golden nose ring and large pointed horns. From the neck down was the body of a large muscular human male. He grinned, showing his powerful rows of white teeth. They were equally massive, but like a bulls and he spoke with a grunt.

'I am sorry..uum..my lady. Some ..uum..last minute checks,' he said, apologetically. He was followed by his nine companions.

'Chiron leads a group of twenty of his kind and Bellerophon a group of ten of his kind. They are my most loyal friends and my father's creations. My father is a bio-engineer of Imperial stature. He was transferred from Eden to Earth in the early days of bio-regeneration, but remained. They were not made from human or animal genes. It's a new process that can synthesize and create virtually any type of genome from basic genetic material.'

'That is incredible!'

'Don't be misled by their gentle appearance or the arrows they carry. Their tips are of special explosives that can destroy Javols, and Bellerophon and his group use giant clubs that can do as much damage,' she said.

'Well, I see, and now I believe. Perhaps we should take them along to see a little action on the field of battle. Everything here seems to be shipshape and calm at this time,' Michael said, and she was quite curious about the wars in Andromeda and most of all, the whereabouts of her father.

'Tell me the name of your father, so I can trace him for you and perhaps bring him up to date on his brave daughters exploits?' Michael asked.

'My family name is Lennox and my father is Andrew Lennox,

but everyone calls him Andy,' she replied.

'I know of your father and of your family's history. You should be proud that you are all grand children of Lord Harry Lennox, one of our most famous fathers and professor of bio-genetics. He is also currently fighting the wars in Andromeda,' Michael said, but she was almost in tears.

Kazok was sorrowful for a moment, but soon change the topic.

'My Lord, I wish I was there with them.'

'Have you had any action recently,' asked Carl.

'These days we observe them on a daily basis, but we only defend ourselves if they come too close or attack us. Usually we win such skirmishes with little damage to our ships, personnel and base, but recently they have become more numerous, a lot more determined and are changing tactics.'

'That can only mean they are in constant communication with their superiors within Andromeda and elsewhere,' he replied.

She took them through the station and showed them the massive plasma and laser projectors. There were several sealed docks that shielded the fighters from the Javols' beam weapons. Those ships could be used locally by base computer or with a human or android pilot when fighting remotely from the station. However, they could only be used by pilots with brain implants. Then she took them to a concealed room with strange crystal controls and glowing lights.

'These are the inter-dimensional controls for taking the station into another space-time away from this location,' she said.

Michael realized that advanced technology was of Octans design, but he was still worried for their safety should the station be overrun by numerous Javols.

Suddenly the sirens sounded throughout the station and she hurried towards her war control room. They followed her to observe that section of space.

'Two large spheres and a giant carrier approaching, Captain Kazok!'

'Good God! I've never seen them in such quantity before.' She was bewildered.

'Lower screens and place all shields to maximum. Computer,

analyse firing strategies and ready weapons to fire. Chiron and Bellerophon take your groups over and secure the tail section,' she ordered and they were away.

'Please keep them safe,' Michael interjected.

'They will be safe enough in that area of the station,' she replied, showing equal concern for her mythical friends.

Suddenly the complete station was in a state of frantic activity never experienced before, as all its many androids hurriedly departed to take up positions at their many stations.

'I am afraid you will be in great danger by remaining here,' she said. Michael saw the approaching Javols' force to be in excess of several hundred thousand and realized no single station could have withstood the force of such an onslaught, so he immediately sent word to Lucia and Venusa.

'You may observe the battle, but remain hidden for now. Please despatch a protective suit for one human controller,' he said.

Before long the silvery suit had appeared in the local portal and Michael took it to the captain.

'This will protect you from their weapons. However, you must use the oxygen mask while vectorized. Only then will you be able to travel through solid matter or remain within empty space. I shall now update your implants with all necessary information.'

Realizing she had no choice, she took the heavy cloak and began to fit it above her uniform. When she was finished it automatically adjusted to her shape.

'I shall inform the Federation to supply all its captains in the front line with such suits in future,' he said.

'Estimated time of interception... two point three hours and closing,' the computer continued to make its announcements every fifteen seconds.

This was going to be his first real battle against the Javols and Michael wondered whether he should place Carl and John in the midst of it. Despite their many weapons and almost indestructible cloak, there was still some danger. Finally he decided such risks had to be taken by novices in order to become proficient fighters. Even so, he would assign Carl to himself and John to Joan.

He had to test the weaknesses and strengths of that station. That was the only way he could know the true power and resolve of the enemy. Most importantly, he would have a better insight into the future designs of all such federation stations.

Although fitted with the latest weapons, its structure was several decades old and he wondered whether it could really withstand the might of the more numerous and determined types of Javols.

'By now they would have already detected our presence and will soon be splitting apart to attack. Their large storage containers have nuclear devices that can be used as missiles against us. However, they will first begin to charge themselves by initiating local explosions. The radiation will also help them to wake from their long hibernation. To them it's a kind of refreshing energy bath, during which time they charge themselves and become more energetic,' she said, with some knowledge of past operations. She had obviously been well educated and briefed in the strengths, weaknesses and tactics of her foe.

'What do you think their attack strategy will be?' he enquired.

'Since they would only recently have awakened from several thousand years of hibernation in deep space. They will assume that our technologies are as they were in ancient times. However, we've recently learnt that their MasterMind have knowledge of our more advanced methods and weapons. Therefore, once they communicate they will learn of most of our technologies and plan accordingly. If all fails, they will simply turn themselves into high speed projectiles and target us en masse, like one enormous swarm of meteorites,' she said and he listened patiently.

While they watched, one of the large spheres began to unreal into hundreds, then thousands of Javols. They formed themselves into an array and began to fire off several local explosions which brilliantly lit space in that area. However one large sphere still remained in tact and continued to follow the large supply vessel toward its distant destination. They obviously did not view the station as a major threat, but would remove it all the same and take whatever resources it contained.

Barely five thousand light years from Osmaron, they would feed on most of their food supplies before the attack, and would not return into hibernation. As they approached the more populated globular clusters and outer worlds, they would be further replenished and begin to multiply their numbers.

CHAPTER 39

Space in turmoil

For efficiency's sake, Javols tended to travel in large condensed swarms called globes. By so doing they would form into large spheres containing many thousands of their kind. Only the external level or shell of those spheres would be exposed to the rigours of space and the under layers of Javols would be well protected while in hibernation. Further, only a few of their LPDs (Linear Progressive Drives) were required to take a mass of them across space.

However, unlike primal animals with relatively high metabolic rates and the requirement to breathe gasses like oxygen constantly, Javols did not require a constant supply of energy, neither did they require oxygen or indeed any gases to breathe. Any energy requirements could always be acquired from their next victim and if they had enough of the relevant minerals all that would be required was heat energy in any of its many forms. While in space they could always pass close to a star to recharge, but they needed iron and other elements to repair their Nano-bot or microid systems.

That made them the most adaptable and efficient life-form in the universe.

They could remain in a dormant state of hibernation for thousands of years and in seconds be revived to full consciousness with virtually no discomfort.

They could comfortably survive in the cold vacuum of space or equally well within the outer atmosphere of a star, at many thousands of degrees Celsius.

They were unique survivors, with high intelligence but with virtually zero patience and creativity.

They gained most of their technologies through the art of copying. To them it was like a religion and they combined their ferocious eating skills with their copying skills.

Only useful life-forms and devices were collected and that also applied to the smaller and more intelligent life-forms discovered during their conquest of space. Others that posed a threat were soon exterminated.

Over the centuries they had enslaved many obedient species whom they used to construct the more intricate mechanisms that were beyond their own capabilities, either due to their lack of patience or non-existent creativity in taking such designs further.

Their main communication system was not verbal and used a type of H-wave which propagated through the higher dimensions and was based on a form of symmetry. That type could traverse great interstellar distances almost instantaneously. Unlike electromagnetic waves, it didn't rely on the speed of light and like LPDs, had been discovered and copied over three thousand years before by their predecessors. They were created by the Andromedan Ancients, on the world of Silo, but had since destroyed most life in that galaxy.

However they could communicate in most ways using air-borne vibrations and only used electromagnetics in planetary environments, particularly within their bases.

The groups now approaching Osmaron had left Andromeda over three thousand years ago. That was how long it had taken them to cross the space between the two galaxies with the more primitive LPD systems.

When they left, most of the food supplies within their galaxy, Andromeda, had been exhausted by their large numbers and ferocious appetites. They now saw the distant galaxies as a new source of food and adventure, while on their way to conquering the universe, and that philosophy was constantly driven into them by their MasterMind.

Those arriving were the older and more primitive types with basic atomic weapons. As they approached the outer rim of Osmaron the bright lights of the galaxy and local stars made the exposed few awaken from their hibernation.

Their leader would communicate with their MasterMind several times during the lengthy voyage and be instructed of any change in plans.

After awakening, they would be extremely hungry and

ferocious. That attitude was probably due to the after effects of long-term hibernation. At that time they would ignite many nuclear explosions for their energy bath. Then they would feast on most of their food supplies.

Solarian humans could never sympathize with Javols. They were obnoxious in every sense and only tolerated their own kind, who they considered to be the most superior in the universe. They cared not a jot for primal life, which included all naturally evolving species and considered them to be a constant threat to their survival. All such primal life-forms were incompatible with their vision of the Cosmos. However, Javols could blackmail and enslave intelligent primals during the process of enacting their plans. There were also the few greedy humans that could be bought for a price.

As far as Javols were concerned, wherever possible, all advanced life should be restricted and the most intelligent forms used for sadistic entertainment, technology and food. The very small and intelligent would be enslaved and trained to fulfil their purpose. The very large and dumb would be farmed like cattle for food. All those in-between would be processed for food.

Because of their dense molecular structure, their micro-robotic cells could not easily be destroyed by heat, explosions or acidic poisons. Those factors made them almost indestructible.

With the exception of psychological and biological weapons, only intense plasma heat and powerful lasers could destroy them. Even when severely wounded, they could quickly repair themselves or duplicate into a brand new pair after absorbing too much radiant energy. That process could only be initiated if they had enough food reserves within their bodies.

After replication, both halves retained the knowledge of all previous generations and would specialize in any available niche. However once specialized they would never be interested or be involved in another's profession if different to their own.

Captain Kazok watched the approaching swarms with dismay and bewilderment, realizing that this new year would in all probably be her last. Yet she would give up her life gladly if she knew her friends and families would survive the evil Javols.

'In a situation like this, we should call for assistance from the nearest stations, Sire,' Captain Kazok said to Michael.

'Don't worry, Kazok. We are more than enough for our unwelcomed friends and you will be quite safe with your phasor adjusted to thirty degrees. Just follow your normal procedures without any assistance and completely remove us from your strategy for now.'

'But, Sire! We can never win against that many. We should make plans to transpose out of this place!' she shouted from the high landing, but Michael ignored her plea.

'I want to observe your stance against the enemy. Such first-hand information could be invaluable to the federation and I require it for my report. They will not use their nuclear missiles and devices if they think there is food on this station and you are quite visible,' Michael said unconcerned and she was dismayed by his kamikaze attitude..

'For your report, my Sire... at a time like this?'

'Yes, Kazok. Be patient. All will be unfolded in the fullness of time.'

'I am beginning to feel like a plucked chicken in this station, already' she argued, nervously.

'Do exactly as I command and you will not be harmed. Carl and John will remain with you while we explore and survey the vicinity,' Michael said and the little captain took very little comfort from the fact that she was not going to die alone.

To get the most from their weapons the station waited until the Javols were within a one hundred thousand kilometre range. That was the maximum distance for hot plasma projectors, which tended to expand with distance and partly obeyed the inverse-square law. That was after their strong containment fields had dissipated.

Hot Lasers could be used over much greater distances but because of narrow beam width could only be targeted on a single individual. Nevertheless the war computer could target thousands of different Javols simultaneously.

All the sirens sounded and the three, with Michael at the lead, floated out of the station through its thick walls, leaving behind their two companions and the captain as bait. They took positions at the control level dressed in their special protective cloaks and in full view of the Javols.

Michael and his colleagues maintained constant communication with the station and Venusa's ship.

'Fighting these monsters in space is the most ideal. Unlike a planet with its many obstacles, places of concealment and innocent bystanders, within such empty volumes of space any type of energy can be released against our fore. Nevertheless, on this occasion we will only destroy them after our task has been completed,' Michael said. Then he found a local star and all three transposed within its surface.

As the Javols approached, their larger sphere and container changed direction to miss the station and the individual Javols from the second sphere began their approach.

They would not decelerate or attempt entry through the station's locks if crashing into it at incredible speed would serve both purposes. However they also realized the damage the vacuum of space would impose upon their live quarry, so that was not their first choice.

The moment they were within range the weapons were set to fire and every part of space in that area was ablaze. The incredible energies released awoke the other sphere, now many minutes passed the station on their way to Osmaron. They would have to de-accelerate and change direction before joining their comrades, losing precious minutes in the process.

By that time the Javols had reduced their speed to about fifty thousand kilometres per hour, but there would be a few kamikaze individuals undeterred by such weaponry. Those few were determined to crash at high speed into the station, destroying most of it in the explosion that followed. Although they could be vaporized in the process it gave their group much better survival odds.

Observing the strategy of her enemy, Captain Kazok made sure all fast moving targets were initially destroyed. Although their small fragments would hit the station, its shields and screens would hold out for a while.

Now within the large star, Michael and his two companions suddenly felt the surge of energy through their bodies. By that time they had become balls of pure and intense energy held by incredible inter-dimensional bonds.

For some time they could feel their minds displaced outside of their bodies in a different dimensional plane as if they had become at one with the star. It was as if the star was itself conscious and aware of their presence.

While energies bubbled and heaved all around them their bodies became more at one with each other and the star, until they were fully satisfied. That was the phase when they became true stellar beings as opposed to being mere planetary life-forms. The energies they now contained could easily have obliterated a large world.

Within their new matrix they were still able to transform into their original human forms, or any other for that matter. However, they needed to screen their powerful energies and neutralize their heavier masses from planetary environments.

When they ascended from the star they were three brilliant spheres of different colours. Michael was bluish, Joan as crimson and David was orange.

'Guys, this is fantastic. It's like getting everything I have ever wanted and more. What a super charge. I feel I can take on the whole universe. I wonder if it's addictive?' David transmitted those thought to his two companions who were equally drunk with energy.

'I could quickly get addicted to this way of existence,' Joan replied.

'I wonder if there are many like us in the universe?' Michael said, not expecting a quick reply.

They spiralled several times in and out of the groups of Javols, temporarily distracting their attention and taking some away from the station.

When the Javols had followed far enough away from the station they would disappear, leaving their astonished pursuers many parsecs away from the station.

Finally they took position equidistantly about the station, several hundred kilometres away and waited for the right moment.

During all this time Captain Christina Kazok and her two human companions were fighting for their lives. A small section of the station had been blown away and that section had lost all communication and power.

Several Javols had entered the gaping hole and were being repelled by the human lookalike Androids with hand-held plasma guns. Many were everywhere carrying out makeshift repairs, only to find themselves in the midst of yet another explosion.

Bellerophon and his group led the assault in his section, with Chiron and his group working on either side, but being careful only to target those Javols who were not very close to either group. They soon found a simple way to entice Javols to their positions. They would release several external air locks through which many Javols would enter. When their quantities were sufficient, they would seal the locks after them and open the inner ones. Then they would take them on one by one.

Although that strategy worked for a while, the area soon stank to high heavens with their remains and the air became filled with smoke and all kinds of obnoxious gases. Some of which could have been poisonous to their kind, so once more they shut the locks and retreated. By that time three of Bellerophon's people was severely wounded by hot plasma ejected from damaged Javols and five of Chiron's had breathing problems.

All Javols were now involved. They had deserted their now empty food carrier for the richer pickings of warmer flesh and blood observed in the station. At that distance they were unable to tell the difference between human and android, since all federation androids looked and acted like human, and the Javol's were determined.

The Federation strategy was working. If everything went according to plan in such a no-win situation, Captain Kazok, Carl and John could evacuate to the nearest station via their portals just before their own went into self-destruct. During such an explosion every Javol in that volume of space would be vaporized. However such drastic measures were a very last resort.

After all, stations were very expensive structures and should never be easily abandoned.

Venusa and her guests observed the strange moving lights, tracing their path from the brightest object in the stellar canopy which was also the nearest star. Yet she was at a loss to consider any type of life that could willingly exist within the surface of a blue star. She closely observed developments from her concealed position with the Javols attacking the station.

Back on the station Carl and John adjusted their cloaks and took position behind semi-portable plasma projectors. They could easily be aimed and triggered by signals from their brain implants via their small convertors, without any physical intervention on their part. Their present stance was taken in the vacuum of space close to a gaping hole in the stations outer shell. That was the only safe place from which they could take pot-shots at the enemy during their downward swoops.

Bravely they stood their ground, targeting each Javol as it swooped close to the weapons to deliver their small missiles. Until finally both weapons had melted into useless junk. They sailed through the walls in darkness towards the captains control room, but that area was also gone. They wondered whether she was still alive and hoped she was not blasted into space by that last explosion.

Then they were suddenly held from behind by the captain. She could affect them because their protective cloaks were equally phased.

'Thank goodness you are alive!' Carl said.

While they stared for the last time at the final approach of numerous Javols, they held tightly and said a prayer. At that time all their weapons and computers had been either destroyed or disabled and even the portals were no more.

'I'm afraid, everything is gone. Not even a single portal remains to take us out of here,' Kazok replied, sadly.

Suddenly there was a brilliant flash in that volume of space, to be followed by utter tranquillity and everything including the Javols vanished. It was like they had all been blown to atoms by a gigantic explosion.

The three on the semi-destroyed station still held hands, wondering whether they were on their way to heaven, but were suddenly confronted by a new and most beautiful stellar canopy with numerous stars and dust clouds.

The picture they beheld was like the heaven of which they had always dreamt. Suddenly the scene vanished to be followed by another blackness, but still with no Javols.

Everything within that volume of space had been transported to the nucleus of Andromeda. The three points of bright coloured lights then moved close to the station and transposed it back to its original position in space, leaving behind the numerous Javols close to their MasterMind at the centre of that galaxy.

When they arrived back at the station the three were still firing their hand weapons at shadows.

'Stop! Stop!' Michael shouted and they lowered the weapons.

'What happened? I thought I was on the way to heaven.'

'Not yet, Kazok!'

'They just vanished from space. And did you see that enormous flash, a blueish world and all those stars?' the captain said in a state of utter bewilderment.

'Those Javols will not be seen in this part of the universe again.

'You all did well today. It was a formidable task. Where is Bellerophon and the others. I hope they have survived?' a contented Michael remarked. Michael soon found the mythical worriers. All he did was follow the trail of numerous dismembered Javols who were still smoldering.

'You guys have done well. You have my congratulations on a most difficult job done most perfectly well. However, we must save our energies for the greater battles ahead. Therefore, all of you must now leave this station to repair your wounds and celebrate our first real victory,' he said. Everyone on that station was soon dispatched to Venusa's ship where they were tended.

He had planned the complete operation to the minutest detail. Now he knew how to deal with them before they came too close to Osmaron.

During their attack, Michael had learnt a lot about the enemy, including their moth-like craving for bright lights.

Energy had quickly returned to several sections of the wrecked station as androids worked around the clock to restore normality. They worked on their own volition without the intervention of their main computer, which had been destroyed during the second assault. However, all federation androids were designed to operate independently in times of emergency. Even so, it would be several weeks before that station was fully operational again.

Michael took them all to Venusa's ship for debriefing during which time he would explain the methods used during the grand assault.

What continually frustrated him was the enormous numbers of Javols on route to Osmaron. It appeared that their numbers were increasing to a maximum, which was too numerous for any single station to cope. It was also difficult to re-site stations in close proximity to others, to improve their chance, since it was not apparent where the next group would be encountered. If that situation continued unabated, all remote stations would eventually be overrun and within ten years the whole of the galaxy would be swamped by their very numbers. The time had come to take the war to the invaders in deep space before they came too close for comfort.

The Shadite, Lumak, knew who they were, but Venusa, Bawaki and the others were ignorant of their true nature and astonished when they realized they were not normal people. Further, since their stellar bath, they had become much more powerful and apparently knew everything relating to their present environment.

It was as if they were tuned to some greater cosmic mind. They could even sense moods and emotions as if their own. Nevertheless, Michael and his two companions decided much earlier on to never invade the private thoughts of others without their express permission. Yet, some parts of their being seemed to permeate all matter to a point of oneness. That aspect could be used to control matter or absorb information from it in great detail.

'From this moment on, we move on the offensive. No more will our front-line stations be sitting ducks, waiting for the enemy to approach and report their numbers.

'All space between the local galaxies will be seeded with microscopic sensors that are undetectable by Javols. When they are detected they will be located and sent back to their Master Mind in Andromeda. From there, it will take them several decades to travel the distance to the human civilizations toward the outer rim. By that time we shall have a method to destroy them at the centre.

'As for now, I shall propose the construction of inter-galactic portals the likes of which we have never seen before. Yes, with very powerful lights that switch on when they are detected. That way they can be lured more easily into our traps.

'Like large vacuum cleaners they will systematically clean space of the threat to our home galaxy. Even the large black hole, Terminus, between our two galaxies can be utilized for that purpose.

'And the larger portals can be programmed to transpose secondary portals in regions of space where more numerous quantities are detected. Such designs can be easily replicated by our Octan and Lodorian friends. If not, we three will do the job ourselves. Anyway, most will die when passing through our portals. So friends, we now have a method that can keep our approaching javols at bay, but sadly not so with the Muts. Those are much tougher and are more advanced. They even appear to come from places like Triangulum. Therefore, we might have another organization to defeat before this war is at an end.'

'You mean, There will be another battle for Triangulum?' Joan inquired.

'Yes, I'm afraid so. That one will be even more deadlier than the Andromedan one. Finally, I propose we take Captain Jane Kazok Lennox and her mythical group of warriors along with us as a reward for such bravery in the face of an indescribable foe,' Michael said and Kazok and her group saluted him as she would her commanding officer.

'Thank you, most gracious Sire!' Kazok saluted.

'I'm sure Kazok and her pedigree will come in quite handy, and the more the merrier!' Venusa replied.

They were finally on their way to caefon in Andromeda, with the sole intentions of joining Martia's ship in the thick of battle.

CHAPTER 40

Planet Caefon

For security reasons very few of the citizens of the new surface city of Cantor knew of the underground city of Lower Cantor. It had been concealed from the surface population for thousands of years and continued that way as the main centre of operations for the war effort in Andromeda. Since it was linked to Mars through the Omegron Portal, that part of Andromeda was now considered a part of Mars and no one knew differently. Unless, of course, when they took the lifts to the planet's surface, which was in many ways similar to Earth, although in another galaxy.

Cantor itself was just a small but growing city with a modest population of three point five million. Most of its population consisted of last century Infilates from the larger cities on Earth, but there were also a few Martian miners, Specials and others. They had followed the Son of Destiny to that world, because of the promise of a new life with their own children if they assisted in the war effort against the Javols. Since that time tens of millions had found homes on the parent world, Caefon. That world was truly beautiful with mauve coloured moss everywhere. There was no grass as on Earth so that moss covered the land and was used by most of its herbivores. Nevertheless, since the migration of Earth's humans green grass had been introduced in some areas of farming for Earth-type herbivores.

They had established themselves mostly as farmers, while their sons and daughters became able fighters in the Federation navy.

Most of their weapons and technology was imported from Osmaron via the great ships and the Omegron Portal. Nevertheless the Miners were allowed visits to Terminus City on Mars on short leave to see friends and relatives and it was hoped those facilities would be extended to the Infilates and others after Earth had been fully converted.

That world had slowly returned to agriculture and most of its previously extinct life-forms had been revived genetically from frozen gene-pools and reintroduced into their original habitats. Many new life-forms and non-indigenous plants had since been added. Those included several varieties of plants and animals from Earth and elsewhere. Those were deemed neutral and would not unduly affect the eco-systems of any inhabited world.

After a span of many thousands of years, finally many birds and bats could be seen gliding the air currents above a breathtaking landscape with violet undulating meadows interspersed with green trees as far as the eye could see. Violet was the colour of the thick moss which took the place of grass on that world.

About Caefon orbited its two large moons. They were used mainly as special bases for weapon testing and trials. Those were joined in orbit by numerous satellites for their defence and communications.

The planet was very similar to Earth, with a star of almost identical age and mass. However its primal evolution had taken a slightly different route to Earth's, leaving its original humans and animals with four digits (three fingers and one thumb), instead of Earth's five.

Its secondary and most recent primary life-form were very similar to Earth's human and only a few had returned since their evacuation to Eden.

The new Infilate population from Earth had close social and religious ties with Terminus City and had adapted the Pa-Baptist and Senot religions with the Son of Destiny as their saint.

Interplanetary space within that system had been thoroughly mined during the previous decades, making any form of physical travel within the system almost impossible. As a result, only ships with the most advanced inter-dimensional drives could transpose in and out of its atmosphere.

There was also the Omegron Portal which linked Caefon with Terminus on Mars, but access was through the underground city and its use restricted to important officials and special troops.

Being counted as an important federation world, all aspects of day-to-day control were via its own Central Macron. However most aspects of law and order were handled by its councillors and Senate, many of whom were Infilate elders with a keen sense of organization and justice.

Caefon was presently considered to be the main Solarian planet in Andromeda, with its capital, Cantor, as the Federation's capital in that galaxy. Planet Caefon was also made sister with Earth, so it followed Earth in matters of law and culture.

Because of limited space, Venusa's ship could not transpose into the underground city. Therefore, to avoid suspicion by surface dwellers, she had to give good reasons for her visit while transposing personnel and resources to the underground city. She found the most genuine of all reasons were the delivery of foodstuffs and technological products from Earth. That aspect kept the underground city unknown to the surface dwellers.

'I never thought Uncle Meron's world would be so beautiful. Apparently it was the most perfect world in this galaxy before the Javols came. Now look at the beautiful flowers again. It's as if not a single Javol was ever here. I just hope we can revived all our habitable worlds in like manner,' Michael said and Joan nodded in agreement. She carefully scanned the local meadows and hills from the ships positions but signs of Javols could not be seen anywhere.

'All the Javols on this world were destroyed by my father and others many decades ago. Only their base and dens remain as an historical museum for the natives to observe,' Michael said in answer to her curiosity.

On this occasion, Venusa would visit the Senate for yet another of her brief speeches about the current situation on Earth and Osmaron, and the progress of the wars in Andromeda. During that time the many crates would be unloaded and sorted for distribution to shops and farmers.

Soon thereafter Michael and his companions transposed into the upper part of Lower Cantor and were surprised by its enormous size and facilities.

The small forest and lake had been restored and the whole place was showered by rays from powerful sun-lamps in its spherical canopy. Its many projectors gave the illusion of blue sky with fluffy clouds in an artificial horizon.

'This is some feat of engineering. They must have been a truly brilliant race to have avoided the Javols for over 3000 years in such an isolated place. However, for an underground city it's not in the least claustrophobic,' David said.

He was right. The whole place was specially designed not to be claustrophobic, but was conducive to comfortable living in a sealed environment.

Its great elevators were still actively transporting personnel and weapons from their training camps to despatch points close to the museum in Southern Cantor on the surface.

Michael and his comrades beheld the giant feat of engineering with awe and took the moving walkway to their point of destination.

'Here we are!' said Lumak and they followed him to the largest building on that level. It was a square block with no windows and appeared to have been constructed for a single unknown purpose.

As he got closer a large part of the building's front lifted and they entered into an area of many rooms that were brilliantly lit.

'Ah! There you are! We have been expecting you!' Lord Meron said. He looked weary and unshaven. Much like one without sleep for many days.

Lumak proceeded to introduce the newcomers to him, but by their Christian names. Then they shook hands as was customary on Earth.

'We have a major emergency on our hands at this time,' said the tall figure dressed in his Edenian robe.

'And we are extremely pleased to have you on board,' said his female assistant. Michael realized she was Lucia, Meron's wife.

'I am also pleased to be here, Lord Meron and Lady Lucia,' he replied.

'How do you think they were able to enter and leave this confined environment?' Michael added, and Lord Meron was amazed by his intuitive abilities.

'We are not sure, but think some Muts are able to use portals. They are not like normal Javols and could have been engineered specifically for that purpose... to infiltrate our organizations and steal our secrets.

'They could even have been transported here through the Omegron Portal from Mars. Failing that, the only other alternative is from one of our concealed portals on the surface. Since the security breach, we have closed all portal systems in favour of the elevators, which are now more heavily guarded.'

'Any such move on their part would have been carefully planned and implemented. If they arrived from the surface there is a good chance they are still within this city. In which case, we will find them with our Primorphs or dogs,' Michael replied.

He communicated his intentions to his colleagues and the six simply vanished through the thick walls of the structure and were travelling the mile distance to the lower part of the city to search the area.

He took stance with both legs apart, hands outstretched and slowly rotated his head, feeling and sensing the psychic emanations from every life-form within that volume of space. Finally he could observe two small reddish glows within the extra-dimensional scene he closely observed. They were two Muts disguised as soldiers.

'Have you located them yet!' Meron shouted, but also transmitted the same thought to his colleagues.

'Your two Muts have been located. They were posing as new recruits. I am sure they used other forms for cover and infiltration. You must check your records for any recent disappearances from scheduled duties.

'Where do you want them?' Michael inquired, but Lord Meron was utterly bemused by their capabilities. It was then he realized Michael carried with him a strange aura of power and knew he was a lot more then he let on.

'I know, you and the others are not ordinary people. I could sense your powers when you first arrived,' Meron said.

'That is very perceptive of you, Lord Meron' Michael replied and smiled.

They took the elevator to the lower level where they met Hamil and others. Then they followed Michael to one of the barracks.

Malik, Bawaki and others from the ship had also been informed of the prize catch and were also on their way. Not having met a

Mut before they didn't know what to expect and were very apprehensive at first. Soon Michael arrived at their location and with a simple wave of his hands they were transported inter-dimensionally to the holding cages. Those changes took place so quickly that they were unable to even blink an eyelid before realising they were in a different place and inside a cell of thick bars. Nevertheless they realized something was amiss and did not attempt transformation in order to escape through the bars. Instead the captured Muts decided to bluff their way out of their present situation.

Both Muts were held in the large metallic cage and were kept apart by powerful magnetic clamps. Once Meron realized prisoners had been captured, he turned the cages on. Their restraining fields prevented the Javols from changing into a form more appropriate for escape. There they remained, struggling violently against the fields but not able to escape its more intense hold which were targeted to specific areas of their bodies. The fields also prevented transmission to their bases or Master Mind. Joan and David remained close to the cage while Carl, Lucia, John and Jane (Captain Kazok) stood close by with hand-guns, pointing towards what appeared to be their heads. With Muts there were no specific vulnerable areas and the head was just an embellishment.

'So we caught you at last! What have you got to say for yourselves?' Lord Meron shouted, not expecting a response.

'You are making a grave mistake. We are not who you think we are.'

'In that case, who are you really?' a sarcastic Michael asked.

'We are from another very distant world and decided to visit out of curiosity. We also have very advanced technology and can transpose over great distances,' the smaller of the two said.

'Is that why you are also shape-shifters like our enemies? And why take the shape of our recruits? Where did you hide their bodies?' Meron asked. Because of the situation they were in, by this time their body odour began to surface and they began to smell for what they were.

'Yes! My companion is correct! We have come here out of

curiosity... to meet a similar life-form from an advanced civilization... with the intention to join forces against our mutual enemies,' the taller said. Then he began to struggle again.

'Did you transmit any of our technologies to your MasterMind?' Michael asked.

'No, we haven't had time to do anything. And who is this MasterMind you speak of?' was the taller one's reply.

'I don't know much about you guys, but I smell a dirty, filthy, Javols' Mut!' Bawaki exclaimed and pointed her weapon at the creatures head but did not fire.

That Mut, having considered his task impossible, decided to save energy and went into a state of semi-hibernation. By now they would have erased all information relating to their mission if it had been completed. Otherwise, they would have stuck to their overriding story of visitors from a distant world. That one they would replay until death.

To the surprise of all bystanders, Michael went into the cage and walked directly towards the smaller individual. His presence aroused and irritated both individuals and they tried to attack him. He pointed his index finger toward them and they froze in their present positions.

'So much for friendly visitors!' he shouted. He moved closer to them and focussed to read their minds. All data was simultaneously down-loaded into their Central Macron for thorough scrutiny.

'Our people will remain in constant danger if they are left alive. They must be destroyed!' he shouted to his bemused onlookers.

'Let me do it. I will take it apart limb by limb and feed its carcass to one of our plasma furnaces,' Bawaki said. But instead Michael calmed her fury.

Then he sent a thought to Joan and David who immediately came forward.

Stretching their hands forward they touched the Javol statues and they began to glow and change into statues of solid bronze.

'Their bodies have been transmuted to solid bronze. Let these two statues be a constant reminder of our mutant enemies and the need for constant vigilance in all our efforts and endeavours. Luckily for us, their mission was not completed. Nevertheless, all their memory records have been relayed to your Central Macron for interpretation.'

'Have you found every one of the monsters,' Lady Lucia asked.

'Every single one, Mam,' Michael replied.

'Any idea where they came from?' Bawaki asked.

'Unlike ordinary Javols, Muts appear to operate universally. They could have come from Triangulum and may have left Terminus Base as recruits. They seem to have a hidden passage or portal close to the Solar System.'

'Then it's imperative that we locate their device!' Lord Meron stressed.

'Don't worry. When we get back we shall run a thorough scan of the whole Solar System. If anything is there we shall find it,' Michael replied and Lord Meron was awed by their powers.

Luckily for us, they were not loaded and hadn't set nuclear devices throughout this enclosed city. Next time we might not be so lucky. Nevertheless, Cantor's location is now known to their MasterMind and others of importance, so they will be back,' Michael said. The thought sent shivers down Queen Bawaki's spine.

When the onlookers had recovered from the incredible images and powers they beheld, they began to cheer the young visitors from Osmaron. Meron went up to them and embraced Michael. He reminded Meron of his old friend George Peterson, now doing his dues in Triangulum.

The young ones aroused the fighting spirit in all those present, who were now intent on following them into battle.

'I must immediately inform Martia of our success in catching the infidels,' Lord Meron said, happily.

CHAPTER 41

At the battle's front

Somewhere within Andromeda on one of its habitable moons, within the Santoran System.

'Captain, we have received report from Caefon. The infidels have been located and neutralized and Venusa's ship will be joining us within a few hours with three special warriors,' Martia said.

'Three special warriors. What can three special warriors do at a time like this, with half the Javols' forces in the whole galaxy descending down upon us,' Andy murmured to himself while viewing the still peaceful world beneath.

'Commander, several large spheres and carriers have been sighted in sector 9, they are moving towards our location,' the operator advised.

'What's their E.T.A?' Andy inquired.

'Just less then 5 hours, Sir,' he replied.

'I suppose Venusa will come in handy in keeping them at bay while we tackle the world below. Martia's ship can watch our backs and prevent any of their scouts or supplies from getting in or out. Now we have to wait for our Grand Lord to complete his mission on the world below,' he thought.

'Captain Lucien get your men ready!' Andy shouted. During such missions even the fighting women were thought of as men.

'On it, Sire!' she shouted back.

The world they viewed had special significance, hence the visit from the Son of Destiny to make his own survey and checks with his two demonic friends. He had also found the area to be mined with the most explosive plutonium bombs, large enough to blow that part of the world into orbit.

Andy and his soldiers had remained inactive in Martia's ship since her arrival several days ago while they patiently awaited word from Caefon. His men were primed and ready to attack at a moments notice. Any further delays could only help to make them softer fighters and even lose morale, not to mention a better prepared enemy.

Andy wondered why the world below held such significance for the federation and the Grand Lord, George Peterson, but also on the approaching Javols' forces from every corner of Andromeda.

Venusa's ship suddenly appeared close to Martia's on the habitable moon of Trivan and all her important crew members immediately transposed to Martia's ship.

Within the grand hall were Andy's finest officers and men, patiently awaiting their important visitors from Caefon. Andy was even more nervous and irritable, to the point where he had to take a weak sedative to calm his nerves.

His feelings of frustration was more to do with the long wait before facing the enemy, than a few visiting officials from Caefon. Despite those unnerving feelings and indignation in the face of an overwhelming enemy, he decided to grit his teeth and wait for the new arrivals.

They calmly walked into the great hall with Michael and Joan in the lead, followed by Carl, David and the others. Meron and his five Ancients walked behind, followed by Malik, Bawaki and others.

Jon and his five colleagues were assisting the Grand Lord in Triangulum and Mallory and his group were in control of one of the federation's fleets that was also to be in that area before too long.

Martia greeted the many visitors and finally embraced her twin sister, Venusa, before walking to the rostrum.

'I would like us all to welcome some very important visitors from Osmaron and Earth and of course my sister, Venusa. So without further ado, I would like you to listen to our chief military commander, The Supreme Lord of Earth!' she said and they all stood up while Michael made his way on foot to the rostrum.

'Please be seated, everyone!' he shouted.

Andy was astonished by the young figure standing in front of him. He could well have been his grandson and wondered how anyone that young could become a supreme lord.

'I know many of you are worried by current events and the approaching enemy forces. I can assure you that very soon everyone here will witness their permanent demise from this galaxy. However, that is a very minor task compared to the one ahead. That one will be fought against a much more advanced form in Triangulum and elsewhere. Some of them are now entering our own galaxy.

'Even as I speak, massive devices of incredible power straddles the inner nucleus of Andromeda. Once initiated, they will disrupt every atom of matter, causing an end to all life within the centre of this galaxy. By so doing, every Javol, including their Master Mind will be obliterated,' Michael said.

Then Michael transmitted a thought to Joan and David and they followed to the rostrum. Suddenly their bodies began to glow, until they became as brilliant as two stars. Then they flew through the walls of the ship leaving it undamaged.

'To prevent any more loss of life, my two colleagues will prepare the world below. It must be kept in tact for technical reasons. However, everyone of its Javol life-forms will be terminated forthwith,' he said.

Even as they viewed the program on the large screen, images of the underworld were being displayed. They could observe the two brilliant lights travelling through the corridors at great speed and like Medusa the Gorgon, everywhere they went Javols fell to the ground as blobs of silicate, seemingly transformed into pillars of stone.

Andy was astonished by the horrific scene. Almost feeling deprived of the chance of taking a few of them himself. How could anyone human or otherwise possess such incredible powers even to transmute elements by some type of elemental virus.

Suddenly he became a happier man, knowing that his veterans would not be fighting them in their death-traps and to die and rot in the bowels of such an alien world.

The great lights were very thorough and unstoppable in their efforts, even able to transmit their contaminating powers through all obstructions and barriers.

Wherever they went solids melted into vapour. Out of the thousands of Javols, not a single one remained. The underworld was full of clouds of gas and blobs of stone. Andy thought, a befitting graveyard and monument to Javols. The scene was nightmarish and ominous. Like one visited by fiery demons from hell.

'Our purpose here is of a two fold nature. We are to distract their MasterMind away from other important operations and in the process attract as many as we can from local stellar systems into this area of the galaxy. By so doing, we remove a permanent threat in these regions. Therefore, let them come in the hope of saving that world and its installations. We have set a trap they are unable to detect. It's a good thing that you planned to attack one of their most important worlds.

'By careful planning, their MasterMind has been deceived and misled by erroneous reports from their many occupied strongholds, giving them the impression they are in control of the whole galaxy. However, new information has come to light, to indicate there are others of superior intelligence acting on the side of our enemies within this galaxy and elsewhere.

'You must maintain your current position and purpose, but be prepared to depart at a moment's notice.

'I must now leave you to join my colleagues. However, our three aides will remain to advise you,' Michael said and transformed into a brilliant bluish star which floated through the side of the ship in similar manner to the other two.

With a superficial grin, Andy had to retract and swallow his thoughts and impressions of the young leaders from Earth. He realized they were not humans as originally thought, but probably the children of the Grand Lords and Masters of the universe, with the powers of gods.

This time Michael and his companions transposed into a giant star for another exhilarating and refreshing energy bath. They needed lots more stellar energy for their future tasks.

'Wow! This is one fantastic feeling. I don't think I will ever get used to life without this pastime. I only hope we will be able to continue our lives as normal humans on Earth when it's all over,' David said.

'Every star is so different. It's like they have their own

personality and individuality. Who would have thought a star had a consciousness of being. This one has a darker and lonelier heart than our last. Perhaps it's because it hadn't mothered any worlds and has a shorter lifespan. Even so it enjoys our presence. Perhaps we should visit all such lonely stars for friendship and attempt some form of communication,' Joan said.

'Like people, everyone is so different and yet full of a common purpose. I suppose they are much like the human consciousness. This must be what the Greater Cosmic Purpose is all about,' Michael said.

'Let's go kick some butts,' a happy David said and they followed towards the nucleus of the galaxy.

CHAPTER 42

At final destination

During the previous months, Lord Vektron and his Hexes continued on their way to the galactic nucleus of Andromeda. At that time they were attacked by numerous Javols, but had deceived the Javols into thinking their main installations were on the surface of the large moonlet stations. When they dived into such installations they found themselves in portals which blasted them into oblivion.

Having attained their final destinations, the six hexes were stationed equidistantly at their relative positions about the nucleus of Andromeda. The Patriarch Vektron and the remaining sixty defenders would remain until the device was initiated to its final ten minute countdown.

Grand Lord Vektron, being in control of the whole project also considered himself the ship's captain and was therefore the last to leave its annihilation after it went into self-destruct.

He had made sure all obvious access points had been permanently sealed. His only route to safety and the outside universe being through a booby-trapped interstellar portal linked to a remote planet well away from that part of the galaxy.

He constantly viewed the self-destruct mechanism on his circular desk and found the waiting a source of constant irritation. If no Javols tripped the external sensors on any of the hexes he would have to complete the ceremony himself and enter the special code at the allotted time. He wanted to be blameless in this operation, where countless souls would lose their lives. So he prayed that the Javols would swarm in numbers at his soldiers risks and by so doing be ensnared to trip their own downfall.

He was presently on number three or H3 hex. The five others were over a thousand light years apart from each other on an imaginable concentric circle with their focus on the black hole close to the galactic centre.

Each one of the hexes had its own overriding self destruct

mechanism which would have the same effect and trigger the units into their irreversible transference mode. They were designed to convert simultaneously and all six were required during that phase. If a single one failed, it could have catastrophic effects on large parts of the galaxy for a very long period of time.

Soon most of the soldiers had been evacuated from the stations, taking their powerful Vipers with them so all six stations were left without fighters. Their only means of defence being the plasma cannons, lasers, missiles and protective screens. Those could easily be knocked out by the enemy kamikaze fighters.

King Malik's son, Captain Filo Olav, was in charge of the remaining fifty-nine soldiers. Ten remained on each of the hexes' stations and he was on H2 with nine of his best. His hex had taken a route through the highest density of stars and had so far survived eleven attacks. They were sporadic and did not pose a major threat when there was a full company of over six hundred trained fighters and their ships. But with just a handful of men he prayed the Javols were in another remote part of the galaxy.

Since their arrival to their fixed location all surplus troops had been sent home, leaving behind the minimum necessary to defend the stations with computer assistance. Those had drawn lots in the old world ways, however, Filo remained out of caring for his men.

As the time approached, Lord Vektron became even more irritated by the waiting, until he decided to float up to the ceiling and spend the remaining hours pondering his past.

He didn't mind dying if at all possible in his present form. To him it was a natural process of release and renewal. Having existed for several billion years, his type of being was probably the oldest in Osmaron. Only he and a few other males had survived the intervening aeons and they could only exist over long durations in their present spherical form, permanent enclosed and served by their brand of technology. Sadly, no females of his kind had survived and he considered that fact the greatest loss of all.

They were no longer in a truly material form, having grown away from their physical bodies after the first few billion years of their evolution. It was partly as a result of advanced technology, but also because of an advanced mind finding a physical body too restrictive for their purpose of universal existence. Yet, they had found technological ways to contain and revector themselves.

Once the process of change took hold, it was not possible to return to any of their previous forms. Each one was found to be deficient and wanting in many respects. Their present forms gave ultimate longevity, mobility and near indestructibility at levels unattainable by any other means. However, it also brought with it loneliness. The loneliness felt without a close lifelong female companion. Nevertheless they could create a physical form of their previous selves for a short time when necessary.

Over the past he had made many friends but no one could replace his wife, even now, a most distant memory in the sands of time. That's why death was a happy release for him from a turbulent universe where its more peaceful salient species were constantly defending themselves from the ravages of sadistic predator species like the Javols.

Over three thousand years ago he had promised Meron and his people he would be with them to witness the demise of their mutual enemy. Now, here he was all alone and a person of his word, enacting a small part of a plan they had initiated thousands of years ago. The hopes and dreams of so many depended on the events of the next few hours and there was always the smallest of chances something would go wrong.

Lord Vektron remembered with clarity the devastating periods of the Hexolytes, Drondytes and others who had ruined so many young and promising civilizations in Osmaron and elsewhere.

Their ruined worlds are strewn all over the local galaxies. They had a knack for corrupting worlds and when they were through, they would lay them waste with nuclear mines. That way, they left no witnesses and their competitors could not gain an advantage. Finally, the Hexolytes were back in the form of the more advanced Javols. How history constantly repeated itself but never with the same players.

Vektron's almost weightless spherical containment form bobbed up and down on the generated air currents above his desk. He pondered thoughts of his friends and enemies long deceased and wondered whether his own death would take him to the Plains of Gohenna, where every dream was possible and every possibility a dream. Then he realized such possibilities of death, the final release, was wishful thinking on his part.

The universe itself was intangible and a form of virtual reality to all those outside. After all, that is what consciousness was. It had to be somewhere to experience something and during the process, to justify its own existence.

Suddenly his meditation was disturbed by an urgent communication.

'Sire, H2 is under attack from several small ships. They appear to be automatics loaded with nuclear devices and mines. Their high command will not risk their soldiers against our more superior fire power,' Filo said.

'Hold your end as long as you can. Make sure their projectiles are kept well away from the disruptor modules.'

'We will try our best, Sire!'

'Our screens will shield against all above-surface explosions. However, solid missiles and projectiles at ground level will cause damage. In an emergency you must transpose to any of the other stations,' Lord Vektron ordered and the carrier wave went silent.

Just thirty-six hours were left before the six disruptor stations became in sync and were initiated. Whatever transpired, they had to repel all enemy forces before that time.

The large stations were designed so that the powerful generators and storage cells were kept well away from major explosions and were over one kilometre beneath surface. They were not detectable from space and were well hidden to avoid detection. Further, all essential equipment were in triplicate and that also applied to the computers and control circuitry.

The military and weapons were placed on one hemisphere of the large moonlets and that area was brightly lit to attract the enemy. However, although the dark side was bare of all devices and projectors, it was mined and wired with many sensors and explosive traps. Even when attacked by a very large force with many nuclear explosions at ground level, that area was expected to hold.

Many decoys and complex arrays on the brightest side of that moonlet made pretence there was a large force with extensive military equipment in that area.

Captain Filo and his soldiers remained to control the targeting computers in that area. They were used to track the fast moving missiles of the enemy and would pick them off several kilometres before they could do any surface damage.

Currently, only the plasma projectors were in operation and most of the enemy's ships were being vaporized. Their missiles were not as fast and they were easily disabled by secondary lasers which were very accurate.

As captain in charge of security and defence, he had seen many of his loyal comrades die in recent battles against an enemy, who were very resourceful and determined. Out of the nine hundred and fifty, only four hundred and twenty five remained and three hundred and sixty five of those were back with their families on Caefon.

He was pleased with the relatively high rate of their survival, which was mainly due to good training, true grit and firm resolve in the face of a relenting fore, and had remained behind out of loyalty for his remaining men and the future of civilization.

Filo contemplated his lovely wife, Veruna, and their two young sons in the underworld of Under-Caefon and wondered if he would ever kiss them again. Whatever transpired, he knew they would be well provided for.

The enemy had suddenly changed tactics. Instead of their singular array, they now approached with a random mixture. Although appearing to be the same on screen, some of those points had three ships, one in front of the other. The first being used as a shield which when exploded caused the second to break away from the group. By so doing it caused the tracing computer to follow its position while the last maintain its original trajectory through the cloud of debris to its surface target. By the time the plasma projectors realigned it was too late.

The enemy was no longer interested in Filo and his men for

food and saw the base as a much greater threat and one to be permanently obliterated.

They used a clever strategy that exacted too much computational time from the targeting computers and out of the numerous sorties, a few got through with their bombs.

The first one that was missed landed several kilometres away and exploded, leaving behind a small crater of molten metal. When the sky suddenly became filled with those missiles they knew the end was near.

With extensive damage throughout the perimeter and to communications and detection scanners, their only chance was through the portal. By that time missiles were exploding everywhere, until that area became a virtual inferno.

'Let them send us everything they can in this area. They will never win this war.'

'Captain, lets get to hell away from this area. We cant do anything to stop them now!' lieutenant Commings barked and soldiers were running like hell.

'My wife and children see you soon in Gohenna!' he yelled as his tower took the blast and evaporated into cosmic dust. He saw the missile but could do nothing about it.

Filo didn't have time to say a proper prayer. He was vaporized by a direct hit. His death was quick and there would be no remains for his enemies to gloat over.

Lord Vektron sensed a change in their communication carrier and knew that part of the station had been destroyed. He also knew that very soon swarms of Javols would be landing to collect trophies and take control. Luckily for them Filo and his few warriors would not have been the enemy's most important meal of the day.

'Filo was such a very good officer and close friend. What a senseless waste,' Lord Vektron said to himself, filled with utter sadness for the loss.

Vektron realized they would soon shift their efforts to the other more undefended side of the moonlet where they would trip the carefully laid sensors to initiate the stations own defences. Once the sequence started, its core would be sealed from all power sources on the surface and plasmic mines would begin to explode, obliterating all life on the outside.

Carefully, he watch his self-destruct panel for the initiation of a blue light, followed by a siren throughout his station.

Just twenty hours remained and all stations were on final countdown. The enemy, by intergalactic law, had initiated their own destruction, knowingly or otherwise. Now he could finally feel the deep pleasure for having won a sustained war against an enemy who had disposed of so many innocent souls within so many worlds in that galaxy. They had willingly caused the devastation of a complete galaxy.

CHAPTER 43

Javols MasterMind

Michael and his two companions had decided to survey the enemies bases and MasterMind near the galactic nucleus and were surprised by the lack of Javol troops in that area. Despite the extremely brilliant show, it was as if the complete area had been deserted of all life. That world was covered by giant installations of every type, but for a bright area at its equator.

They landed on the partly ruined world with a parent dwarf star and wondered why anyone would choose such a dead world for home. Just a few light years away from that apparently dead system was another much younger star with a world similar to Earth that was used for Timits and larger animals. That area was just inside the nucleus of Andromeda, but the radiation was not too extreme in that volume of space. There were also several magnetic generators and other powerful satellites that deflected harmful radiation away from the planets surface. They soon returned to the dead system to do some more surveillance.

Despite its lack of a bright parent star, the world was showered by incident light from the stellar canopy, which cast shadows in every direction.

The ambient light in that part of the galaxy was many times moonlight, but not enough to support plant life on that world.

They transformed into their human forms and decided to explore.

They could observe a most spectacular metallic dome the size of a large house in the distance with a tall spiky spire. It had four large square windows several metres across that led unto a balcony which encircled the dome.

The balcony was suspended midway, vertically. That area was obviously used for viewing the beautiful skies, with their many gaseous nebula and swirling giant black hole close to the centre of the galaxy.

They entered the building and could smell phosphorous and

sulphur. Judging from the thick layer of interstellar dust, it had been unoccupied for several decades before.

Within the dome's shell were several passageways and a central lift. All led to the lower floors through sealed enclosures. They entered the first floor and were astonished by their discoveries. The room was filled with alien furniture that was made of metal. There were two large helmets for mind use and on a distant desk were two small computers with many blinking lights.

They took the form of small semi-transparent cubes and appeared to be very active. Both were tied into their MasterMind, the main interface of which was sited in an adjacent underground block. The MasterMind and its many transmitters and auxiliaries had occupied a large area of the planet.

'Apparently, their leaders must have left this galaxy several decades before. Since that time all Javols within this galaxy has been under the control of these two small AI computers. Their two leaders were obviously the real MasterMind behind the Javols and had left in a hurry for some unknown purpose,' Michael said.

'They have programmed these AI computers with their knowledge and strategies for the future, and in such a manner that their underlings would be forever kept in ignorance of their departure. What a devious plan.' Joan replied.

'I wonder if they intend to return at some future date?' David said, not requiring an answer.

'Somehow I doubt it. I think they had little choice in remaining here and could well have been the Javols' prisoners. An advanced intelligence used to maintain order and supply them with advanced technologies,' Michael replied.

'If that is the case, why remain in such a place for thousands of years, as indicated by this numerous installation?' David interjected.

'Perhaps it had taken them all this time to plan their escape. It could take that long if they had to travel to another galaxy. In which case, their special equipment would have to be developed and built in secret. I think they might have gone to Triangulum for help or for another more serious purpose,' Michael said.

The main core of MasterMind was in a large sealed underground room close to the dome and was powered by fusion reactors driven from the planet's core. Here, elements of matter were transformed directly into energy. Such power stations had a lifetime of several million years, aided by self-repairing robots and androids. They could use the raw elements of the planet and transform them to any element down the periodic table. Then they would be combined to form any number of elements for fabrication and such like.

As far as they could observe, the place was on automatic with numerous servicing robots. They could perpetually create components to repair themselves and mend the occasional failures throughout the station. When their services were no longer required, they simple went into a state of hibernation and were placed on slow energy charge.

The MasterMind was connected externally to numerous aerial arrays and other H-Wave sensors that collected data from every point across Andromeda. There were other even more powerful devices collecting from Triangulum, but those appeared to be one-way receivers. Judging from the intricacy of the devices, they could not have been designed or constructed by Javols.

They took the elevator to the basement and were aghast by their observations. The four walls were covered with drips of blood long since decayed.

There were many intricate instruments for releasing pain in its most excruciating forms. The shackles on the four walls were of a size suitable for human-like creatures and two skeletons remained hanging from the wall. Although female in shape, their incisors were long and pointed.

'They were their last victims. What cruel sadism!' Michael complained.

'Only Hexolytes have such an appetite for cruelty,' David said, while closely observing the primal's skeleton.

They passed through another large room with many skeleton operators at controls with communication helmets. They could have been the ones replaced by the two small computers. They had obviously been poisoned before that area was sealed.

Having checked most of the enclosures, they could observe another pyramid in the distance and wondered what secrets it held. On route, there was a small shielded place with thick walls and Joan entered to investigate.

'I have found something!' she shouted and the others rushed to observe the find.

It was a two-metre sphere that was dotted with numerous circular iris type entrances.

'Do you think it's a home of some kind?' David inquired.

'Yes, and there are live occupants,' Joan replied, using her powers to scan the interior.

'Where can anyone find food in a place like this?' David inquired again.

'There could still be underground reserves. Their masters have considered them too valuable for poison. Perhaps they intend to collect them at a later date,' Michael replied.

'What intelligence can be that small?' David again inquired.

'I think they are the Thoraxi. One of the first civilizations to be conquered by the Javols. They are probably the designers of the more intricate computers and machines,' Michael replied.

'Goodness! That's incredible for any creature that size,' David said.

'You of all people should realize nothing is impossible. In all probability they could have evolved on a very harsh world and had to slowly adapt to changing conditions and resources. The process could have taken millions of years. What do you think would happen if we had to shrink in size to survive and still retain our intelligence? Mother nature always finds a way.' Michael said.

'I see your point!'

'We must take them with us for safekeeping, and any other life found on this world,' Michael continued.

The Thoraxi were extremely shy and frightened individuals, so he didn't wish to communicate his presence at that time. However they remained tranquil in their sealed enclosure while expecting the very worst from their new masters.

They entered the large pyramid and within its thick and shielded structure were a fountain with running water that supplied a large pool. They couldn't believe water could exist in such quantity and on such a barren world.

Most of its atmosphere had been blown away by the nova of its parent star billions of years ago and whatever little remaining atmosphere was mainly nitrogen with about six percent oxygen.

Closer observations indicated large quantities of water to be still locked in the lower rock strata, much like fossil fuels on Earth. A simple drill and pump mechanism released as much as their needs required. That area was obviously used to supply the whole station and its many Timit operators before they were poisoned.

While they viewed the pool, they could observe several green octopus-like creatures frolicking about in the water. They abruptly stopped their games when the intruders approached and slowly walked toward the pool's ledge.

They had several eyes around their large spherical heads with a mouth at the very top. Two of the tentacles extended into fingers with sharp claws.

'What a hideous looking form. I wonder if they are as ugly as they look?' David commented.

'They are the Praille. They are from a watery world and live most of their lives in the horizontal. This is why their mouth is in that position.'

'Yes, I heard about them when I was a kid from Granddad,' Joan said.

'I shall have to gain their confidence before removing them from this place.'

'Yes, you should. Most of these species are completely innocent in all this.' Joan said.

'Contact Venusa's ship. Tell her it's urgent,' a sympathetic Michael said and David immediately transmitted a powerful thought.

'We are your new friends and wish you no harm. However, this world and all its life is soon to be destroyed. You and your people will be taken to a new galaxy and given your own world where you can rebuild your civilization without interference,' Michael said.

One of the braver and more senior member of the several dozen creatures cautiously went forward to touch his hand with his clawed one, then he moved back. Michael could feel a thought forming in his mind and knew they had powerful minds and language.

'We accept your hospitality and offer our full cooperation in return, as we have with our previous masters,' it said.

Michael couldn't tell the difference between male and female as they all looked identical and realized they were probably all of a single sex.

'You must make urgent preparations. A ship is on its way to collect you,' Michael said, and several previously hidden robots immediately came alive, unwound themselves and began disassembling and shifting things around.

The creatures were placed in large watery tanks for the trip. They were sealed with several pressurized canisters of oxygen and their supply of seemingly live eels. Soon every part of the fountain and its mechanisms were packed in metallic trunks. It was then that Michael realized the difference in the technology used on that world.

It appeared to him that the robots and heavier equipment were constructed by the Praille, while the more intricate computers and fusion generators were by the little Thoraxi, who were more like a cross between a beetle and reptile, with a larger than normal head to body ratio.

They were enslaved by unforgiving and brutal masters, who had saved them for no other reason then their small size and large mental potential.

Michael also wondered whether any of their kind had survived the Javols on their original home world. Then he realized they would have been considered a perpetual threat and terminated like pests. Only those few would have been the remnants and survivors of a once great civilization. Nevertheless, he would ensure that one day many of them returned to their home worlds to make things right.

CHAPTER 44

The destruction of MasterMind

Three small brilliant stars suddenly appeared in front of Lord Vektron's circular desk and immediately transformed into human forms, making his containment sphere jolt backward in a protective manner. He soon realized anyone so powerful could halm him at any chosen time, so he floated forward to greet his uninvited guests.

'Although your plans have been intricately laid, you have been out-manoeuvred. Every Javol in the most central parts of this galaxy are presently on their way to Osmaron. They have been given the technology of a much faster ship. As a result of which, they will arrive ahead of their primary fleet.

I am afraid, your Hexotron is almost redundant,' Michael said and Lord Vektron immediately floated back to his seat to take stock of their original plans.

'Are you absolutely sure?' a disturbed Lord Vektron interjected.

'We have just come from that part of the galaxy. Their MasterMind is just a computer program and their masters have long since left for Triangulum. We have to prevent them flooding our own galaxy. The world we visited called Trivan was just a giant manufacturing complex for producing their special ships en masse. It also contained a large inter-galactic portal with links to Triangulum. That strategy must have been initiated by their leaders decades ago.

'Don't worry, we have a plan that is guaranteed to send them back, but one in which you and the Lodorians will also be involved... and perhaps the Praille and Thoraxi. I think the latter two will also want a little justice for their enemy's evil efforts of the past,' Michael said and Lord Vektron was humbled.

'Can the Hexotron be adjusted for continuous operation over a long cyclic period of say... one month?' David inquired.

'It's now on final countdown. All the inner chambers have been sealed and are now inaccessible. Only I have the relevant knowledge to adjust the transformers and energy pulsators,' Lord Vektron replied, disappointingly.

'In that case, come with us. We will make you like us and give you a new body.'

'What?'

'Hurry! we have little time left before the main attack!' Michael continued in a most determined manner.

They transposed to a distant quasar and there joined energies, each giving a little of themselves to create the new form. It was the beginning of a new life that contained Lord Vektron's memories and consciousness.

Lord Vektron was astonished by the miracle and could not get over the feeling of release from his self-made prison of several billion years. That was when he returned to this plenum from the negative universe.

The spherical container with its many sensors and converters was then designed to shield him from the destructive and chaotic energies of this universe. However, once he and his few companions entered, there was no turning back and their life-forces were forever trapped within its core. They could however transform into a human form, but that process required lots of energy and could not be sustained for long periods. But now, with such freedom, energy and enthusiasm, Lord Vektron swooped in and out of the local stars until he realized there were more urgent matters at hand. Then they went through the walls of Hex to make intricate adjustments to its core.

The same procedure was urgently carried out on the other five hexes. The countdown still remained and was set at twelve hours before initiation. Lord Vektron then gave the command to clear all stations and the remaining men left.

Michael sensing a disturbance on H2 realized many soldiers had been recently lost. He also knew one of them was Captain Filo, the son of Lord Malik.

'I want a list of all those with life-savers,' he said and Lord Vektron complied, realizing in that distant part of the galaxy such life-savers could not be registered after death. There was no means of communication back to a main station.

Having disabled the MasterMind, Venusa's ship collected the Praille and Thoraxi from the main world and were on her way back to join Martia's ship. She materialized within the system and were immediately set upon by elements of the Javols' attacking fleet.

As far as she could observe, her canopy was filled with swarms of spheres, ships, food carriers and individual Javols.

A large part of that moon had been obliterated and the area where Martia's ship lay was covered by a large plume of dust which extended several miles into the upper atmosphere.

The Javols' fleet was still attacking with its many small automatic fighters loaded with bombs and missiles. They obviously believed there was a great threat on the world below.

Her sudden presence had focussed their attention to a new target and once again a new set of fighters began to approach and give a more accurate sight to their missiles. Numerous missiles were released unto the nearby target only to be foiled by her sudden disappearance. When they reached the spot they all exploded at once with the brilliance of a thousand suns.

Knowing of the more deadlier weapons of their enemy, the Javols high command kept well away from their automatic frontal assault. Their robotic fleet would take the brunt of their assault. They would only get directly involved after the enemy was completely subdued.

Venusa's ship played hide and seek with them for a while, appearing in and out of her enemy's lines and taking several small explosions in the process, but she was trained for that purpose and could quickly repair her outer shell.

The whole purpose of the game was to attract as many Javols possible in that area of space and their ploy was working.

Suddenly Martia's ship appeared out of the blue and Venusa was happily surprised that her sister was still in one piece. She had her worries that the plume of smoke on Trivan was the gaseous remains of her and her crew, but now that fear had been abated.

Martia' ship had led even more Javols into the trap. They had been collected from denser populated regions by her aggressive fire power. The Javols' newer ships contained a type of super-drive, giving speeds somewhere between their LPD's and inter-dimensional. With those new ships they could traverse the complete galaxy in just seven days. Luckily for many, they were limited in range and could not visit Osmaron before the end of the year.

When Venusa's ship had collected the Praille and Thoraxi they made it as soon as possible to Martia's position. During the trip she had communicated with the Praille and Thoraxi and explained the Greater Purpose and the long wars against the Javols, who were their mutual enemies. She had communicated those thoughts to the Praille via her brain implants and they inturn had communicated the information to the Thoraxi through their own technology.

They immediately asked to be involved and take revenge for the loss of their past civilizations, to which she agreed.

'In future you may observe all our battles against our mutual enemies via your own systems,' she said and they were pleased and relaxed.

She had prepared several comfortable areas on board for them and they were free to roam as they pleased. However, she still could not get used to the little Thoraxi, who had two rear stumpy legs for bipedal use and six beetle-like hands. On their backs were greenish vestigial winglets which could never bear their full weight in flight, but used mainly for balancing.

On their iguana-like heads were large semi-protruding eyes, with two long hairs for feelers and their mouths were sunk inside what appeared to be their necks.

As far as she could observe they didn't wear any protective clothing and were extremely hardy survivors, being able to survive many years in a semi-dehydrated state without food. She was determined to communicate with their chief of science, to find what their needs were and welcome their kind to their temporary home. She had learnt from her previous communication with the Praille that his name was Melco. She went towards their large spherical home and gently tapped on the closest entrance. Suddenly the iris opened and out he jumped.

'Melco, I would like to take this opportunity to welcome you and your colleagues to our ship. We are from the distant galaxy called Osmaron and are currently at war with your past masters,' Venusa said, and the little Thoraxi bowed his head and communicated his thoughts through her implants. It was probably one of the technologies they first discovered and was used extensively to increase the powers of their small brains.

'My companions are pleased with current developments. However, having observed your very advanced technologies, we might not be in a position to assist greatly. Nevertheless, we shall do as you command,' he said and bowed again.

'You and your companions are not in a prison devised by us and are free to view this ship at will. We of the Federations of Worlds are all free within the constraints of law and order.

'Very soon, you and your people will be given a world in Osmaron for your kind, to do with as you wish and your friends the Praille will also be given their own world within that very same system.

'One of the Grand Lords of the universe have so decreed and I am very happy and thrilled for you,' she said.

The little creature was also full of emotion. He flapped his little wings in a frenzy and began to dance on his stumpy little hind legs.

He soon returned to their enclosure to relay the good news and very soon thereafter there was over fifty of their kind surveying the ship to observe in detail its technologies and cultures.

They were dependant on the small computers and wherever possible could also operate larger robots and androids, much like the Lodorians.

During their long captivity they had learnt to cooperate with the Praille for their mutual survival and both were very respectful of each other and worked efficiently together as a single race.

Michael never liked the idea of live people fighting against robots and automatics, even with the most advanced weapons. To him people were far too important, but he also realized the frustration felt by many, when not being able to partake in the final battle.

He realized the Javols' high command had placed all their faith in their forward fleet, who were expected to move well ahead of the main fleet and clear the way. Those were the kamikaze of the fleet who also had at their disposal sensitive mine detection equipment.

Within the complete Javols' fleet, there may have been as many as a thousand units, each with a thousand fighting ships, giant spheroids, massive food and weapon carriers and separate Javols following their flanks.

For reasons of safety, they formed into a single queue of units and each unit was organized in a long pyramid formation. That method was the most efficient for movement through the enemy's minefields.

The forward fleet comprised of only two units with about two thousand ships between them and kept a good distance from the main fleet.

Suddenly three bright lights appeared ahead of the main Javols fleet. The first group of more energetic Javols under their more ruthless commander were several minutes ahead and not visible to the others by electromagnetic detection. Javols had no reason to look behind, so they could not observe the disappearance of their main forces.

The three lights had got between them and the main attacking force. Suddenly, there was a major disturbance in that part of the galaxy as strange energies emanated from the bright stars to engulf them.

That volume of space with all its millions of Javols and ships had simply disappeared. Seconds later they appeared in a much denser part of the galaxy and a lot closer to the world of their MasterMind.

Almost every Javol had been dispatched to that part of the galaxy and the canopy was littered with their many spheres, ships and food carriers. From the numerous advanced utilities and dishes throughout its moons and elsewhere, they assumed their computers were at fault and if that was the case there was also the remotest chance that the world in their present path was Caefon, their enemies stronghold.

Their attitude was a simple one; when in doubt let everything out and they began blasting that world with everything they could release unto its surface, until nothing remained but clouds of gas above a severely cratered landscape.

Gone was all evidence of a prior civilization or its large underground facilities that once contained an active Javols' MasterMind.

CHAPTER 45

Commander XO-ZIR-00033-MIR-008135076810

Commander Exo Ziro or XoMir, and his Javol's offensive.

'A nak no ta ke no ata ke ho,' he jeered with fury.

'Ana no Clots ka no ata ka no! no! no!' his second in command jeered with anger.

His remaining Javols' fleets were finally on their way to Caefon with no communication from their MasterMind and he wondered why. After much consideration they assumed it was for security reasons. In any event, they had been given their orders, which was to destroy one of the enemy's main bases on Trivan followed by their only major stronghold on Caefon.

After taking that world, their home galaxy would be secured and there would be no more opposition to their conquest of the other galaxies. With their new interstellar ships in mass-production and inter-galactic ones to follow, both local galaxies could be invaded and conquered within a decade.

Their strategic and targeting computers were as always, a marvellous piece of Thoraxi engineering and much better than the enemies' own at finding weaknesses in their strategies. They could each control a thousand ships and target half that many at any given time. However they didn't realized they were players in a much bigger game that were contrived by their clever masters years before to destroy them along with their enemies.

Since their masters didn't want the Javols to destroy the whole of Osmaron and Triangulum, as they had done to Andromeda, their faster ships were built to last only so long before their drives became inoperable. That single feature would prevent them from visiting any of the local galaxies.

Lupher and Dracma, being Hexolytes, didn't like the idea of the Javols eating all their sadistic pleasures from the universe. After all, once they had eaten all the intelligent life what would be left for their own entertainment and cruel pleasures. They wanted to rule a chaotic universe filled with life and not a dead one with the sole occupation of boring and uninteresting Javols. They had created the Muts for a purpose and that purpose was to take over the roles of the original Javols. Therefore all remaining Javols in Andromeda were surplus to requirement.

Javols identification numbers had been assigned to them by their MasterMind almost from birth and represented the attributes, rank and hierarchy of every Javol, from their adopted careers of specialization to their position in the family hierarchy.

Only their seniority changed with time and that aspect was represented by the first few letters of their name-number. Loosely speaking, the first two parts of their name-number were used as their Christian name during greetings.

They could not communicate acoustically while in their more natural forms. Nevertheless they tended to adopt the forms of primal life-forms of significant power. Then they were able to adopt all their emotions and functions. They could also communicate electromagnetically in vacuum or use the H-Wave over greater distances. H-Wave was a type of order imposed at a higher dimension. This form of communication had been taken to a fine art since their creation. It was really inter-dimensional communication but travelled mainly through the fifth dimension. It could be considered a form of advanced symmetry.

That method did not rely on distance or the speed of light and could traverse galactic distances almost instantaneously, but only between Javols and their MasterMind. However its symmetries could be neutralized and reduced over great distances. Nevertheless special collectors were engineered to reconstruct and boost those signals.

Every Javol was able to communicate with all others, but only their commanders and leaders were allowed to communicate with their MasterMind. That was also one of the reasons why they used a code instead of a name. Further, too many Javols communicating at once could cause noise and distortion, thus leading to misinformation and confusion.

Any code that was not preceded by the seniority prefix was

automatically discarded by their MasterMind, that way it couldn't be flooded by irrelevant and erroneous calls. However that aspect also restricted data collection by the military, who were not always aware of the true facts.

Their many underlings were good at taking orders from their trusted superiors, who wielded the powers of life and death over them. Not preferring the alternative of the plasma pit and utter meltdown, they would do anything to comply.

Like most predator types, they lived for the moment of conquest and relished rubbing their victims faces in their own blood. To Javols it was just two words, the KILL and the FEED, anything else was incidental. The FEED also included copying their victim's technologies. However excessive feeding caused them to multiply in number and for that reason it was restricted by their MasterMind. Despite their cravings, all such food had to be stored for future use and each was given a ration. That way Javols only reproduced when ordered.

Because of the way Javols were constructed, they craved the more natural biological molecules and easily found them within the bodies of animals. Therefore like deprived addicts they could not keep themselves away from their victims blood. That aspect also caused them to be contaminated with every type of disease in the universe, to such an extent that their normal breath was lethal to humans and they carried with them a permanent stench of decaying flesh. Then there was their microid breath that could tear a body apart from inside. They were Nano-bot or micro-robotic and could not be affected by the diseases they carried.

Over the years, their original language had evolved to one richly embellished, with the crudest forms of intonation and vulgarity. They could also quickly adopt the languages of their prey.

Not being sexual, they made up for that deficiency in their sadism to all kinds, including their own. Javols had no humour, no art, no hobbies, no loved-ones and no human feelings. They were a thousand times worse than the sea pirates and pillagers of old and completely void of any compassion. Nevertheless they believed in their own god called Voth, who was the supreme

Javol and as far as they were concerned controlled their MasterMind.

Since the creation of their original parent, formed within a laboratory on the planet Silo over three thousand years before, there have been many generations, yet everyone contained the knowledge and experiences of that first parent Javol.

Whenever the individual separated to form two new Javols, their parent would become the two new children, with all the original knowledge. However those two tended to be opposite in their desires to specialize in limited fields for their mutual survival. That aspect made them singular in the way they viewed the universe, but formidable when grouped together for their mutual survival. Much like ants in a large nest, their long-term survival depended on the harnessing of their many limited specialists by a single coordinator or queen in the form of their MasterMind.

Like most Javols of his kind, Commander Exo Ziro or XoMir to his close relatives, did not like his High Command, neither did he relish his present company on board his new ship. His new officers were young and soft, and far too eager. After all, his enemies were not Timit. They had equipment and brains, and would be waiting with every weapon imaginable.

Of all the ranking officers in the galaxy, why choose him for the dangerous task of first-run. It was like placing him and his command in a plasmic bath without any lawful rights of appeal. He was annoyed by the thought that he might not be around to partake in the spoils of the greatest battle of all time.

He remembered clearly the original parent, thirty eight generations removed. That experience always sickened him and every other Javol in existence. Despite his dislike for his superiors, his dislike for the primals were a billion times more.

'Nano Clots ka bat!' he always thought. To him all Cloths were bad, were a constant threat to Javols and should be exterminated whenever possible.

He knew his original parent-self was an experiment which had given birth to all his other selves throughout the universe and the disgrace of their unfortunate beginnings would forever haunt every Javol in existence.

The primals had subjected his parent-self to such unnecessary distortions and pain. At the end, they were determined to destroy his kind with every weapon imaginable. Who gave anyone the right to create life and take it away in like manner, just because it was not to their original plan.

Some of his underlings had been from as many as a hundred generations. During most of their previous births the galaxy was rich in primal pickings. Most of their unwilling prey were spread far and wide, and free for anyone to harvest.

Since harvesting and farming, everyone was allowed a small ration by the MasterMind and that type of regime did not please the majority. They carried knowledge of the days of pleasure, when they were free-roamers and saw little reason to remain in a dormant galaxy, free of its varied and un-expecting prey. After all, their true nature was that of a predator and hunting was part of their being.

Although still tied to their MasterMind for the purpose of mutual survival, the majority took to invade the local virgin galaxies where live food would be unwilling and in plenty.

'Commander Exo, our forward automatics have detected the enemy's mines. We are getting ready to cut a way through them,' the globular form said. He would change into many surface colours and shapes while expressing those words and his commander would show his regard for the message in like manner.

H-wave was seldom used for close range communication. Since it was of the mind, it was not always easy to distinguish between individuals in a local group, particularly when an order was given, so simpler more discriminating methods were utilized, including vocal when they were of a similar adopted form. In their natural forms Javols had no eyes or ears and relied on sensitive detectors throughout their outer skin to receive and transmit such communication. Each sensor would relay information for all their senses, so their sight was not only in colour, but could hear, smell, feel and touch. Over the years they had learnt ways to encode and decode such sensory information into a language, which was equivalent to any complex human language.

The many mines laid by their enemies had concealed the even more deadlier limpet mines, which were virtually undetectable, extremely small and mobile. Once they found their target they would weld themselves on and wait for a signal to explode. That signal was transmitted by Central at the appropriate time.

The first nuclear devices exploded, taking with them a large part of the interplanetary minefield and they continued through at a relatively slow pace, with senses keenly glued to their forward sensors, checking for even worse dangers as they progressed towards Caefon.

Caefon was just visible on their broad-band detectors and they continued firing their long range missiles only to be intercepted by the carefully laid mines. However Exo Ziro knew they would have a safe tunnel cut through the field after enough missiles had been dispatched and decided to send them well spaced and in a direct line.

Suddenly, three bright lights appeared from another direction and he felt the urge to follow. They reminded him of the three eternal, all-knowing and all-powerful beings revered in their fire sacrifices.

Iadin represented fire, Mok the harshness of empty space suffered by the lonely traveller and Sakn, the ever changing form. They were the messengers of Voth and their powers held the universe together. They beckoned as if asking him to follow them to a more exalted position beyond the stars.

Before long, Exo Ziro and his escort broke away from their automatics and decided to follow the bright lights to wherever they led. The automatics followed along their line of attack only to be approached by numerous limpet mines.

Then they and the volume of space they occupied exploded into a small nova. The conflagration was extensive and it took several minutes for the fireworks display as seen from Caefon's surface to die. Gone were the automatics and most of their deadly payloads of nuclear missiles.

All that remained were the numerous Javols, their spheres and supply ships and like moths to light, they were being taken to an area away from the minefield and Caefon.

When the bright spherical lights disappeared, the Javols found themselves facing many federation fighters and weapons began blazing from both directions.

Exo Ziro realized it was a trick by the enemy to lure them into a trap. He also knew his troops outnumbered them a thousand to one and gave the order to destroy the enemy with whatever means possible. Large spheres uncoiled into numerous Javols and food and weapon carriers emptied.

CHAPTER 46

Fighters from hell

Martia and Venusa's ships had arrived on Caefon, to be greeted by three other giant ships of the realm. There also was poised the Enterprise, Jupiter and Neptune. They had all been designed on the same technology and scale of Venusa's ship by the Lodorians and Polokans.

Jon and his six with their warriors were on the Neptune; Mallory, his family, Ebony and the other five female Amazonians were on the Enterprise. On the Jupiter was Sarah, Jerry senior, Jerry Junior, Miranda, George Peterson (Jull) in his human form and Cathy, Clair or Corra, now a grown woman with several of her priestesses, and members of their families.

They were all hardened veterans and determined to take a last shot at their mutual enemy. However they were also there to help their friends on Caefon and defend the thoughts and aspirations of all primal life throughout the galaxy of Andromeda. They realized that during the last stand of the Javols against civilization virtually everything nasty and destructive would be unleashed against Caefon and its defenders. Therefore they wanted to stand their ground and teach the Javols who were the real boss.

Martia had communicated the loss of Captain Filo to his father, King Malik, who had immediately began to weep. However they were unaware that he had received a life-saver before his dangerous mission with the Hexes, so his body could be revived at a later date. But as usual with most humans, it was never the same as their original. That was because the new body and mind would only contain the memories and experiences of the time before it was scanned by the Psyrotron and Megotrons. In some cases a period of ten years could have passed since their last scan. So in a sense, a small part of that person's memories had died for good, since they couldn't relive that part of their life. Fortunately, for most Federation fighters with implants, life-savers were standard issue.

Nevertheless, it was always up to his spouse and family to fill him in on the blanks via their brain implants. That process was not too difficult since all storage through implants could be downloaded to personal macrons, which acted as extra storage for most minds so fitted within the federation. Most macrons also knew most of the past histories of most important individuals.

Solarians had become so advanced that it was possible to exist even without a body, which was considered a mere suit of clothes for interfacing with the reality of this universe and its dimensions.

'I shall have to pass the bad news to my daughter and her family. These bastards will pay dearly for my son's death!' an overwrought Malik cried and left the room, knowing how badly his son's wife would take the shock of his death.

Soon enough, Andy heard of the disaster and communicated his feelings to his warriors. They immediately stood up and began to jeer.

'We want action! We want action! We want action!' Martia quickly went to the rostrum to calm them.

'Please! Please! Please! There is no requirement at this stage for direct intervention or involvement in the final battle. Some of you will surely lose your lives in the process and there is not enough time to give you all new life-savers.'

Nevertheless, only a very few of the younger warriors hadn't brain implants.

'I don't care! I want some action! If I can take just one before I go, that will give me enough pleasure for a lifetime,' shouted Lucien, and Kazok at the front of the group and the other warriors cheered.

Martia sensed a mutiny in progress and had no idea how to disperse or channel their mounting frustrations. However, she was sure many would die uselessly if they remained adamant to fight the enemy at all cost.

Lord Vektron was finally free to transform into a material form and preferred his original human type that resembled one of the Ancients. He decided to remain on Martia's ship with Andy's warriors, who he thought were the best trained for action. He would remain close at hand to protect anyone in trouble with his newly acquired godlike powers.

Suddenly four bright lights appeared, which changed into human forms and Michael immediately walked to the rostrum amidst cheers and excitement.

'We have won! Even as I speak, their main fleet is timed for destruction in six hours.

Over a billion Javols including their main fleet have been dispatched to the nucleus of this galaxy. In the process, they have obliterated the world of their MasterMind thinking it to be Caefon,' he said and there was a joyous uproar.'

'Ha! Ha! Ha! Ha!, Bloody idiots!' a happy Andy shouted.

'Only a small part of their fleet now approaches Caefon. Our plan is to eliminate their robot ships in our hidden minefields. Then we can fight our enemies man and woman to Javol. So do not dismay, you will all have your chance in the final battle.'

'Thanks, My Lord!' shouted Kazok.

'Now I can have some payback!' shouted Lucien.

'Within three hours they will be here and in another three, those at the nucleus will be destroyed by powerful matter disrupters, so be patient and greet our friends from Earth and elsewhere who have recently arrived to assist us,' Michael said and they cheered with utter excitement.

During the cheering the minotaurs and Centaurs Bellerophon and Chiron led their two fighting groups forward and stood for a while at the side of the large theatre with weapons in hand. They looked truly magnificent and everyone suddenly went silent in awe and amazement. They were straight out of Greek mythology and to many they signified the human spirit, steeped in myths, notions and ideas. But that was not all, they also brought to mind that the war against Javols was a fight for all primal life throughout the universe and not just human life.

On the large screen were the many faces of their friends from the other ships of the realm. Some included the bird people of Colnn and they were many other so-called alien life-forms. All partaking in the final battle against the Javols. There were numerous dogs with special shielding collars that were trained to sniff Javols. Even cats and other alien life-forms were involved. They were going to stand up for all primal life in the universe and teach the Javols a final lesson by their destruction.

With only three hours left, Andy and his Specials left to change and arm themselves for the glorious fight ahead.

Fighting in space was never the most desirable and every warrior had to use the heavier armoured environmental suits and mobile packs. Not knowing how long the fight would take and where it led, they also took along basic rations and oxygen for several days. Javols always had a supreme advantage in space, being even more mobile in that environment than on the surface of a planet.

Andy and his officers wore their special protective cloaks and so did many of the Federation's finest. However in deep space they also had to use tight fitting well-armoured environmental suits with helmets underneath and more powerful shielding.

In order to target the enemy, the cloaks were neutralized just before firing. That process was tied in to their implants and the fire trigger on their weapons, giving them a narrow window of operation and minimizing any damage from their enemy's weapons. Further, they could not use powerful plasma weapons, since their recoil would act as jet rockets and propel them in the opposite direction. Therefore, they were limited to personal lasers, disruptors and such weapon with a massless discharge. That was when they were not holding on to one of the ships outer rails or landing platforms.

In a situation like this, Exo's strategy was a simple one; surround the enemy on all flanks and let them have the full force and weight of his troops. However he didn't realize the enemy used phasor cloaks and inter-dimensional drives. Those were technologies lacking with Javols, so he didn't allow for them in his deployment.

Exo was not an idiot regarding military matters and decided to analyse the strengths and weakness of his enemy before he deployed his main force. Therefore he didn't mind sacrificing a small part of his fleet to gain that knowledge.

'Fen Zo take six spheres, platforms and carriers, and locate our enemies. Then I want you to engage all their ships at once. Inflict as much damage as you can to those Clots!' Exo commanded and they could not refuse his command.

The Javols' fleet took up positions in two groups at right angles to their approach. They took the bait and decided to attack them from their rear, thinking it would have taken them time to turn around to retaliate in full. However, they were sadly mistaken.

After their first confrontation, the giant federation ships disappeared in the void leaving the Javols' heavier weapons directed toward their own fast moving troops coming from the opposite direction and sending them into oblivion.

Realizing there was a lot more to the enemy than met his senses, Exo immediately changed his strategy by splitting the main fleet into three parts. One he sent on the original course to Caefon, the other remained with him to spearhead the attack and the third remained on the outside to guard their supply ships and prevent any enemy movement away from the centre.

Andy never relished the idea of one-to-one combat in deep space. The process was too long-winded and time-consuming. He signalled Martia's ship and he and his officers were transferred behind enemy lines. Their main interest was to sabotage the enemy's weapons platforms and container ships.

Using small H-wave converters, they would kill the crew, mine the ships and steer them into the heart of their forward fleet. Then they would propel themselves elsewhere. The explosions that ensued vaporized hundreds of thousands of Javols.

The battle went on between the Javols and the Federation, many new ships joining to assist, until the numerous Javols were severely reduced in number. By that time almost everyone of their supply ships and weapon platforms had been destroyed by Andy and his brave veterans while using their guerrilla tactics.

Although three of his officers and Lucien were injured on board one of their supply ships, the wounds were superficial and had not been contaminated by any of the many Javols' diseases. Anyway, they had taken several antidotes before the fight, expecting the worst if anyone was captured.

The remaining Javols, included their commander Exo escaped towards the planet Meron to regroup and take the fight to Caefon itself.

Just one group of about two hundred thousand Javols remained, from several hundred million. The losses on the federation side were few and included many automatic fighters and their androids. However, despite direct hits to two of the giant ships they managed to transpose away from explosions, thus minimizing the damage and repairing those areas in the process.

During the battle most of the minefield in that volume of space had been destroyed and the route to Caefon lay free and exposed, and Exo also realized that simple fact. But he didn't know that it was well guarded by all the veterans of old in their many phasor cloaks. Then there were the giant ships of the realm and finally, the starry gods of the universe, presently known to many as the Titans.

Suddenly, there was a communication from Michael to all the troops.

'They have taken shelter on Meron's planet to lick their wounds and will not continue the battle today, so return to your ships and watch the destruction of their main fleet marooned at the centre of this galaxy. The Hexotron is on final countdown and only ten minutes remain.'

'Wow! That's got to be spectacular!' Lucien yelled.

They watched the large screens in silence and awe at the sight of the almost stationery Javols' fleet at the centre of the galaxy. Such information could only have been relayed via H-wave to get to the distant observers in time. It was also being recorded for future analysis.

A small Javols' force had destroyed the world of their MasterMind in error and having realized the folly of their ways their high command had decided to make a few scapegoats before returning to Caefon to take revenge in every horrific manner possible on their Federation enemies.

Their fleet was just getting ready to leave the system when there was a blinding flash, followed by enormous cosmic waves which tended to distort space and the stars in that volume of space. They appeared to be awash in a sea of inter-dimensional G-waves.

Their distant points of light bobbed up and down against the crest of those immense space-time distortions when viewed against the more distant stellar canopy. The process continued until they became mere brilliant clouds of gas. It was like they had returned from the primordial dust from which they had condensed billions of years before.

From that moment on, all life within that part of the Andromeda galaxy ceased to exist. The gigantic waves were held in place by the six sections of the powerful Hexotron, thus preventing its deadly effects to be felt by matter and civilizations outside of the Hexes.

The waves continued for about fifteen minutes and when it ended no stars or planets remained. All that could be observed in that region of space was raw hydrogen gas.

No one within the federation cheered, but many said a prayer for the death of so many ignorant and un-expecting Javols. Due to the high levels of radiation at its nucleus, that part of Andromeda was never highly populated with primal life. Further, the planets that were populated had since been ravaged, to reduce any threat to their MasterMind.

In time, large volumes of those gaseous nebulae would condense to form new stellar systems and many would once again begin the process of life. That was providing the large black-hole cycler at its nucleus didn't devour them first.

CHAPTER 47

New MasterMind

While on Meron's planet with his remaining troops, Exo attempted contact with the main fleet, but as on previous occasions during the battle, there was no response. It was as if they had disappeared from the galaxy all together.

In one final desperate attempt he broke curfew and signalled the MasterMind with greater power. There was no response and neither did he sense the H-wave sub-wave carrier with its greenish background as seen through his displays. It was as if MasterMind had been switched off. Only a few Javols could be sensed within the whole galaxy and they were just insignificant farm controllers and their guards.

'The primal Clots must have some new and very powerful weapon that could have projected them away to another galaxy or to wherever they had disappeared. Either that or they had taken MasterMind out. Bloody Clots! They will pay for this deception.'

'We are now hidden from their main scanners. Let us plan a new strategy to destroy their settlements and bases on Caefon. We must sacrifice ourselves for our race and empire!' Barked Bulta-005.

'When I am through with the world, Caefon, they will wish they had never established a settlement and bases there. The bloody Clots will pay for their deceits.'

'Yes, Commander! Let it be so!'

'Bulta, you are now my second in command. Check the equipment, supplies and soldiers. We shall have a busy day from star-rise.'

Realizing he was now completely on his own, Exo had to quickly hatch a clever plan if he was to take on the might of the Federation or Clots as he called them.

He soon found his only real chance was to lie low for a while, during which time his troops would multiply. If luck prevailed, they would collect more strays from around the galaxy. He could then attack the Federation week spots when they were least expecting. But that plan would take a long time to put into operation. By that time the enemy would have been doubly prepared for their invasion.

His only real chance against them was as terrorist, with terror as the effective word but using guerilla tactics. It would be a lengthy war of attrition against his enemies. However he would have to take his troops to an unsuspecting world where they could be better prepared with the few fast ships remaining.

He remembered the bombardment of the moon, Trivan, and its mother planet, Santora III, and thought that world was the best place for a temporary base.

Exo soon gave orders to seal the food carriers and other essentials. He was not in the best of moods and would take revenge on any primal he met on the way.

Before long they had left planet Meron and were on their way to the Santoran system.

Being prepared for almost any eventually, he emptied the containers of inhibitor capsules which were to be absorbed by his soldiers. The bluish substance prevented them from multiplying and specializing into anything other than Javol soldiers.

The spectacular swam of Javols went on a rampage throughout Santora III, plundering and consuming any Timit along with their bovine catelac herds, until their hunger was fully satisfied. Then they flew off to the parent dwarf star where they would bathe in its surface heat until every virus and disease in their bodies were consumed, then they divided into two new warrior Javols. However, Exo and a few of his seniors took no part in the process.

Michael and his companions had observed the battle from afar. They didn't want to partake and deprived their human colleagues of their moment of glory and their satisfaction from the sense of justice served. After all, they had lost many friends and family members to the Javols over the decades and had waited a long time to partake in the final downfall of their enemy and they got lots of payback in the process. Never again would Javols be a real threat to any civilization in Andromeda. This was mainly because there was little primal life remaining as in the past on which to feed and create large numbers of their kind. Also, current technologies and weapons could easily cope with their present numbers.

He had taken care of their main fleet, by transposing them to the nucleus of the galaxy where they had been destroyed and now only the minor mopping-up remained.

That mopping-up operation was better suited to specially engineered hunter-killer Primorphs, many of whom had been kept in storage for that very purpose. Like the Javols before them, they would be controlled by their own MasterMind in the form of a macron and search the galaxy throughout its length and breath for their quarry.

Michael had also traced Exo to planet Meron and had decided to keep a close eye on his movements.

Suddenly the renewed Exo felt the powerful H-wave carrier in his mind, its greenish hue saturated his every thought until they became as one. Then he could see the red star insignia and knew it was MasterMind.

'You have done well, Commander Exo Ziro, but we have suffered a defeat in the face of great treachery. Our main fleet has been stolen from us by our own high command.

'They have, with the aid of our enemies, taken them to one of the local galaxies. I have not been able to communicate this deceit to you because our own security was temporarily compromised.

'You must maintain concealment, but send communication to all others of our kind within this galaxy. The time has come for us to regroup and invade the traitors galaxy for vengeance and much richer pickings.

'You will soon be given newer ships and I shall rebuild myself in several new locations within our local galaxies for the survival of our kind.

'There is little need to pursue the few remaining Clots in this galaxy. As far as I am concerned, they can have it. After all, it's

now a virtual primal desert.

'Yes, let the primals have it for now while we go for richer pickings elsewhere and when they have multiplied and replenished it, we shall return to reap a rich harvest.

'Here is an up-to-date report of circumstances since their treachery,' the thought said.

Exo received information of the destruction of his main world by the forces of their own high command and of the disappearance and reappearance of their main fleet in a distant galaxy with many rich stars, and swore he would revenge their attack on his sovereign deity, MasterMind.

Michael had planned the deceit well, with the help of the vengeful Praille and Thoraxi. They had rebuilt the Javols' MasterMind and knew their communications. They knew their command structure well, and had rigged a temporary MasterMind on Venusa's ship for the purpose. That one they christened Mastermind of singular name. Unaware to all Javols in Andromeda and elsewhere, the two computers taken from their head world was once more relaying information to a new MasterMind or Mastermind.

Very soon several Masterminds would be constructed in Andromeda and elsewhere as part of Michael's diabolical plan to fight Javols against Javols, while they were being hunted by Primorphs.

Soon a powerful coded H-Wave signal had been received by new Mastermind from Triangulum.

'Inter-galactic prototype to follow within one Santoran month at base location XX5492053. You are to make all necessary preparations to urgently manufacture for our new invasion fleets.

'H. Out,' the message said.

'It was a message Michael was expecting from his enemies in Triangulum. He immediately relayed the same message to Exo with the location of the underground base on Santora III.

Exo assumed providence had led him to the very same world of the production facility and gave instructions to immediately occupy the base.

During the days that followed he and his Javols were disturbed by the observation that so many of their kind had been changed into stone by some unknown force of incredible power. He assumed the Clots had used a new weapon and they would not be back, thinking everyone on that world was dead. That gave him and his group time to repair their base and manufacture the new ships with the remaining robots left at that base.

For the first time in his existence, Exo felt important. Apparently he was the only remaining commander within the galaxy and also the only loyal one in contact with Mastermind and that must count for something.

He had always kept his troops well fed and he knew they were the most loyal that would follow him wherever he chose to go. Anyway, there was greater safety in numbers and they had little choice if they were to survive. He was also in key position for promotion, with all its ensuing perks.

He realized everything Mastermind said made sense, even regarding the remaining Clots. Although he would have dearly liked to get his knives and teeth into them, they could wait when there was much more important fish to fry and a brand new galaxy from which to choose.

Anyway, there was only a few remaining Clots in a galaxy that had become unpopulated and uninteresting. Therefore why not give them some time to breed and multiply, then the harvest could be worthwhile. No wonder the majority of his comrades had already left for the nearest galaxies, and were prepared to suffer temporary death and dormancy in the coldness of space and in the arms of Mok, with all the unexpected dangers, to get there.

In time the Clots will procreate and repopulate its many habitable planets with their most advanced technologies. After a thousand years or so they would return to harvest a complete galaxy full of fresh and unwilling prey, and in the process also copy some of their most advanced technologies.

Before long Exo communicated his intentions to every Javol in Andromeda and they were being prepared for the long journey to Triangulum. The purpose of that plan was to collect all stray Javols throughout that galaxy and get them in a single place. That way they could be controlled as one by Michael's new

Mastermind that took the place of their original MasterMind. They were also made aware of the Clots latest weapons that could transform their comrades into stone, which would further scare them into leaving.

The many sensors planted on Santora III would constantly observe and keep track of their movements and inform Michaels new Mastermind of any abrupt changes in their plans. Then his Mastermind could initiate countermeasures.

The Primorphs would perpetually seek them out, making their existence within Andromeda a Javol's hell, until not a single Javol remained.

CHAPTER 48

Victory celebrations

After the confirmation that the Javols had left the system and hunter-killer Primorphs released, Caefon was taken off red alert and orders given to repair the mine fields in orbit and replace all equipment damaged during the brief battle. The whole of Caefon was to be made ready for the victory celebrations that followed.
 In the following years, every world within Andromeda would be cleared by Primorphs and repopulated. Then the whole of that galaxy would be filled with sensitive observation bases as were Osmaron. Since the leaders of the Javols had left for Triangulum, the chance of their returning in the foreseeable future was considered slim. Nevertheless, the Hexolyte's main portals were to be dismantled, making any transmission by Muts through that media impossible in the following years.

The main reception was to be held on Martia's ship, but Venusa's ship was also decorated to accept the overspill. She had rescued the Praille and Thoraxi celebrities and new additions to the Federation were never taken lightly.
 After extensive discussion with Venusa and Michael, their alien guests had realized the universe to be a much better place then previously considered and had finally become enthusiastic in their efforts to assist in the Javols downfall.
 They also wanted to show gratitude for their rescue from bondage by handing over all relevant data on the Javols' previous high command.
 Both species uttered an enormous sigh of relief when they observed the destruction of the Javols main fleet, along with the world of their painful experiences.
 Michael was still worried about the not so intelligent Timit people, but couldn't interfere before Exo and his Javols had left for Triangulum.
 However, he realized many would be consumed in the

intervening period. He also knew Exo and his Javols would not return. Their special ships would begin to fail just after the completion of their trip to that distant galaxy. The master portal within the production facility on Santora III would then be set to only transmit and their production facility completely dismantled.

That very same underground facility would become one of the main federation bases within Andromeda, with its alien portal already linked to Triangulum. Nevertheless, they had to find what lay at its preset destination point and control it before the portal could be used and set to receive.

Michael, Joan, David and the others wanted desperately to meet their real parents, but so far had little chance to break off their present surveillance activities to socialize. Nevertheless they would attempt to pluck the necessary courage and visit them during the break that followed.

Grand Lord Vektron found his new body to be quite sensational, but also realized that although he was a Ploran and several billion years old, he was officially the offspring of Michael and Joan. After all, he was formed from the material of their bodies.

Michael's father, George Peterson, also known as the Son of Destiny and Jull the Supreme Patriarch, knew of their existence and had kept his distance so they could practice their skills and sharpen their wits against the enemy. After having observed Michael and his devious plans from afar, he realized he was a chip off the old block and his second in command. Suddenly he had become very proud of his son, Michael.

Meron and his Andromedan Ancients had already began their celebrations and couldn't wait to thank the bright stars in person for the swift defeat of their enemy. They could now revive the many extinct species on as many habitable worlds throughout the galaxy as necessary.

Micol, the ship, Jon and his six, with their sons and daughters had assisted Andy during the last moments of the battle. Despite slight damage and one loss of life, that life was soon revived with Martia's ship Megotron.

King Malik's son, Filo, was soon recreated within the time

limit. Although he had lost most of his memories and experiences during the trip with the Hexotrons, that was a small price to pay for their glorious victory. His grieving wife was overjoyed to see him in person. She completely forgot that his former body was no more. Well, when a body was re-created within the specific time interval which was a matter of days, the identity of the individual was still available, so all that was required was the new physical body, past experiences and memories. All that information had been previously recorded and stored by the Psyrotron and Megotron. A lifesaver device within their implants would set the process of re-creation into action. Soon all lost memories would be updated by their acquaintances and macrons through their implants.

Bellerophon and Chiron, the beautiful Minotaur and centaur, along with their mythical troops were much too important to fight in further battles. Michael made them honorary members of the Federation and they were given the responsibilities as Animal Welfare Officers, to observe and report on the development, well-being and freedom of the wild life-forms on Earth, now Solaria. They would be based at his Hearst's Mansion on arrival back to Earth.

The original Javols' population within Andromeda were estimated at just under three thousand billion. During the ensuing wars and other disasters that followed over two thousand billion had been destroyed, leaving approximately two hundred billion. Out of that number, about one hundred and twenty billion were presently on their way to Osmaron. Within the galaxy remained some seventy billion until the final battle. There were an equivalent on their way to Triangulum. Most of those would be converted to Muts for the infiltration of Osmaron and Federation worlds.

Despite the destruction of their main fleet, about one billion Javols still remained throughout Andromeda. However, those were dispersed over a complete galaxy within numerous habitable stellar systems.

Only about five hundred thousand soldiers remained under

Exo's command, the other Javols were mainly farmers and technicians with little inclination to fight and were scorned by their military masters as being week and impotent. However those did not feel secure and would not remain without Exo's protection. Therefore the majority were expected to follow Exo and his fleet to Triangulum.

As far as the federation was concerned, Javols no longer posed a threat within Andromeda and because of its sparse food supplies, neither would they or their newer and more deadlier forms return in the foreseeable future.

Those very few remaining Javols that were caught by Primorphs and found useful to the federation, would be harnessed to prevent further multiplication of their kind and used to produce for the federation. After all, despite their savagery, no one in the federation wanted them completely obliterated once the threat was removed. Further, they could now be cleansed and through Subliminals, transformed into less ravenous and more obedient servants. Their dangerous diseases could be destroyed by emerging them in molten led for long periods. The extreme heat would completely sterilize their bodies. Then their new synthetic food would prevent further diseases from taking hold.

Javols and their Timit people were good farmers and could be educated in the ways of their new masters through their new Mastermind.

Michael had also realized many of the more capable species would have hidden themselves from the Javols and might still be inhabiting their under worlds or large caves. Some might even be in long-term hibernation awaiting the time of awakening. So it was essential that a search party was formed to survey every habitable world within the region of the galaxy that was unaffected by the Hexotron waves. Because of their toughness, Primorphs were ideal for locating all such species, and were also giving that task through their new Mastermind.

To be continued with
Battle for Osmaron

Epilogue

With the Hexolyte bosses gaining a stronghold in Triangulum with their new Muts and Demons, its only a matter of time before the whole of Triangulum and Osmaron are infiltrated by the servants of the evil Dracma and Lupher.

They are set on universal domination and with their new suits, ships and weapons will pose a great threat to all life within the known universe.

However our enemies seriously underestimate the powers of the Grand Lords and New Titans of Osmaron. While Andromeda is being resettled by Earth's humans, the whole of that Galaxy, including its original Javols, are being won over for the Greater Good. Many advance civilization are being discovered and released under the flag of freedom.

Earth, now Solaria, is presently the main world of the Federation and is made a sitting target for a purpose. It will draw the enemy and confuse them into a false sense of security. Soon the complete Solar System will be mined, allowing only the Inter-dimensional ships of the realm passage through. Nevertheless, a clear path for ships are allowed to Mars via special space corridors called Spaceway. From henceforth, interstellar portals will be used for travel. Those contain all the sensors necessary for detecting Muts, but not the enemy sympathizers. Who can also be Primal. That is human or other aliens.

The way ahead is fraught with many difficulties. The enemy is very clever and treacherous, and will not stop until the Federation is brought to its knees.

Dracma, Lupher and their superior underworld demons are gaining strength and will give us a run for our money until the final battle for Osmaron. That final battle will seal the faith of all life within the universe.

www.ingramcontent.com/pod-product-compliance
Lightning Source LLC
Chambersburg PA
CBHW030521120726
47904CB00005B/1567

* 9 7 8 1 0 6 8 7 9 0 2 8 7 *